THE WHOLE TRUTH

"Ladies and gentlemen," Doyle began softly with as much humility as she could generate in her voice, "everything you've just heard from Mr. Jehnke is absolutely true." She stopped, walked a few steps, and allowed the drama of that remark to take effect. "On May 15, 1990, Dimmy Pappas"—she turned and looked back at Dimmy—"seated at the defense table"—she brought her eyes back to the jury—"did enter the bedroom of his father, Nikos Pappas, and did, in the darkness of the night, stab his father seventeen times." She sighed deeply. "That's the truth. We will not deny it."

She paced for a moment as if collecting her thoughts.

"But it's not the whole truth ... You see, it's the defendant's claim that he's not guilty of the charges against him because he was acting in self-defense. Whoa! you're thinking. In the night? While the victim was sleeping?"

PROOF OF INNOCENCE

A novel of legal suspense
by Morton Reed

PROOF OF INNOCENCE

MORTON REED

JOVE BOOKS, NEW YORK

PROOF OF INNOCENCE

A Jove Book / published by arrangement with
the author

PRINTING HISTORY
Jove edition / April 1994

ISBN: 0-515-11353-0

A JOVE BOOK®
Jove Books are published by The Berkley Publishing Group,
200 Madison Avenue, New York, New York 10016.
JOVE and the "J" design are trademarks belonging to
Jove Publications, Inc.

PRINTED IN THE UNITED STATES OF AMERICA

10 9 8 7 6 5 4 3 2 1

For Ruth, Roni and Julie

With special thanks to Joel Isaacson

PROLOGUE

Nikos Pappas tiptoed into his second-floor rear apartment in the run-down stucco building on Cahuenga just north of Hollywood Boulevard. It was four in the morning, and for a change, he was more weary than drunk. His collar was too tight and pinched the loose flesh under his chin. The waistband of his trousers cut into him so badly that he had opened the top button and covered the gap with a loosely buckled belt. He felt his swollen feet press angrily against the pointed toes of his tight Italian shoes and knew his feet were losing their struggle for survival.

He was still eating too much salt, he told himself again, swearing for the hundredth time to be more careful in the future. He was eating too much salt, drinking too much ouzo, fucking too many weird women, and keeping too many late hours. He was not taking care of himself. He continued to mistreat his body as if he were still a young stud with a lifetime ahead of him.

Without turning on the lights, he moved through the living room into the short hall and then into his bedroom, pleased that he had navigated through the dark apartment without bumping into one piece of furniture, knocking anything over, stumbling, or falling. He had managed to walk the entire way without mishap, which indicated to him again that he was not as drunk as he could have been after half a night in the back room with the boys.

He pulled out his gold cuff links and dropped them on the dresser along with his wallet, keys, handkerchief, and loose change. He kicked off his shoes without unlacing them and dropped his jacket onto the floor as he shuffled in his stocking feet toward the bed in the corner. Almost too weary to make it, he felt his knees buckle just before he reached the soft mattress. He turned and fell across it, then swung his legs up off the floor.

It had been a long evening. He had played a little backgammon and eaten some dinner with Louise, the bottled blonde who worked for him off and on, now and then. Then they'd spent an hour in the sack upstairs over the restaurant in what was supposed to be a storage room, and Nikos had done some drinking—not too much, because Louise was in a program and he did not want to tempt her because she was such a low-down dirty drunk that he could not stand the sight of her when she was loaded. They'd had a late supper before he sent her home in a cab. Then he spent a few hours playing high-stakes panguingue in the back room with Guido and Jack Browning, his bodyguard, and the rest of the boys.

Nikos was glad to be home at last, on his own bed, sacked out and free to sleep as long as he liked. No obligations. No duties. No one to take care of. One of the advantages to having been dumped by Laura, he frequently told himself, was that he did not have to worry about pleasing the bitch. There was no need to come home late and then have to give her what she needed. This way he was his own man, the way he had always been before her. The way he liked it. Only after she was gone had he realized how much he disliked being married. Only then did he realize that she had pressured him into getting married in the first place. She'd blackmailed him! The cunt had held it over his head. God damn! And he hated her guts for that. He was glad she was finally, once and for all, out of his life forever. He had been telling himself that over and over for the year and a half since she had taken off.

He sighed and let his eyes close. He let go of the thoughts of Laura and allowed himself to drift toward sleep. He had no sense of anyone being in the room with him—until he felt the stunning blow to his abdomen. As the air rushed out of his lungs, he was propelled up into a sitting position and saw the dark shadow looming above him with its arm raised, long knife in its hand, poised to strike again.

A fire raged in the pit of his stomach and extended outward toward his limbs. He could not draw a breath. He sucked at the air through his open mouth but could bring none of it into his lungs. He wanted to scream but could not. He could only watch as the knife fell again, and he heard as well as felt it tear into his shoulder. He rolled away as it was pulled from his flesh, but caught another blow to his upper back, which slammed his face against the wall beside the bed. He fell back and lay staring up at the ceiling, his entire body racked with unendurable pain, helpless to ward off his attacker. Blackness invaded his vision like a curtain slowly drawn across a window. He knew he was losing consciousness, feared he was dying, could not believe he was being murdered. *Why?* He shouted the question silently because he could not speak, and even the thought began to diminish, like a distant echo, as he lost his sense of self.

The very last thing he remembered was a final blow that caught him in the neck and seemed to sever his head from his body.

PART
ONE

ONE

The voice from the receiver sounded concerned. "Mrs. Pappas?" it insisted. "Mrs. Pappas? Are you there?"

A year and a half had passed since she had last been addressed by that name. During that time she'd been plagued by terrifying nightmares, startled by sudden sounds, frightened by innocent shadows. She had grappled with her private demons in what felt like a life-and-death struggle each time she visited Dr. Benson's office. Although she pretended to feel safe when she was cloistered with him in his office, the memories of her past hung over her like the blade of a guillotine.

But thanks to his quiet support and assistance she had slowly grown confident that she had managed to escape after all. She had succeeded in disappearing into an old, poor neighborhood of Dayton, where he would never find her. She had stopped expecting him to jump out at her each time she passed a dark alley or entered the hallway of her apartment building. She had not yet completely eliminated the apprehension that lay buried deep within her, the fear that infiltrated her dreams nightly, but at least she had learned to put the terror out of her mind for long periods during her waking hours.

"Hello? Mrs. Pappas?" the voice continued.

She shook her head slowly as if refusing to be recognized, as if she wished to deny who she was. Soft tears traveled quietly down her cheeks, and she pressed her eyes shut as if to conserve the precious drops. Outside her apartment window, through the sheer beige curtains, drawn back and tied off to allow filtered early light to spill across the floor, the sounds of morning escalated as increasing numbers of motorists entered the streets on their way to work. She heard the remote wail of a siren, plaintive, compelling, in the distance. She heard young girls shouting and laughing as they walked and ran playfully to school in the early spring Ohio morning, full of energy, full of the joy of living, unconscious of the brittleness of their fragile existence.

With her left hand she pulled the lapels of her blue terry-cloth robe together at her throat. She was not cold, but the motion comforted her. She felt safer wrapped tightly in the cloth cocoon as though she were being protected by a delicate woven mantle.

"Hello?" she said softly.

The voice brightened. "Hello! I'm trying to locate Mrs. Laura Pappas. It's very important."

"There's no one here by that name," Laura said. Her lip trembled and she caught it between her teeth as if to prevent the caller from observing her anxiety through the phone.

"Look," the voice said, sounding eager now, sounding excited, as if sensing the end of his quest.

She strained to detect some trace of accent, the slightest hint of dialect. Was it Nikki or one of his friends?

"If you know her, I'd appreciate any help you could give me. It's urgent that I locate her."

"What for?" Laura asked after a moment's hesitation.

"I'd prefer to discuss that with her. It's a very personal matter."

"I don't know where she is," Laura blurted.

The caller sighed deeply. "Look," he said. "I've been on the phone half the night. I'm tired. I've got other things to do, and I'm running out of patience. I've talked to half a dozen people already—all of whom, by the way, were as cagey as you are. I want to finish with this and get to bed."

"How did you get this number?" Laura asked, unconcerned about the caller's discomfort. "Who are you?"

A long silence followed during which Laura pictured the caller wondering how to get through to her. A large part of her wanted to end the deception, wanted to be found out and confronted. Yet she clung to her anonymity, longing to return to the precious shadows of concealment.

"You're Laura Pappas, aren't you?" the caller asked gently, softly.

"Who are you?"

"I'm a doctor," he said. "My name is Perez. I'm associated with the County of Los Angeles."

She disguised her surprise. "What do you want?"

"Are you Laura Pappas?"

Laura hesitated. "I don't know," she finally said, sadly surrendering. "It depends on who wants to know and for what reason."

Perez chuckled softly. "I got your number from Patricia Devon in Toledo."

Laura flashed on the face of her mother and was annoyed that she had been betrayed. "Go on," she said.

"She gave me your number in Dayton and told me to call you here. Believe me, it wasn't easy to get that much out of her. Why are you all so secretive? If I hadn't told her about your son, I think she would've hung up on me."

"I don't have a son," Laura said firmly. "I don't know what you're talking about."

"The boy asked me to find you," the doctor said kindly.

"And if I didn't think it was important I wouldn't have gone to all the trouble of tracking you down. I don't know what's going on between you and your son, but he needs you now."

Laura's instinct was to slam the phone into its cradle, break the connection with this stranger, and send him and his sympathetic voice into oblivion. What could he possibly know about need? How could he possibly understand the painful alliance between Laura and the boy? The boy! My God, she thought, how long had she been thinking of Dimmy as "the boy"? How distant had she grown from his memory? How far had she drawn away from the person who had saved her life, the only person in that family who had truly loved her. How easily she had turned her back on him!

She tried to recall the effort that had been required to exorcise him from her recollection. How had she fashioned him into an indistinct shadow, a distant dark spot on the legend of her past. But actually, she recalled, it had taken no energy. None. She had merely turned and walked away from him. She had simply adopted a fresh identity and forgotten him as quickly as if he were an insignificant speck of dust.

"What's wrong?" she asked in a hoarse whisper, her lips barely moving. "I haven't got any money. I have a job, but I make just enough to—"

Perez interrupted. "Mrs. Pappas—"

"Don't call me that!" she snapped. "Don't ever call me that."

"I'm sorry."

"Just don't call me that name."

"Your son is in a lot of trouble. He needs you."

"*Who* needs me?"

The doctor sounded exasperated. "I'm talking about Dimmy. Demetrios Pappas."

"He's not my son," she said. "He's my stepson. I'm not

his mother. God! He's only twelve years younger than I am.''

Perez sounded thoughtful. ''He didn't tell me that. I thought—''

''It doesn't matter,'' she said sadly, and there was a shrug of resignation in her voice.

''He seems to think you're the only one who can help him,'' the doctor said.

Laura recalled Dimmy's soft face—round, cherubic, wide-eyed, and innocent, promising eventually to be as beautiful as his father's. How easily that face had registered excitement at the introduction of a new thought or idea. How freely it had broken into a sparkling grin that stretched almost from ear to ear. His was a face that could easily entertain her, soften the severity of her bondage, even after hours of grueling, ruthless abuse. She remembered his desperate concern for her, the tears of frustration he had shed so frequently for her, and she remembered how daring he had been, how heroic. A helpless little boy who had risked his own safety, perhaps his own life, in order to protect her.

Clutching the phone to her ear, she shivered as she recalled the last time she had seen Dimmy. In her memory she could re-create that bizarre incident in intricate detail if she allowed herself to sink into the sensations of terror it had evoked. As if she had observed the action from above, had been gazing down at the players as they moved about in their individual attempts to control her life, she viewed it all once again as though it were a motion picture projected onto the screen of her mind.

She could see Dimmy in his beloved navy blue pea jacket, embattled high-top sneakers flopping loosely around his ankles, ears and nose red from the cold, racing wildly up all five flights of stairs, puffs of clouded moisture popping from his open mouth in rhythm with his awkward gasps for breath as he ran through the dark hallway, the odor of stale waste offending his nostrils as he fumbled with his key, then pushed the apartment door open. She could imagine it now as if the scene were being played out once again before her eyes.

The boy plunged into the ragged living room—torn and stained carpeting on the floor, ancient, abused furniture exposing springs like tiny reptiles pushing stuffing through its ruptured skin as though wounded in battle. Two dull standing lamps—their scorched shades cracked and peeling, warped and misshapen; their stems scarred from their frequent use as weapons—stood like forlorn guards in the corners. Yellowed walls, unadorned but for the many gashes inflicted on them during maniacal fits and rages, surrounded him like warped and distorted borders.

Dimmy allowed the door to swing shut behind him and moved quickly toward the bedroom that belonged to his father and Laura. Draped in wrinkled pajamas, silky hair tousled, sleep sheltering her face like a play mask, his older sister, Irene, appeared in the doorway of the second bedroom. She was taller than her younger brother and almost too thin, model thin, her ribs protruding like faint ridges through the light cotton pajama top. Her long, straight dark hair framed the delicate softness of her face in velvet shadow accentuating the depth of her piercing eyes, highlighting her classic features. She licked her lips nervously with the tip of her tongue. Her hands fluttered before her like slender birds as she stared in wonderment and fear at the fury on her little brother's face.

"What, Dimmy?" she said fearfully.

"Go back to bed," Dimmy whispered.

"What?" Irene whined, an uncomprehending expression on her face.

"Go!" Dimmy snapped. "Do what I tell you!"

The older girl started, pouted, turned, and disappeared into the darkness of their bedroom. "What're you so angry at me for?" she mumbled.

Slowly the bedroom door swung closed and Dimmy could hear the sounds of soft sobbing through it. He was instantly sorry he had been so sharp with her, immediately remorseful that he had used his fourteen-year-old sister badly, that he had deposited his anger once again on the innocent, modest girl, as he had been doing so frequently of late. He promised himself that he would make it up to her, that he would repay her for all that he had stolen from her. Crossing himself, he swore that he would respect Irene and give her deference as an older sister rightly deserved.

He moved to Laura's bedroom door and, pressing his ear to the thin wooden panel, eased it open slightly. He peered into the darkness, then opened it farther so that light from the living room could illuminate the bed on which Laura slept wrapped in a rough woolen blanket.

"Laura?" he whispered.

Laura, eyes closed, her troubled, swollen face lined with weariness, stirred, rolled onto her back, and lifted her throbbing head.

"Laura?" the boy repeated.

"What is it?" she asked, peering at him in the dark through puffed eyes, his handsome features obliterated by the light behind him.

He rushed to her, fell to his knees beside her as she lay back on the bed, and clutched her rough, scratched hand in both of his.

"Hurry," he breathed. "Get up!"

"What's the matter, Dimmy?" she asked, rubbing stiff pain from her bruised, reddened eyes with her free hand, instantly frightened, wary.

"Come on!" He pulled at her urgently, lifting her to a

sitting position. "He's coming. He'll be here in a minute. Come on! Please!"

"Nikki?" she asked, fear clearly etched into her voice.

The boy nodded. "He's on his way. Hurry up!"

She sighed, then reached out and touched the boy's cheek with gentle fingertips. "Why, Dimmy?" she asked. "What's the matter? What's he done?" She sighed resignedly. "What's the use?"

He turned his face away from her and averted his eyes. "Don't ask me," he said. Then, returning to her, he pleaded, "Don't talk now. There's no time. Come with me, please."

"Tell me!" she demanded.

His full, wet childish lips begin to tremble, and his eyes softened as they rested on her bruised face.

"I can't," he said. "It's terrible. Please!"

For a moment Laura inspected him, seeming to plunge deep into him with her sad eyes as if she wanted to read the silent message that was hidden there. But he would not tell her. He would say no more. He would not totally betray his father.

"All right!" she said, too fatigued to argue with him.

She slid her bare legs out from under the blanket and stood shakily beside him. She wore only one of Nikki's old T-shirts, which hung halfway to her knees, exposing most of her long legs, exposing the dark purple abrasions on the insides of her thighs. As she rose, the little boy turned his eyes away from her partial nakedness and a thin flush of embarrassment flooded his face.

"I'm sorry," she said, attempting to cover herself.

He turned and walked to the open door. With his back to her he spoke. "Please get dressed," he whispered, quickly disappearing from the room.

While she slipped on a pair of jeans and a sweatshirt, she heard him puttering in the squalid kitchen and felt ashamed at how poorly she maintained their home. She heard the scrape of a chair as he pulled it across the scratched linoleum floor, the creaking of cabinet doors as he opened and shut them, the metallic clink of flatware, the lids of jars being lifted and replaced. As she put on her brown loafers over thick white sweat socks, Dimmy reappeared carrying the small cardboard suitcase Nikki had brought with him when he arrived from Greece many years before. He treasured the valise because it reminded him of his humble beginnings.

"Here," Dimmy said, holding the suitcase out to her. "Pack your things."

"What?" she said, failing to understand his intention. "I don't need anything."

The boy rose up to his full height. "You're leaving," he said. "You're going away from here for good. Far away. And you're never coming back. Pack your things."

"No, Dimmy," she said, terrified. "That's crazy. I can't. I won't run away."

"Yes, you will!" Dimmy said emphatically. "You better, if you know what's good for you."

"If he finds me," she whispered tremblingly, "he'll kill me. Oh, God!"

His eyes did not waver as he held out the suitcase, and she began to realize that he was truly serious.

"I don't understand," she stammered, trembling like a frightened animal. "You don't want me around anymore? You don't love me?"

His usually soft eyes blazing, whitened lips pressed tightly together, nostrils flared, the boy glared at her as if enraged by such a thought and bobbed his head toward the dresser that stood against the far wall.

"No," she whined as fear consumed her. "No, Dimmy, don't do this to me. Don't make me do this."

The boy turned and with two long steps was beside the

dresser. After dropping the suitcase to the floor, he flung drawer after drawer open and emptied the delicate under-clothing into the valise—filmy pink panties, white silk half slips, sheer stockings. Garments belonging to his despised father he flung across the room to lie askew, littering the floor.

Finally, when he was finished, Dimmy turned to her. "What else?" he asked.

She shook her head in perplexity, her eyes pleading with him to stop.

"Don't you get it?" he asked. "I'm getting you out of here. I'm saving you. He's never going to touch you again. Can't you understand?" He moved to her, a heartbroken boy, and took her trembling hands in his. "Don't you under-stand?" he whispered. "I'm setting you free."

Tears flowing down her cheeks, she pleaded with him. "But I don't want to go," she said. "This is my home. I want to stay here with you and Irene and—"

"If you stay, it won't be for long," Dimmy said omi-nously.

"What do you mean?"

"Please don't argue with me," the boy pleaded. "Believe me. If you don't go, you'll regret it for the rest of your life."

Reaching down, he slammed the suitcase shut and lifted it.

"Wait," she said, seeming befuddled.

She dashed to the closet and, reaching up to a shelf above the many suits hanging in a row, located a small red velvet box. She turned back to Dimmy and showed it to him.

"My jewelry," she said, nodding as if to indicate that she was resigned to leaving. "I can't go without these things." She gazed around the room anxiously seeking, searching. What had she forgotten? She patted her pockets. "I don't have any money, Dimmy. I can't go anywhere."

From the pocket of his pea coat, Dimmy pulled a large roll of bills. "This is for you," he announced quietly.

Her eyes opened wide in blank amazement. "Where did you get all that money?"

"I got it," the boy said.

"Where?"

He shrugged and waved off her inquiry.

"I'm not going unless you tell me."

His face clouded and he finally spoke angrily. "I took it from him. From the kitchen. From all the places he hides it."

"Oh, my God!" Laura breathed. "He'll kill you."

The boy shrugged bravely. "Maybe," he said. "But he won't hurt you anymore."

She moved to him and laid her warm hand on his cheek. "You can't do this, Dimmy," she said softly.

"It's done!"

"I can't . . ."

He nodded once sharply, grasped her elbow, and guided her firmly out into the disorderly living room. As he pushed her toward the front door, he noticed that Irene's door was slightly ajar, that an eye was pressed to the tiny opening watching their every move.

A moment of fear flashed across his face. Observation by his sister meant automatic exposure, he knew. For an instant he wanted to stop it, wanted to pull back from this dangerous course. He thought of returning Laura to the bedroom, undressing her, pushing her back into bed. He wanted to save himself, of course. But he wanted to save Laura even more. He was filled with love for her. The feeling swept over him and enveloped him. It was the final experience that persuaded him to continue.

Dimmy pushed Laura out into the hallway, leaned back inside to shut off the overhead light, and slammed the door closed behind him, leaving the lonesome eye to stare into the darkness.

"I guess he wouldn't look for me unless he was really desperate," Laura said into the phone. She breathed deeply, sighed, and composed herself. "He wouldn't betray me for just anything."

"There's no question that the kid feels desperate all right," Perez said. "His behavior has certainly indicated that."

"How?"

Perez hesitated. "Dangerous behavior in an adolescent is usually a cry for help."

"What kind of dangerous behavior?" Laura asked suspiciously.

"Self-destructive behavior," Perez said, being intentionally evasive. "Walking on the edge. Doing stuff that can't possibly result in a positive outcome."

Laura stiffened. "What did that bastard make him do?"

Perez was surprised. "What?"

"Never mind," Laura said. "What's Dimmy done?"

Perez cleared his throat uncomfortably. "He's committed a serious crime. He's been in custody, in the county jail, for the past six months, Mrs. . . . What can I call you?"

"My name is Laura," she said. "What crime?"

"He's awaiting trial . . ." Perez let his voice trail off as if wishing to avoid telling her.

"What did he do, Doctor?" she insisted.

Softly Perez said, "He tried to kill his father."

"Oh, my God!"

"There's a question of self-defense, and he's got a good lawyer," Perez hastened to add, "but . . ."

"But what?"

Perez sounded sheepish. "He isn't handling jail very well."

"My God!" Laura said. "Who could? He's just a kid."

"He's worse than we expected. No one likes jail, Laura, but most inmates manage to adjust, if only to survive psychically."

Perez paused and Laura said, "What kind of doctor are you, Dr. Perez?"

"I'm a psychiatrist." He let a moment pass. "Actually, I'm Dimmy's psychiatrist. At least, I've been assigned by the court to care for him temporarily. During this trying time, I mean. Until . . ."

"Till he gets out of jail?"

Perez wavered. "No. Not exactly. He's out of jail at this moment."

"What are you talking about, Doctor?"

"Dimmy's in the county hospital prison ward." The doctor sounded apologetic, as if he felt responsible, as if Dimmy had been treated unjustly and he was to blame.

"What are you doing, Doctor?" she asked coldly. "Parceling out your information as if it's rationed?"

Perez said, "I'm sorry, Laura." He coughed and cleared his throat. "The truth is he's been in jail too long. I cautioned the court that he was not adjusting well. I told them he was reacting in an especially abnormal manner, but you know how it is."

"No, I don't," Laura said. "I don't know anything about jail."

"Yesterday," Perez continued, "Dimmy tried to hang himself."

"Oh, no," Laura groaned. She suddenly realized that she had not simply run for her life that night a year and a half ago. She had, in reality, abandoned Dimmy and Irene as well.

"Look," Perez said. "He's okay. They cut him down in time, but he really needs somebody. That was a very desperate act and I'm afraid it won't be his last suicide attempt. He's feeling very much alone, isolated and helpless.''

"Oh, God," Laura sobbed, her face burning with shame.

"I think it would be wonderful if you could call him. I'll give you the number. It can't hurt, right? At least it'll buy me some time."

"No!" Laura said.

"What?"

"No!"

"Come on, Laura," Perez said. "That's not so much to ask."

Laura swallowed. Her throat had tightened, and she was having difficulty breathing. She blinked blinding tears back from her eyes. At that instant she drew near to despising herself. Had she identified so completely back then with Nikki, with her tormentor, that she had actually become cold like him? Had she managed her own survival through conversion, by emulating her tormentor? Had she learned to repay simple, unconditional love with abandonment, pain, and suffering, as Nikki did?

She spoke firmly. "No!" she said. "I won't call. I'm catching the first plane out. Tonight. I'll be there in the morning. Give me your phone number, Doctor. I'll call you as soon as I get to the airport."

TWO

Before going into the office, Laura booked a seat on an evening flight to O'Hare, where she could connect with a flight that would arrive in Los Angeles at 12:27 in the morning West Coast time. She even paid for the ticket at the travel agent's so that she could not talk herself out of going.

Her next concern was her job. She was uncomfortable about asking for a leave of absence because she felt obligated to the woman who had hired her when no one else would—without experience, without references, without even a permanent address. First, she phoned in ill, intending to call again from the West Coast when it would be too late for the office manager to argue with her. Later, however, after withdrawing her meager savings from the bank, phoning her mother in Toledo, and packing a few clothes appropriate for the climate of California, she decided to go to the office and do the honorable thing.

The real estate office, though coldly furnished, seemed warm and secure when she stepped through the door, and she hated the thought of leaving it. For the past year the place had served as the closest thing to a home and family that she had been able to create while in exile. Lazarus Realty, run effectively by Franny Gouch, the middle-aged office manager, had been the refuge, the haven, she had so desperately needed when she was running from Nikki Pappas, fearing his pursuit, fearing capture and a return to bondage. For the past year the office had been her safe house, and she worried about how confident she could feel away from it.

Franny had taken Laura to her heart almost immediately, like a mother hen with a newly hatched chick. Franny had hired Laura when no one else would. At the interview Laura had been nervous and agitated, with suspiciously darting eyes that could not maintain contact and anxious fingers that did not cease their continual picking. But Franny Gouch had sensed something worthwhile in the disturbed girl who literally begged for any kind of useful work through which she could earn enough to rent a bed for the night and buy a warm meal. Franny, who had a thing for the downtrodden and the defenseless, saw in Laura her own little sister, Milly, who had not survived childhood, the little sister whose death had left her devastated.

"Can you type?" Franny had asked.

"A little," Laura had answered shyly.

Franny grinned. "How little?"

The girl had looked away. She chewed her lip the way Milly used to when she wanted to lie. "Very little."

"I thought so," the older woman said, smiling softly. "You're cute, though, aren't you? Were you thinking of getting a job on cuteness alone?"

Laura's eyes opened wide at Franny's words. The last word she would have used to describe herself was "cute." In her own perception, she was an ugly, bedraggled throwaway to whom people gave a wide berth when passing.

"I guess," she had said finally, willing to acquiesce to anything at that point. She smoothed her hands down over her lightweight coat, touched her hair self-consciously, and wet her lips with the tip of her tongue. She had dressed as best she could in a blouse that buttoned up to her chin, hiding the few yellowing bruises that still remained as mementos of Nikki's brand of love and affection. Her eyes, wounded and sad, seemed to be imploring Franny for some consideration, for some sign of kindness.

And Franny had felt the girl's need reaching out to her like an open hand. "I'll bet you could do lots of things," she said, clearly trying to comfort the girl. She examined Laura and thought she was seeing a replica of what Milly would have become had she lived. They differed in physical appearance—hair color, skin tone, height, and size—but in luck, fortune, and destiny, Franny sensed that they were identical. Milly and Laura.

Laura nodded shyly. "I'm sure."

"You could sort the mail and do the filing and things like that," Franny said, feeling a sudden desperation, the sense of urgency felt by a rescuing swimmer as she pulled and tugged at a helpless cramp victim to prevent him from drowning. She knew she was creating an unneeded job. She knew there was a good chance she would regret what she was doing. But she also knew, as surely as she knew that the girl before her was down and out, at the bottom of her luck, that Laura desperately needed compassion if she was to survive, and her mind flashed to sister Milly once again.

"I'm sure I could do that," Laura said hurriedly, realizing that she was being offered a helping hand.

Franny smiled warmly. "I can't pay very much," she said. "But I'm sure I can get you started."

"It's okay," Laura whispered softly. "Anything you can do . . . I'll be grateful for. Anything."

Much later Franny told Laura how touched she had been by the girl's obvious plight. She had felt melancholy, remembering her sister, remembering how she had felt, how helpless and abandoned, so much like Laura, herself praying for a benefactor to ease the pain of Milly's death. She had forced herself to shrug off those feelings before they led to more complex remembering that would certainly have destroyed the remainder of her day. But she had felt pressed to take a risk, to trust the strange girl, although her common sense reminded her that she was far too inclined toward sentimentality and that all too often good turns were repaid with betrayal.

"Even though you confessed to being desperate, broke, and lonely, a difficult confession for any girl to make," Franny had told her later, "I sensed you had another secret. It was like a shadow following you. I felt that bad luck was pursuing you. And I knew that it would stay with you. It would probably hang over you forever, unless a friend intervened." The older woman sighed deeply. "And at that moment, against all reason, I resolved to be that friend."

Though fully aware that Laura knew nothing about real estate, Franny had hired the girl as a part-time file clerk, had taught her, supervised her, nurtured her, and eventually promoted her and elevated her to the position of assistant office manager.

She had given Laura three weeks' salary in advance and helped her find a small semifurnished apartment near the office. For several Friday evenings running, they had scouted used-furniture stores together, seeking the little additions that would transform the apartment into a home, and on a succession of Sundays, they had painted and papered together, getting covered with glue and paint and grime. And though to observant strangers they might have appeared to be mother and daughter, they felt more like high school buddies. Each related to the other's loneliness and fears. They had both been alone in the midst of an indifferent crowd—Laura cut off and isolated from her family, Franny mourning the loss of the sister she had loved so deeply. Now they had found each other, and suddenly they were together. They did not speak of it, but they knew without articulation that they were together in a very special way and soon their bond would become so strong as to be unbreakable.

They had stood back one day, having finally finished painting the apartment, and examined their work.

Franny swiped at a gash of blue paint streaked across her forehead and swore under her breath. Laura turned, smiled, and handed her a rag.

"There's more paint on this rag than there is on me." Franny laughed.

"That's what you think." Laura laughed easily with her. "Here. Let me do it." She retrieved the rag and rubbed paint from Franny's face. She stepped back, examined her work, then returned and rubbed some more. "There. That's better. Now you're cute again."

"Thank you," Franny said, and there were sudden tears in her eyes.

They stared at each other for a moment, each examining the face of the other.

"I think it's time to celebrate," Franny finally said, as if wishing to break the spell. "Let's open the wine."

"Oh, good!" Laura said, her eyes flashing with happiness. "I'll get it." She dashed off to the kitchen.

Franny watched her depart and abruptly felt fulfilled, settled, accomplished. In the four weeks since she had first met Laura she had lost the sense of emptiness that had perpetually accompanied her and her memory of Milly. Laura had unwittingly filled the terrible void within her, increased her sense of validity, helped her feel whole rather than impaired and wasted. The girl had given a purpose to Franny's life. To outside observers it might have appeared to be the product of a unique friendship, but Franny knew it was something deeper, more profound, more fundamental than mere cama-raderie.

"Here!" Laura reappeared from the kitchen carrying two glasses of champagne. She moved to Franny's side and handed her a glass.

"What shall we toast?" Franny asked.

"You decide," Laura said.

Franny grinned. "To your new life, free of specters and apparitions."

Laura nodded slowly. "And to my new best friend," she said, touching her glass to Franny's, then sipping and wrinkling her nose as the bubbles tickled it.

"Okay," Franny said, deeply touched, her voice husky and almost inaudible. She slipped her arm through Laura's and raised the glass to her own lips so that they could drink together, arms entwined. But her eyes did not stray from the girl's face. Over the rim of the glass, she studied the childlike features, the sad, wounded eyes, the slightly arched brows, the long eyelashes that curled upward like tiny brushes. And the warmth of her feelings washed over her and engulfed her.

"What?" Laura asked, sensing a change in Franny.

The older woman wanted to speak of the mysterious churning inside her, to confess the extent of her feelings, which she could barely comprehend, but she was unable to utter the words that caught in her throat.

She leaned forward instead and touched her lips to Laura's warm cheek. "I love you, Milly," she whispered.

"What?" Laura asked, moving away from Franny, gazing at her, perplexed.

"Oh, God!" Franny said, frantic. "God! I'm sorry." She covered her face with her hand and began to weep quietly. "I'm so sorry."

"For what, Franny?"

Agitated, Franny turned from her. "I called you Milly. I called you by my sister's name."

"I didn't know you had a sister."

"I shouldn't have done that," Franny whispered. "That was a terrible thing to do."

Laura touched her shoulder. "Why was it terrible?"

Franny shook her head. "Because she's been dead for a long time, and I had no right to make you into her."

Laura followed Franny to the bathroom and watched as she splashed water on her face to cool her cheeks.

"Franny," Laura said, speaking the woman's name faintly, "I'm honored."

"I don't know what came over me," Franny said.

Laura wrapped her arms tightly around her and spoke like a comforting mother. "Don't worry, Franny," she said. "I couldn't ask for a better sister."

"You're not angry?"

Laura shook her head. "No," she said, touching Franny's disheveled hair tentatively. "I love you, too."

"You'll never know how that makes me feel, Laura. I need your friendship as much as you need mine."

"You have it," Laura said.

"Thank you," Franny said. "You'll never regret it. I'll be the best sister you could ever have—better than a real one." She clutched Laura's hand in both of hers. "I'll always be here for you. I'll never let you down. I swear to God!"

And Laura, knowing that Franny would abide by her words, took the older woman in her arms and held her as she sobbed softly and quietly grew calm once again.

Now, after more than a year of working together and being close friends, the older woman was frightened by what Laura was telling her.

Over the past year Franny Gouch had watched Laura become more self-reliant, less anxious, happier. She had settled into a relatively normal way of life and the phantoms behind her eyes had slowly, gently, faded away. The two women had settled into a comfortable routine, relying on each other, sharing. Franny did not dare think of Laura ever leaving.

For a brief moment after entering the office, Laura felt hesitant; her resolve to fly to California seemed to dissipate in the light of her daily reality, and she was tempted to forget Dr. Perez and his early-morning phone call, to push it from her memory as she had learned to do with her nightly bad dreams, and to carry on with her new life as if no interruption had occurred.

"Good morning, Laura," Franny Gouch bubbled, rushing over to Laura. "Poor thing," she moaned. "Are you feeling any better?" Her bright blue eyes sparkled, and her puffy gray hair bobbed when she moved. "You shouldn't have come in," she said. "You should stay in bed until you're fully recovered. Otherwise it lingers. You'll never get rid of it. There's nothing as persistent as a spring cold."

Laura smiled weakly. "I need to talk to you, Franny," she had said, biting her lip, her eyes darting about the room. "Privately."

Franny's exuberance faded. "What is it, dear? What's the matter?"

"Please," Laura said.

Franny nodded. "Yes. Of course. In my office."

In Franny's office Laura fidgeted nervously. "I need some time off," she said at last.

"Of course, you do," Franny said worriedly, knowing instinctively that Laura was not asking for a day or two. "You're not well. You have to rest until this cold is—"

"No, Franny," Laura interrupted. "Not because of the cold. I need to go away for a while. To California."

Franny stared at Laura as the shadows of the old demons

slipped in behind the girl. She did not want to believe what she was hearing. "What for?"

Laura shook her head sadly. "I can't tell you."

Franny waited, then nodded slowly. "Okay," she said, controlling herself with great effort, "but I thought we'd gotten beyond distrust. I thought you knew you could tell me anything. I would never divulge your secret or use it against you."

"I know that," Laura said.

"Then what?"

Laura shook her head. "I'm afraid of what you'd think of me." She raised her hand and silenced Franny, who was about to protest. "There's so much you don't know about me, that I hoped you'd never know. I wish I could forget it all, but I can't." She sighed, and her shoulders sagged wearily. "I have some unfinished business. No matter how well I hide, it will find me eventually."

Franny, saddened by Laura's apparent pain, spoke softly. "You know I'll do anything for you." She clasped her hands before her as if in prayer. "Let me help you. I have so much to give. Let me give it to you, Laura."

Laura smiled gratefully at the woman, but shook her head. "There's nothing you can do about this," she said. "But just knowing you're here, caring about me, maybe that's good enough."

Franny studied her young friend for a long moment. She examined the near-perfect features, the petite chin and nose, the high cheekbones accented with a natural blush, the soft ivory skin, the gleaming hair reflecting shards of light like a mirror, and she felt proud, as if Laura were her sister, as if she had created this young woman instead of having found her floundering about in despair.

"Anything," Franny said, the word catching in her throat. "No matter what. Just call me. I'll be here for you." She slipped one arm around Laura's shoulders and held her gently. "You can count on me."

"Thank you, Franny."

Franny nodded. "Nothing, not the worst sin in the world, could change the way I feel about you, Laura. Remember that. I know you. And nothing you've ever done has anything to do with who you are."

"Thank you."

"Someday you'll need me, and I'll be able to prove to you just how much I love you."

Laura nodded.

"Someday," Franny said. "I'll prove it to you."

Laura knew that when Dr. Benson was through questioning the wisdom of going to California at all, he would then question her decision to arrive in a strange city in the middle of the night. He would probe her motives for scheduling her trip at night, and he would suggest that she unconsciously wanted to make the journey more arduous than it had to be so that she could once again feel thoroughly victimized. He would point out that she continued to punish herself, that she still sought to assuage her overwhelming guilt with self-inflicted retribution.

He lingered interminably on what he regarded as her craving for punishment, and she dreaded her last visit to him. She was weary of answering his questions. She despised the feelings of guilt and shame that he contended she secretly enjoyed. Sometimes she hated Dr. Benson for insisting that she examine why she so frequently placed herself in situations where she became a victim, why she was attracted to people who were willing to abuse her. His voice served as a prod, moving her along in a single direction, pushing her back into line, keeping her on the straight and narrow, forcing her to face her own dangerous fascination with cruel and sadistic men.

She could not get in to see him until one o'clock that afternoon, and then only during his lunch hour, which he finally agreed to sacrifice after she insisted that her need for a short session to discuss this new, radical turn of events in her life constituted a real emergency. On the one hand, she felt she needed his endorsement in order to follow through on her decision. On the other, however, she feared his disapproval and was secretly glad that he could not see her right away. She was glad she would have time to set her plan in motion before he could talk her out of it.

When, finally, she was settled in Dr. Benson's office, Laura knew from his voice that he was not in favor of her decision to fly immediately into an unknown and potentially dangerous situation. He regarded her hasty resolution as impulsive, an example of her self-destructive tendency. He pointed out that she was inclined to leap into situations without thoroughly considering the possible consequences of her behavior. That, he said, was the single most significant cause of the difficulties which had brought her into therapy in the first place.

She thought it was unfair of him to take the information she had given him and use it against her, but she did not tell him so. She was practicing assertiveness out in the world, as he had suggested, but she was still far too frightened of being abandoned to assert herself with Dr. Benson. She was too afraid of his displeasure to risk antagonizing him, and yet, for Dimmy she had found the courage.

"Have you considered carefully the possible ramifications of such a trip?" Benson pushed his glasses up his nose.

She stared at the gentle therapist in his familiar brown leather chair. He was bald except for a fuzzy white fringe, and he looked like a wise owl in his huge horn-rimmed glasses.

His office, so familiar to Laura that she felt protected there, looked like a small living room. Done in earth colors—browns, tans, greens—it contained only a soft leather couch and a matching chair, a kidney-shaped walnut coffee table, walnut bookcases, and a dozen soft leather cushions that could be scattered around the room or stacked in a corner.

Finally she nodded and shrugged her shoulders. "The consequences don't matter," she said.

"Don't they?" the doctor asked.

"Dimmy didn't think about the consequences when he helped me."

The doctor nodded. "He was a child. You're an adult. Don't you think adults need to be more responsible?"

"Yes," she replied. "I think going to Dimmy's aid now is the responsible thing to do."

"Do you?"

"Yes."

He contemplated her quiet confidence for a moment. "Why do you say that?"

"Because a year ago I wouldn't have had the courage to go, and I wasn't very responsible then at all. But I am now, thanks to you. And I'm not nearly so afraid as I used to be."

"You're saying that therapy has helped you make this decision?"

"Yes," she said. "If you could help me, I can help Dimmy."

Benson shrugged. "I had nothing to risk. You do." He held out his hands, palms upward, as if to emphasize the indisputability of his statement.

She smiled and nodded. "Then you should be proud of me," she said. "I'm going anyway. I'm taking a risk."

He glanced away from her for an instant. "I'm worried about you."

She smiled. "That's nice."

"I mean it."

"It's still nice."

He laughed. "You're a mischievous child, you know that?"

She shook her head. "I'm not a child anymore, Dr. Benson. Thanks to you, I'm all grown up. I don't stew in my anger anymore. I don't hide in my apartment avoiding the world anymore. I don't think of myself as worthless anymore."

He gazed at her incredulously.

"Well," she said, "hardly ever."

He smiled. "I see."

"Doesn't that mean that I'm all grown up?"

He touched his eyeglass frame with a forefinger and nodded to her. "I suppose so."

"You did a pretty good job with me."

"You did the good job," he said.

"You think so?"

"Yes."

"Hmm," she murmured. "That makes me feel good."

"It should."

"Then why don't you trust me to go to California, if I did such a good job?"

"You know why, don't you?"

"No, I don't."

"Think about it," he said.

She pressed her lips tightly together, then relaxed and even smiled slightly. "Okay," she said. "I'm scared of Nikki."

"Of course you are," he said softly.

"But that shouldn't stop me. It didn't stop Dimmy."

"The threat was different. For both him and his sister."

"What do you mean?" she asked, puzzled.

He shrugged. "The worst that Dimmy and his sister could fear was more of the same. He had done just about every despicable deed one could perpetrate upon a child. What more could he do?" He nodded slowly, his eyes locked onto hers. "But for you there is a much greater risk."

She was with him now, suddenly cognizant of where he was leading her. "What's that?"

He squirmed uncomfortably in his brown leather chair and spoke hesitantly as if not convinced of the appropriateness of what he was about to say. "You fell in love with him once," he said.

"Yes." She nodded.

"He's a charming and handsome man."

"Yes, he is."

"Very appealing to you."

"He was," she agreed.

He hesitated. "You've made phenomenal progress here."

"I know, and I'm grateful."

"You've come a long way," the doctor said. "At a great price—a lot of hard work, pain, suffering. It's been a most difficult therapy."

"I'll say."

The doctor wet his lips, and his eyes appealed to her. "I don't want you to lose all you've gained. I don't want you to slip back into that dependent mode." He stared at her with eyes as hard as diamonds. "I don't want you to go back to him," he said.

"That monster?"

Benson cleared his throat. "He was a monster when you met him, when you fell in love with him, and when you married him, wasn't he?"

"Yes."

"You knew it, and yet you gave in."

"Yes."

"You took a monster to your heart and then were shocked when he behaved like a monster."

"That's right."

The doctor lowered his eyes. "I don't want you to do that again."

She looked at him lovingly. He was not just her doctor. He had become a comforting voice, a friend, a comrade, a kindred spirit, a nurturing, accepting, caring parent, and she did not ever want to lose him.

"You need to have more faith in your skill, Doctor." She smiled brightly at him, laughing at him just a little, as a loving sister would laugh at a socially inept brother. "I'd never go back to him." She leaned forward and spoke emphatically. "I would die first!"

He shook his head sadly. "I hope and pray it never comes to that."

THREE

Having made the connection at O'Hare just barely in time and then rushed through the crowded passageways of the terminal hauling her own luggage, bumping and jostling strollers as she weaved through slower traffic, Laura finally boarded the 747, located her window seat, and settled back hoping to relax during the remainder of her journey to Los Angeles.

However, she could not free herself from the memory of Dr. Benson's warning of the dangers that lay ahead for her when and if she encountered her husband. The psychiatrist had instilled a persistent apprehension in her. The admission of his own fear for her continued to trouble her. Laura had believed that Dr. Benson feared nothing. She had believed that he was superhuman, near-perfect. Seeing his fear out in the open was a new experience for her.

She wondered about her own progress. Had she been deceiving herself? Perhaps she had not moved far toward personal courage during the past year. Was Benson's view of what she had accomplished more realistic than her own? Had she deluded herself into thinking she possessed more self-confidence than she'd actually gained? Had she simply become a more proficient deceiver? A better liar?

What had she really learned while in Benson's care? she wondered. To deceive herself in a more sophisticated manner? To avoid the pain of change by pretending to have already achieved the strength she was still far from gaining? She recalled her early sessions with him and felt an involuntary stiffening of her body, a physical resistance to the memory of that struggle.

"You don't want to be here," he was saying as she twisted and turned on the soft leather sofa to avoid his penetrating eyes. His office was still unfamiliar to her, still strange and forbidding. It was her third visit, and earlier that morning she had toyed with the idea of calling to cancel, but finally she had forced herself to go.

"Yes, I do want to be here," she lied. Her whisper was barely audible, and she turned away from him so that he could not read the lie in her eyes.

"There's no reason for you to want to be here," he continued gently. "To subject yourself to the scrutiny of a stranger, to bare your soul to a person you hardly know." His face remained expressionless, even when he reached up and pushed his spectacles up onto the bridge of his nose.

"No," she said. "I don't mind. Truly I don't."

"You trust me?" he asked, the corners of his mouth dipping downward slightly.

"Of course," she said.

He nodded. "Of course," he repeated. "Why not? Why shouldn't you?"

"Yes," she said. "Why shouldn't I?"

"Yes," he said. "Your life experience has proven to you that strangers are trustworthy, hasn't it?" He watched her carefully, waiting to see if she had noted his sarcasm.

"I guess so," she replied unemotionally.

"What do you mean, you guess so?"

She shrugged. "If you say so."

"If I say so, it's automatically true. Is that it?"

"I suppose."

"What do you mean, you suppose?"

She held her breath for an instant, then released it, controlling her annoyance. "I mean, you're the doctor and you know more than I do."

He nodded thoughtfully. "That's right!" he finally said. "I'm the doctor, and you're the patient. I'm sitting here, and you're sitting there. I'm always right, and you're always wrong. Because I'm educated and you're not. Because I'm an expert and you don't know anything. Because you're stupid and I'm smart. Right?"

She lowered her head, feeling ashamed, guilty, worthless. She responded to him docilely. "Yes," she said so softly he barely heard her.

"Do you believe that?" he asked.

"Yes."

He nodded again. "Really believe it?"

"Yes." She began to sob.

"How does it feel to know you're insignificant?"

She glanced at him through tear-filled eyes, half expecting to find him gloating, his face twisted into a sadistic grimace of joy at her discomfort. She was sure he enjoyed tormenting her. After all, she thought, what could make her think that she deserved better? Had she expected him to be kind to her simply because she was paying him?

But she was surprised to note that he remained unmoved and expressionless. The exchange had not been pleasurable for him after all. He looked as though he had merely stated a fact, and she despised herself further for being so unimportant. She covered her face with her hands and sobbed aloud, her tears flowing freely. Great heaving sobs escaped her.

"I'm not insignificant," she moaned. "I'm not." She continued to sob, and tears poured down her cheeks.

"Of course not," he said.

"I'm just as important as anyone else." Her chest heaved as she fought to control her sobbing.

"Exactly," he said.

"I'm tired of being treated like dirt."

"I hope so."

She studied him then. Was he laughing at her, mocking her? Did he see her as some foolish girl? Would he treat her like an ignorant, immature child? Would he punish her in some sly way? She focused on his appearance—his thin body, the large head, the soft hands resting lazily on the arms of his chair. The hair that ringed his head stood like tiny electrified spikes. His spectacles were large and thick and horn-rimmed. He wore neatly pressed trousers with fresh wrinkles across his lap, and a blue and white checked wash-and-wear shirt.

"Oh, God!" she whispered. "What's happened to me? What am I doing here? Why do I always hurt myself?"

"How are you hurting yourself now?"

She shook her head sadly. "I need help. Don't torture me. Don't do this to me."

"So," he said softly. "You don't trust me."

She hesitated in confusion. What did he want from her? she wondered. "No," she said, not looking at him.

"Good," he said warmly. "That's a better beginning."

"What?"

"You have no reason to trust me, Laura. You should be wary of me. You should be cautious of me. As the Bible says, respect but suspect. You don't know anything about me. I could be a charlatan. I could be incompetent. I could be a fool. It's perfectly normal for you to be guarded with me. It's more than normal. It's intelligent."

"I don't understand," she said shaking her head in bewilderment. "What are you telling me?"

He moved for the first time. He leaned forward in his chair as if to emphasize what he was about to say, and he spoke in a soft, conspiratorial voice. "You don't need to trust others, either, Laura. You don't need to trust me or anyone else. What you need is to trust yourself." He smiled at her almost affectionately. "Maybe that sounds silly to you. Maybe it sounds like a cliché. But it's the most important truth you will hear in this room."

He leaned back again and nodded shortly. "When you have learned to trust yourself—when you know that it doesn't matter what others do or say, that it doesn't matter if people fail you or deceive you or try to rip you off, that what really matters is that you will always be there for yourself, that you will survive no matter what, that you are strong and capable and competent and can rely upon yourself—*then* you can trust me if you want to. Because, then, when you decide to make yourself vulnerable by trusting me, it won't be devastating, it won't be a tragedy if I fail you. Then you'll have yourself to fall back upon, and the worst that I can be, no matter how evil I turn out to be, is a disappointment to you." He sighed and shrugged his shoulders. "That's what you'll be doing in here, Laura, for the next year or so. You'll be learning how trustworthy you really are."

Laura wondered how successful she had been in learning to trust herself. Why did she feel such trepidation if she had successfully thrown off the shroud of her past self? She could almost hear Dr. Benson warning her that she might always have some doubt, might always remember how she used to be, might always fear regressing to her old dependent self, but he had said she would come through each crisis because she was no longer that old self. Now, as she clutched the armrest with tense fingers and braced her back stiffly against the soft cushions, she wondered if she truly could trust herself.

She was encouraged to note that as the plane prepared for takeoff and the harried passengers settled down, no one sat beside her. In her present agitated state she preferred to be spared idle conversation. She lifted the armrest that separated the two seats, kicked off her shoes, and swung her feet up to occupy both spaces.

She braced herself for takeoff, grimacing as the engines' thrust pressed her back into her seat, and recalled how much she disliked flying, though she hated to admit to her fear. She knew that flight was the way of life for contemporary people, but still she suffered through the experience and wished she had lived in an earlier time when it was acceptable to speed across country in a railway car on steel tracks. She liked to believe that she had been meant to remain on the ground and was unhappy to be suspended in the air.

She propped a pillow between the edge of the seat and the window and rested her head on it, then closed her eyes and allowed her mind to wander. She remembered her first time on an airplane, the sheer terror of it, when she had flown to Miami with Nikki on their honeymoon. She recalled how understanding he had been at first and then how he had teased her as his patience wore thin. Finally he had become angry when her fear did not subside. Nikki had wanted her to stop being afraid upon command, but she had been unable to accommodate him, nor had she ever flown with him again, although she paid for that privilege many times over. Nikki expected obedience on demand. He tolerated no disagreement, especially from a woman.

''Don't argue with me,'' he was saying, twisting her hair in his fingers. He held her pressed up against the wall beside the mailboxes, his other hand holding her hip, his thumb digging into the flesh of her thigh.

"You're hurting me, Nikki," she said and squirmed to escape the pressure he was applying to her.

They were standing in the poorly lighted hallway on the ground floor of her apartment building on Amsterdam Avenue where she shared a fourth-floor walk-up with Liz, an aspiring actress. Nikki had just told Laura that she would marry him, and she had made the mistake of suggesting that he ask her rather than tell her.

"Where I come from," he said, "women don't argue with their men. You understand? I take care of you, and you do what I tell you. You understand?"

"It's not like that in America," she said, pulling futilely at his fingers, which were digging painfully into her hip. "If you want that, go back to Greece."

"When I go back, I take you with me. You understand?" He laughed and pressed his lips upon hers. She resisted mildly, pretending she did not like what he was doing. In truth, she loved the way he kissed her. She loved the power in his lips, the strength of his tongue as he thrust it into her mouth, the feel of his teeth urging her to surrender. His hand left her hip and traveled up to her breast and clutched it, kneaded it like bread dough, and though the action hurt and disgusted her, it somehow thrilled her as well.

"You belong to me," he whispered into her mouth, the words traveling down into her throat. She shuddered as his voice vibrated in her. "You are mine, chérie. My little Laurina. Mine. You will marry me. Believe me. You will marry me and be mine for the rest of your life. Until you are dead."

They had met some weeks earlier at the Iliad, a small Greek restaurant in the lower seventies near Laura's apartment. She and Liz, having developed a taste for moussaka, were in the habit of dining there once or twice a month. They usually sat at a table covered with stained white oilcloth in a dark corner of the long whitewashed room. From there they could watch the darkly handsome young mandolin player who played traditional Greek folk music from a tiny platform in the rear. They enjoyed watching the customers who, carried away by the musical reminder of home, would often dance in front of him. Though Laura and Liz had been invited to join in at times, they had never accepted.

The mandolin player had brought Nikki to their table one evening and shyly introduced him as Nikos Pappas, a friend from the old country only recently arrived in America. Then, appearing more afraid of Nikki than affectionate toward him, he had backed away and returned to his tiny stage.

Nikos, however, did not depart. Without benefit of invitation, he pulled out a chair, turned it around, and straddled it, facing Laura and Liz as if they were old friends.

"Call me Nikki," he had said, smiling brightly. His eyes moved from one to the other and finally settled on Laura as if deciding that she presented the more interesting view. "You want a drink?" He asked Laura first, then turned briefly to Liz and repeated the question in English that sounded practiced and belied the assertion that he was new in America.

Laura shook her head but Liz, obviously attracted to him, smiled and nodded.

"Good!" he said happily. He twisted around on the chair and signaled the waiter. "Two ouzos," he shouted, raising two fingers. He leaned toward Laura. "You want something? Anything!"

She shrugged helplessly, fascinated by his charming manner.

"Sure," he said, nodding emphatically. "One coffee," he told the waiter.

He was small and dark, his thick black hair cut close to

his head and shaved neatly at the back of his neck. His thick but neatly trimmed mustache reminded her of the policemen who patrolled Times Square. He wore black pants with a silver-buckled black belt and a black cotton shirt unbuttoned halfway down his chest, exposing thick, curly black chest hair. He wore no jewelry, but around his neck, on a slender silver chain, hung a long, thin crucifix.

"You want to dance?" he asked Laura.

"No, thank you," she said tentatively.

He pouted. "You don't like Greek music."

"No! I like it," she protested. "I like it very much."

He smiled broadly again flashing his large white teeth.

"I'll dance with you," Liz said impulsively.

He turned his eyes to her and studied her for a moment. He hesitated as if pondering a puzzle. "Okay!" he said dramatically. He jumped to his feet, extended a hand to Liz, pulled her to her feet, and led her toward the dance floor.

"Dance!" he shouted.

Laura watched as the mandolin player ended the slow, sad dirge he had been playing and launched into the vibrant, melodic cadence of a familiar Greek folk song. Nikki handed Liz a small glass of the thick, milky ouzo mixed with water, touched his glass to hers and threw the liquid down his throat. Liz, observing him, lifted her glass to her lips and sipped carefully.

"No!" he shouted. "Like this!" He mimed the aggressive downing of the drink, then, clutching her wrist, lifted her hand to her mouth and forced her to swallow the entire contents of her glass. She choked and coughed, and he laughed as he slapped her back. Then he grabbed her by the waist and swung her into a calculatedly sensual dance.

He danced slowly and powerfully. As he moved in a tight circle, one arm encircling Liz's waist, the other half raised in the air, he bent his knees and sank low to the floor, pulling her down with him as the music dipped downward, then lifting her upward again as he raised himself with the lofting of the music. He kicked out emphatically, stiffly but gracefully, his movements taut but symmetrical. Proudly, arrogantly, his head high, he moved Liz around the tiny floor, in total command of her. She moved awkwardly, her eyes focused on his feet as she attempted to follow his lead, always just a bit behind him. He made her look statuesque by his mere presence beside her.

The room grew silent as patrons turned to watch the couple. As the tempo of the music quickened, Nikki's feet stamped more commandingly and his guttural shouts punctuated the increasing passion of the dance. Without missing a beat, he scooped another glass of ouzo from the waiter's tray and passed it to Liz, who was helpless to refuse while squeezed against his side. Together, each with one free hand on the glass, they raised it to Liz's lips and held it there as she swallowed the opaque liquid. Then he flung the empty glass against a far wall, smashing it to bits and laughing boisterously. Liz, mesmerized by the dance, by the liquor, by the heat of Nikki's body, threw her head back and laughed with abandon, surrendering to his demands, to the demands of the sensual dance.

The music intensified, and their dancing grew more frenzied. He whirled her in tight circles, finally holding her around the waist and turning her to face him so that he could examine her as if she were a succulent morsel about to be consumed. Their movements became frenetic, hysterical, savage. He pulled her closer, rubbed himself against her, clasped her tightly to him as if they were joined pelvis to pelvis, and the patrons, now caught up in the exotic ritual, clapped in rhythm, urging the couple on, pushing them toward an erotic conclusion.

Laura, too, was captivated by the scene. Her breath had

quickened. She could not pull her eyes from the dancing couple. She felt warm and wet, as if she had been running, as if she had exhausted herself. She watched the simulated lovemaking and envied Liz, wished she had not refused to dance. She wished the dark stranger had dragged her out onto the floor. She wished he had filled her with ouzo and clutched her ardently to his body. She cursed herself for being so timid, for missing one more opportunity because of her lack of self-assurance. She became furious with envy, hungry with jealousy.

She saw herself out on the floor whirling with Nikki, held tightly by him so that she could not fly away as he whipped her around in reckless circles. She saw herself responding to him, her body surrounding him, her hands ravaging him, her lips swallowing him, and a low moan escaped her as she leaned forward and pressed her thighs together. She clutched herself tightly and rocked in time to their rhythm. She grew sad with the realization that sitting off on the side rocking to the music of someone else's adventure was as close to romance as she would ever get.

When the dance had been played out and Nikki had led a staggering Liz back to their table, Laura—flushed, ashamed, self-conscious—could not meet his gaze. He smiled at her as Liz insisted that he sit with them. Then Liz called for more ouzo and teased Laura for not at least trying the tasty liquor.

"Yes," Nikki had said, warmly urging her. "You should at least taste."

"No, thank you," Laura said softly, like a polite child. "I don't like liquor."

"Ah," he sympathized. "You cannot know until you try. Only one sip." He became enthusiastic. "One tiny sip. You will see. You will love it."

She smiled, lowered her eyes, shrugged, and then nodded.

"Yes!" he shouted, then signaled to the waiter for more ouzo and slowly slid onto the vacant chair, glancing lasciviously from one young woman to the other.

"Tha's a girl," Liz said, patting Laura's hand. She giggled, and Laura noted that her eyes were slightly unfocused. She saw also that Liz was feeling possessive of Nikki; she had laid her hand on his leg and was massaging his upper thigh. She was ashamed that Liz was flirting so blatantly with Nikki. Laura glanced at her reproachfully, but Liz seemed unaware of her disapproval. She seemed grateful that Laura had finally acquiesced, as if she believed that would keep Nikki interested and allow her to pursue him further without feeling guilty about deserting her friend. And when the ouzo arrived, Liz reached for it first, drank it quickly, and demanded more, eventually drinking most of Laura's.

Laura, caught up in the frenzied drinking and teasing, rubbing and touching, unable to excuse herself and gracefully escape, remained with them through it all. She hardly drank at all, merely sipping at a small glass while Nikki urged her on gently, demanding to know if she did not, after all, love the sweet liquor. Laura marveled at Nikki's capacity for the potent drink, which he quaffed like water, showing no effect, not appearing at all drunk.

But Liz grew progressively drunker and louder and less controlled. She latched on to Nikki, clutching him as if he were a life preserver and she were a drowning woman. She stopped making sense and spoke in loud drunken riddles. She laughed foolishly at nothing and several times slipped off her chair onto the floor and needed assistance to rise again. Laura was grateful when Liz finally passed out on the table and she and Nikki were forced to carry her home.

She let him into their apartment and held the door for him while he carried Liz, cradled in his arms like a sleeping child, through the living room and into her own bedroom.

She watched from the doorway as he stretched her out on top of the bedspread, pulled off her shoes, and commenced to undress her.

"Don't do that," Laura said.

He looked over his shoulder at her, his hands on Liz's shoulders.

"She can sleep in her clothes," Laura continued. "It's okay."

He straightened up, nodded, and moved toward her. He seemed to stumble slightly, and she noted that for the first time he appeared to be feeling the effects of all his drinking. She backed out into the living room, and he followed her. For an instant she feared that he was about to pounce on her, but he moved beyond her, found her couch, and fell upon it.

"What are you doing?"

He shook his head weakly. "I can't move," he mumbled.

"Well, you can't stay there," she said.

He lifted his feet onto the couch and stretched out, indicating that he intended to remain. "I can't move," he repeated sleepily.

"No," she said. She lifted his limp arm and pulled gently at him. "You've got to go home."

Suddenly she felt him reach up under her skirt and grab the soft flesh on the inside of her thigh. Stunned, she pushed his arm down, but he raised it again until his hand was cradling her warm crotch. She jumped at his touch and stumbled slightly. While she was off balance, he pulled her down on top of him, his hand between her legs, holding her with the ferocity of a pit bull.

Before she could cry out, he pressed his mouth onto hers and pushed his thickly coated tongue against her teeth. She could taste the licorice flavor of ouzo trickling down her throat, and she gagged slightly.

Feeling the involuntary jerking of her body, he seemed to

mistake her resistance for passion, thinking that she, too, was caught up in the throes of lust and was abandoning herself to him.

He rolled her onto the floor and fell on top of her.

"Oh, Jesus," she breathed. "What are you doing?" She pushed at his heavy chest with both hands. "Please! Don't!"

His lips were at her ear. "I'm giving you the greatest moment of your life," he said.

"Oh, God! Get off me," she begged in terror.

"Come on. You will love it," he whispered wetly.

She pushed upward with her entire body.

"Now you got the idea," he said.

She kicked and squirmed when she felt him pulling her skirt up around her waist and tried to punch him and scratch him when he pulled her panties down. He did not bother to fend her off, as though he hardly felt her blows, but used his hands instead to force her legs apart and guide himself into her. Just a bit at first and then, finally, deep inside her, painfully deep. She cried out, and he thrust more vigorously, deeper, mistaking her cries for howls of pleasure and her resistance for passionate cooperation.

She wept for herself then, accepting what was happening to her as preordained. She had often wondered what it would be like, how it would feel, to be taken violently like this, and her prurient thoughts had left an invisible mark on her, a signal that she was available for the taking. She felt that what was happening was her fault, that she had asked for it by sending out messages to the world that she was ready to be used. And now she was getting what she deserved.

Afterward, feeling burned, raw, and wounded where he had rubbed and scraped her during the attack, she silently called him every filthy name she could think of, although she was angrier at herself than at him. She pushed him off her easily. He was spent and he lay back on the carpet grinning contentedly.

She lifted herself from the floor and sat on the couch, her legs crossed, clutching her pain. She hated the feelings that churned in her. Disgust, self-loathing, and revulsion mingled with the secret unfinished, hungry yearning that lingered in the lower regions of her body. She stared at him on the floor at her feet.

"Bastard!" she whispered unconvincingly.

He grinned drunkenly up at her and wet his lips with his tongue. His eyes lingered upon her, took her in approvingly.

"I'm calling the police," she said. "I can't believe I've been raped."

"No," he said, shaking his head, offended. "Not raped." He wore a petulant expression, as if he had been insulted. He rose up on his elbows and stared into her eyes. "We make love. You're so beautiful."

"I feel dirty," she said, wondering why she did not.

"Did I hurt you?" he queried, surprised. "Did I beat you? I don't see that. We made love."

"I'd like to kill you," she said with little emotion.

He pursed his lips and shook his head. His eyes were smiling now. "Not a good idea. Better idea is to do this all the time. I like you very much."

"You do?" she said.

"Sure."

"Then how could you do that to me?" She pointed toward the floor. "Hurt me like that?"

"You were wonderful," he said softly.

"Oh, God," she moaned.

He laughed softly. "Come on," he said. "Not so bad. It's normal to want. Yes? You want me like I want you. I saw your eyes in the restaurant."

"Stupid. Stupid," she said shaking her head in self-disgust, amazed at what he was telling her.

"Come on," he coaxed. "You know you like me. I can feel it. On my back. Where you scratched me. I know this. We're good together."

The stirrings in her continued to grow, and she began to wish he had taken more time, had not forced her. She was fascinated with him but ashamed to admit that he might be telling the truth. She placed her foot on his chest and pushed him gently back down onto the floor. She dug her heel into his sternum.

"You know what?" she said softly.

"What?"

"You're never going to see me again for the rest of your life." She shook her head. "You've ruined it."

He started to interrupt, to protest, but she quieted him with the regret in her voice. "If I ever see you again, I'll kill you. I swear it. As God is my witness."

"Jesus Christ!"

"I mean it."

He nodded.

She smiled grimly. "I want you to go now."

"*Chérie?*"

"Out!"

He shrugged and rose from the floor. Scooping up his clothing as he went, he moved to the front door and without looking back said, "Tomorrow, *chérie*, you'll wish you had me here." And by the time the door had closed behind him, she partly regretted sending him away, because what he had said had the sound of truth about it.

Laura was aroused from her reverie by the stewardess's gentle but insistent prodding. She opened her eyes, aware of a motion all around her, and stared up at the smiling young face hovering over her.

"You'll have to fasten your seat belt," the stewardess said softly. "And the captain's lit the No Smoking sign."

"What is it?" Laura asked, suddenly frightened.

The stewardess attempted to reassure her. "It's nothing. We're encountering some turbulence. We usually do when we cross the Rockies."

"Oh," Laura said, attempting to sound composed but very aware of her terror.

She quickly pulled the belt around her and buckled it across her lap. She looked up for approval and found that the stewardess had moved on and was waking other passengers behind her, offering the same instructions she had offered Laura.

Suddenly, the plane seemed to drop out of the sky, only to catch itself in midair and right itself. Laura's breath caught in her throat, and she dug her fingers into the seat. Around her she could hear the murmurs of worried passengers. One man gently encouraged his wife; then his voice grew harsh and parental when she refused to be reassured.

The incident turned Laura's attention back to her memories of Nikki and his insistence that she enjoy flying as much as he did. She recalled his dogged persistence, his obstinacy. Nikki was not a quitter. He was obsessive and inflexible and would pursue a goal with the tenacity of a bulldog—as he had pursued her, smothered her with attention, saturated her with his own energy, and overwhelmed her with his strength of will. Nikki got what he wanted. Perhaps that tenacity was what she feared most about him. He had taken on the establishment dozens of times without losing once. He had beaten the Immigration and Naturalization Service, had beaten the Athens police, had even taken on the New York

City Police Department and beaten them as well. That ability was the greatest threat to her safety, both for herself and Dimmy.

Perhaps that was the real motivator behind her flight to California. Dr. Perez might think that she could help Dimmy. He might believe that the dangers facing Dimmy stemmed from his own depression and sense of isolation. But Laura knew that the real threat to Dimmy, to them all, for that matter, was Nikki Pappas, who did not know how to lose, and could not tolerate losing. He would have to win no matter what the cost, even if it meant sending his only son to prison. Nikki Pappas would do anything to exact revenge. He would go to any extreme, even to the extent of goading his son into threatening to take his own life in order to bring Laura out of hiding. She knew Nikki was capable of anything. When it came to Nikki Pappas, nothing, no act, no contrivance, no manipulation, no matter how impossible it sounded, was too farfetched.

She remembered filling the tub that first night after Nikki had left the apartment. When the small bathroom was fogged with steam, she had lain back in the near-scalding water, her legs spread apart, to cleanse herself by soaking out the recollection of his awful touch. Then, wrapped tightly in a robe, she had visited Liz and found her asleep, unmoved, as if nothing had happened to disturb her. She had felt a twinge of irrational anger at the thought that her friend could calmly sleep through her brutal devastation.

She had made hot chocolate, filled her favorite mug, floated a marshmallow on top, and settled down on the couch to regroup. She had become a story, the sort of tale told in whispers about some other person, some unknown person, never oneself. Tears flowed down her cheeks again. She did not feel herself crying. She felt no sadness. She was aware of the wetness on her face, but was devoid of sorrow or grief. Somehow, having been victimized by Nikki had left her with a sense of righteousness. She felt vindicated because of it.

When the telephone suddenly rang, startling her, she jumped and almost dropped her cup. Fearfully, she hurried to the phone across the room and lifted the receiver on the sixth ring.

"Hello," she whispered, fearful of who might respond.

"Hello?" Nikki's voice was friendly, playful.

She recognized the voice immediately and was terrified and thrilled by it but desperately did not want to disclose those feelings.

"Who is it?" she asked as if confused.

"Are you feeling better?" he asked. "You know who this is. Don't you, *chérie*?"

Her shoulders fell as she realized that her deception had failed. "What do you want?"

"To hear your voice."

"Do you remember what I told you?"

He sounded pained. "Don't be cruel, *chérie*."

She chewed on her lip to suppress the wave of emotion sweeping over her. She did not want to sound weak to him. She hated the sound of a victim seeking pity. She did not want to sound like an abused woman. "I'm hanging up," she finally said.

"Is it a crime that I miss you already?" he asked. "You want to punish me for missing you?"

"I'm hanging up," she repeated.

"No!" he said. "I'm sorry. What can I do? Talk to me for a minute."

She relented. "What do you want?"

"I want to come back," he said. "Right away. Only for a minute. I need to talk to you."

"What will that accomplish?"

"I need to see you," he whispered. "I need you not to be angry with me."

"Oh, my God!" She could not believe what she was hearing.

"No! Don't hang up!"

"You go straight to hell," she said and slammed the receiver down onto its cradle.

Back on the couch, she pressed herself into the soft corner and pulled her feet up under her. She trembled uncontrollably, but not with fear. She was not afraid of his voice on the telephone. She was not afraid of what he could do to her. But she was horrified by her attraction to him. When he spoke to her she could feel the weight of him on top of her again. She could feel the largeness of him inside her again, and as much as she despaired about that, she was immensely aroused by the memory.

God, she thought, I must be going mad. Such behavior had to be crazy, such fantasies a sure sign of insanity. And yet such dreams and desires had been with her most of her life. What was it about her, she wondered, that caused her to do such harm to herself? Why was she so desperate to hurt herself? Why did she search for personal pain? Why did she find it so easily?

Recognizing her weakness, she resolved to resist him as she would resist the devil. She could imagine the phone suddenly ringing again, could feel the awareness of him on the other end of the line. She could see herself dash to the wall and pull the phone wire violently from the jack, then fling the instrument against the wall, smashing his voice into a thousand bits. All that she could imagine while secretly wishing he would call again.

She was not, however, prepared for the knock on her door and, though startled, did not leap to her feet but remained seated, frozen in place. She knew instantly who was on the other side, and though she felt angry and trapped, a tremor of excitement ran through her. She despised him for thinking he could rape her and then be forgiven and permitted to return. She loathed his touch, his breath, his laugh. She wanted desperately to hurt him as he had hurt her, to wound him as he had wounded her. Yet she was excited that he had come back to her.

She rose, strode to the door, and threw it open. He stood before her, leaning on the doorjamb, one hand in his pocket, a boyish grin on his face, as if he had pulled off something really clever and was expecting her to acknowledge it. He held the other hand conspicuously behind his back, and she knew it contained a peace offering of some sort.

"Hello, *chérie*," he said tenderly, exuding an oily charm.

"How dare you come back here?" she said.

He grimaced. "I feel terrible that you don't understand me." He brought his hand out from behind his back. It contained a large box of chocolate candies. "These are for you."

She eyed the gift suspiciously. "I don't want anything from you."

He seemed hurt, pouting at first, then breaking into a mischievous smile as if he could draw on a store of petulant facial expressions at will. He said, "I see that you want to hurt me. Go on." He shrugged. "Maybe I deserve it. Go on. Maybe I have it coming. But I didn't want to hurt you. I swear it."

She whispered sadly, "I hurt enough. I just want you to go away and leave me alone."

He squinted at her, never losing his endearing smile. "Are you sure that's what you really want?"

She frowned to hide her uncertainty. "Go away, please." She tried to push the door shut.

"Am I so bad?" he pleaded. "I hurt you with my love?"

Biting her lip, she turned her face away from him.

"I think we should talk," he said, looking at her sheepishly. "Come on," he begged. "Don't leave me out in the hall like this."

She hesitated as her anger dissipated in the face of his humility and was replaced by curiosity. "All right," she said, finally relenting. "You can come in for a minute."

He entered and waited humbly while she closed the door behind him. She stepped around him and returned to her place on the couch, from where she stared at him. She brushed her hair back from her face. Fully aware that she had invited a tormentor into her home, totally cognizant of the fact that he was quite capable of brutalizing her again, that he was playing on her confusion, on her terrible loneliness, she felt helpless to protect herself from him. Arms folded across her chest, a look of consternation on her face, she glared at him.

"What do you want?" she said.

"I feel so bad for you," he said. He cast sad eyes upon her and pouted like a child seeking forgiveness.

She shuddered under his gaze. "It was terrible," she whispered.

"I'm so sorry," he said. "I don't want to hurt you. Please believe me and forgive me."

"I should call the police," she murmured. "I should have you arrested."

"No, *chérie*," he said shaking his head. "Don't do that. I swear I'll never hurt you again." He walked slowly toward her, set the box of chocolates on the coffee table between them, and stood directly in front of her.

"I don't lie to you," he whispered softly. "You see, I love you." He placed his hands on the sides of her neck, then lifted her to her feet and drew her close to him. She leaned forward and dropped her forehead onto his shoulder.

He continued to whisper softly to her. "You know you like me. Don't fight it. Just because I've been a fool once doesn't mean that we won't be good together. You're smarter than me. You're stronger than me. You can make me your slave."

Almost unwillingly she uncrossed her arms and slid them around his waist. Touching him electrified her. She raised her head and pressed her cheek to his.

"Am I right?" he asked, one hand cupped behind her head holding her to him.

He slipped his other hand up inside the back of her robe and caressed her soft skin. She resisted with only a gentle pressure of her hands on his waist. He pulled his hands around and massaged her abdomen.

"We are perfect for each other, you and me," he said.

He undid the belt of her robe and pulled it open, exposing her naked body. He dropped to his knees and pressed his face between her warm thighs, tenderly biting the silken flesh.

She trembled and, frightened by her own passion, pulled him to his feet. Then she pressed her lips to his mouth and, while deep in a probing kiss, fell onto the couch and pulled him on top of her.

"Wait," he whispered into her ear.

"I can't," she breathed.

He quickly pulled his clothes off and threw them across the room. The tips of her fingers trailed along his back and traveled around to wrap themselves around him and gently urge him to return to her.

In an instant he was inside her, thudding into her repeatedly in his familiar rhythm, and she was surrounding him, swallowing him like a tropical flower.

Afterward she slept in his arms for a while, her face

pressed against his chest. Surrounded by his arms, she felt secure, loved, protected.

He shifted his weight, waking her, and she clung to him more tightly and nibbled at his arm.

"I'm going now," he whispered.

She moaned, "No!"

"I must," he said.

He slid away from her and sat up. She held on to him, but he gently pulled her hands away and began getting dressed.

An old familiar feeling of abandonment swept over Laura. The feeling had followed her around since childhood and had possessed her whenever she drew close to a man. She felt tears accumulating in her eyes, and her throat constricted into a series of almost silent sobs. She knew he was leaving because he had gotten what he wanted and there was nothing more she could offer him.

"I'll call you," he said, looking down at her nakedness.

She nodded silently, sadly, unbelieving.

"I will!" He sounded impatient. "I'm telling you."

"Yes," she whispered.

"Well, what's wrong, then?"

She shrugged and turned her face away from him.

"I will call you in a couple of days."

"Yes."

From the doorway he said, "You are a wonderful girl, Laura."

When he was gone, she dragged herself to the shower and washed off every trace of him again. She stood under the pounding needles of scalding water for a long time and rubbed her skin where he had bitten and kissed her. She wanted every speck of him gone.

She despised herself and her weakness almost as much as she despised him. The more she thought about her behavior, the more she hated herself. She had actually wanted to be degraded as much as he had wanted to degrade her. She felt sick to her stomach. And yet she knew she would wait for his phone call like a lovesick schoolgirl. She knew that if he did not call she would search for him, visit the restaurant, walk the streets of the neighborhood seeking a glimpse of him. She knew that he had touched a very deep part of her that desperately needed the kind of degradation he was so skillful at administering.

She sat up suddenly, straining against the tightly buckled seat belt, aware of being confined in an airplane. The plane had passed through the poor weather, and most of her fellow passengers were asleep in their seats.

She became aware that her heart was racing at an incredible speed. Her hair was wet with sweat, and her clothing clung to her damp body. Her hands trembled slightly. She was profoundly afraid. Terrified. She was flying toward that man. She was once again seeking him out. And she was petrified that somewhere deep down inside her, some part of her still longed for his kind of debasement.

FOUR

He fluttered gently, as if in a dream, wafting from side to side, then settling slowly downward. He floated as if suspended from a parachute or held by an unseen hand.

He heard the wind rushing by with a steady, unrelenting whoosh. He heard it fill the void as he settled into the softness and sank beneath the billowing surface. Then, slowly, in tight circles, he rose to the top and rested.

The orderly noticed that, as the boy awoke, he moaned and sighed as if being released from a persistent pain. The careful orderly moved quickly to his bedside.

Beneath his eyelids the boy's eyes darted from side to side as if in frantic search for escape from their imprisonment. Another, much deeper, sigh emerged from his pale lips, and his soft, rhythmic breathing became more labored.

The orderly, shifting the leather restraint, fingered the boy's wrist and found a pulse. He gazed at his watch as he silently counted. Satisfied, he released the wrist and touched the ice pack surrounding the boy's neck. It had turned warm with time and was no longer effective. It would have to be replaced. He adjusted it minutely as if needing to do something, even if that something meant nothing.

The boy sensed a presence near him and grew tense. His body instinctively tightened as if anticipating a blow, and he pressed his eyelids even more firmly shut.

"Hey! It's okay," the orderly's distant voice insisted. "I ain't gonna hurt you."

The boy, as if coming from darkness into light, began to realize that he was alive, began to feel the dull throb emanating from his neck and slowly rising to his head. He became aware of the restraints on his wrists and ankles and knew that he was whole. Before memory could return, he opened his eyes and stared up at the round black face hovering over him.

"What?" he heard himself croak in an unfamiliar voice, as if from a long distance away.

"You're gonna be okay," the orderly said softly. He smiled and nodded reassuringly.

The boy let his eyes roam around the room, taking in the sterile white walls, the small barred window just above him, the overhead light encased in tight wire mesh, the absence of tables, chairs, mirrors. "No," he murmured and slowly shook his head. Tiny tears hovered at the corners of his eyes, then rolled down his cheeks.

"Hey! You're gonna make it," the orderly insisted. "You're gonna be all right." He stared down at the boy, placed his hand gently on his shoulder. "Ain't nothin' that bad," he whispered. "Believe me. Ain't nothin' in the whole world bad enough for that."

"For what?"

"You know." The orderly was embarrassed. "To do . . . that."

The boy stared at him, puzzled. He shook his head slightly, felt pain caused by the movement, and coughed.

"You thirsty?" the orderly asked. "You want something to drink?"

The boy nodded and croaked, "Yes."

The orderly disappeared from the bedside and returned almost immediately with a glass of water and a flexible plastic straw. Holding the glass carefully beneath the boy's chin, he moved the straw toward the dry lips.

"Go on," he said. "It's good for you."

The boy sipped, grimaced with sudden pain, and turned his face away.

"Sore, huh?" the orderly asked. "It's gonna be that way for a while. But that ain't nothing. Hell! You're lucky you're still with us."

The boy's eyes opened wide as if in astonishment. "Where am I?" he whispered.

"Hey!" the orderly chuckled. "You're in the prison ward of County General Hospital. That's where you are. Where'd you think you was? In a hotel on the West Side?" He emitted a short laugh much like a snort. "Hell! You ain't out from behind them bars, boy. You just changed beds, that's all. You just changed your sleepin' accommodations."

Dr. Zeke Perez was jarred out of a half sleep by the shrill ringing of his desk phone. "Yes?" he mumbled, raising the receiver to his ear.

"Dr. Perez?" a woman's voice asked professionally.

He straightened himself in his chair. "Yes," he said.

"This is Nurse Draper at County, Doctor. Dr. Griffith asked me to call you and tell you that the Pappas boy is conscious."

Perez rubbed the sleep from his eyes. "Oh, thank you. How is he?"

"I don't know, Doctor," the nurse responded. "I was asked to inform you that he is awake and lucid. That's all."

"Thank you."

Zeke rose wearily and, pushing himself away from his

cluttered desk, rubbed his burning eyes with the back of his hand. He felt thoroughly exhausted, rough and raspy, as if granules of sand had somehow gotten into his works. His wrinkled shirt felt sticky on his back, and he imagined its slept-in appearance. He was stiff and grimy and tense.

But he was content. The boy was awake, and Zeke Perez was playing detective for the first time in his life. He had achieved a goal that had seemed nearly impossible at the outset of his quest several hours earlier: he had found the Pappas woman.

He gathered together the notes that lay scattered across his desk—names and numbers he no longer needed, pieces of a puzzle he had solved, corridors of a maze he had successfully navigated. As he gazed down at the papers representing the trail he had doggedly followed to locate Laura Devon Pappas, he shook his head slowly. He thought back over the trail that had led him from New York City to Chicago, Cleveland, Toledo, and finally Dayton, and he remembered the faceless voices of people who had either denied knowledge or blatantly refused to help. He had encountered suspicion and distrust and fear time and time again.

He had done all he could—more than he should have, perhaps—to locate the woman he had more than half suspected was a fantasy. He knew he had no business searching for her. His sole function was to evaluate Dimmy Pappas's mental status and report to Bob Haines on the boy's ability to stand trial. That was what the defense had hired him to do. Anything more than that could be viewed as a violation of the code of ethics of his profession, place his objectivity in question, and perhaps disqualify him as an expert witness.

And yet, as he grew closer to the case, as the boy's plight began to impinge on his conscience, his sense of fairness and justice, locating the missing mother had become a matter of major importance.

From their very first meeting, in the lockup on the fifth floor of the old county jail, which occupied the top floors of the archaic Sheriff's Building in downtown Los Angeles, Zeke had known that getting to the essence of the boy was going to be a difficult task. He felt the wall of ice around Dimmy, the invisible barrier that separated them. There is not an ounce of trust in this boy, he had told himself then, and God knows if there ever will be again.

"I know about that stuff," the boy had said at their first meeting when Zeke asked him if he knew what a psychiatrist did. "Yeah, I know." His fingers had trembled slightly, and he had wet his dry lips with the tip of his tongue. He slouched on the chair. Like those of a marionette, his limbs had seemed to hang loose, and his body had seemed to sag. He had looked off at nothing in the empty room, pretending to be unafraid. "You're going to shrink my head, right?"

He had sat across from Zeke at a plain wooden table in a small, empty green room on a straight-backed green metal chair. A small boy, his feet barely reached the floor, and his hands seemed ludicrously tiny peeking out of the long sleeves of his large faded blue county jail shirt. But his dark eyes, under close-cropped black hair, were bright and intense and, though they darted about fearfully, he frequently forced them to focus on Zeke's face, encountering the psychiatrist's own eyes, struggling not to avoid contact, struggling not to seem afraid.

"Have you done any of this before?" Zeke asked, indicating the stack of material on the table beside him.

"The ink blots? I've seen them." The boy shrugged nonchalantly.

''Where was that?''

''I don't know.'' The boy shrugged again and glanced away. ''Here and there.''

''Oh,'' Zeke said. ''Then you don't mind doing it with me?''

''What for?'' he murmured.

''So I can learn some things about you.''

''You want to know something ask me. I'll tell you.''

''Will you?''

''Sure!'' the boy said flatly. The dull expression on his face did not alter, and he spoke without inflection, without feeling or emotion.

''Well then,'' Zeke said. ''Tell me about yourself.''

''Like what?''

''Like anything. Where do you go to school? Do you have a girlfriend?'' Zeke paused. ''What are you in here for?''

The boy stared at him. ''Don't you know?''

''Do you?''

''What? You think I'm crazy?''

They sat in total silence staring at each other for a long moment.

''No,'' Zeke finally said. ''I don't think you're crazy.''

''Sure, I know why I'm here,'' the boy said. ''Why don't you talk to my lawyer, Mr. Haines? He'll tell you why I'm here.''

''Can't you tell me?''

''Sure, I can.'' The boy leaned his head back and stared up at the ceiling. His lips moved soundlessly as if he were counting the light fixtures. ''You know, I been here more than a year,'' he said softly.

Zeke nodded. ''I know.''

''That's a long time.''

''Yes, it is.''

''I was fifteen when they brought me here. Now I'm

almost seventeen." He lowered his eyes and watched Zeke's face. "Can they keep me here forever?"

"I don't know," Zeke said. "What does your lawyer say?"

The boy shrugged. "Mr. Haines don't say nothing. He wants me to cop a plea."

"What do you mean, cop a plea?"

The boy smiled for the first time. "He wants me to plead guilty."

Zeke nodded his understanding. "Are you guilty?"

"Of what?"

"Of whatever they say you did to get you in here?"

The boy shook his head. "I don't know," he said. "What do you think?"

"Well, did you do what you're accused of?"

The boy tilted his head slightly as if listening to some distant sound. "Did I?" The young face grew rigid, and the muscles in his jaw rippled as if he were biting down on something hard.

"The only thing I'm guilty of," he stated, his voice flat once again, "is that I didn't finish him off. I should have killed the bastard." He nodded once and locked his eyes onto Zeke's in a challenge.

The diminutive boy looked younger than his actual age. He was no more than five feet four, weighing perhaps one hundred and ten. He seemed even smaller in his oversized clothing, and he looked powerless and helpless in his desperate situation, and yet he had dared the psychiatrist to underestimate him.

Zeke smiled at the memory of that day, that first encounter, at how effectively the boy, distant and withdrawn, had enticed the doctor into his web. He lifted his telephone and punched in a familiar number.

"Law offices," a young female voice announced on the second ring.

"Bob Haines, please," Zeke said. "This is Dr. Perez."

"One moment, please."

He drummed his fingers nervously on the desk top as he waited.

"Zeke!" Bob Haines's effusive voice boomed at him through the phone. "How the hell are you?"

"I'm fine," Zeke said. "And I've got some good news."

"Good!" the lawyer said. "I could use some."

"First of all," Zeke continued, "Dimmy Pappas is awake and probably out of danger."

"Well, that is good news," Haines said. "I almost lost a client there, didn't I?"

"And on top of that," Perez continued, "I located the stepmother. I spoke to her this morning."

"What stepmother?" Haines asked, sounding confused.

"The missing mother he talks about is not his mother," Zeke said. "She's his stepmother. I found her in Ohio."

"You've been a busy guy, Doc. How the hell'd you manage that?" Haines continued without allowing Perez to respond. "Can she help with the defense fund?"

"I don't know," Zeke replied. "I know that she cares. She was shocked when I told her what had happened."

"Does she care enough to help pay the bills? That's the question."

"I don't know," Perez said, annoyed at the turn the conversation had taken. "You can ask her yourself. She's on her way out."

Haines grunted. "I don't need another fan in the gallery. I need someone to help with the expenses."

"I know," Zeke snapped. "I heard you."

"Listen, Zeke. I appreciate what you've done. I really do. But I hope you didn't open up a can of worms here."

"What does that mean?"

"It means that I don't need a nagging mother on my back.

I know what it's going to take to wrap this case up and I don't need another fly in the ointment.''

"Jesus, Bob!" Perez said in disbelief. "The kid tried to kill himself. It's not a question of just wrapping up the case anymore. Now it's a matter of keeping him alive, of giving him some encouragement, some reason to keep going."

"Maybe that's your priority, Zeke. You're the mental health guy here. But it isn't my primary concern. I'm supposed to defend him, and that's all I intend to do. If I can get paid a little better, there's no harm in that, is there? But I'm sure as hell not going to become his social worker. You can if you want to. But I'm content being his lawyer which I've barely got time for."

"I thought you'd be happy that I found her," Perez said, his voice filled with disappointment.

"I am happy," Haines replied. "I think it's terrific that you were able to do that. Just don't lose sight of what we've got here."

"What *have* we got here?"

He heard the lawyer's deep, patient sigh. Then, "The little fucker's a killer, Zeke."

"No, he's not."

Haines hesitated. "No. You're right. He's not. But not because he didn't want to be. He *tried* to kill his father more than once."

"That's alleged."

"Bullshit!" Haines said. "Don't feed me my own line." He paused, then chuckled softly again. "You're painting this kid like he's some kind of angel, buddy. He's not. He's a rotten little shit who doesn't deserve anything better than he's getting. I'll do the best I can for him because that's my job, but there's just so much anybody can do with a case like this."

"That doesn't sound very encouraging."

"What do you think I brought you in on this case for? You get me an opinion and I'll go for an insanity plea. Anything. I'll go for what I can get."

"That boy's not insane," Zeke said. "He's depressed. He feels hopeless, abandoned, and betrayed, but he's not legally insane."

"I know that and you know that, but what will the jury buy?" Haines asked. "You know I don't sell reality, Zeke. But I can tell as good a story as the next guy."

"Then tell the jury how badly Dimmy has been abused all his life. Tell them what his father is like, what he did to his kids. Tell them that."

"Shit, Zeke," Haines said, losing his patience. "They don't want to hear any of that. We're all sick and tired of hearing that society is responsible for all the little gangsters running around the streets. Nobody buys it anymore. Everybody wants the little hoodlums punished. Get them off the streets and into cages. Get them the hell away from me and mine, for chrissake. That's the new battle cry. Who the hell wants to hear why they are what they are? The American people want these kids burned, Zeke. You go out into the street and take a poll of the citizens walking up and down, and ninety percent of the people will tell you to nuke 'em."

"I don't believe that," Perez said.

"Well then, you're really out of touch. That's all I've got to say. If you're a bleeding heart, Zeke, keep it to yourself, because you can do our client a real disservice if you let him believe he can get an easy shake out of a jury of his peers. They'll lock him up and throw away the key. I guarantee it. If you want to do him a favor, persuade him to take the deal the state has offered."

"What deal?" Perez asked.

"Dimmy pleads guilty to attempted voluntary manslaughter, saves the state the cost of a trial, and gets a straight seven years, three off for good behavior. They'll even throw in time served, so he'll be out in less than three years. It's the best we can do."

"I don't think he can handle that," Perez said.

"He won't serve his time in the county jail. He'll be on the prison farm. It's wholesome. He'll work, get lots of fresh air. It'll be good for him."

"God!" Perez said. "I can't believe what you're telling me."

"Believe it."

"You make it sound like summer camp."

"Listen," Haines said slowly, emphatically. "He's going to have to do time, Zeke. The only question is how much. You think about it. He can do the three years standing on his head or he can take his chances with a jury that could give him life."

"Life!"

"That's the new law, Zeke. The Singleton Law. Premeditated attempted murder. And it carries a life sentence."

"Jesus!"

"Just remember this, pal: juries are made up of adults, and adults don't like the idea of kids killing their parents. Adults are sick and tired of being scared to death by angry kids with guns and knives and Molotov cocktails. They want to feel safe in their community. They don't want to live in fear of the children around them. Hell, adults don't even like to lose at Ping-Pong to kids. How do you think they feel about being at some crazy kid's mercy? You think about that, buddy. And you think about how safe it is to put your patient's life in the hands of twelve angry citizens."

Dr. Paul Griffith removed the warm ice pack from around the boy's neck and pulled open the threadbare hospital gown. He listened to the healthy heart pumping inside the youthful chest, then nodded and hung his stethoscope around his neck. He patted Dimmy on the shoulder and smiled at him. "How do you feel?"

"It hurts," the boy said.

"Your throat?"

Dimmy nodded.

"I should think so," the doctor said. "You stretched the hell out of it."

"How'd I do that?" the boy croaked.

Griffith eyed him cautiously. "You don't remember what you did?"

Dimmy shook his head slowly.

"Do you know where you are?"

Dimmy's eyes went to the sterile ceiling, then traveled around the impeccable white room. "The jail hospital?"

The doctor nodded.

Dimmy grimaced at the pain in his throat. His eyes grew fearful and his lip commenced to tremble. "Why am I in jail?" He pulled on the restraints that bound his wrists to the metal bed rails. "Why?" Tears rolled down his cheeks.

"Take it easy," the doctor said. "You've got a little loss of memory. No big deal." He shrugged. "It happens."

Dimmy squirmed like a trapped animal, his face twisted with terror.

Dr. Griffith rose. "I'm going to get Dr. Perez in here."

"Who?"

"Dr. Zeke Perez, your doctor."

Dimmy's agitation slowed. The boy became thoughtful, then nodded. "Zeke," he whispered as if tasting the name for the first time. "Yes."

"Okay," the doctor added. "I'll go call him. Meanwhile, just lie back and let your mind wander. Let the memories come. Okay?" He smiled and patted the slender shoulder.

"It'll all come back to you. You weren't up long enough for any real . . . damage. I'm sure it's not serious."

As the boy stared at him, Dr. Griffith grew uncomfortable. He preferred to deal with ailments that could be explained quickly and understood easily—broken bones, bleeding ulcers, the flu. Amnesia and other psychiatric disorders were not in his purview. He thought of himself as a physician, not a mystic, and he held little respect for the various psychotherapies, which he thought of as ways of intellectualizing malingering. Besides, this boy was not his patient. This was a shrink's job, and he would gladly let Perez deal with it.

When he turned to leave, he smiled tightly at Dimmy and tried to sound reassuring. "It'll all come back to you. You'll see."

The boy watched Paul Griffith disappear from the room and wished he understood what was wrong with him, why he was in the hospital. Something had happened to put him there, some accident. But he had no idea what it was. He had been washing dishes in the back of the restaurant, and then suddenly, as if he had been propelled through time and space, he was in a hospital bed in a jail, recovering from . . . what?

He believed what Dr. Griffith had told him—that he was suffering a loss of memory, that he could remember if he tried. He shut his eyes, moved his mind away from the present, sent it back in time, and tried to remember.

And then Dimmy remembered. . . .

PART TWO

FIVE

Mrs. McNamara had cooked dinner.

The apartment was permeated with the pungent odor of moussaka baking and lamb roasting. The tiny lamb chops, which were such a delicacy and so rarely affordable that the children's mouths watered just thinking about them, were slowly crisping in a deep roasting pan far back in the oven. Mrs. McNamara had ground up the lamb breast and rolled the meat into short, fat cigars, which she wrapped in grape leaves and set into a deep pan to stew and bubble in a rich tomato sauce in the oven alongside the eggplant moussaka.

She had allowed Dimmy's sister to cut the vegetables for the salad. Irene was in heaven. Dimmy watched his sister. The tip of her tongue protruded from the corner of her mouth as she concentrated on producing perfect pieces of green pepper and cucumber. He felt envious that Mrs. McNamara had trusted her with the razor-sharp knife.

He got to cut the feta cheese into small cubes. That safe task was often reserved for him as the younger child, but it was of little consolation since it was performed with a dull knife and required no trust on the part of Mrs. McNamara. He was usually happy to do it because he was able to eat some of the cubes when Mrs. McNamara's back was turned.

But on this day he was not happy, nor was he proud of how carefully perfect his cubes were. On this day he did not want them to be perfect, not for the guest they were expecting. On this day, he ate none and cut them quite crookedly.

When the meal preparations were complete, Mrs. McNamara guided the children into their bedroom and dressed Irene in her special Sunday outfit. With loving care she piled the girl's hair high on her head to expose the child's lovely long neck. Dimmy, looking underfed and scrawny in his underwear, sat on the edge of his bed watching as Mrs. McNamara slipped a soft pink chiffon dress over his sister's head, straightened the large silk bow at the back, smoothed the front with her gentle hands, and stepped back to admire her work. Irene, nervous and excited, jumped to her feet, which were clad in frilly white socks and shiny black Mary Janes, and, twirling in wild circles, modeled for her brother.

"Am I beautiful, Dimmy?" she asked, giggling.

"Of course you're beautiful," Mrs. McNamara said. "You're the most beautiful little girl in the entire city of New York."

The little girl's face reddened, and she giggled happily behind her hand. "I am not," she said.

Mrs. McNamara turned to Dimmy, but the boy would not allow her to dress him. He did not want to dress up on this day. Not for the woman Papa was bringing home for dinner.

After he had put on his tailored black suit with its single-breasted jacket and sharply pressed pants, however, he did permit Mrs. McNamara to straighten his tie, tug the cuffs of his white shirt out from under the jacket sleeves, wipe the dust from his shoes, which he had neglected to polish, and brush his untamed black hair out of his eyes.

She stepped back and appraised her two charges with a critical eye. Irene preened. Dimmy dropped his eyes and scraped the side of his shoe sullenly on the floor. He hated being scrutinized like an item on sale. He hated being found imperfect and unacceptable.

"Straighten up, Dimmy!" Mrs McNamara said as if she had read his mind. "Stand straight. It's impolite for a boy to stand like a chicken."

He raised his head and glared at her. A chicken?

"Show me your hands," she said.

The two children extended their hands toward her, palms downward. She examined the fragile skin, checked out each knuckle for a sign of grime, seemed satisfied, and said, "Other side."

They flipped their hands over, palms upward, and subjected them to a similar inspection. "Very good," she said. She nodded and smiled with satisfaction.

Much to their father's pleasure, she had unofficially adopted the two children who were being raised by a lone man after their mother's untimely death the year before. Her arrangement with Nikki required only that she would cook for the family. Twice a week she was to prepare large amounts of food. She would freeze it in individual portions to be heated and eaten as needed. They had not agreed that she would care for the children. On the contrary, Nikki pretended to be of the opinion that it was healthy for children to be on their own, to be self-sufficient, at an early age. He told her that he had been dumped on the streets of Athens when he was seven years old and that he was a better man for it—more self-reliant, competent, trustworthy. He asserted that he was the kind of man who could be dropped from the sky into any environment and he would land on his feet ready to do business. What he was not capable of, Mrs. McNamara thought sardonically, was raising two small children—not with his style of playing around all night and sleeping through most of the day.

In the beginning she had tried to avert her eyes, to avoid

seeing the two little kids trudging home from school together, the older girl, a mature nine-year-old, clutching the hand of her rambunctious eight-year-old younger brother, as they hurried down the street and climbed the five flights to their apartment. As she watched them through the window of the McNamara family grocery and delicatessen on the ground floor of the dirty old building on Second Avenue, she imagined them feeding themselves, getting themselves up in the morning, washing themselves, dressing themselves, cleaning house together like a miniature married couple, and her heart hurt for them. Better not to see, she told herself. Better not to know. But in her mind's eye, she continued to see the two lonely children as they cared for each other like friendless refugees in an alien society.

She was incapable of ignoring them, each one more beautiful than the other. So, without Nikki being aware of it, Mrs. McNamara slowly took upon herself the task of surrogate parent. In the morning, before setting off for school, while their father slept, they visited her in the back of the deli, and she inspected their appearance, saw to it that their clothing was clean, if not bright and new, and asked them if they carried lunch money. If they did not, she made them sandwiches and put them in brown paper bags along with some ripe olives and large slices of garlic pickle. By the time they returned from school, their father had already risen and departed for wherever he spent his evenings, so she would visit them in their apartment to make sure they did not feel totally alone in the world.

She remembered how she herself, as a small girl, had rushed home each day after school, fearful that her parents had left for parts unknown without waiting for her. She recalled the terror, the insane beating of her heart, the gasping as she ran up the stairs and burst into the apartment half expecting it to be empty. Remembering, she wept for the two Pappas children as she imagined them suffering the same fearful fantasies.

But today was Sunday, and she was not cooking for the week but for that single day. Nor was she dressing the children carefully for school or for church. This was a special day, and she was preparing a feast to celebrate the arrival of Nikki's fiancée, who was coming to meet the children for the first time.

Mrs. McNamara motioned for them to drop their hands. "You want to be neat and clean for your father's lady friend. You want to make a good impression, don't you?"

"Yes, ma'am," Irene said, nodding solemnly, her dark eyes passionately wanting to please.

Dimmy grunted and shrugged as if to say that he personally did not care very much what kind of impression he made. As a matter of fact, he would have preferred to make a terrible impression on the woman who dared to think she could replace his gentle, silently suffering mother.

He was aware that Irene felt differently. She was hoping that this Laura person would turn out to be a loving friend for her, someone with whom she could talk about girl things. But Dimmy knew in his heart that this woman would never be able to replace the greatest loss of his life. No matter what kind of person she was, Dimmy knew there was no room inside him for her. He also knew that if he did reach out to her, she would fail him and abandon him, just as as his real mother had. After all, if one's blood mother could disappear like that, who could expect a girlfriend to stick around?

"Come on," Mrs. McNamara said then. "Let's practice."

Irene nodded enthusiastically while Dimmy groaned as if his shoes were too tight.

"Come on, now," the old woman coaxed. "This is very important."

Dimmy shrugged. "Okay."

"Good!" She beamed. "You first, Irene."

The girl pressed her eyes shut for a moment and bit her lower lip while she concentrated. Suddenly her eyes popped open and she broke into a huge smile. She clutched the sides of her dress, drew the skirt out like a fan, and lowered herself slowly into a graceful curtsy.

"Wonderful!" Mrs. McNamara applauded. "That was simply perfect, Irene." She moved to the girl and hugged her, then drew back slightly. "You're such a little lady," she said somewhat breathlessly, thoroughly impressed.

Irene grinned with pleasure.

Mrs. McNamara turned to the boy. "Now you, Dimmy."

"Aw, do I have to?" The boy's face wrinkled into an expression of severe pain.

"Yes," she said. "You have to."

"I won't do it when she comes," he said.

"Yes, you will," she insisted.

"Won't!"

"Will!"

She could be as stubborn as he, even more so if need be. She braced her hands on her hips and stared at him ferociously.

"Aw," he groaned, relenting under her burning stare. "It's such girl stuff."

"Do it!" she demanded.

He glared at her, dark eyes narrowed, nostrils flared, humiliated at having lost to her once again. He mumbled something unintelligible under his breath.

"What was that, young man?"

"Nothing." He did not want to be disrespectful to her. He knew Mrs. McNamara loved him and worried about him. He loved her, too. He sighed and finally surrendered. Folding his right arm across his midsection, his left straight down at his side, he bowed from the waist, straightened up, and said,

''Pleased to meet you, ma'am.'' Then he grimaced as though he had eaten something awful.

''See?'' the old woman said. ''You can do it.''

''Ugh!'' he said. ''It's stupid.''

''It's not stupid to be a gentleman, Dimmy. It's never stupid to have good manners.''

Irene watched her brother squirm. ''Dimmy thinks good manners make you a sissy,'' she said.

He glared at Irene with loathing. ''Don't talk for me,'' he said. ''You don't know what I think.'' He hated her when she played know-it-all big sister. His mother had never made him bow from the waist. His mother had never made him practice saying things like ''Pleased to meet you, ma'am.'' His mother had never told him what he was thinking.

He longed for her at that moment. He wished so desperately that he could run into her bedroom and find her there, in bed, under the covers, alive. He wanted to crawl under with her and rest his head on her shoulder and tell her what he was thinking. He wanted her to listen to him. He wanted someone to listen to him. He would tell her how frightened he was of the impending visit. He would tell his mother how much he hated the monster his father was bringing home. Without even knowing her, he hated her. He knew she would be ugly and mean and angry. He knew she would punish him every chance she got, with or without reason. He knew she would prefer Irene to him right off.

''Don't be mean to your sister,'' Mrs. McNamara said gently, sensing that the boy was becoming upset. ''She didn't do anything.''

''Tell her to leave me alone,'' he said sullenly.

''I didn't do anything,'' Irene said, haughtily mimicking Mrs. McNamara.

''You were lording it over me,'' Dimmy snapped.

''Was not!''

"Was too!"

"Okay! I'll leave you alone," Irene said angrily. "I'll never talk to you again."

"I wish."

"You'll see, brat!"

The old woman stepped between them and laid a gentle hand on each of their shoulders. "Listen, children," she said softly. "Your father will be home any minute. You don't want him to find you fighting like this. And you don't want his lady to think you're a couple of bandits, do you? You don't want to scare her away."

Irene pouted and a tiny tear appeared in the corner of her eye. But Dimmy stood firm, his face determined, because that was exactly what he wanted. He would have loved to scare her away. He wished he could do that without even meeting her, before she even arrived. He wished there was no Laura and his mother was still around and, bad as it was back then, he wished things were still the way they had always been.

When they heard Nikki's key in the door, they scurried about frantically to get into the positions they had rehearsed half a dozen times. They lined up in the center of the living room, prepared to greet the guest as if she were visiting royalty. When Nikki guided Laura through the foyer and into the living room, the three of them stood rigidly at attention, plastic grins painted on their faces, not knowing exactly what to expect.

"Ah!" Nikki exclaimed. "Here's my family."

He clutched the young woman's hand and pulled her along with him as he did with Dimmy when they were going somewhere together and the boy dawdled. She seemed breathless, as if she had been dragged along more quickly than her legs could carry her, as if she were there against her will.

She seemed to be scared to death of Papa, Dimmy thought.

He knew that feeling well, had felt it himself many times. His father had no patience for argument or discussion. When he wanted something, he got his way by sweeping others along with him, like those big yellow plows that pushed mountains of snow off the street and onto the curb in the winter.

She was like a lamb, Dimmy thought. She hung back, obviously as nervous and afraid as he was, as if Nikki's arm were a tether to which she had been tied. She did not look mean, as he had expected. Dimmy thought that she was the most beautiful person he had ever seen. She was small and almost blond, not dark like them, but fair like Mrs. McNamara. Her face was gentle. It had the same quality of kindness that Mrs. McNamara's had, and she smiled tentatively as if she wanted to grin but did not know if that would be appropriate. She seemed confused, as if she wanted to please but did not know exactly how. He felt an instant kinship with her.

"Everybody," Nikki said. "This is Laura." He pulled her into the room so that she faced Mrs. McNamara.

"How do you do?" the older woman said, extending her hand, which Laura shook uncertainly. "I'm Maureen McNamara. I live downstairs, and I cook for the family."

"Hello," Laura said softly.

"And this is Irene," the older woman said proudly.

"Hello, Irene," Laura said warmly and extended her hand to the girl. But Irene had dipped into a deep, flowing curtsy, and Laura's hand hung suspended for a moment, then fell back to her side.

"And this," Mrs. McNamara said boastfully, "is Dimmy."

Laura stepped in front of him. He stared at her as if mesmerized, watching her graceful movements as if she were a ballerina performing just for him.

She smiled directly at him, a genuine smile. He knew the real thing when he saw it.

"Hello, Dimmy," she said, and there was a lilt in her voice as if she were singing his name.

He bowed deeply, straightened up, and said, "Pleased to meet you, ma'am."

She moved closer to him and placed her hand on his hot cheek. "That's so sweet," she said.

Ignoring the flush that swept over him, he grinned at her with pleasure and suddenly knew that all was lost, that he had gone and done it. He was hers—hopelessly, irrevocably, unalterably.

Dimmy loved her the instant he saw her.

"Shut up and go to sleep!" Dimmy whispered.

"It's true," Irene insisted. "I can hear them right through the wall if I close my eyes and listen real hard."

"You're crazy," Dimmy said.

"Am not!"

"Are too."

The near total darkness of the bedroom they shared prevented them from seeing each other, but they were used to conversing in the dark.

"Why would you say a thing like that?" Dimmy continued after a thoughtful pause.

"That's what people do when they get married. Don't you know anything?"

He hesitated again. "Well, Papa and Laura don't," he finally whispered. "And they're not married."

"Of course, they are," she said.

"No, they're not."

Irene sighed. "You're such a child, Dimmy."

"Am not!"

"Why do you think she brought all her clothes with her?"

Dimmy grunted.

"Why do you think she's always here?"

Dimmy remained silent.

"She sleeps here all the time, Dimmy."

"If they were married, they'd have had a wedding," he murmured.

"You'll see," Irene responded.

He paused for a long moment, then spoke. "Shut up and go to sleep," he said weakly.

"Next thing," Irene continued, "they'll want us to call her mommy."

"Never!" Dimmy was aghast.

"You'll see," Irene said. "Just you wait."

"Goddammit!" Dimmy spat.

Irene was shocked. "You talk like that, Papa will give it to you."

"You gonna tell him?" Dimmy said sarcastically.

She laughed softly in the dark. "Papa knows everything." She fell silent for a moment. "Except about women," she added quietly.

"Yeah," Dimmy agreed.

They lay in silence for a short time, each hoping that the other had fallen asleep. Dimmy did not understand what he was feeling, but he knew that he did not want his father to marry Laura. Faint, unwanted recollections filtered through his mind causing a jumble of conflicting impressions that pulled him every which way. He wanted Laura near him. He wanted to smell her soft, clean, sweet scent. He wanted her gentle fingers touching him, caressing his hair, grazing his cheek. He wanted her to remain in their home, to remain in his life. Yet the thought of her being his father's wife tormented and enraged him.

Suddenly, without wanting to, he remembered his mother. He could see her again—dark, silent, melancholy, beautiful.

He relived her confusing pain, her frequent tears poorly hidden from view, the ugly purple bruises on her face and body that pained her when he touched them with curious fingers while she held him close and rocked him in her arms.

He recalled, as if in lightning flashes, the way she had crouched in the face of Papa's onslaughts, seated on the floor, knees pulled up high, one arm covering her head and face, receiving the blows, one arm clutching Dimmy with fearful desperation. He could not forget feeling helpless, unprotected, as he struggled to breathe, to free his face from her breast where he lay gasping for air as she held him pressed to her.

"Dimmy?" Irene's voice penetrated his half-dream. "Are you asleep?"

"No," he mumbled.

"What are you thinking?"

"Nothing."

"Tell."

"Really! Nothing!"

"I don't believe you," Irene said forlornly. "Tell me."

"I don't want him to marry her," he suddenly blurted.

"I knew that's what you were thinking."

"How did you know?"

"Me too. I was thinking the same thing."

"It's a very bad thing," he said. "I don't want it to happen all over again."

"I know."

Dimmy stifled a sob. He pressed his eyes shut and squeezed a solitary tear out of each. He wanted to beg for help. He wanted to turn to someone and plead for protection. He wished he had someone to turn to, anyone. But there was no one, and he felt as alone as he had always felt, even before his mother died.

He knew he had to be strong. He could hear his mother's voice telling him to be strong. He could sense that his frightened sister, pretending to be so sophisticated, needed him to be strong, too. But he felt so vacant, so abandoned, that strength eluded him and he wished he were tiny once again and back in that time when he did not understand what the world was all about.

"Dimmy?"

"Yes."

"Do you hate her?"

"No."

"I do," Irene confessed.

"Why?" he asked without enthusiasm.

"I don't want her to take Papa away."

"She wouldn't do that," Dimmy said. "Where would they go?"

"I don't mean that," she said. "I don't want him to love her. I want him to love me."

Dimmy brushed the tears from his eyes. "Forget it," he said. "Love is for grown-ups."

"That's not true."

"Yes, it is," he said with some bitterness. "Just keep your mouth shut and stay out of it. Forget all that love junk."

He rolled over so that his face was turned away from her and pulled the covers up close under his chin. He was not sure if he believed what he had told his sister, but he was convinced that it was a safer belief than one that might cause him to expect something he might never receive. He could trust Mrs. McNamara's cooking. He could trust his papa's temper. He could trust that the bigger kids at school would steal his lunch money. He could trust lots of things. But love was not one of them.

Irene's voice came to him as if from a great distance. "Dimmy," she said, "I love you."

Startled, he hesitated for a moment, then replied from equally far away. "Yeah, Reenie. Me too."

Mrs. McNamara had gone out of her way to help Laura. Without her the young woman might not have been able to adjust. Laura's initial fear had been that she would not be able to coexist with the children. Though she had not intended to play at being a parent, had no desire to replace their mother—Nikki had promised her that she would not be required to do that—she feared they might perceive her as trying to do just that and that they would resent her. She expected them to be cold and distant, rude and rebellious, intruding on her and Nikki in order to damage their relationship. She feared they would behave monstrously to her and make her miserable, make her regret her decision to move in with them.

Consequently, attributing to the two children, in her own mind, the power to control her in their home, she began to quietly resent them. Being so young and inexperienced herself, she doubted that she had the patience and common sense to guide and counsel them as they grew up. They were not her children, and she knew that she had no maternal feelings for them. She could not force herself to love them simply because they were Nikki's children.

Years later, when she confessed these fears to Dimmy and Irene as they huddled together in the darkness of the bedroom to protect one another from the common enemy, the boy had been shocked and amazed at the similarities between their unspoken anxieties.

But it was Mrs. McNamara who reminded Laura time and again that she need only reach back and remember herself at that age.

"Remember the things that caused you pain back then," she said. "What were your greatest fears? What were your loftiest, most secret desires? Think of those things and you'll cope quite well with Irene and Dimmy."

She smiled encouragingly. "They're not any different from you and me. We're really only children ourselves, after all. Just stuffed into bigger bodies."

The two women had sat at the square plastic-covered table in Nikki's kitchen and sipped coffee together soon after Laura moved in. Mrs. McNamara had come up to see how things were going as soon as she saw the children return from school. She had been surprised when they had come knocking meekly at her door early that morning looking for their little brown-sacked lunches. She had felt confident that, now that Laura was living with them, they would be receiving a proper lunch to take from home. A proper inspection, too. But when the children's presence at her door suggested that that was not so, she made a point of visiting upstairs to see what was going on.

"They watch me," Laura said. "When I turn around suddenly, I catch them watching me." She shook her head in puzzlement. "And they look so angry, so—I don't know— resentful."

Dimmy—seated on the floor in his bedroom, the door slightly ajar, his ear at the crack—grimaced at Laura's remark. How could she think such a thing? he wondered.

Irene—stretched out on her stomach on her bed, her chin propped up on a pillow, her eyes glued to an open textbook— whispered, "You better get away from that door. She'll catch you and tell Papa, and he'll skin you alive."

Dimmy put his fingers to his lips and motioned her to be quiet.

In the kitchen the older woman smiled warmly at Laura. "You have to give them time, love. You're a big unknown in their lives. You have to let them test you before they'll be ready to trust you."

Laura shrugged dejectedly. "I don't know what to do. I try to do things for them, but they won't let me."

"Like what?"

"Like this morning," Laura said. "I wanted to make breakfast for them, but they insisted on making their own."

"Well, the little darlings have been doing for themselves for a long time. It's an old habit, but they'll give it up soon, especially if you can cook better than they can." The older woman grinned at her. "Why don't you start with something easy?" she suggested.

"Such as?"

"Fix 'em a little lunch to take to school. Something they really like."

"They don't take lunch," Laura said matter-of-factly. "Nikki gives them money to buy lunch."

Dimmy heard Mrs. McNamara laugh, and he grinned humorlessly along with her.

"No, love," he heard her say. "You can't count on that. Trust me. You want to do something for those kids, you make 'em a good lunch every day."

"I don't know . . ." Laura sounded hesitant.

"There's nothing to it," Mrs. McNamara said, misunderstanding Laura's misgivings. "A peanut butter and jelly sandwich would do. An apple. Maybe a cookie or two."

"You think so?" Laura sounded unconvinced.

"I'll make a deal with you," Mrs. McNamara said. "You agree to send those kids off every morning with a bag of eats and I'll teach you everything I know about cooking for your . . . for Mr. Pappas."

"You will?"

"I'm the best Greek cook the Emerald Isle ever produced. Besides, I've been cooking for him long enough to know what he likes and what he don't." She leaned forward and touched Laura's arm. "What do you say?"

Laura hesitated, seemed to ponder for a moment, then smiled. "It's a deal," she finally said. "I hope I'm doing the right thing."

"Oh, it's the right thing, all right. Believe me."

It was, too. From that day on, Dimmy and Irene found two brown sacks with their names written on them in crayon waiting for them in the kitchen each morning. Sometimes the bags contained simple sandwiches like peanut butter or luncheon meat, and sometimes they contained more complicated sandwiches like turkey, bacon, lettuce, and tomato on toast or salmon croquettes and sliced cucumber. Sometimes the lunches were dry and hastily thrown together; other times they were very special, and the children knew Laura had taken time with them. At all times they included a a special treat—an Oreo cookie or a Fig Newton or half a Twinkie. It seemed to Dimmy after a while that he had only to mention his interest in some food item and it would magically appear in the brown bag the next morning or the morning after.

Mrs. McNamara held up her end of the bargain as well. For several weeks Nikki and the children were treated to extravagant Greek dinners prepared by Laura under the secret supervision of Mrs. McNamara. She learned well and discovered that she had a natural knack for cooking exotic dishes. She mastered moussaka—Nikki's favorite—easily. Then she learned to prepare pastitsio, a ground lamb and beef casserole with pasta and béchamel sauce; arni fricasse, a spring lamb casserole with artichokes, celery, and onion in an avgolemono sauce; and payidakia, the tiny char-broiled lamb chops they loved so much. She also quickly became proficient at preparing saganaki, a flaming cheese dish; spanakopitta, a spinach-cheese pie baked in phyllo pastry; and dolmades, grape leaves stuffed with chopped lamb and rice.

Dimmy was dazzled by the delectable aromas that greeted

him each day when he returned from school. They wafted out from under the apartment door and seeped down the dingy stairs to meet him and his sister as they climbed the many flights, slowly at first then eagerly as the wondrous aromas grew in intensity and served as a friendly greeting. They would burst into the apartment, rush to the kitchen, pass by Laura and Mrs. McNamara, who by that time were usually seated at the small kitchen table sipping coffee, and lift the lids of the pots and pans that bubbled and gurgled on the stove.

Dimmy and Irene had created a game out of guessing what spectacular repast Laura would be preparing on any given day. The winner—if there was one—got to eat the loser's dessert—baklava or galactoboureko—an extreme price to pay for wrong guessing. But neither child minded losing that much, for Laura was sure to insist that both children have extra dessert anyway, and they loved being surprised when the dinner was new and unfamiliar.

"You can't give up your favorite dessert," Laura would say, sliding a sticky square of baklava onto Irene's plate. She would smile and touch the girl's silken hair lightly. "You shouldn't let your brother swindle you."

"It's not a swindle," Irene replied. "He's just a better guesser than I am."

"Oh," Laura said. "He just has a bigger nose." She reached over and caught Dimmy's nose between two fingers and tweaked it slightly.

"Ow!" he would shout and jump away from her hand as if he had been mortally wounded while secretly enjoying the way Laura played with them and teased them affectionately.

"One day I'm going to steal that magical nose of yours," Laura sometimes said. She showed him the end of her thumb protruding from between her two fingers. "See? I'm going to keep it. Maybe I'll give it to Irene and she'll become the better guesser." Then she smiled and caressed his cheek with her soft hand. "No," she would say. "Your nose is too beautiful right where it is. I would never think of changing it."

That was a time of great joy for Dimmy and Irene, that early time when Laura first came to live with them. Their apartment had not smelled so Greek, had not been filled with so much laughter and playfulness, had not been so much like a home, since long before their mother had fallen ill. The new ambience reminded them of a better time.

"You're getting to be a big boy, Dimmy," the tall man said, leaning his pockmarked face close enough to shout into Dimmy's ear.

The heavy scent of his aftershave lotion fused with the pungency of his breath, filling Dimmy's nostrils and nearly bringing tears to the boy's eyes. He pulled back and turned his face away in search of breathable air.

"You got on a suit with long pants and everything." Uncle Stavros nodded and grinned, displaying a row of yellow teeth. He motioned toward the dance floor where Irene danced falteringly with their father. "And your sister's gonna be a beauty, ain't she?" He smirked lasciviously. "She's gonna break a lot of hearts when she grows up, I'm telling you."

The children had been instructed to address him as "uncle," but Stavros was not a relative. Dimmy did not know exactly who he was or where he had come from, although it was clear that he was of Greek descent. They did not know how he had become involved with their father, but the two men were business associates. They were in and out of quiet ventures and spent whole days and nights away from home together. Stavros was sinister. He smiled too much; he scowled and became angry without reason; he frightened

Dimmy and Irene. His appearance was terrifying; the rough face, the close-set and penetrating black eyes, the straight dark hair slicked back with pomade, and the yellow grin like that of a mad dog sent chills up and down their spines. He always wore gray pinstripe suits with wide lapels over black or dark maroon shirts and white or beige ties, just like the gangsters in the old-time movies that were shown on television late at night.

On this night, however, Uncle Stavros wore a tuxedo. His shirtsleeves, extending beyond the shiny cuffs of his jacket, were adorned with square black links that matched the studs on his frilly white shirt. His perfect black bow tie was not a clip-on; Dimmy could see the ends peeking out from behind the bow.

As a matter of fact, all the men in the hall wore tuxedos. The young boys wore dark suits, and all the women wore evening gowns and had purple flowers pinned to their shoulders or wrapped like bracelets around their wrists. Only Laura wore no flowers. She did not need them, Dimmy thought. They would only have detracted from her beauty. He watched her as she came into view weaving through the dancers, speaking to everyone she passed.

"Ha!" Stavros squeezed Dimmy's arm in his powerful fingers. "Your old man is a lucky guy. Your new mama is some piece of work." There was admiration in the man's voice as he regarded Laura moving around the room in her white satin wedding gown, laughing brightly, veil and hat gone, her long almost-blond hair flowing behind her. "This is my dance. Stay here, kid. I'll be right back."

Dimmy watched Uncle Stavros swoop down on Laura like a bird of prey, catch her in his hard hands, and swing her into a wild dance. The pleasure he had felt at watching her diminished once Stavros had her wrapped in his arms, and the boy turned and moved off toward the buffet table. He picked at a meatball, popped it into his mouth, found it hard to swallow, and decided that he was not hungry. He helped himself to a glass of pink punch that had a floe of green sherbet melting in it and leaned back against the wall to observe the crowded dance floor, which was now filled to capacity with almost all of the wedding party.

He realized that he was confused. He did not understand what he was feeling and was not sure that he was feeling anything at all, other than a strong urge to weep, which he kept in containment. He was consumed by the strangest combination of odd, unwanted thoughts and bits and flashes of sadness and joy and fear. He was calm and yet nervous. He was tired and yet filled with an excited energy.

In a way he was pleased that his father and Laura had married, because it meant that she would not leave them, that she would be with them forever, waiting for him when he returned from school in the afternoon, there, in the kitchen, in the morning to send him off, to place a brown bag in his hand, to inspect his fingernails, smooth down his unruly hair, straighten his collar, which did not need straightening, kiss his cheek with her cool, soft lips. Yet he was also sad and frightened that they were married now, because he suspected that her attitude toward him might change. His father might insist that it change. He suspected that the brief, wonderful system which Laura had brought into their home would be altered now that her status had changed. He feared she would devote less time to him and his sister, that she would care less about him and Irene. She would be drawn away from them. He did not understand how he knew this, but he knew the truth of it as well as he knew his own name. There would be less for him from now on and more for Papa.

His father and mother had argued about that. Dimly he could remember his father screaming those very words: "Less for him. More for me." He did not actually recall hearing it, but it was there in his memory as clear a recollection as the softness of his mother's skin. He had always known that men would begrudge him the women who loved him. Men were the enemies of little boys and would always hurt them and take their mothers from them.

"Come, Nikos," he heard Uncle Stavros, in his gravelly voice, shout from the dance floor. "I'll trade women with you."

Dimmy, who had drifted away from the present, lost in his baffling thoughts, looked up in time to see Stavros swing Laura toward his father and grab Irene and twirl her to him, pulling her into his grasp, as though she were a yo-yo. Now the filthy man was touching Irene, and Dimmy's heart seemed to stop beating. His breath caught in his throat, and he had to stifle a cry of fear. Touching Laura was bad enough, but to contaminate Irene was intolerable.

"Hupa," the ugly man shouted, one crooked arm held over his head, the other, like a snake, encircling Dimmy's sister's tiny waist. He lifted the little girl off the floor and swung her around in wide circles. Dimmy expected her to scream with terror, but instead, she laughed loud, the sound rising above the din of the music and the crowd, and shrieked with delight.

Without realizing what he was doing, Dimmy dropped his cup of punch and rushed out onto the dance floor, pushing through unsuspecting couples until he was beside them. He flung his arms around one of Uncle Stavros's legs and, holding on as if for dear life, buried his teeth in the meaty calf.

"Aaaaagh!" Stavros roared in pain. He dropped Irene, grabbed Dimmy by the head, and shook his offended leg wildly, trying to pull the boy off him.

At the sound of the big man's scream the music stopped. The dancers all turned toward the strange confrontation and watched in stunned silence as Stavros balled his hands into tight fists and pounded on the top of Dimmy's skull. The dull thud of each vicious blow resounded in the now silent room.

Dimmy grew dizzy from the blows, but he was determined not to release Stavros's leg. Eyes shut, teeth clenched, arms locked around the leg, Dimmy hung on, unrelenting.

While Stavros continued to pummel the small head that seemed attached to his leg, Nikos clutched his son around the neck.

"Get him off me!" Stavros sputtered between teeth clenched in pain.

"Idiot!" Nikki shouted. "Let go!" He began pulling on the little boy. He squeezed and pulled on the slender neck while Stavros hammered on the top of the small head.

The boy began to choke as his father's fingers closed more tightly around his throat. He felt his own grasp loosening as his vision grew dim and he struggled for air. His arms weakened, and he sensed himself being pulled away from his quarry. His thirst for air became too great and he opened his mouth, releasing his hold on Stavros's leg.

Then he was hanging by the neck from his father's hands. Laura, worriedly wringing her hands, stood beside Nikos with concern on her face. With one hand under Dimmy's chin, holding him steady, his father struck him across the face. The sharp pain in his cheek awakened him from his stupor, and he saw the rage in his father's eyes. He knew he had humiliated his father and was going to pay the price for doing that.

"Idiot!" his father shouted. "Idiot!"

The open hand struck again, and it seemed to Dimmy that the only sound in the world was the crack of his father's palm connecting with his face. Again he was struck, then again and again in a slow calculated cadence, until he tasted blood. As he began to lose consciousness, he hoped it was Uncle Stavros's blood rather than his own.

"Stop it, Nikki!"

Faintly he heard Laura shouting at his father. "Oh, my God!" she cried. "Let him go! You're killing him."

Dimmy felt himself land hard on the floor as his father dropped him. Gasping and choking, he gazed up, one arm ready to cover his head to protect himself from the kick he expected his father to launch at him. But Nikos had lost interest in him. He was glaring at Laura, who was clutching his arm as if to restrain him.

"Get him out of here," he breathed at Laura, shrugging her hands off him. "Go home and take the little bastard with you."

Nikki reached down and lifted the boy from the floor. With a hand on each of them, he pulled Dimmy and Laura off the dance floor, through the circle of tables covered with remnants of half-eaten meals, and out into the vestibule.

"Nikki! What are you doing?" Laura protested. "Don't do this, Nikki. Don't treat us like this."

As Nikki flung them both out into the street, Dimmy heard his father say, "You take his side over mine, bitch? You can walk home with him."

"Why did you do it?" Irène asked from her bed in the darkness where she lay sobbing.

"I don't know," Dimmy answered. He lay flat on his back staring up into the blackness. He had discarded his pillow because his head throbbed more when it was elevated. He wondered himself about his bizarre behavior. He wished he could go back in time and stop himself. He wished he could rewrite history.

They had lain awake for the past hour, since Nikki had brought Irene home from the disrupted wedding party, listening to the muted sounds of Laura's weeping through the wall between their bedrooms. They had shuddered at the tenor of their father's voice reverberating throughout the apartment as he chastised Laura viciously. The rise and fall of his anger had lifted them and dropped them as if on the crest of a wave. They had trembled as his voice escalated to thunderous shouting, and they had frozen in terror as he lowered his volume to a seething whisper.

"She's getting it now," Irene said as they heard a harsh slap followed by Laura's sharp intake of breath.

Dimmy chewed on his lip to control the sobs that reached up from his throat. Silent tears slid down his cheeks and fell on the sheet under his aching head.

Irene was crying now, too. "That's the end for us. She'll hate us now for sure."

"I'm sorry, Reenie," Dimmy mumbled.

"What you did was dumb, Dimmy. It's going to be just like Mama again. The same all over again. Just like it was. Like nothing changed."

"I know."

"I thought it was going to be fun. But it looks like it's going to be the same."

Dimmy rolled over and buried his face in the wet mattress. His tears tasted bitter.

"I'll never do that again, Irene," he said softly, sobbing between words. "I swear! I'll never do anything like that again."

"It's okay, Dimmy," his sister said gently. "I know you won't." She paused and sobbed loudly herself. "I just hope he doesn't kill Laura like he killed Mama."

<u>SIX</u>

It was clear to Dimmy that Mrs. Morrisey, his teacher, had gotten up on the wrong side of the bed. She marched into the congested classroom, dumped her huge purse into the deep bottom drawer of her desk, slammed it closed with a bang, and faced the class, her thin, colorless lips pressed uncomfortably together.

Joey Trafficanti, seated directly behind Dimmy, poked him in the back with his stubby fingers. Joey, who had been held back one year and who was much bigger than the other children, loved to make trouble. This ability to disrupt the class and frustrate the teacher without being held responsible was his only skill.

"I love to see the teachers pop their buttons," he had said to Dimmy, who suffered as Joey's unwilling accomplice. "I like it when their faces get all red and they stutter and they don't know what to do. I love it!"

Trafficanti was especially fond of irritating Mrs. Morrisey. To him she was a challenge, an inviting victim, an obstacle to overcome. Whatever his reasons, his deviousness was not news to Dimmy who had been thrust into Joey's company in the third grade and had, until recently, been relatively content to remain there.

But the chicken episode the day before had been a bit too much for Dimmy to accept. Joey had put several eggs in Mrs. Morrisey's desk drawer, knowing she would toss her large carry-all purse on top of them, shattering them and spreading their gooey contents everywhere. The prank had sent the teacher into paroxysms of rage. The cow sounds that Joey planned for this morning would certainly put an additional strain on the tentative relationship between the two boys. At the risk of being accused of cowardice, Dimmy had been begging Joey to ease up on the teacher for the past week. But Joey contended that it was the privilege of children to harass their teachers.

"Don't do it," Dimmy whispered over his shoulder. "Don't!"

"Why not?" Joey responded.

"Enough already."

"You're chicken, Pappas," Joey taunted. "You're a wimp."

No sooner had Mrs. Morrisey turned to the chalkboard than a soft, mellow lowing emanated from the rear of the crowded room, interrupting her. The long, mournful moo, like the saddened cry of a wayward calf lifting and filling the room, caused Mrs. Morrisey to spin around and search for the culprit. Her eyes wandered futilely over the herd of children who giggled loudly behind their hands.

Mrs. Morrisey, a tic developing in her right eye, quietly placed the chalk on her desk. "I would like to ask whoever is making that grotesque noise to please stop," she said. "Please! Let's not have another day like yesterday."

She stared at the sea of silent, innocent faces, then lifted the chalk and returned to the board. Almost instantly, as Dimmy received another poke in the back, the cow cries rose up and filled the air.

"Quit it!" Dimmy snapped just as the teacher spun around to face the class again.

Her eyes fell on Dimmy and remained fixed on him. As her expression smoldered, she stepped around to the front of her desk and pointed a long, accusing finger at him.

"What did you say?" she demanded.

Dimmy, his eyes widening in innocence, returned her stare and squirmed slightly. She had settled on him, he knew, and he had not done anything. But she had settled on him and he became frightened.

"Nothing, ma'am," he murmured.

She fumed quietly. "Are you a cow, Dimmy?" she finally asked quaveringly, barely able to control her voice.

"No, ma'am," Dimmy whispered.

"I can't hear you," she snapped. "Have you suddenly lost your voice?"

"No, ma'am," he said, his voice rising to a high pitch.

"Well, are you a cow?"

Dimmy felt desperate. He sensed that he had to do something quickly. He could not afford to be sent to the principal's office again. He could not afford incurring his father's wrath again.

"I didn't do it, Mrs. Morrisey," he said finally.

"I saw you," she accused.

"I swear I didn't do it."

She sneered. "You only make it worse by lying."

Around the room, his classmates turned away from him. They found new interests in different directions. Behind Dimmy, out of his sight, Joey Trafficanti pointed at the back of his head and nodded emphatically at the teacher.

"Fortunately," she said, "not all the children in this class are liars." She lifted her eyes from Dimmy's face. "Is Dimitri the culprit, Joseph?" she asked.

Trafficanti nodded sadly. "Yes, ma'am," he said.

"Thank you, Joseph," she said to Trafficanti. "I'm grateful to you for your cooperation."

Dimmy turned to glare at his tormentor, who smiled at him guilelessly. "I can't lie, Dimmy," he said. "You know that."

"God damn you!" Dimmy spat. "You son of a bitch!"

It was three o'clock in the afternoon, and they were on the sidewalk in front of the school where hordes of children milled around them. Joey laughed defiantly at Dimmy while Irene, frightened of the worsening situation, tugged on her brother's arm, trying to drag him down the street. He resisted her. Clutching the teacher's bad-conduct note in his left hand, Dimmy shook his right fist at Joey Trafficanti.

"What's the matter, Pappas, can't you take a joke?"

"It's not funny," Dimmy shouted, struggling to hide his tears. "Now I've got to bring my father to school."

"Tough," Trafficanti sneered. "Mine comes in all the time."

"Damn you! Stay away from me. You're always hanging around me, getting me in trouble."

"Oh, yeah?" Trafficanti grinned, enjoying himself. "What're you gonna do about it, weenie?"

Dimmy, red-faced, breathing rapidly, grimaced at the bigger boy threateningly, but could not break loose from Irene. "Lemme go!" he screamed. "Lemme go!"

"Aw," Joey Trafficanti said, waving a hand at him in disgust. "You greaseball Greeks are all chickenshit!"

"I'll kill you," Dimmy shouted.

"Get real, dickhead."

Suddenly Dimmy broke loose from Irene's grip and flew at the larger boy. Joey Trafficanti, who had not expected such courage, was unprepared for the ferocious attack. Dimmy, thin arms flailing, lunged at him and rammed the top of his head into the bigger boy's soft stomach. He felt gratified when he heard the sudden whoosh of air shoot out of Joey's mouth. The big boy grunted, doubled over, and covered his stomach with both hands.

"God damn you!" Dimmy screamed as he battered Joey's back and shoulders. "God damn you!"

Joey Trafficanti sucked in a deep gasping breath and stepped away from the small windmill that was hovering over him. Dimmy followed him and continued to throw blows at him with his tiny fists, but most of the punches fell on the big boy's arms and shoulders.

"Get off me," Joey said, pushing Dimmy away. "I'm warnin' you."

Dimmy continued to bore in, head down, blindly throwing punches, kicking and crying, swinging wildly. Joey, stiff-armed, held the little boy at bay. "Quit it, ya little bastard. That's enough."

Dimmy, near exhaustion, kept swinging wildly at Joey's body, now out of reach and unattainable. As he swung and missed, again and again, he sobbed loudly in frustration.

"You gonna quit?" Trafficanti demanded.

"No!"

"I'll bust your face off."

Dimmy reared back and aimed a kick at his adversary's groin.

Joey turned quickly and caught the kick on the side of his leg. "Ow!" he shouted. "You goddam little son of a bitch." He released Dimmy's head suddenly and allowed the smaller boy to rush in toward him, off balance, his forward motion making him vulnerable. Then Joey stepped aside and, balling his big fist, punched Dimmy with all his might in the eye, knocking the little boy flat on his back.

Dimmy, shaking off his dizziness, covered his injured eye with one hand and struggled to his knees.

"You get up, I'll knock you down again," Joey warned.

Dimmy rose to his feet. His eye was nearly closed with

the immediate swelling. Slowly, deliberately, he started toward the big boy. Joey waved him away, but Dimmy was resolute, and he continued to pursue his opponent.

"You asked for it," Joey said. He hit Dimmy again in the same eye and knocked him down for good.

Irene, weeping loudly, rushed to her brother and leaned over him. She took his head in her hands and looked up at Joey Trafficanti.

"I warned him," the big boy said, clearly indicating that he was not responsible.

"Idiot!" she screamed. "Get away from here. I'll kill you myself."

Joey Trafficanti grinned at her. "Shit," he said. "You're as crazy as he is."

Laura and Mrs. McNamara were talking in the kitchen when the two children rushed into the apartment, slammed the front door, and dashed into their bedroom without a word. Laura called out to them, but they pretended they had not heard. Irene was of a mind to confess to Laura and enlist her aid in treating Dimmy's injury, but Dimmy would not hear of it. It was too soon for him to face another confrontation. He felt emotionally exhausted as well as physically bruised and wished he could hide for about a week, hibernate like a bear for a while, and return to society whole, without a mark on him.

"What're we gonna do?" Dimmy asked his sister, who had taken command of the situation.

"Don't worry," she said. "I'll take care of it. You get in bed. Get under the covers and I'll tell her you don't feel well. I'll get some ice for your eye."

A lump the size and shape of a large egg had risen on Dimmy's cheekbone, and his eye was squeezed tightly shut by the massive swelling. She helped him get out of his clothing and into pajamas. She saw to it that he climbed into bed and pulled the covers up almost entirely over his head. Then she went to get an ice pack and left him alone.

He found himself trembling, even while huddled under the heavy quilt, and knew he was still terribly frightened. What frightened him more, he wondered, the fight with Joey Trafficanti or the thought of his father's anger? He had agonized over bringing still another disciplinary note home. He vividly remembered the punishment he had received the last time Nikki was called to school. Dimmy could still feel the stinging blows across his back. This current transgression could warrant something much worse. Dimmy had compounded the school offense with brawling in the street, and that might be more than his father's bad temper could endure. Losing the fight to boot would surely bring Nikki's rage crashing down on his head.

"Dimmy!" Laura said worriedly as she charged into the room with Mrs. McNamara right behind her and Irene following them both. "Let me see you."

Laura sat on the side of his bed and lowered the quilt to expose his abused face. "Oh, my God!" she said. "What happened to you?"

Dimmy's one remaining functional eye glared at his sister who stood behind the two women.

"I didn't say, Dimmy," Irene protested. "I swear I didn't tell."

"She should have," Laura said. "Why were you hiding from me? Did you think I'd be angry with you?" She caressed his hot cheek with the cool palm of her hand. Her soft skin felt comforting on his face.

"Give me the ice pack," Mrs. McNamara said to Irene and snatched it from the girl's hands. "Here, Laura. Press it right on the eye."

Laura placed the ice on Dimmy's face and moved his hand

up to keep it in place. "Here, hold it." She smiled down at him and he grinned back at her. He was already feeling less afraid. He had nearly forgotten the fear of his father's reaction.

"So you're a street fighter," she said with a laugh in her voice.

Dimmy shrugged. "I didn't start it." He pointed to his clothing. "There's a note from my teacher in my pants pocket."

"Uh-oh," Laura said.

"I didn't do that, either."

"What?"

"The mooing," Dimmy said.

Irene giggled and turned away.

"What mooing?" Mrs. McNamara asked.

Laura read the note from school, and then Dimmy related the events of that day. He told of his humiliating punishment at the hands of Mrs. Morrisey and his subsequent confrontation with the true offender. The boy's lips trembled as he concluded. "I can't ask Papa to go to school again. I don't want him to know."

"Well," Mrs. McNamara said, "if you didn't do anything and you're being wrongfully punished, I should think you'd want your father to go there and straighten it out."

"Oh, no," Dimmy whimpered and started to weep softly.

Laura silently lifted him from the pillow and held him in her arms. He cried onto the front of her dress like the child that he was.

"We won't tell him," Laura whispered. She was rocking the boy ever so slightly. "We'll just take care of this ourselves and not bother him about it. That's all."

"Bother him?" Mrs. McNamara said.

Laura turned her head to the older woman. "Nikki's too busy for all this school stuff. He doesn't have a head for it."

She returned her attention to Dimmy. "We'll take care of it, won't we, Dimmy?"

Dimmy, his face pressed against her shoulder, nodded.

"Tomorrow, we'll march into that principal's office and put them straight."

Later, as Dimmy lay quietly in his bed, he heard Mrs. McNamara at the door. Just as she was leaving, she said, "And you weren't going to be a mother to those children, remember? You weren't going to take their poor dear mother's place." There was warmth in her voice, and she laughed softly. "I guess there's no danger of that happening, is there, my dear?"

"You don't understand," Dimmy heard Laura say quietly. "It's not what you think."

"You don't have to be ashamed," Mrs. McNamara said. "You never have to be ashamed of loving children. They're lovely children, and it's wonderful how well you've taken to each other."

"I know," Laura said quietly and there was fear in her voice. "But you mustn't say that I've taken their mother's place. You mustn't ever say that."

"But it's true," Mrs. McNamara said.

Laura hesitated for an instant. "If Nikki ever heard you say that, I don't know what would happen," she finally whispered.

They almost pulled it off.

While Dimmy lay awake in his darkened bedroom, his heart beating rapidly, his hands sweating with fear and anticipation, silently hating Mrs. Morrisey for having unjustly placed him in such jeopardy out of her own frustration, he heard Laura explain to Nikki that he would not be joining them for dinner, even though she had prepared lamb souvlaki, his absolute favorite dish, because he was not feeling well. She sounded concerned, as though he were truly sick, and Dimmy admired her ability to do that so sincerely and convincingly. He was never able to lie to his father. Somehow, no matter how good an acting job he did, his father could always read Dimmy's mind.

Dimmy heard his sister say, in an offhanded manner, that she thought he might have a slight fever, and Laura added that it might even be a touch of the flu, which was going around. Half the kids at school had it, he heard Irene say, and he could almost see her head bobbing up and down frantically as she made her case.

Nikki was sincerely sympathetic and wanted to comfort his ailing son, but Laura quickly suggested that they let him rest. "Sleep is the best thing for him," she said. "I stuffed him with liquids, and he should sleep as much as he can."

Irene agreed. "Poor Dimmy," she said. "He's so miserable and uncomfortable. He'll feel much better after a good night's sleep."

He could just barely make out their dinner conversation. He heard his father heartily compliment Laura on the wonderful lamb. He heard Irene agree, although she usually only picked at the succulent chunks of grilled lamb and ate only the vegetables. He heard Laura's subdued thank-you and the tiny self-conscious giggle that meant that she was embarrassed. His mouth watered for the dinner he had chosen to sacrifice in order to deceive his father.

After dinner, Irene crept stealthily into the room, as if he were truly sleeping, and turned on the night lamp beside her bed.

"What are you doing?" he asked, sitting up in bed.

She put her finger to her lips. "Shh," she said. "Papa will hear you."

"Did you bring me anything?" he whispered.

"Like what?"

"To eat, you dummy. I'm starving."

She frowned. "How could I bring you food? You're supposed to be sleeping. Don't you remember? You're sick."

"Oh, God!" he moaned. "I will be if I don't eat something soon. I can feel the front and the back of my stomach rubbing together."

She giggled. "Silly." She kicked her shoes off, then sat cross-legged on her own bed.

"Couldn't you sneak me anything?" He shook his head despondently. "Maybe Laura will come in later and bring me a snack. I hope, I hope."

Irene laughed. "Serves you right for not behaving yourself in school."

He grimaced. "Don't you start on me now. You're supposed to be on my side."

"I am," she said.

"So go get me some food—a piece of bread, a cookie. Anything."

She smirked. "And what if Papa catches me?"

"Don't tell him it's for me. Tell him it's for you." Dimmy grinned at his cleverness.

"I just had dinner. He'll know I'm lying."

They sat in silence for a long moment staring at each other obstinately. Finally Irene shrugged at her brother's downhearted appearance. He looked so little to her, so slight, with small hands and small feet and a small, lean body. Everything about him was petite except his swollen eye, which protruded grotesquely like the bulbous appendage of a movie monster.

"Please?" he begged.

"All right!" She slipped off the bed and out of the room, leaving the door slightly ajar.

Dimmy lay back contentedly, wondering what she would

bring him—a plate of cold lamb cubes, perhaps, or a handful of chocolate chip cookies and a glass of cold milk, which he loved and she hated, or a pita stuffed with cold grilled vegetables with olive oil and garlic. His stomach churned with hunger and he could hardly wait.

He was dreaming about tender, tasty lamb when the bedroom door suddenly burst open and Dimmy saw the formidable figure of his father dragging Irene behind him. Nikki stood before the boy, his legs spread apart, one hand on his hip, the other entwined in his daughter's hair.

"You're too sick to eat!" he shouted. "Too sick to come to the table and eat with your father like you're supposed to." He reached out and flipped the wall switch, flooding the room with light, then took several steps into the room, pulling the little girl in after him while Laura, who had suddenly appeared, hung back in the doorway. He was moving toward the boy when he stopped abruptly, stood still in the center of the room, and released Irene, who sank to the floor, sobbing.

"What happened to you?" Nikki shouted, pointing his rigid forefinger as if it were the barrel of a pistol.

Dimmy, terrified, pressed his back against the head of the bed and pulled the quilt up to his chin. His legs began to tremble uncontrollably, and he bit down on his lower lip to prevent it from quivering.

"What happened to your face?" Nikki demanded. He looked back at Laura. "What's going on here? What're you telling me about the flu?" he screamed.

He whirled back to face Dimmy. "What happened?"

"I . . . I . . ." the frightened boy stammered.

"Speak up!" Nikki shouted, his face contorted and flushed.

The speechless boy began to weep.

"Answer me when I talk to you!"

"It wasn't his fault, Papa," Irene cried from the floor.

"You shut up!" he snapped at her without taking his eyes from Dimmy's tortured face. "How'd you get that eye?"

Tears flowed down the little boy's face. "I had a fight," he finally muttered with great effort.

"What you fighting for?"

The boy shrugged and threw his hands up to cover his face.

"Answer me when I talk to you."

Dimmy swallowed and forced his lips to stop trembling. "A boy got me in trouble."

"What trouble? Where?"

"In school. He got me in trouble with the teacher," he sobbed. "He lied about me."

Nikki seemed to inflate until he loomed over the boy. "I gotta go to the school?" he roared. "I gotta listen to some old dyke tell me what a rotten kid I got?"

Dimmy nodded silently, and when Nikki raised his hand to strike him, the boy threw his arms up to protect his head. The two of them remained frozen in that posture, the puny cringing boy overshadowed by the huge enraged parent. Then suddenly Nikki, seeming to resolve a dilemma, dropped his upraised arm, wheeled around, and stormed out of the room, brushing roughly past Laura.

She stepped quickly away from him, letting him pass, then hurried into the room to lift Irene to her feet and stand beside Dimmy's bed. Almost instantly Nikki reappeared in the room. In his right hand he clutched a makeshift whip fashioned from several strands of clothesline, which he slapped across his left palm as he advanced.

"Roll over!" he ordered Dimmy. "Get your pajamas off."

The boy whimpered but knew better than to disobey his father at this juncture. He pulled his pajama shirt over his head and dropped it onto the floor, then turned over and lay down on his stomach.

"What are you doing?" Laura shouted.

"You stay out of this."

"You're not going to whip him!"

"None of your business what I do with my boy."

"Yes, it is," Laura said loudly.

"He's not your boy. He's my boy."

Laura left Irene and moved quickly around the bed. She grabbed Nikki's arm in both hands. "You're not going to whip him," she said coldly. "I'm not going to let you."

Nikki studied her for a moment, Dimmy thought, with admiration in his eyes, then nodded emphatically. "Okay," he said. "You want to be the boss around here. I'll show you what it takes to be the boss of me and my kids."

He clutched her around the throat and dragged her from the room. They heard her shoes scraping along the floor as he pulled her into their bedroom and slammed the door behind them. The children heard the whistle and thwack of the whip as it sailed through the air and landed on Laura's back.

Much later, when the apartment was dark and quiet, when Dimmy could hear Irene's measured breathing from the other bed and knew that she was asleep, he heard his door open and looked up to see his father standing beside him. He lifted his head from the pillow and peered at the shadowy figure. Nikki reached out and touched the boy's head, caressed the top of the small head, and the boy shivered.

"Dimmy," he said, sitting down on the edge of the bed.

"Yes, Papa."

"You hate me?"

The boy could not answer. The words he wanted to utter stuck in his throat and a terrible fear kept him silent.

"You hate me." The man nodded. "But you're still a little boy. You don't understand these things. Someday, when you're grown up, you'll know what it's like to have responsibility for a family. When you grow up you'll be just like me."

"No, Papa," the boy whispered, surprising himself with his own courage.

"No?"

"No, Papa. You hit too much."

Nikki nodded thoughtfully. "Sometimes you have to hit. To make people understand. To teach. To show right from wrong. You'll see. Someday, when you're a man, you'll do the same."

The boy shook his head mournfully. "No, Papa," he said. "I hate hitting. I'll never hit again. I swear to God. I'll never hit anyone again."

Dimmy and Irene waited outside as they had been instructed. There had been no discussion. There had been no debate. They had nodded their agreement and watched silently as their father led Laura, draped in a black veil, up the steps and into the old building on Ninety-second Street where, the children had deduced incorrectly, dead Greeks went to be buried. Dimmy wore his little black suit, wrists protruding from the cuffs too far now that he had grown another inch, and Irene was dressed in her white and pink chiffon, the belt tied in a bow in the back, the bodice stretched tightly across her budding breasts in the front. They clung to each other, fingers interlocked, wound together like the fibers of a rope, for greater support, and though Irene sniffled and sobbed softly now and then as if mourning fittingly, Dimmy was not sure exactly what was expected of him. He did not know how he was supposed to behave or how he was required to feel.

Unquestionably he was in awe of this fearful place. This was the same forbidding establishment that had claimed his mother several years earlier and, he sensed, would claim them all someday. He was just as happy not to have been invited inside, as he had been at his mother's departure. Then he had been pushed before his father, dragging his feet unenthusiastically while Irene clung to him much as she was clinging now.

Dimmy shuddered at the recollection of that misery and decided that he and Irene were lucky that their father had decided to spare them the pain of viewing this body. It had been difficult, Dimmy understood, to put this one back together in a recognizable way.

"Are you cold?" Irene asked.

"No," he replied, mystified by her question. "It's hot out here."

"You shivered. I thought you were cold."

"I didn't shiver," he said.

"I felt you. You shivered."

He shrugged. "Whatever." He squeezed her hand. "At least I'm not crying."

"Who's crying?"

"I hear you."

"My nose is running. That's all."

"Sure," he said mockingly,

"It's true," she insisted. "Why would I be crying?"

Dimmy leered at her. "You're going to miss his hands all over you, that's why—his clammy hands on your face and his fat, wet lips on your mouth. That's why."

"Ugh!" She grimaced. "You're disgusting."

"I'm not the one he was kissing all the time. He didn't pinch my little titties every time Papa looked away."

"Don't talk dirty!" she snapped. "You're a disgusting little boy."

She turned away from him, red-faced, and sniffled.

He had one more shot he could take at her, but he decided against it and closed his lips silently. What was he hurting her for? he wondered. It wasn't Irene he was angry with.

When he stopped to think about it, he realized that he did not harbor any anger toward Stavros, either. It was true that Stavros had inconvenienced him by dying. Otherwise, he would not be standing in the street dressed up like a monkey, feeling stupid and hot and uncomfortable, wasting a Saturday morning when he could be at the playground shooting baskets, slapping a handball around, playing stickball with the guys. But Stavros had not planned to ruin his Saturday. At the moment of his death Stavros had not been thinking of the impact it would have on Dimmy's weekend.

Dimmy doubted that there had been anything on Uncle Stavros's mind at that fateful moment. He tried to imagine the accident. What had Stavros felt at that very instant? He waved away the thought of the pain, for that was not the kind of feeling he was curious about. He wondered about the other kind of feeling, the kind that one felt in the soul rather than in the body. Ouzo had most likely flattened out any thoughts the man might have had. But would it have stifled feelings of, say, regret or sorrow or anger at suddenly being snuffed out like some insignificant light?

He could imagine Stavros staggering down the dark alley searching his pockets for his keys, wondering where he had left his brand-new Jaguar, wondering where he was going and where he had been. In a flash Dimmy could see him flattened by a huge speeding pickle truck whose driver did not even bother to stop and examine the remains of the man he had crushed. How he knew it was a pickle truck was beyond him, but for some reason the thought pleased Dimmy. He did not want to remember Stavros in any way that might be considered even slightly heroic. It could have been a garbage truck or a *New York Times* truck, but Dimmy preferred to think of the weapon as a pickle truck. That was a fitting end for his father's partner whom Dimmy had hated so deeply for such a long time.

"Goddammit!" he had heard his father roar at Laura the night he learned of his friend's death. "I told the crazy bastard a thousand times—a million times—that's what happens when you don't listen to me."

Dimmy had heard Laura say something unintelligible. He could still see her, in his mind's eye, shoulders sagging, head bowed in fear and submission.

"Bastard!" Nikki had shouted. "Dumb bastard."

They had been in the kitchen, which they all jokingly called "Laura's room." His father had come home from the restaurant more than a little drunk and spoiling for a fight, itching for someone to take him on. It was two in the morning, and Dimmy had been awakened by the slamming of the front door and his father shouting at Laura to wake up and make him some coffee. The boy had sneaked into the dark hallway and sat on the floor with his back against the cold wall, listening, fearing another beating for Laura.

"Now what do I do, huh? Tell me that. What do I do now?" His father's speech was slurred and he was slobbering.

"I don't know," Laura said.

"You don't know nothing," Nikki replied. "What good are you?"

"I didn't kill him, Nikki," Laura said softly.

"Don't get smart with me," Nikki said. "I know who killed him all right."

"You said it was an accident."

Nikki laughed. "Some accident. Anybody can make it

look like a hit-and-run accident. It's easy. You get a big truck and you hit somebody and you drive away. Anybody can do it.''

He pulled a chair out from under the kitchen table, scraping its legs on the linoleum floor. ''What am I gonna do now?''

''Sit down,'' Laura said. ''Drink your coffee.''

Nikki's speech was slurred. ''What I'm gonna do now, Laura? I don't have a partner no more. How'm I gonna run the restaurant? How'm I gonna take care of business alone?'' he shouted. ''Oh, Stavros, you crazy bastard, why'd you do this to me?''

Dimmy could not remember having seen his father so enthusiastic about anything, not even at his wedding to Laura or that day when he had first brought her home to them and was so delighted with the beautiful young woman, not even at Irene's first communion. Dimmy was pleased that his father was so cheerful, but, at the same time he did not trust the longevity of the mood, for Nikki's enthusiasm was similar to a beautiful blue, sun-filled, cheerful sky just beyond the farthest horizon of which lay heavy black rain clouds waiting to unleash a relentless downpour on him the moment he relaxed his guard.

''To the future of two Greek millionaires,'' Nikki shouted as he uncorked a bottle of ouzo wrapped in a brown paper sack. He filled two small glasses, one for Uncle Stavros and one for himself.

Dimmy watched Laura, familiar apron tied around her slender waist, standing with her back pressed against the kitchen sink. There was a look of frightful despair on her face as she watched Nikki and Stavros begin a night of serious drinking at her kitchen table. The two children sat across from each other at that same table and shared worried glances, even though they tried to avoid each other's eyes.

The two men had come home together, having already launched their drunken excursion elsewhere, to loudly announce to Laura that Stavros was staying for dinner. No matter, Nikki had said, that there were only four chairs around the small kitchen table. Laura would stand and Stavros would sit. After all, Laura would be busy serving, anyway. This was a celebration. He laughed loudly and Stavros nodded supportively. They both knew how to keep their women in place.

"What are we celebrating?" Laura asked flatly, almost as if afraid of the answer.

"Today Stavros and I went into business together," Nikki said, waving his glass in the air.

"*Legitimate* business," Stavros added softly, making clear that this was not the first joint venture for the two. This was different from the knockoff watches, the counterfeit theater tickets, and the forged designer jeans they had been known to peddle in the past.

"What business, Papa?" Irene had asked, her eyes lighting up with interest.

"Okay!" Nikki shouted, a huge grin on his face, his eyes shiny and wet with drunkenness. He banged his glass against Stavros's and said "Skoal!" Stavros replied with "Chin-chin," and they both laughed boisterously at their Continental sophistication and drank deeply.

"Oh, Papa, tell us," Irene begged, getting caught up in the excitement.

He grinned at her like a conspirator, then winked broadly, crinkling his nose. He nodded his head toward his wife, who stood silently across the room. "Laura, you remember that little restaurant where we met?"

"Yes," she said.

"You like it?"

Laura hesitated. Dimmy understood that it was safer not to respond too quickly to questions posed by Nikki when he was in such a mood. "It's okay," she said carefully.

He jumped to his feet. "Only okay?" He turned to face her. "You love that place. It's our place. You said so yourself a thousand times. What do you mean, it's okay?"

"All right!" Laura recanted. "It's a lovely place. I like it very much."

"Hah!" Stavros said and poured himself another ouzo.

"Good," Nikki said. "Because we bought it today."

Nikki was the greeter, the wheeler-dealer, the suave, good-looking, affable partner who kept the customer flow going with his bright smile, his sexy looks, his flattering patter. He kept the single girls coming in night after night, hoping for one shot at him, although he and Stavros had agreed on a hands-off policy when they had started and Nikki had lived up to that agreement pretty well, barring a minor slip now and then.

Stavros was the businessman, the buyer, the maker of deals, the pilferer, and the borrower. The muscle. Stavros carried a gun. Nikki was never armed. Stavros sat in a dark corner, his back to the wall, observing the goings-on each night. Nikki was out in front in a suit and tie, high polish on his shoes, hair carefully styled and trimmed, hopping from table to table, charming the customers, making them feel that they were special.

On those occasions when he was allowed to hang around, as long as he stayed out of everyone's way, Dimmy had marveled at just how smooth his father could be. He was pleasantly disposed toward Nikki at those times, both because his father was always amiable in public and because

Irene was never allowed to hang around and Dimmy enjoyed being one up on her.

Initially, business was good, and the partners prospered. Though Nikki worked long hours, he was generally in a happy mood and seemed to become less short-tempered both with the children and with Laura. He hardly ever got drunk and was almost never depressed anymore. On Sundays, when the restaurant was closed, he took them all out to a special dinner. Sometimes they went for Chinese food, which was Dimmy's personal favorite, and other times they went out for Italian, Irene's absolute favorite food being pizza with a thin crust and loads of green pepper and sausage.

Laura was content for them all to be together; the style of food did not matter at all to her as long as she did not have to prepare it. Cooking, which she had taken to so lovingly, so passionately, had grown into a wearisome chore after three years of being obliged to do it. It seemed to Dimmy that she was hardly ever out of the kitchen. She was growing drab and bleached-out from being stuck so many hours in the steam that poured from the pots and pans boiling and bubbling on the stove.

Laura did take time away from her chores to sit on the living room floor each evening and help Dimmy and Irene with their homework. Those were delightful times for the children. They practiced arithmetic and spelling and memorized dates from American history. Irene sometimes got to braid Laura's hair and take it down again, and Dimmy occasionally taught Laura the finer points of stickball and kick-the-can and ring-a-levio and Johnny-on-the-pony, traditional New York City street games.

But Stavros's single greatest weakness eventually caught up with the happy-go-lucky restaurant owners. Stavros was growing accustomed to carrying more money in his pockets than he had ever seen at one time as a young man. He kept it in an ostentatious gold money clip in the shape of a rearing horse imprisoned by a large dollar sign, and he could not resist spending it freely, playing the big man on the block, the high roller.

"What do you need to tip the chick twenty bucks for?" Nikki would argue after breakfast at Nate's on the corner.

"You know what your problem is?" Stavros had grown used to responding.

"Yeah, I know," Nikki would say.

"Hah! That's right!" Stavros would say, a huge grin on his face. "You ain't large. Me, I'm large. You, you're small. You know what I mean?"

"I know what you mean."

"You, you're large sometimes with the babes. With your cock. Hah! That's as large as you ever get, Nikki. Me, I'm large where it counts." He would rub a thumb and forefinger together. "With the dinero. You know what I mean?"

"Yeah! I know what you mean."

"So, lay off. Don't hassle me on my largeness."

"Bullshit on your largeness," Nikki would end up saying. "Your largeness is full of shit. You used to bet fifty bucks across the board on a horse when I bet twelve, and you thought that was pretty large. Now you bet five hundred to win, and that's getting to be not large enough. You get any larger and you'll be either as tall as the Empire State Building or as broke as a junkie in a back alley."

Dimmy must have heard that same conversation ten or twenty times without realizing what the two were talking about. What he did understand, though, was that Uncle Stavros was winning the strange argument, because Dimmy soon noticed his father becoming more and more like Stavros, behaving like Stavros, talking like Stavros, dressing like Stavros.

One Saturday Nikki took Dimmy to Saks, where he bought

himself two new suits, dark gray with a fine white stripe. "One chalk and one pin," Nikki explained. "Different and yet almost the same, like a signature. Like they see you coming and they know right away who you are."

Nikki turned this way and that and gazed at himself in the full-length mirror while the tailor danced around him, making chalk marks on his cuffs and sleeves. His black shirt had been lain open at the collar when they left home, but it was now closed beneath the knot of a white silk tie.

"You look like Uncle Stavros," Dimmy observed.

Nikki wheeled on him. "Never!" he snapped, frightening the boy so that Dimmy felt as if his heart had fallen to his feet. Nikki smiled and flashed his white teeth. "He's ugly and I'm beautiful. Right?"

The boy nodded silently, relieved that he was not going to be punished for speaking his mind.

"Right?" Nikki demanded.

"Right, Papa," Dimmy said.

"You betcha," he said and returned to the mirror.

But Dimmy was confident with the comparison. It was true that his father was handsome and Stavros was ugly, bullet-headed, and jowly, with huge bushy eyebrows that grew every which way and tiny beady eyes set close together over a large, flat, wide nose. But that was the only difference he could find lately. Nikki had not only taken to dressing like Stavros but had begun sucking on a wooden match as well, so that he spoke with his teeth clenched like a movie tough guy. The things he said sounded more like Stavros than like Nikki. He had begun to punctuate all his speech with Stavros's "hah!" and to talk about the ponies and exactas and football score spreads and vigorish. He started using Italian slang words in his speech like *capisce* and *gumba* and *fongu*, as if English and Greek were not adequate to express what he was thinking. He joked and bragged a lot about Bruce the bookie and how Nikki and Stavros had grown to be such large bettors that he had extended unlimited credit to them.

"The problem with credit," Dimmy overheard Laura saying one morning to his father, who was in an expansive mood, "is that it doesn't feel like you're spending, but eventually you've got to pay the bill."

"Hah! No problem," Nikki said. "First, we hardly ever lose. That partner of mine has the magic touch. He can close his eyes, stick his finger in the paper, and come up with a winner damn near every time. And second, even if we do lose now and then, we can afford it. We got plenty. Hah! We got so much we don't know what to do with it."

"Business is so good?" Laura asked.

"Am I a winner or what?"

"Maybe we could move to a better apartment, a better place for the kids," Laura offered hesitantly.

"Hah!" Nikki exploded. "What for? We got it made here. We got rent control. We got plenty of room. We're in the middle of the city. What more you want?"

"But if we can afford—"

Nikki's voice grew harsh. "I got plenty for what I need. I don't have for wasting on things like fancy apartments for you. *Capisce?*"

Dimmy agreed with his father. He was perfectly content in their apartment and was frightened by the thought of moving. His life had become relatively good where he was, and he was not prepared to gamble that it would stay good if the family moved. Dimmy liked things the way they were, and he did not trust change.

He knew something was up when he and Irene came home from school one afternoon and found their father at home pacing the living room floor in a rage, a large swelling under his eye and his lower lip split in the middle. The children came in laughing and slammed the door as they always did to let Laura know that they were back so that she could get out cold milk and Oreo cookies for their after-school snack.

"Shut up!" Nikki screamed from the living room. "God-dammit!"

They froze, stared at each other, and silently realized they had best not be seen or heard further. They slinked through the long hallway to their own room and shut the door silently behind them.

Once in their room, they relaxed somewhat. Irene dropped her books on her bed and sat facing the wall. "You better get away from the door," she said. "He'll catch you listening."

"I'm too quick," Dimmy responded. "He can't catch me."

"I wonder what happened," the girl said.

"Something terrible, I bet."

She shuddered. "Did you see his face?"

He nodded. "Somebody worked him over good."

She hesitated, then said, "Can you hear?"

"Not with you talking."

"What's he doing?"

"Nothing."

"Where's Laura?"

"I don't know." He pressed one ear against the door and stuffed a finger into the other. "Lemme listen."

"God damn him!" He heard his father grumble.

Then he heard the soft sobbing, like faint perpetual street noise underneath his father's muttering.

"Stop your goddam crying," he heard Nikki say. "I'm sorry I hit you, okay? Now, stop crying."

The sobbing seemed to cease suddenly.

"You shouldn't interrupt when I'm talking," Nikki said.

"You shouldn't get in my way." The pacing footsteps stopped. "You can see I'm angry. Why do you provoke me?"

"I only said—"

"I don't want opinions," Nikki shouted. "Do you always have to talk? I don't need you to talk all the time. I need you to listen to me. *Capisce?*"

Dimmy could envision Laura nodding in humiliation. He sympathized with her. He knew what she was feeling. He had felt it himself many times. He knew what it was like to be unable to do anything right.

"I caught him stealing from me," Nikki continued. "My partner. My best friend. Stealing money behind my back to pay that goddam Bruce. That goddam bookie. I say to him, 'What the hell you stealing from *me* for?' And he says, 'Who else I know's got any money? Anyway,' he says, 'it's half mine, ain't it?' 'But you're stealing my half,' I says." There was a pause and silence in the room, then, "Ahhhh!" Nikki roared in frustration.

" 'You goddam son of a bitch,' I says to him. 'You goddam bastard.' And I hit him and knock him down. So when he gets up we go out to the alley to settle it. And I get him good. Sure, he gets me a little, too. He ain't no slouch, my gumba Stavros. But, I got him better. You think I look bad, you should see him. He used to be ugly. I think now I made him beautiful."

Nikki roared with laughter at the memory and applauded himself.

"What's the matter? You don't think that's funny? I think that's funny as hell."

He suddenly grew serious. "But I don't know what he's gonna do. I don't know how he's gonna take care of Mr. Bruce. He owes a lot of money, more than we got. More than I got. Goddam son of a bitch. He wants to sell the restaurant. No goddam way I'm gonna sell that restaurant. I told him. No goddam way. He says I should buy him out, but I ain't got that kind of money. I don't know what to do. I can't buy him out, and I don't want to give it up. I don't know what to do.

''He says we should borrow on our insurance and I should give him my share, but I don't wanna do that. Insurance is too important, you know what I mean?''

Nikki was pacing again, and his heavy footfalls sounded like beats of a drum vibrating through the closed door into Dimmy's ear.

After a long moment he heard his father stop pacing. ''I don't wanna take no chances with the insurance, Laura,'' he said, ''That's my ace in the hole.''

It was late in the afternoon before they got home from the cemetery. Irene had slept in the back of the limousine, her head resting in Laura's lap, her feet curled up beneath her. One of her hands clutched Laura's dress and pulled the skirt close to her face so that the delicate material was pressed against her cheek. His father sat solemnly in the other corner staring out the side window, watching the devastation of the Bronx slip by as they headed back toward Manhattan. Dimmy, perched on a jump seat facing the rear, watched with fascination. He was pleased that his father seemed to be suffering. Nikki was anxious and upset, and his fingers picked nervously at a loose thread hanging from a button on his jacket sleeve. Dimmy was even more pleased that his father was unhappy when Laura lifted her veil and displayed the dark purple bruise on her cheekbone just below her left eye.

''Now everybody works,'' Nikki said.

Trapped in traffic several blocks from home, Nikki smiled at Irene's sleeping figure, then lifted his eyes and grinned at

Dimmy. "It's gonna be hard now," he said. "Without Stavros I'm gonna need help. I can't do it all. You all have to help me."

"What can we do?" Laura asked softly, protecting Irene's sleep.

Nikki shrugged. "You be the hostess instead of me. You greet the people. Take them to their tables."

Laura's fingers drifted up to the large bruise on her face. "I don't know how to do that."

"Anybody knows how to do that," Nikki insisted. "A baby knows how to do that."

"Who will stay with the children?" Laura asked.

He smiled sadly. "They work, too."

"Really, Papa?" Dimmy said excitedly. "At night? In the restaurant?"

"He's only twelve years old," Laura said.

Nikki stared at her for a moment. "Irene, too," he finally said. "Everybody works."

"That's crazy," Laura said, and Dimmy was surprised that she was willing to express her anger. "These little children in that filthy place."

Dimmy cringed. He expected his father to explode and strike out at her. But instead, Nikki shook his head slowly, patiently, as if he were speaking to simple children who did not understand.

"I have no money," he said quietly. "I need you all to help. Dimmy will work the kitchen, helping the chef, washing dishes, whatever. Irene also. Everybody works. It's necessary."

"What do you mean, you have no money?" Laura said, refusing to accept his demands unchallenged, and Dimmy knew that she would never have taken such a risk for herself as she was taking for them. His father tensed, and Dimmy could sense Nikki's desire to slap her face. He silently prayed that would not happen.

"I have no money," Nikki said emphatically.

Laura's eyes blazed. "What about your partner's life insurance?"

Nikki returned his gaze to the window. He shrugged and spoke as if no one else were there. His voice contained a strange, sad, defeated quality, as though he were announcing the inevitable, as if there were absolutely no choices for him in the matter. "It all goes to the bookie," he said. "Every penny goes to Bruce to pay off Stavros's debt. That was the deal."

SEVEN

"Oh, my God, child," Mrs. McNamara breathed. "You look like death warmed over."

She knelt beside the bed and brushed the damp hair back from Laura's eyes. She moved the covers, which had been pulled tightly up under Laura's chin, and the oppressive odor of human waste wafted up at her and offended her nostrils. She allowed her hand to rest briefly on Laura's forehead, then moved it gently down to her bruised and reddened cheek. "You're burning up," she whispered. "What's happened to you?"

Irene, squeezed into a distant corner, sobbed softly and chewed on her finger nervously. Her terrified eyes darted about the room as if she were a stranger there, lost in an odd new world and fearful of what would become of her. Dimmy hovered behind Mrs. McNamara, straining to see over the woman's shoulder, keeping a worried eye on Laura's feverish face.

Upon returning from school he had found her in bed, sweat-soaked and delirious. When she failed to recognize him and would not respond to any of his questions, he had called for Irene. The girl had run into the room and stopped short at the sight of her battered stepmother, looking more dead than alive, staring out into space from dazed and sightless eyes.

"Go get Mrs. McNamara!" he had shouted, but Irene had backed into the corner and become immobilized. "Go!" he had shouted.

The girl, her eyes fixed on Laura's face, pressed her hands behind her and shook her head stupidly.

Dimmy stared at her for a moment, then flew down the stairs and pounded on Mrs. McNamara's door.

"All right!" she said, opening the door. "Where's the fire?"

"You better come," Dimmy said breathlessly. "It's Laura." Dimmy grabbed her hand and pulled her into the hallway.

Mrs. McNamara headed up the stairs behind him. "Have you called a doctor?" she asked as they entered Laura's room.

"No," Dimmy said.

"Well, go do it!" She began working over Laura.

"I can't. It's not allowed."

The older woman turned to him. "What do you mean it's not allowed? Who ever heard of such a thing? This woman's sick."

"My father doesn't allow us to call the doctor," Dimmy said.

"Never? Has this happened before?"

Dimmy, eyes cast to the floor, responded quietly. "You have to fix her."

The woman fumed. "Get me his number and I'll call him."

Dimmy shook his head, frustrated that she could not understand the rules. "We're not allowed to call the doctor or to tell anyone."

She stared at him for a moment. "Well, *I* don't need

anybody's permission," she said finally. "I'll call my own doctor." She took one step toward the door before Irene stopped her.

"No!" the girl cried. "Don't do that, please."

Mrs. McNamara stood in the center of the room, her gaze moving from Dimmy to Irene and back again. "What are you children so afraid of?"

They both turned away from her stare. Dimmy suddenly regretted having summoned her. He could not understand what had possessed him to breach the rules like that. He knew the price he would have to pay if his father ever found out, and suddenly he was more frightened for his own safety than for Laura's.

"Can't you just help us?" Dimmy pleaded. "Can't you just fix her up?"

He watched the woman struggle with the request. He could see how angry she had become and knew, from his own feelings when he was angry, that she wanted to do something hurtful, that she wanted to strike out at someone, hit someone, punish someone. He understood what power he had given her. She could turn his life into a disaster if she chose to. She could end it all for him right then and there. He watched her mind working. He could almost see the calculations flashing across the chalkboard of her brain. He watched and waited and held his breath.

Mrs. McNamara shook her head despairingly, then gave in. "All right!" she said. "Get me a pan of hot water. Irene, you get me a thermometer so we can see how much fever she's got."

She turned and gazed down at Laura but spoke to Dimmy and Irene. "And get me a clean nightgown, clean sheets and towels, and some aspirin."

As the children left the room, she called after them. "And heat up some tea or soup."

Mrs. McNamara's take-charge attitude galvanized Irene into action. She ran from the room and returned shortly with the things the older woman had requested. After discovering that Laura had a temperature of 102 degrees, she helped change the bedding and Laura's nightgown.

Mrs. McNamara gasped at the sight of the dark bruises on Laura's torso, over her ribs, under her breasts, along her lower back. She and the girl, each armed with a hot wet towel sponged the dried fecal matter off Laura's legs and pelvic area and as Laura became more aware of what was being done to her, she wept with shame. She wept softly, quietly, as though she had not the strength even to cry decently.

"Don't look at me," she begged.

"Hush, child," the older woman whispered. "I'm your friend. You don't have to be ashamed in front of me."

She sent Irene to fetch cold water, then laid cool compresses on Laura's body and pressed a cold towel over her forehead. She lifted Laura's head and helped her drink some warm tea.

"Thank you," Laura murmured, holding on to the older woman's wrist. Her eyes had become focused once again, and the odd, dazed expression of astonishment had faded from her face. "Thank you so much."

Each sprawling purple blemish on Laura's white skin pained Dimmy deeply. Each groan tore at his heart, wrenched at him as though it expressed his own agony. Stoically, he resisted the urge to cry with her, as she had cried with him during the years since she had entered his life. As she had done many times with him, he wanted to take her head onto his lap and hold her, rock her, comfort her.

When they were finished and Laura was feeling more comfortable, her fever brought down by the aspirin and the cold compresses, Mrs. McNamara shooed the children from the room. They were reluctant to leave, as though leaving the room might mean losing Laura permanently, and Mrs. McNamara finally had to usher them out.

Once they were outside, with the door closed and their ears pressed to the thin paneling, Mrs. McNamara sat on the edge of the bed beside her wounded young friend. "How long has this been going on?" she asked.

Laura shook her head.

"Come on, now. You think I'm stupid or something?"

Laura turned away and chewed on her trembling lip.

"You can't hide something like this forever, Laura. I'm surprised you were able to keep it from me for as long as you did. You're a good actress. I'll say that for you. You certainly had me fooled."

Laura shook her head. "It's the first time," she murmured.

"Nonsense," the older woman said. "You've got old scars and fading bruises all over you. Your thighs and the insides of your legs are covered. Why are you lying to me?"

"You don't know him."

"I've known him longer than you have, Laura, and I know he's beating you, and you don't deserve that. You hear what I'm saying? You don't have to take this anymore."

A long silence ensued while the two women stared at each other, one with intense determination, the other with fear and anxiety.

"I love him," Laura whispered.

Mrs. McNamara nodded. "'Course you do. Who ever said you didn't? It doesn't mean you don't love him when you stand up for your rights. One doesn't have anything to do with the other. You hear me?"

Laura nodded, but her eyes were disbelieving.

"What are you thinking?" the older woman demanded.

"I can't be disloyal," she whispered. "Loyalty is very important to Nikki."

"That's the stupidest thing you've said so far." The older woman had grown angry. "You think that punching you is a sign of loyalty? Is that what you're telling me? Or doesn't he have to be loyal? Only you? Is that it? He gets to kick you around, and you get to tolerate it to show how loyal you are? I see. That's a very interesting relationship you've got there."

Laura began to weep softly. "Don't!" she said.

The older woman relented. "I'm sorry, honey. I don't mean to be cross with you, but I got to find a way to shake some sense into you. You can't go on like this. It's gonna get worse all the time. After a while, you're gonna get seriously hurt, end up in the hospital maybe, maybe die."

"That won't happen."

"How do you know?"

"I know." Laura closed her eyes. "You don't understand."

"Explain it to me."

"It's not Nikki," she said. "It's me. I provoke him. I always realize it after it's too late. I know I'm being bad, but I can't help myself. Things just come out of my mouth before I can stop them."

"That's hogwash, love."

"It's true," Laura insisted. "If I could just leave him alone, he wouldn't have to punish me."

"Who told you that?" Mrs. McNamara seethed. "Did he fill your head with that crap?" The woman's voice rose an octave. "You wanna tell me that because you say you don't like his tie or ask him to take out the garbage or try to stop him when he's mean to his kids, he has the right to beat you? You cook and clean and take care of his children and take care of him and God knows what else." She stared at Laura in silence for a moment, fuming. "Forget that nonsense!" she finally said, "because it's the biggest lie since the invention of the little green people."

"What do you want me to do?"

"Start taking care of yourself. Go to the police," Mrs. McNamara said. "He'll stop beating you if he gets hauled in for wife abuse."

"I can't do that."

"You like being beat up?"

Laura shook her head.

"Then you've gotta do something about it, Laura."

"I will," the girl said. "I promise."

"What?" Mrs. McNamara persisted.

"I don't know," Laura mumbled.

"If you don't call the police, I will."

"I hope not."

"Why are you so dead set against protecting yourself?"

"Please," Laura begged. "Don't do anything foolish."

"I can't just stand by and watch."

Laura's pleading eyes rested on the older woman's face. "If you really care about me," she said, "don't do anything. Don't say anything. Forget what you saw today. Make believe it never happened. If you really care about me."

"Of course I care about you."

"If you report this," Laura said, "you'll make things worse. You'll be the one killing me."

Later, after Mrs. McNamara had gone home, Dimmy slipped into the bedroom and stood sheepishly beside the bed listening to Laura's measured breathing. He was very frightened for her now that he realized how fragile she was. He had grown to think of her as strong, perhaps because she defended him so courageously so frequently, and he was shocked to see how breakable she was. For a moment, standing in her bedroom in the near dark, he felt much bigger and sturdier than Laura, and he resolved to watch out for her in the future, to protect her from his father, who was a threat to them all. He would step between the two of them and act as her shield in the constant struggle that raged between the two of them.

She opened her eyes and saw him standing over her. "Dimmy," she whispered.

He knelt beside her. "Are you better, Laura?"

"Yes, thank you." She smiled weakly, then reached out and touched his cheek.

He took her hand and kissed her fingers. "I was so afraid for you," he said.

"I'm sorry." She retrieved her hand and slipped it under the covers. "I can't get up to make your dinner."

"That's all right. Irene is making it. She can cook almost as good as you," Dimmy said proudly. "Well, maybe not yet, but soon. She's learning from José in the restaurant. Do you want something to eat?" he asked. "Anything. Whatever you want. I'll go to the store and get it."

She shook her head. "That's very kind."

He watched her eyes close, her smile vanish, and she seemed to diminish, to shrink within herself while lying in bed, helpless.

"Papa will be home soon," he said.

Laura did not respond, and he thought she had not heard him.

"Papa's coming to get us pretty soon, Laura."

"I know," she said.

"We have to go to work."

She nodded. "I know."

"What'll you do?"

"I don't know, Dimmy," she breathed. "Maybe he'll forgive me tonight."

"Yes," Dimmy nodded. "If he knows you're sick, he won't make you go. Maybe he won't go, either. Maybe he'll stay home and take care of you."

She bit her lip and nodded. He saw that she was crying softly, soundlessly. Tears appeared in her eyes and drifted down her cheeks in single file. He was unsuccessful at withholding his own tears, and he wept with her, as silently as she.

"I'm not going to let him do this to you anymore," he finally mumbled. "I swear it. I don't know what I'll do, but I'll think of something."

"You must never speak like that," Laura cautioned. "Never turn against your father." She smiled wetly at him. "You're such a sweet little boy."

"I'm not a little boy anymore, Laura," he said in a voice so strong that it surprised him.

"Yes. I'm sorry," she said contritely, genuinely sorry that she had hurt his feelings. "I shouldn't have said that. You are a big boy now, aren't you?"

"Yes," Dimmy said solemnly. "And I'm going to protect you from now on."

When Nikki came home, he found Dimmy and Irene alone in the kitchen. They sat opposite each other, a cup of thick black coffee set before each of them. They had fallen silent when they heard him enter. He appeared in the doorway and glared at them angrily.

"Get ready," he snapped. "We have to go."

They slid off their chairs in unison.

"Where's Laura?" he asked.

The children remained silent.

"Where the hell is Laura?"

Irene answered with a tremor in her voice. "In bed."

"What's she doing still in bed? We have to go to work. Get ready!"

He stormed down the hall and slammed into the bedroom.

"What the hell are you doing in bed?" they heard him shout. "We've got a restaurant to run. Get up and get dressed."

A short silence ensued, and then their father shouted again. "Sick? What the hell do you mean, sick? You don't have time to be sick. Get out of that goddam bed before I drag you out."

"I can't," they heard her moan. "Not tonight."

"That's what you say every night, you lazy bitch. If I let you, you'd stay in bed the rest of your life. What do you think this is, a free ride? You think I'm gonna support you like a queen while you lie around doing nothing? That what you think?"

The children followed and crowded into the small bedroom doorway. They watched him looming over Laura, his hands planted on his hips, his body bent forward, shouting down at her as if she were a dog who had wet the floor.

"I can't," she wept.

Nikki raised his fist and showed it to her.

"She's too sick, Papa," Dimmy shouted from the doorway.

Nikki wheeled around and glared at his two trembling children cowering in the doorway. "And what the hell do you know about it, Mr. Smartass?"

Dimmy swallowed and found some additional courage. "She's been sick all day, Papa. Really sick."

"Goddamm it, how do you know so much? You think you're ready to take over this family?" He advanced on them, his eyes burning with anger, and Dimmy steeled himself for the blows he knew would soon rain down on him. Behind his father, he saw Laura swing her legs off the bed in an attempt to rise.

"I'm okay," Dimmy heard her whimper. "I'm getting ready. See?" She staggered to the closet and pulled a dress from its hanger.

But Nikki had not heard, was not listening. He was slowly approaching Dimmy, enraged at the boy's audacity.

"Mrs. McNamara said so," Irene blurted out, frightened for her brother.

Nikki stopped and slowly turned back to Laura, who was weaving dizzily. "You brought a stranger into our private family affairs? Did you cry on her shoulder? Did you tell her how mean I am to you?"

Dimmy straightened up and started to speak, but Laura spoke sooner.

"Yes," she said defiantly. "I asked her to come and help me. I was sick and I needed someone, so I called her."

"God damn you to hell!" Nikki screamed. He turned, pushed past the children, knocking them to either side of the doorway, and raced out of the apartment.

"Oh, my God!" Laura said, her fist to her mouth. "What did I do?"

Dimmy followed his father out of the apartment. When he got to the landing, he could hear Nikki's heavy footsteps hammering quickly down to the ground floor and moving swiftly to Mrs. McNamara's door. When he heard his father's huge fist pounding on that door, he cringed in fear.

The boy crept down the stairs slowly. His heart beat so loud, so frantically, that he feared it could be heard down the length of the stairwell.

"Open up this goddam door!" His father's voice rushed up at him like a booming echo in a deep canyon. "Open up, goddammit!"

Then Mrs. McNamara was at the door sounding as defiant

as his father. "What d'ya want, using that kind of language around here?"

But Nikki was not to be outshouted. "What you doing in my house when you're not supposed to be there, you old biddy?"

"What are you talking about? I been in your house hundreds of times. I used to cook your food for you. Or have you forgotten that?"

"You know what I mean," Nikki shouted. "I didn't tell you you could go up there and play priest with my old lady, did I?"

"Well, *somebody* needs to look after the poor girl."

"I look after her. You mind your own business. You understand?"

The older woman laughed ironically. "I seen how you look after her, all right. I've seen the bruises and all."

"You just shut up about that."

"I will not shut up about it. I'll tell the whole world. I never seen anything like that up there. You ought to be ashamed of yourself."

"It's not your business," Nikki shouted, and his voice began to sound uncontrolled.

"It's everybody's business." Mrs. McNamara's voice was as shrill as Nikki's.

Suddenly there was silence, as if the angry energy that had motivated both of them had dissipated. Dimmy rose on his toes and leaned far over the banister to look down at the bottom landing. He could just make out his father's back but could not see Mrs. McNamara. The silence lasted for a long moment until, finally, Dimmy heard his father speak.

"Stay away from my house," Nikki said quietly. "Stay away from my wife. Stay away from my children. Never speak to them again, and never speak to me again. You are my enemy, and I don't do business with my enemies. To you, we are gone; we don't live here anymore. And to us, you are dead and buried!"

Dimmy saw his father turn and start climbing the stairs. Then he saw Mrs. McNamara step out onto the landing and gaze up at his father.

"You can pretend all you want, you criminal!" she shouted to him. "But I ain't dead. I've got eyes and ears, and if I see or hear anything more like what you did today to that girl, I'm going straight to the police."

Dimmy dashed up to his own landing and into the apartment, closed the door quietly behind him, and shut himself in his bedroom, where he quickly changed into the clothes he wore when working as José's helper in his father's restaurant. He glanced at Irene, who sat on her bed cross-legged. He kicked off his shoes and pulled on his sweat socks.

"What did he do?" his sister asked hesitantly.

"He told Mrs. McNamara never to talk to us again," he responded sadly without looking up, without pausing in what he was doing.

"Oh, no," she said. "That's not fair."

"He told her she's dead and we moved away."

"Oh, God!"

"He told her we're enemies." Dimmy paused in lacing up his sneakers and, still bent over, looked up at her. "I'm gonna miss her."

"What are we going to do?"

He stood, stamped his feet into the soft shoes, and frowned. "Same thing we always do," he said. "Keep our mouths shut and pray."

Dimmy could not believe what he had heard.

"Five thousand dollars and she's yours," Nikki said. "Any time you want her. Anywhere. I don't care."

"You sure about this?" Mr. Caprisi said around the gold toothpick clamped in his mouth.

Nikki shrugged, "I need the money."

The two men were sitting in Nikki's private booth at the rear of the restaurant beside the swinging doors to the kitchen. Nikki sat with his back to the wall so that he could watch all the action in the room. Mr. Caprisi, large and round, was stuffed into the seat across from him, his stomach pressed up against the edge of the table, a napkin tucked into the collar of his shirt to protect his expensive cashmere jacket. He was an exotic food importer and was reputed to be very rich, but Dimmy thought that all the money in the world could not help Mr. Caprisi. The man was too fat, too ugly, and too gross. He drooled and leered and belched in public. Dimmy despised the look of him and hated his habit of chucking Dimmy under the chin and commenting on how small he was for his age. The man was an insensitive slob.

Recently, Caprisi and Nikki had taken to dining together once a week. Caprisi had almost replaced Stavros as Nikki's best friend. They went to the racetrack together and bet with the same bookie. Nikki even began to talk like the rich Italian, just as he had mimicked Stavros's way of speaking. Mr. Caprisi was also a lover of high-stakes poker and was a regular player in Nikki's weekly after-hours game in the back room.

They had shared some lamb and rice and were smoking cigars and sipping retsina when the subject of Laura came up. Just as Dimmy passed by the door, he heard Mr. Caprisi express his disappointment that Laura was not present that night.

"She brightens the place up, Nikki," he said. "As good as your food is, she's better. She's a hot woman. I like to watch her move. She has a body that rattles the windows."

Caprisi chuckled under his breath and shook his head in admiration.

Nikki beamed. "That she has! That she has!" he said enthusiastically as if he thoroughly enjoyed the lewd compliment.

"She's a very sexy lady," Caprisi continued dreamily. "You look at her, you want to do things to her and have her do things to you." He chuckled again, louder. "Hot stuff where it counts, Nikki."

Then Dimmy heard his father apologize, with a leer in his voice, and tell Mr. Caprisi that Laura had become ill suddenly—something she ate, he was sure—and had gone home early. Nikki implied that Laura was faking her illness, and Dimmy fumed at hearing such a lie. He was tempted to burst in and tell Caprisi the truth, but he would never contradict his father in public. Causing his father to lose face might very easily cost him his life. Besides, he dared not let Nikki know that he could overhear his private conversations by crouching inside the kitchen doors and pressing his ear to the crack. He had not intended to spy on his father, but after seeing Laura hurt once again, and watching Nikki hurl her into a taxi and send her home with curses, he could not help but eavesdrop when he heard her name mentioned.

In the past few months Dimmy had watched the changes taking place in Laura. She had started sipping wine while alone at home. It was not long before she switched to vodka in the afternoon, reserving wine for the mornings. She had become depressed and moody. She began to spend much of her time in bed; she no longer rose to make the children's breakfast and prepare their lunches. Their study time together had diminished also. When Laura was not working in the restaurant she slept or moped and had little patience with them.

Dimmy realized that his greatest fear was becoming a reality: he and Irene were losing her. As she became bitter about her life with Nikki, Laura had begun to withdraw even deeper into a dark, secret world she had created for herself.

Earlier that evening Laura had already been walking at a tilt and speaking with a definite slur to her speech. Dimmy had worried that she would stumble and fall over some customer's table, bringing Nikki's wrath down on all of them. An eight-ounce tumbler was hidden on the top shelf of the hostess's lectern. The glass appeared to be filled with ice water, but it contained, in reality, nine parts vodka and one part dry vermouth. Laura had sipped so frequently from it that she was soon feeling no pain.

Peeking out from the kitchen at every opportunity, he had watched her guide the first diners to their tables at six o'clock when she was still walking straight and still seemed to be in control of herself. She had looked very elegant and impressive in her black silk sheath. But later, as he watched her gearing up for the eight o'clock turnover by bolstering herself as often as she could with gulps from the hidden glass, he saw that she no longer walked with confidence. Her flushed cheeks, glazed eyes, and fixed smile bore witness to the fact that she was swiftly losing control.

Nikki had been watching her, too. Dimmy ducked out of sight when his father moved down the center aisle toward the hostess's station. He signaled a waiter to take over Laura's station, then pulled her through the room and into the kitchen. Inside the swinging doors, he dragged her to a corner and pressed her up against the wall, holding her in place with both hands on her shoulders.

"You're drunk again," he snarled, within earshot of the kitchen help.

José, the chef; Malcolm and Eli, the two helpers; and even Ramón, the dishwasher, wisely pretended not to have heard or seen a thing.

Nikki had Laura backed up against the rear wall, near the

stairs to the basement, and was leaning over her. His face was pushed into hers as he towered over her. He was so close to her that Dimmy was sure she would choke on the smell of garlic and feta cheese on his breath.

"How many times I warned you?" he seethed. "You think I tell you that to hear myself talking?"

"I had one drink," she said innocently, her slur a dead giveaway that she had had far more than one. "Wha's wrong with havin' a drink?"

Nikki pressed his thumbs into her flesh, and Laura writhed under his hands. "You're hurting me!"

"I'll break your head for you," he whispered. "You make a fool out of me."

"I'm not doin' anythin'."

"You're drunk!"

Laura straightened up and grimaced as though she had been insulted. "I am not!"

"The hell you're not. You can't see straight, you're so plastered."

"I'm not drunk!" she insisted.

Nikki slapped her. "Shut up!" he shouted. "How many times I told you I don't allow no drinking on the job?"

"You drink all the time," Laura said through the sobbing she tried to stifle.

Nikki grew red in the face. "You gonna tell me what to do now? Since when you became the boss around here?" He twisted her arm up behind her until she cried out in pain. "You think this hurts? Wait till I get you home, you think this hurts."

She was crying in earnest by this time. Her chest heaved with the sobs she could no longer contain.

"Shut up!" he said. "Don't make a scene here!" Nikki gazed around to see if the kitchen helpers were watching.

Dimmy quickly turned his eyes away and pretended to be occupied with chopping lettuce.

"I told you to shut up," he said to Laura when she continued to cry. He opened the basement door. "Get in there!" he said, shoving her onto the landing of the cellar stairs and closing the door on her. "You stay in there until you can control yourself. When you can clean up your face and go back to work, you let me know."

"Please, Nikki," Laura cried through the basement door. "Don't leave me here!"

Nikki leaned close to the door. "You gonna clean up your act?"

"Yes," she whimpered. "I swear, Nikki," Laura cried.

Nikki turned and gazed at the kitchen workers, who all pretended to be occupied with their own chores. He grinned contentedly, as though he really felt good. Then he opened the door, stepped onto the basement landing, and pulled the door almost closed behind him.

"Look at your face." Dimmy barely heard his muffled whisper. "Look at your goddam face."

"I'm sorry, Nikki."

"You can't work no more tonight."

"Yes, I can."

"Look at you! You can't hardly stand up, and your face is red and puffy. What kind of hostess you gonna make all burned out like this?"

"I can fix myself up. Just give me a chance."

Dimmy heard a thud and made a move toward the door.

"You can't even stand up," his father said. "How you gonna work?"

"I'm sorry, Nikki," Laura cried.

The door opened slightly, and Nikki leaned out. "Ramón!" he shouted.

"Yes, boss." Ramón, the dishwasher, jumped away from the sink as if he had been shot.

"Go get me a cab," Nikki ordered.

"Right away." Ramón pulled his latex gloves off and headed for the door.

"Fast," Nikki shouted. "Bring the cab around to the alley in back."

Nikki closed the door after shouting his instructions, but Dimmy continued to hear Laura crying softly. He was not sure if he was truly hearing the sound of it or if its memory was planted in his mind in such a way that he would always hear it. His face was flushed and he burned with the fever of outrage. He wanted to save Laura, to stop his father. He wanted to do something terrible to Nikki. But his fear paralyzed him, and he stood over the cutting table consumed with shame.

"I'm sending you home," Nikki said.

"No, Nikki," Laura pleaded. "Don't do that. I promise, I'll be good."

"It's too late," Nikki snapped. "I want you out of here. Go home and get into bed and stay there. When I get home, we'll see what we can work out."

"Whatever you say," Laura said. "I'll do anything, Nikki."

The door opened, and Nikki stepped out into the kitchen just as Ramón stuck his head in the back door. "Cab's here, boss."

Nikki grasped Laura's wrist and pulled her with him. "Come on," he said. "Let's go."

Her face was streaked with tears, and her expression was pitiful as Nikki pulled her to the back door and shoved her out into the alley. He turned in the doorway and shouted back to no one in particular, "Show's over! Get back to work!'' He stepped out into the alley and slammed the door behind him.

Later that night Nikki made his offer to Mr. Caprisi. It was simple, he said: Caprisi wanted Laura; Nikki needed money. They were friends. Why not? It was strictly business, and it made good sense. There followed a long silence while Dimmy, shocked and frightened, waited for Caprisi's response.

''What if she don't wanna do it?'' Caprisi asked. ''What if she don't like me?''

Nikki laughed. ''She does what I tell her. In my family I'm the boss. That's how it is with Greeks. I don't know how it is with Italians.''

''It's the same,'' Mr. Caprisi said. ''But I don't know about something like this.'' He shook his head. ''Anytime I want? Day or night? Anything I want?''

''Just give me the money,'' Nikki said. ''You'll see how much I mean it.''

Dimmy guided Laura through the huge but almost silent bus terminal like a lost child. Only a few of the wooden benches were occupied at this late hour. Some weary and bedraggled men were attempting to steal some sleep, but a uniformed guard moved around the terminal prodding them awake with a nightstick. Other forlorn travelers, waiting for the departure of their buses, sat reading, resting, or daydreaming, their legs wrapped tightly around their luggage to protect it from wandering off in strange hands.

Laura had resisted Dimmy continually from the moment he had dragged her from the apartment, where he had found her fearfully waiting in bed for his father to come home and mete out another punishment. Once they were outside and settled in the backseat of a cab she continued to complain all the way to the bus station.

Dimmy had fled the restaurant and rushed home, convinced that if he did not get her away she would be sold into sexual slavery to Caprisi, and he knew she could never tolerate that. It would be the end of her, he was sure. He had no doubt that his father would go through with it, so he knew he had to spirit her away.

Dimmy also knew that Laura did not understand the seriousness of her situation. He knew she would not believe that Nikki intended to sell her. She would want to stay and make him love her again, and Dimmy knew she would lose against Nikki. His father always had his way, and this time Laura would later regret not having escaped in time. Therefore, he did not try to explain anything to her. He did not plead with her or appeal to her ability to reason. He had watched her slowly lose the ability to think clearly, and he could no longer trust her judgment.

The ticket agent stared at Laura, who stood before her looking confused. ''Well?'' she asked after a long silence.

''A one-way ticket to Cleveland,'' Dimmy said to the agent with as much conviction as he could muster.

The woman swung around to her store of tickets.

''Okay?'' he said to Laura. ''Cleveland?''

She nodded and fumbled with her purse. ''I'll give you my aunt's telephone number.''

''No!'' he said. ''I don't want it. If I don't know where you are,'' he said, ''I can't tell Papa.''

''That'll be eighty-eight dollars one way,'' the clerk said.

Dimmy pulled a roll of bills from his pea coat pocket. He stepped around Laura, counted out the exact amount, and pushed the money through the grille. The ticket agent accepted the payment with a mechanical thank-you, slammed a stapler several times, and pushed the ticket through to him. ''That bus leaves from gate nine in twenty minutes,'' she said.

"Here!" he said, stuffing the rest of the money and the ticket into Laura's purse.

"Dimmy—"

"If you don't go," he said, leading her away from the ticket windows, "I don't know what'll happen to you."

They sat on a bench near gate nine. He took her hand in both of his, and they sat together silently until her departure was announced over the loudspeaker. He carried her suitcase to the sliding glass doors where the driver was collecting tickets from the few passengers in line.

"Come with me," she said without conviction, not looking at him, just before her ticket was taken from her.

He smiled. "Good-bye, Laura."

She leaned down and kissed him. "Good-bye, Dimmy." She passed through the doors, then turned and waved.

"See ya!" he said.

"I'll call," she said.

"See ya!" Dimmy said again. Still so young, and he was losing his second mother. He turned and walked away, brushing the tears from his eyes.

Dimmy touched the tip of his tongue to the cracked tooth and bleeding gum on the left side of his mouth and grimaced in pain. He could still taste blood, and he swallowed it quickly as it oozed from his lips and gums. He would like to have felt how badly his teeth were damaged, but his hands were tied behind his back and he could barely wiggle his fingers. His shoulders and back ached where he had been beaten repeatedly, and his knees burned where they had been scraped while he was being dragged along the floor of the apartment to the kitchen.

He lay back against the pillow his father had graciously thrown to him after stuffing him under the kitchen sink. He would like to have had a blanket as well; he was shivering severely either from the cold or from shock. But he could not ask for any additional comforts while his father was still angry enough to kill him for his betrayal. Besides, the bicycle chain wound around his neck and attached to the drainpipe caused him much more discomfort than the cold floor did.

From his cramped position, he could hear Irene sobbing in their bedroom. He suspected she would cry all night. When she was through crying over the beating he had taken, she would fully realize that Laura was gone for good, and she would cry over that loss as well. He loved Irene very much at that moment. He felt proud of the way she had come to his defense. He could still hear her screams as she pulled on his father's arms in an attempt to break Nikki's hold on Dimmy's throat.

"Papa! Stop it!" she had screamed over and over as she tugged on him until he finally released one hand from around Dimmy's neck and slapped her so hard that she flew halfway across the room.

His father, screeching at him through clenched teeth, continued to beat and choke him. "Where is she? Where's my money?" He pounded Dimmy's back with his fist while still clutching his throat with the other hand. "How did she know about my stash?"

Dimmy had pretended to be asleep when his father came home after closing the restaurant. He had heard Nikki enter, slam the front door, and stomp into his bedroom. After a moment there had come a loud crash from the bedroom, and Dimmy burrowed deeper under the covers. He heard Nikki pound into the kitchen and knew what was coming next. His father slammed the cabinet doors one after the other, smashed jars and dishes, flung chairs against the walls, and filled the apartment with loud drunken curses.

When silence finally fell, Dimmy knew it was his turn.

He steeled himself, pressed his eyes shut, and waited for the inevitable. He was not surprised when his father jerked him out of bed and flung him into a corner.

"You little bastard," Nikki spat at him. "Where did she go?"

"I don't know, Papa."

"Don't lie to me, you little shit! You helped her, didn't you?" He moved toward Dimmy, and the boy cringed farther into the corner. "She couldn't go anywhere by herself. You had to help her, God damn you!" He grabbed Dimmy around the neck and lifted him off the floor.

"Papa!" Irene shouted from her bed. "Don't!"

"You shut up!" he screamed at her and shook Dimmy like a rag doll.

"Papa!" Irene shouted. "Don't kill my brother."

"I won't kill him," Nikki said. "I'll just make him wish he was dead." He began to beat Dimmy viciously.

When Nikki was exhausted from delivering the cruel beating, he dragged Dimmy into the kitchen, tied one end of a bicycle chain around his neck and the other to the drainpipe, and stuffed him, bleeding and broken, under the sink.

"You stay there," he raged. "You sleep under the sink from now on. You bite me like a dog, you live like a dog." He turned and stomped away.

Now Dimmy lay in the dark examining his wounds as best he could.

"It'll be all right," he whispered to himself. "The worst is over. It'll get better now."

Later, when the early light began filtering through the window, he heard his father enter the kitchen and approach the sink. He looked up, squinting through his bruised eyes, and watched Nikki sink slowly to the floor until he was lying beside him. His father stared at him grimly, white lips pressed tightly together, but Dimmy was no longer frightened. He could see that Nikki's rage had dissipated and had been replaced with a sad resolve.

After a moment Nikki said, ''What am I gonna do now, boy?''

Dimmy shook his head painfully.

''It's a terrible thing you did. You went against your father. No loyalty. That's a bad thing.''

They lay together in silence for a while. Dimmy watched his father's face as the man seemed to ponder his situation. Nikki sighed deeply.

''Maybe you think you did the right thing,'' he said finally. ''Maybe you think you did something good by getting between a man and his woman.'' He shook his head slowly. ''You didn't. You made it worse. It was a dumb thing you did. You made it worse for me. You made it worse for you. And most of all, because you took my woman away and now there's no more woman in the house, you made it a lot worse for your sister, too.''

PART
THREE

EIGHT

"This is it," Dr. Zeke Perez said.

Laura shivered. "Oh, God!" she whispered, staring at the ominous old building before her.

"Are you apprehensive?" he asked her, without taking his eyes from the road as he turned off the street and into the narrow driveway.

"Terrified."

He nodded. "That's understandable," he said. "You two haven't seen each other in a long time."

She smiled sadly, hearing Dr. Benson's voice in the recesses of her mind. "It seems like a lifetime."

They were in Zeke Perez's automobile and had pulled into the doctor's parking lot at County General Hospital.

"Dimmy's anxious to see you," Zeke continued. "It took me a long time to persuade him to let me look for you."

"Yes," she said.

"After you visit with him," he said, "I'd like to talk to you." He pulled into a parking space and shut off the car's engine.

She stared at him but did not respond.

He turned to face her. "I'd like you to tell me what

happened." He watched her and smiled. "Maybe we can discuss it over lunch."

It had taken an endless series of grueling, painful sessions with Dr. Benson to enable Laura to recount what had happened to her, to form the words that shouted hysterically in her secret distorted memory, and to overcome her shame and guilt enough to admit to the role she had played in her own incarceration. She wondered now how this young doctor could think she would be able to sit down over a tuna fish sandwich and discuss her life with the Pappas family as if it were a simple, commonplace affair. What did he expect? she wondered. Some tale of domestic disruption, perhaps? A sad account of marital infidelity? Perhaps a breakdown in communication? Two adults whose interests had changed? A simple drifting apart of two lovers who had grown bored with each other? What fantasies did Dr. Zeke Perez harbor? What could he possibly understand about her and her bondage to Nikki Pappas? Who was this man Perez? She felt herself growing angry. How dare he attempt to penetrate her darkest terrors as if he were an old and trusted friend instead of someone she had met just that morning?

She had waited for him outside in the morning sunlight, pacing slowly up and back in front of the motel office. She was still feeling heavy, gritty, and stiff; even ten full minutes under a steaming hot shower had not banished the listlessness with which her night flight had left her, and the half hour of sleep she had snatched had merely made her wearier. She would just as soon have taken a taxi to the hospital but for his insistence on picking her up and driving her there. She would need his assistance in getting in to see Dimmy anyway, he had explained.

When he pulled up in a late-model white Honda, she was already annoyed about being made to wait. He jumped out of the car and came around to greet her.

"Laura?" he asked as he approached her, his hand extended.

"Yes," she said as he took her hand and shook it warmly.

"I'm sorry I'm late. Traffic is so unpredictable."

"Dr. Perez?" she inquired.

"Zeke," he said. "Please." He grinned at her. "Don't punish me for being tardy."

She smiled and nodded. "Okay, Zeke."

He led her to the car, opened the passenger door, and helped her in.

"It's short for Ezekiel," he said as he moved around to the driver's side and climbed in beside her. "I was a biblical baby. My mother's really into the Good Book. My brother's name is Zach, for Zachariah and my sister is a Ruth."

She smiled again. He was disarming her, she realized. His easygoing, relaxed manner was meant to make her feel unafraid about where they were heading this morning.

"We've got a little bit of a ride," he said, guiding the car out of the motel driveway. "You'll have a chance to see some of our city. Have you ever been here before?"

"No," she said.

He beamed. "Well, then," he said, "I'm going to have the pleasure of showing you around, aren't I?"

"I guess so," she said, pleased that he seemed to be interested in her.

She studied him as they drove. He was dressed in a light gray jacket over a white shirt with a maroon paisley tie and dark trousers. He was tall, perhaps six inches taller than she, and lean, though strong and muscular.

She was most surprised at how much his features resembled her husband's. His skin was dark like Nikki's, and his hair was black and straight and trimmed short like Nikki's. When he smiled, he was handsome, and his teeth glistened against his olive complexion. But his eyes were more open than Nikki's. They were clear and unsuspicious, and there was no sense of danger in them.

They drove in silence punctuated by Zeke's descriptions of landmarks along their route. They passed along Wilshire Boulevard through the heart of Beverly Hills where every second building was a bank, into what used to be called the Miracle Mile and was now referred to as mid-Wilshire, on past the formerly exclusive but now defunct Perino's, once overwhelmingly expensive and restricted to diners who could afford to wait three months for a reservation or who knew someone who knew someone, and the old Wiltern Theater, which had become a house of jazz and rock concerts, through the corridor of tall office buildings that housed uncounted law firms and advertising agencies, in and out of McArthur Park where paddleboats were stranded in the mud because the drought had failed to replenish the water supply in the great man-made lake, which now resembled a garbage-strewn swamp.

At Alvarado, Zeke swung onto the freeway and edged into the solid, barely moving stream of traffic that inched along like a huge overfed reptile. He entered the maze of the downtown interchange where freeways moved off in all directions like bent spokes in a broken wheel, then exited on the other side into East Los Angeles, where he grappled with surface street congestion the remainder of the way to the immense hospital complex known as County-USC Medical Center.

He did not mention the specific purpose of the hospital visit until they arrived at the medical center and pulled into the parking lot, where they now sat together, him facing her, waiting as if expecting her to confide her innermost secrets to him.

"I don't know about lunch," she said finally. "It depends on how I feel after . . . you know . . . I see Dimmy."

"Of course," he said. "But I want you to know that you could be very helpful to me, and to Dimmy. He's not the most communicative person I've ever worked with, and you could help me fill in the blanks."

She shrugged. "If you think so."

"I'm sure of it," he said. "It's very important to me," he urged. "I've grown to care very much about your stepson, and there's no one else I can turn to."

"What about his sister, Irene?" Laura asked.

He shook his head. "She won't even speak to me on the phone."

"I can't understand that," Laura said. "They're so close."

"Apparently she thinks I'm trying to prove that Dimmy is insane, and she doesn't want to help me do that."

"Are you?"

He thought for a moment before responding, then said, "I want to understand the boy. I want to know his reasons for trying to kill his father. If he was legally insane when he stabbed his father, I want to know about it. It's not up to me to prove anything. I'll simply testify as to my opinion, that's all."

"How can you know if he was insane at that moment?"

"*Legally* insane," he said. "It's not exactly the same as being mentally ill. It means that at the precise moment when he committed the criminal act, for some reason, he did not know the difference between right and wrong. He did not comprehend that it was wrong to stab his father."

"But how can you know what he was thinking?"

He nodded. "That's the problem, isn't it? How can anybody know? How can I know what his mental state was by simply re-creating the past, by learning the history of the event? It sounds impossible." He shrugged and grinned at her. "But you'll just have to trust me when I tell you that I can do it. It's what I've been trained to do. If I can get a complete picture of what his life was like at that moment in time when he was propelled into doing something as terrible as murder, something he might never have done otherwise, maybe I can surmise what his mental status was. But I can't have pieces missing. I have to know everything about him. You understand?"

Laura thought she understood. "Yes," she said tentatively. She flashed back upon how much she had learned about herself during her own therapy and how reliving events from her past had clarified for her how corrupt had been her own perceptions of reality, how perverted her own notions of right and wrong. She nodded. "I understand."

"Good!" he said. "Then I hope you'll agree to help me. I have a lot of questions." He paused and studied her troubled face. "I hope you'll give me as much time as I need, because Dimmy and I desperately need a friend right now."

Zeke placed Laura on one side of the long Formica-topped table. He pulled up another green metal chair for himself beside her and informed the orderly that they were ready to see the prisoner. Laura's immediate reaction to the forbidding room was one of oppressive fear. She felt chilled, as if she had entered an immense refrigerator. The white walls, scuffed with black scars along the baseboards where many pairs of shoes had kicked out over the years, smacked of the sterile atmosphere of a clinic. Her very first visit to a prison, and mild as it was, being in truth a hospital, she felt pressed upon, confined, claustrophobic.

It was a bright corner room, and in two of the walls there were mesh-covered windows that looked out onto the hospital grounds and allowed radiant sunshine to pour in onto the floor. Except for the table and several chairs, the room was unfurnished. A single spotless plastic ashtray sat in the middle of the table like a centerpiece. A TV camera, its red eye glaring, was mounted in one corner near the ceiling where it could continually watch the entire chamber.

The door opened and a white-clad orderly, accompanied by a uniformed, armed sheriff's deputy, ushered Dimmy in. Laura shifted her eyes away as if afraid to look at him. She sensed him standing in the doorway, perhaps with as much trepidation about seeing her again as she was feeling about seeing him.

"Here he is, Doc," the orderly announced.

"Thanks, Ralph," she heard Zeke Perez say. Then she heard the door close, and she slowly moved her eyes toward the sound.

"Hello, Laura," Dimmy said.

He stood with his back to the closed door. His hands, clasped before him, were manacled at the wrists and fixed to a tight chain wound around his waist. He wore a faded blue robe and flimsy paper slippers. A stubble of thin beard marked his young face.

He had changed some—hardened, was taller by at least two inches, older, more haggard in the face, more determined in the eyes, less innocent, less forgiving, leaner in body, and more suspicious in nature—but she instantly recognized the little boy she had known and loved beneath the new, cruel veneer.

"Hello, Dimmy," she said, and she heard the sob of regret in her own voice.

The boy's shoulders fell. "I'm sorry, Laura." Eyes focused on the floor, he shook his head forlornly as if he were surrendering responsibility for his own welfare. "I'm sorry I gave you away. I never wanted to do that."

"Oh, Dimmy!" she sobbed.

He raised both manacled hands and wiped the silent tears from first one eye and then the other. "I don't want him to know where you are."

Weeping herself, she rose from her chair and rushed across the room to him. "Oh, Dimmy!" She wrapped her arms around him and crushed him to her. "It's so good to see you. I'm the one who should be sorry for not being here to help you."

Weeping freely now, like an infant, he pressed his head against her shoulder and rubbed his wet cheeks against the soft material of her blouse.

"I'm back now," she whispered to him. "You can cry. I'll stay with you. I'll make it all right. I swear it." She stroked his hair gently. "I'll get you out of here, and you'll come and live with me," she said, surprising herself by blurting out a thought that had entered her mind only at that moment. "You and Irene. We'll all be back together again."

They clung to each other for a long time. Dimmy remained silent, his only utterance an occasional sob or a deep sigh. Laura continued to whisper comforting words to him, as she would have if he had awakened from a bad dream in the middle of the night. She did not want to admit that this present situation was a ruthless reality. She wanted to pretend that she could make it all disappear simply by exerting her newly found power of will.

Laura felt a gentle hand on her shoulder and turned her head to see Zeke Perez standing beside her.

"Why don't we all sit down?" he suggested calmly.

Unwilling to release her, as if fearful she would vanish as easily as she had reappeared, Dimmy clung to her like an infant to its mother. They moved together to the two chairs placed side by side at the table and sat. They continued to hold on to each other as Zeke took the seat across from them.

"Are you okay?" he asked Dimmy.

The boy nodded and straightened. He held on tightly to Laura's hand.

"I'm going to leave in a moment," Zeke said. "So that

you two can be alone for a while. But I have to say something first." He paused and waited to gain Dimmy's full attention. "Bringing Laura here, Dimmy, was a manipulation on my part. I admit it. I don't want you to suspect me of being dishonest. So I'm telling you that I had my own motives for bringing her here." He turned then to Laura. "I want you to fully understand that, too," he said.

"All right." She nodded.

"I want you both to understand that I have a task to perform. That task requires that you speak to me, Dimmy. That you cooperate with me. If I thought you were mentally incompetent, I would walk away, make my report to your attorney, and forget about you. But I'm convinced that you are capable, that you could talk to me if you wanted to, and that you are choosing, for some reason unknown to me, to remain silent."

He paused, observed the boy for a moment, then leaned forward and spoke emphatically. "I'm hoping that Laura will induce you to help me, to help yourself. As far as I'm concerned, that's the only reason she's here. I'm hoping she will help you see the light."

Zeke pushed himself away from the table and stood. "I'm going now," he said. "I'll be at the nurses' station when you're finished, Laura."

She nodded. "Thank you."

"I'll see you tomorrow, Dimmy."

The boy shrugged and looked away. "Yeah, sure!" he said sullenly.

Zeke turned, moved to the door, pounded on it once, and exited when the deputy opened it and released him.

Dimmy shook his head. "I don't know what that guy wants from me," he said.

"He wants to help you," Laura said.

"What for?" Dimmy asked. "What's in it for him?"

She stared at him in silence for a moment. Such a cynical attitude was not part of the Dimmy she remembered. While he appeared so helpless, so needy, he remained so aloof. He had cried with her, had clung to her longingly, had revealed his weakness. But still, she sensed his distance from her. She sensed that the responsive part of him was shielded from her, protected by a layer of hard, impenetrable distrust.

She sighed. "What happened, Dimmy? Why did you do it?"

He smiled bitterly. "You mean to him or to myself?"

"Both," she said.

"I don't know." He looked away from her as a tremor rippled across his face and rested on his lips. "For him, it was time. I took too much from him already ..." He shrugged. "And for me, I can't spend the rest of my life in prison. I'm not gonna do that."

"You don't have to," she pleaded. "Dr. Perez wants to help you."

"Yeah." He laughed humorlessly. "Like my lawyer wants to help me, right?"

Laura was confused. "I don't know what you mean."

He grew solemn. "The shrink wants me to pretend I'm crazy, and the lawyer wants me to cop a plea," he said.

She shook her head. "What does that mean, exactly?"

He sighed resignedly. "They want me to plead guilty to assault with a deadly weapon, or something like that. To make a deal. That way there won't be a trial. They won't have to work hard. And I'll go to jail for seven years." His eyes suddenly reflected his fear and rage. "I'm not gonna do that, Laura. I don't care if they brought you here from Ohio to get me to agree. Everything I gave him, he had it coming. I don't think I should go to prison for that."

"I didn't come here to help them send you to prison,

Dimmy," she said firmly. "I came to be here with you, for you."

She touched her palm to his cheek and allowed it to rest there. How could she explain how grateful she was to him? How could she make him understand, through the barrier of distrust he had erected, that she would never betray him? On the contrary, she would fight for him to her very last breath.

"You're not alone anymore," she continued, attempting desperately to reach him. "I'm here and I'm going to find out what's going on. I'm going to talk to your lawyer and to the prosecutor and to the judge, if I can. And I'm going to find out exactly what's happening to you. Okay?"

He watched her through half-closed eyes as if trying to remember if he had ever truly trusted her. "Okay," he finally said in a small voice, as if to indicate that what she did was out of his hands.

"And if you don't want to talk to Dr. Perez, then don't talk to him," she said. "Give me a little time and I'll find out whose side he's on. Then you can talk to him if you want to or you can tell him to go straight to hell."

Much to Zeke's disappointment, Laura begged off the lunch invitation and asked him to drive her back to her motel.

"When can we meet?" he asked as she stepped out of his car in front of the motel office.

"I don't know," she said. "I'm going to try to see Dimmy's lawyer, Mr. Haines, tomorrow morning."

"Okay," he said. "How about meeting me at about five o'clock, after my last patient?"

"All right," she said. "I'll call you."

He grinned and looked uncomfortable. "Unless you'd rather make it for dinner," he mumbled.

She smiled. "Maybe," she said hurriedly as if anxious to get away from him. "Why don't I call you tomorrow?"

"All right!" he nodded. "Talk to you tomorrow."

She watched him drive out into traffic and disappear down the street. Then she turned and entered the motel lobby.

In her room she took another shower, let the steaming water pound on her for ten minutes, and changed into blue jeans and a yellow T-shirt. Barefoot, worried, and anxious, she sat unhappily on the side of her bed and stared at the telephone as if it were an executioner's lever.

In the bathroom she had examined herself in the foggy mirror and found that she still presented a calm exterior. She still appeared to be perfectly in control—strong-willed, confident, aggressive. But that was a pretense. In reality she was the very opposite of those things—weak and uncertain.

She had promised Dimmy that she would do battle on his behalf. She had urged him to have faith in her. She had led him to believe that she would be his white knight. She had left him convinced that she could rescue him somehow. But in reality she knew that she could do no such thing. Now, as she sat quietly in the privacy of her motel room, unobserved, she could evaluate herself candidly, and she could see that she had never in her life been strong enough even to rescue herself. How could she possibly hope to deliver Dimmy?

She needed help, but asking for help this early in the game would be an admission of defeat. It would mean that she had not come very far after all, that she had not grown out of her passive, needy, reliable defense. Being incapable, believing that she was incompetent, had been the method she had employed all her life to coerce others to do for her. Was she regressing to that state now?

No! She was not ready to fail so soon. What of those who had supported her? Would Franny still be there for her if she admitted she could not go it alone? Of course she would, Laura told herself. Would Dr. Benson be sympathetic, or would he remind her that he had predicted such an outcome, that he had told her so? Had it all been reassuring talk? Was she ready to take on the world only within the confines of Benson's office?

Wait! Why did any of that matter? When did Dimmy's predicament become less important than her own? How had she allowed the old feelings of inadequacy to overcome her? When had she let the old dependent Laura regain control? Damn! She was feeling like a victim again. Her own sense of worthlessness was not the issue at hand. There would be plenty of time to feel worthless later. At the moment Dimmy needed her, and she would not fail him.

She reached out and pulled the phone closer to her. At issue was not what Dr. Benson would think of her. Hadn't she learned that what people thought of her was much less important than what she thought of herself? Hadn't she passed beyond the need to please? Hadn't she forsaken the need to be loved by everyone, even her enemies?

She punched in a direct-dial long-distance number, waited through several rings, listened to a recorded message, then spoke calmly and clearly.

"Dr. Benson," she said. "It's Laura. I'm in California at the Days Inn." She gave him the telephone number and then said, "I'm a little shaky, but I'm doing okay. I would like the name of a therapist here in Los Angeles whom I could call just in case I need to talk to someone. Thanks," she said, "for everything."

Dimmy, no longer in restraints, lay on his back in the cool bed. His eyes were closed, but he was fully awake. He suspected that the orderly was watching him and would continue to watch him as long as he was in the prison ward. He was tempted to open his eyes, look up, and locate him, but he resisted the temptation. His eyes remained shut.

Actually he believed he could see his situation more clearly with his eyes closed than with them open. Open, his sight was filled with insignificant objects, people, movements. Closed, he had control over what he examined. He observed only that which he chose to explore; he made better decisions, found clearer directions, saw his options more distinctly.

Not so long ago, in the darkness of his prison cell, eyes closed, lulled by the rhythmic snoring of his cell mate, he had seen the path to release. His inner vision had brightened suddenly as though he had allowed sunlight to enter his shadowed mind. He had discovered then the three pathways open to him like three major thoroughfares extending out before him in three different directions.

The boulevard on the left led to the distant horizon upon which loomed the formidable towered walls of the stone prison in which he could remain, if he chose to. There he could learn a trade, he was told. He could become an educated man with an entire lifetime to devote to study.

He could see himself as clearly as though it were midday in his imagination. He was recognizable but foreign, alien, to his own perception, a citizen of terminal confinement. He could see that he had become an old man—decrepit, broken, wounded, shattered. More dead than alive. Inured to the pain. Enduring the sequestered existence in a constant state of anesthesia.

On the far right, another avenue stretched to the horizon. It led to the tiny room in the back of the greasy restaurant his father now owned on Hollywood Boulevard, which he had called home prior to being arrested. That room held unknown horrors in store for him, rare tortures the likes of which he could barely imagine. If he returned there when he was freed, he would again face the punitive serfdom that had nearly destroyed him in the past.

But the highway in the center led beyond the horizon. It moved cleanly beyond this cruel earth and lifted off into the heavens, concluding somewhere beyond mortal vision, in a place where there was no suffering, no anguish. Down that path lay salvation for Dimmy, a final release from tribulation.

He saw himself, as if in a motion picture, rising quietly, taking the coarse prison jumpsuit from the foot of his cell mate's bunk, threading it through the bars high up near his own bunk, tying a noose at the end of one leg, slipping it over his head, tightening it around his throat, balancing himself on the edge of his upper bunk, saying a quick Greek prayer, and flinging himself outward. He saw the noose catch and tighten as he fell and then swung back and crashed against the bars with the force of a battering ram. He saw the cell turn upside down, falter, lie on its side and grow dark. . . .

Dimmy opened his eyes. There was no orderly standing above him. He was no longer back in the cell seeking a road to freedom. He was alone in the hospital bed, in a secured room, in his white world, alone and still alive. But even with Laura close to him, there was no joy for him there. A tear fell from the corner of his eye and rolled down his cheek. He did not know when he would be able to gather up the courage to try again. He did not know when an opportunity would present itself again. But he knew he had no alternative. He would try again and again and again, until he finally, once and for all, escaped his irrevocable sentence.

NINE

Early the next morning Laura phoned Bob Haines's office and made an appointment to meet with the attorney at his Century City office at eleven. She ate a light breakfast in the coffee shop off the lobby of her motel and took a cab to the Century City mall, where she hoped to cheer herself up, breaking the depression that hung like a cloud over her, with an hour of mindless shopping.

Having brooded most of the night before and slept only fitfully, tossing and turning, her body experiencing a seemingly bottomless exhaustion while her mind raced savagely with unwanted and unwelcome thoughts, consistently denying her sleep, she needed some relief from the burden weighing upon her. Her hour alone with Dimmy had not relieved her anxiety. On the contrary, he had achieved just the opposite effect by refusing to discuss his problems with her. He was comforted to have her near him, had missed her terribly, he said, but he was not willing to divulge to her any of the details of the incident that had catapulted him into prison.

"You don't want to hear," he had said to her after she begged him to explain why he would do something so foreign to his nature. "Believe me, Laura, anything I could say to you would only hurt you more."

"But, Dimmy," she had pleaded. "That's why I came to be with you. I want to help you. I want you to talk to me, to make it lighter for you. You know that talking about it will make it hurt less."

He smiled at her sadly, touched with the same kind of loving feelings he used to harbor for her. She had not changed that much, he observed. She was still so naive, so innocent, blind to truth, and adept at distorting her world into a kind of pleasant cartoon community. She still believed in magic.

"No, Laura!" He shook his head vehemently. "I want to hear about you. Tell me where you live, what you do. Do you have a boyfriend? I need to hear about you more than I need to talk about . . . it."

She eventually gave in to him. They did not speak again about the charges against him. They spoke only about her job in the real estate office, her apartment, her therapy, and the progress she had made. She told him about Franny and what a good friend she had become. She could see that he liked Franny immediately. Perhaps he equated her with Mrs. McNamara whom he had loved so deeply during his childhood. Then she told him about Dr. Benson and how much she had come to rely on him, look up to him, and respect him, how she had learned about kindness from him. And as Dimmy scowled darkly during her description, she realized that he was jealous of her feelings for Dr. Benson and probably would have preferred her to work with a female therapist.

When their time together ended, she had reluctantly pulled herself away from him. She felt devastated, as if she were experiencing all over again the same loss that she had felt on that frightful night back in New York when he had put her on that bus and sent her away from him to make a new life.

Later, seated next to Zeke Perez as he drove her back to

West Los Angeles, she had felt despondent, as if a weighty melancholy had pervaded her sense of self. The news of Dimmy's situation, which at first had frightened her, had finally, during the short time she'd spent with him, reached its natural conclusion, and she felt hopelessly depressed and incapable of saving him.

She had rattled on about herself because he had seemed to enjoy it so, but she had learned nothing about him. What had driven him to commit such a desperate act? Did he need anything from her? Was there some secret he could share with her alone? She felt useless and ineffectual, believing she had wasted their precious time together. She knew nothing more now than she had known after that first phone call from Zeke Perez, and she was angry with herself for giving in to Dimmy. Was that not exactly what she had worked on so diligently with Dr. Benson? Was that not her single most serious problem? Her unwillingness to confront, to insist upon, to demand what she wanted from people so that later she could feel unfinished, cheated, used and consequently could retain and reinforce the silent hidden anger that simmered within her? How would she ever be free of that debilitating anger if she did not start to assert herself? How could she ever hope to be fully self-sufficient if she was still so afraid of offending that she sacrificed what she wanted and accepted what others wanted for her?

Those were her thoughts as she strolled through the wide promenade of the mall, up one walkway and down another, glancing at the cleverly dressed windows but not seeing them, preoccupied with her own murky thoughts. She stopped at one brightly colored display window and stared at the gaily dressed mannequins behind the glass. The window display was a beach scene. The painted sky, blue beyond belief, hovered over the heads of three female mannequins, each in a different color of the same cotton flowered sundress and each posing as if draped in a gown of silk. The dress was straight, pinched tight at the waist. It was short, low-cut, and cool, with thin shoulder straps. She examined her own pink blouse, billowy at the cuffs, and charcoal gray skirt that hung halfway to her ankles and realized she was out of fashion in her Dayton, Ohio, outfit.

She reflected that she had determined to do things for herself, that she would no longer diminish her importance in her own mind, that she would no longer discount what she wanted for herself as being unnecessary compared with what others wanted. She had learned from Dr. Benson to pamper herself, but she needed much more practice before she could consider herself proficient at that. Talking about rewarding herself and actually doing it were two different things entirely. With a huge intake of courage-building breath, she entered the store.

Half an hour later when she stepped into Robert Haines's austere reception room, she was clad in a lavender version of the dress that had caught her eye in the shop window. She wore new white pumps and carried a matching white bag. The receptionist, busily typing at a word processor, was dressed so conservatively that Laura thought perhaps she should have worn the clothes from Dayton, which she now carried in a paper bag.

She moved to the desk. "I'm Laura Devon," she said. "I have an eleven o'clock appointment with Mr. Haines."

"Just a minute," the woman said, barely looking up from her typing. She lifted a phone receiver and pressed a single button. After a moment she spoke again. "Your eleven o'clock is here, Mr. Haines." She nodded at the unheard reply and replaced the phone. "You can go in," she said.

Laura pushed open an unmarked door in the wall behind the secretary.

Bob Haines stood up behind his desk and waved her forward.

"Mrs. . . . uh . . ." He glanced down at a slip of paper on his desk. "Miss Devon."

"Mr. Haines," she acknowledged with a nod. She closed the door behind her and moved to one of the soft cream-colored leather chairs across from him.

A minute smile pulled at his mouth, and his eyes roamed down the length of her body admiringly before he spoke again. "Please, sit down."

"Thank you." She sat on the edge of the deep chair clutching her new purse with both hands, knees together, feet flat on the floor.

He sat in his own chair and smiled at her as if he had tested her and she had passed his examination. He leaned back and waited for her to speak.

"When did you get in?" the lawyer asked.

"Yesterday," she said.

He nodded. "Have you seen Dimmy?"

"Yes," she said. "Dr. Perez took me to the hospital."

Haines studied her thoughtfully. "And now you want to talk about the case. Is that correct?"

"Yes," she said. "I would."

"What would you like to know?" he said.

"Everything," Laura said. "Where do we stand? What exactly are the charges against Dimmy? What are your plans for his defense? How soon will the trial begin? What are the chances of him being convicted?"

While she spoke, he nodded with her, at times looking grave and others smiling briefly. "Shall I give you a brief synopsis of the case?"

"If you would," Laura said seriously.

Haines studied her for a moment. He clearly enjoyed what he saw. He was pleasantly surprised at how attractive she was. Her new tight dress accentuated her excellent figure, her narrow waist, her high, firm breasts. Sitting on the edge of her chair, her skirt had hiked up to expose her strikingly long legs.

"Dimmy plotted to kill his father for a long time before he finally carried out his plan," Haines said. "He attacked the man in his sleep, inflicted multiple stab wounds, and left him for dead. Later he phoned the police anonymously. They sent a car to the apartment and woke up the sister, who lives with her father. She let them search the house. They found Mr. Pappas bleeding to death in his bed. An hour later the police picked Dimmy up at the restaurant, where he lived in the back room. They took him into the station for questioning, and he confessed to the attack. He even told them where to find the knife, which he had cleaned and replaced in the kitchen of the restaurant where he worked."

While he spoke, Laura felt the pain Dimmy must have been experiencing. Her jaws tightened, and she began to grind her teeth. Her sad eyes nearly closed as she heard about Dimmy's confession. Up until that point, she had been prepared to deny Dimmy's ability to stab his father. She knew the boy. She knew he could not have committed such a crime. Dimmy was too much like her, like the old Laura, too willing to accept his fate in silence without a struggle. No matter how brutal Nikki became, Laura was positive that Dimmy could never raise a hand against him.

"Did he have a lawyer with him when he confessed?" Laura asked. "Did the police read him his rights?"

Haines smiled. "You know," he said. "All these damned TV shows about cops and lawyers have taken the mystery out of my life. They make everything look so cut and dried on that little screen. They tie it all up in fine little knots at the end. Meanwhile they fill people's heads with catchwords and legal phrases that the public blows way out of proportion because you really think the criminal courts function like those theatrical things you see in your living room while you're drinking beer and eating popcorn.''

"What are you saying?" Laura asked, wondering if she had just been insulted.

"I'm saying," Haines continued, "that real cases don't work that way. You're not going to get that kid off on a technicality. This isn't the movies. The cavalry isn't going to come charging to the rescue at the eleventh hour. It just isn't going to happen that way." He sighed deeply.

"Of course, there was a lawyer present," he said. "Dimmy had a public defender with him from the minute he indicated that he had a story to tell. He was informed of his rights. Protecting a suspect's civil rights is second nature to every cop in America by now. Cops aren't dumb, no matter what the TV lets you think about them."

"What is going to happen?" Laura asked, feeling her anger rising, feeling frustrated.

Haines continued, ignoring her question. "Dimmy has been indicted on a charge of premeditated attempted murder. We're waiting for a trial date to be set." He shrugged. "The court is hesitant to set a date while there is still the possibility of a plea bargain. And that's about the gist of it."

Haines clamped his mouth shut and studied her once again as if weighing her ability to deal with the truth. He nodded finally and leaned forward. "Look, if the kid will agree to a plea, the judge would be very happy to go easy on him. Judge Bauer is a lenient judge. Believe me, he cares about the kids of this community."

"What if Dimmy doesn't plead guilty? What's going to happen to him if he goes to trial and loses?"

He frowned in consternation. "Okay," he said. "If you can take it, I'll give it to you straight."

"I can take it," she said. "I want it straight."

He paused again as if offering her one more opportunity to avoid what she was about to learn. Then, he shrugged as if it was no longer his responsibility and spoke with resignation. "He tried to kill his father. That's worse in the minds of a jury than trying to kill a stranger. Juries don't like kids who take butcher knives to their parents. Sure, there are mitigating circumstances, and if his father had been abusing the kid at that moment, you can bet we'd be screaming self-defense. But in this case the perpetrator planned the attack. He stalked his victim. Lay in wait for him. When the father was out flat on his back, drunk, the kid slipped into the bedroom, walked up to the sleeping man, and stabbed him." Haines dropped a fist into the palm of his other hand as he spoke. "Dimmy stabbed him. Bang! Then stabbed him again. Bang! And again. Bang! And again. Bang! And when he was done, you couldn't see the victim for all the blood. He had been stabbed in four different places. The kid made a pin cushion out of his own father. How in the world can we justify that as self-defense?"

Laura clutched desperately at her purse. His words struck at her like the harsh blows of an assailant. They pounded on her as if she were being physically beaten by them, and they left her pained and breathless.

"That boy is going to prison," Haines continued. "There's no escaping that fact. No judge is going to send a message to kids that it's okay to go after their parents whenever they feel like it." He paused for effect, then spoke emphatically. "Dimmy Pappas is going to prison. No two ways about it. The only question left is, for how long?"

Laura shook her head sadly. "You're not talking about the boy I know. *If* Dimmy attacked his father he must have had a good reason, but I can't believe he did attack Nikki. None of us even dared to talk back to Nikki. The thought of raising a hand against him is beyond belief."

"Well," Haines said, driving his point home. "Dimmy did. And the hand he raised had a big knife in it. You'd better get used to that fact, Miss Devon. Try to adjust to the idea that your stepson is a killer. Otherwise you're not going to be able to help him. If you continue to deny what he is, you're going to do more damage than good. He needs to face up to reality, and in order to do that, he may need you to face up first."

"I *am* facing up," she said angrily. "How much more do you want me to do?"

"I want you to grasp the fact that this boy can go to prison for the rest of his life."

"How can that be?" she said breathlessly. "There are lots of murderers who don't get life."

Haines leaned back and nodded at her. "That's true," he said. "But in this state we have a law brought about by the Singleton case. You remember the Singleton case, Miss Devon?"

Laura shook her head. "No."

"Singleton was a drifter, a handyman, who picked up a fifteen-year-old hitchhiker, raped her in the back of his van, and left her on the side of a deserted road to die after he carefully chopped off her arms with an ax. You remember it?"

"No." Laura could barely speak, she was so appalled by the story.

"She didn't die, and he got fourteen years," Haines said venomously. His face clouded, and his eyes bored into hers. "That was the maximum that California law allowed for attempted murder back then, and the people of this state were up in arms. There was an outcry you could hear all the way to Hawaii. Because Singleton failed as a murderer, he condemned that girl to live out the rest of her life without arms.

"The legislators went crazy with that one. They made mincemeat out of the statute with public opinion unanimously wanting to execute the miserable bastard. The law was changed finally. It now allows a judge, in a case of premeditated attempted murder, to sentence the defendant to life without possibility of parole. It's too late to get Singleton. He's already served his time and been released. But it's not too late for Dimmy Pappas. He's going to feel the full brunt of the law. He could be sent away forever. If Judge Bauer gets mad enough, he's liable to do just that."

If Haines's intention was to frighten her, Laura thought, he had been very successful. She was devastated by the idea that Dimmy could spend sixty or seventy years locked in a cell. Controlled rage mounted within her. She felt it rising, filling her lungs, entering her throat, flushing her face.

"All right!" she said. "What do we have to do?"

"Good!" Haines responded amiably. "Now you're talking. I want you to persuade Dimmy to take the D.A.'s offer. They'll come down as low as assault with a deadly weapon, if he pleads guilty. That's a huge reduction."

"How long?" she asked.

He shrugged. "Seven, but with time served and good behavior, he'll be out in four."

"Four years," she whispered.

"It's a good deal," Haines said. "I'm amazed the D.A. made the offer. I'm even more amazed that the judge agreed to it. Judge Bauer is fair but tough. He could hit the kid hard. But if Dimmy shows that he's remorseful, and if he saves the court the time and expense of a trial, the judge will reciprocate."

"How can I persuade him to plead guilty?" she asked.

"It shouldn't be too hard. He's already confessed to the crime. They've got his confession in writing." He paused and studied her.

She felt numb, as if she had been overloaded and had switched off the part of her brain that allowed her to comprehend what was happening.

"Look," he continued. "You have to keep in mind what's best for the kid. You don't want to take risks with his life. You don't want to let him take risks, either. If you tell him that you've thought about it and decided that the best and safest thing for him is to cop the plea, he'll do it. He doesn't trust any of us, but Zeke Perez tells me he really trusts you."

She nodded. "Yes. He trusts me. That's why I have to be sure that what you're suggesting is the right thing."

"Believe me, if I thought there was one chance in a hundred that we could beat this rap, I'd be the first one out there fighting like a bulldog. But I know better." He smiled at her sadly, sympathetically. "Don't let him put his life in the hands of a judge and jury. Persuade him to take the deal. It's the best way."

"All right," she said, rising from her chair. "I'm going to see him again tomorrow. I'll talk to him then."

Haines came around his desk to take her hand. "I'm glad," he said. "You won't be sorry."

He walked her to the door, then stopped before opening it.

"By the way," he said. "I'm going to need some money—before I go ahead with any additional work, I mean. You know, I haven't been paid very much . . ."

Laura was surprised. "It didn't occur to me that there's no one to pay you."

"I'll need something on account, Miss Devon."

"How much?"

"Well, I'd like ten thousand, but I'll take five."

Laura stared at the lawyer. "You haven't been paid anything yet?"

"Dimmy's sister gave me a retainer," he said, "but that was at the very beginning."

"How large a retainer did Irene give you?"

"Well, you know, it was used up a long time ago. I've spent a lot of time on this case."

"How much did she give you, Mr. Haines?"

"Ten thousand," he said, then added hastily, "but that was a long time ago."

"Where did she get ten thousand dollars?" Laura asked.

"I don't know."

"You didn't ask? A young girl gives you ten thousand dollars and you don't ask where she gets it?" Laura shook her head in disbelief.

Haines looked uncomfortable. He wet his dry lips with the tip of his tongue and backed away from her. "She said something about getting it from her father," he finally said, "but I couldn't swear to that."

Dimmy struggled with the chains that bound his wrists to his waist. He twisted and turned on his chair, crossed one leg over the other, swung it nervously, vigorously, for a few moments, then crossed the other. Zeke Perez watched him closely, quietly, while the boy's body language disclosed his uneasiness.

"You're angry today," Zeke observed.

Dimmy's eyes snapped to the therapist's face. "No!" he said, suddenly growing very still.

They were in the room where Dimmy had met with Laura the day before, Dimmy on one side of the table, Zeke across from him. The therapist rose, moved closer to Dimmy, and sat on the edge of the table.

Zeke shrugged. "I was watching you swing your leg, and I wondered who you wanted to kick."

Dimmy glared at Perez menacingly. "You reading minds now, Doc?"

Zeke smiled. "No. That's not a guess. That's what we call an interpretation. That's when I see something or hear something that has an obvious meaning to me and I point it out to you in case you don't see it as clearly."

Dimmy chuckled. "Maybe I was keeping time with a song I was humming in my head."

"I don't think so."

"Maybe I was doing an exercise," Dimmy challenged.

"No."

"Maybe I just like swinging my leg."

"Maybe," Zeke conceded. "But the question then would be why you liked it, wouldn't it?"

"Because I'm angry?" Dimmy asked.

"Because you're angry."

"So you know what my swinging leg means more than I do, right?"

"It's a possibility, isn't it?"

Dimmy pondered that for a moment. "Yeah," he said. "It's a possibility. Not a very good one, but a possibility." Then he smiled. "You don't know anything about me for sure. You want me to be feeling something—anything—so you take a wild shot. What the hell! I got you figured out, Doc. You're not a bad guy, but you're so obvious. I can see right through you."

"Can you?" Zeke asked.

"Sure."

Zeke nodded. "But, I can't see through you, right?"

Dimmy's face dropped. "What do you mean?"

"Did you ever think that maybe you're as obvious as I am. Maybe I can see right through you, too. Maybe I'm not the only one who's transparent. Maybe we have a lot in common."

"See! That's what you guys always do. You twist everything around."

"I merely commented that you seem angry today," Zeke said innocently.

"Well, I'm not!" Dimmy snapped.

"Okay!" Zeke surrendered, holding his hands up, palms outward, as if warding off an attack. "You win. I lose. If you say you're not angry, then you're not angry. And that's that! Let's forget it." Zeke stood and returned to the chair on the other side of the table.

Dimmy squirmed, moved from side to side, tugged on the chains that bound him. He glanced at Perez now and then as he swung his attention from one side of the room to the other, from the ceiling to the floor, from corner to corner. Finally he said, "Why do you always try to bug me?"

"Do I bug you?"

"Yes."

"When?"

"All the time."

"*All* the time?"

Dimmy hesitated, then said, "When you tell me things about myself."

"You don't like to talk about yourself?"

"I don't like to hear about me . . . from you."

"You don't like to hear the truth about yourself?"

"You don't know the truth about me."

"Maybe I do. Maybe I know a lot."

Dimmy eyed Perez suspiciously. "Like what?"

Zeke hesitated. "I know you're different today."

"What do you mean, different?"

Zeke shrugged. "You're showing your anger more."

"There you go again!" Dimmy said with exasperation. "You and my anger. Goddammit!"

"You don't think you're showing your anger?"

"What if I am? So what?" Dimmy shouted. "Why is that so important?"

"That's the right question, Dimmy. Why? Why are you showing your anger today? What's different about today? What happened that's different? You tell me."

Dimmy grimaced angrily. "I don't know what the hell you're talking about."

"Is there anything new in your life?"

"No," he snapped. "The same old cell."

"Anybody new?"

"No! Same dumb cell mate."

Zeke waited for a moment while Dimmy squirmed. Then he spoke softly. "How about Laura?"

Dimmy dropped his eyes and spoke as softly as Zeke. "I knew you were going to say that. God, I just knew it."

"Sure you did."

"I did!"

"I know you did. I agree with you."

Dimmy searched Zeke's face for some sign of condescension, but found none. "I thought you were being sarcastic," he said.

Zeke shook his head. "I know that Laura's being here has changed you. I don't think you even realize how much her presence has affected you."

"You don't think I know how important Laura is to me?"

"That's right. I don't."

Dimmy turned angrily on his chair. "You're nuts, Doc!"

"No, Dimmy," Zeke said. "Nobody in this room is nuts. Nobody."

They stared at each other silently, eyes locked as if in mental combat. Finally Dimmy could hold the stare no longer. He lowered his eyes. "So how much has she affected me?" he said to his own hands.

Zeke smiled and nodded. What he was about to point out was obvious to him. He knew that Dimmy was aware of what he was doing. He knew the boy was not mentally incompetent, was not stupid, was very much aware of his own behavior and its varied meanings. And Zeke was about to say something that Dimmy already knew. He wanted to avoid allowing Dimmy to believe that he had been caught in something, that he was being criticized, laughed at, or ridiculed. That was a great danger in interpreting behavior to a patient. If the given behavior was desirable, a comment of recognition from the therapist could be misconstrued by the patient as a statement of the therapist's superior insight, knowledge, and intelligence. That could cause feelings of guilt and confusion in the patient, especially in a bright patient, so that the behavior could be instantly discarded and the relationship set back to its awkward beginning. Zeke did not want to play brilliant doctor with the boy at this point. He wanted to embark on a journey that would end in trust, and that meant not being superior.

Zeke cocked his head sheepishly. "We're talking," he said, shrugging as if it was no big deal. "Really talking for the first time. What do you think about that?"

Dimmy reflected, nodded slightly to himself as he mused, then looked up and grinned at Perez. "Yeah," he said, nodding. "That's a pretty big effect."

When Laura returned to the motel late that afternoon, she found one message from Franny, one from Dr. Benson back in Ohio, and two messages from Dr. Zeke Perez awaiting her. Before responding to any of them, she kicked her shoes off, wriggled out of her new dress, and jumped under the shower. She stood beneath the hot water for a long time, letting it pound on her head and fall over her aching shoulders. The meeting with Dimmy's lawyer had disturbed her, but it had also galvanized her into action. It was the afternoon's labors that had exhausted her and heaped stress upon her.

She wrapped a towel around her hair, dried herself, put on her blue robe, and settled down to make phone calls. It was three hours later in Ohio—dinnertime. She dialed Dr. Benson's number, and he picked up on the first ring.

"Laura, how are you?" he said after greeting her.

"I could be better."

"So I gathered," he said. "Listen. I can't talk right now, but I sense that there's much we need to talk about. Will you call me back later?"

"I . . ."

"I don't know any therapists out there, Laura, but we can talk over the phone, can't we? If not, maybe you should come home."

"Well . . ."

"Call me back, Laura."

"Okay," she said. "When?"

"Later," he said impatiently. "I have to go, Laura."

She heard the line disconnect and set the phone down in its cradle. She sat staring at it for several moments. She was angry but was not sure why. Had he disappointed her? He had not sounded excited to hear from her. He had not sounded as if he trusted her. He had sounded hurried, quick. Like a parent. Did she need a parent at this time? What had happened to her conviction that she could handle her new life?

She decided to call Zeke Perez, since her own therapist had not been much help.

"I want to confirm our dinner plans," he said when he heard her voice. "Same place, seven o'clock?"

"Okay," she said. "Zeke, I met with Bob Haines this morning. I want to know what you think of him."

Zeke hesitated. Bob Haines had consulted with him on a

case. Lawyer referrals were Zeke Perez's bread and butter. He needed to practice caution when speaking about the people who produced his income. "He's okay," he said. "Why do you ask?"

"Because he wants Dimmy to plead guilty."

"Yes. I know."

"And Haines wants me to give him some money. A great deal of money."

"Yes," Zeke said. "I expected that."

"Zeke," Laura said, "can't I find a lawyer who will fight for Dimmy?"

"Haines is a good lawyer, Laura. He's very successful."

"Help me, Zeke." She was pleading with him as she would with a friend and it excited him.

"Anything," he said.

"Help me find another lawyer. I don't trust Mr. Haines."

"I know a lot of lawyers, Laura. They all send me clients. They all know one another. I can't recommend one without offending all the others."

"I see."

She sounded so disappointed and helpless that his heart sank. "Look," he said. "Forget what I just said. Let me look around."

"Thank you, Zeke."

He was relieved. "I'll see you at seven, Laura."

She replaced the phone. She felt slightly disrespectful at so shamelessly manipulating Perez. Sensing that he liked her, she had played the role of the needy, helpless female in order to coerce him into assisting her. She smiled and shook her head as she thought about what Dr. Benson would say regarding her reverting to her old habit of feigning dependency to get what she wanted. He would say that although she believed she was feigning, she was truly dependent and resisting being self-reliant in order to experience a neurotic sense of power over a man. That was unacceptable behavior, he would say.

She called Franny, who was overjoyed to hear from her.

"I was beginning to worry," Franny said. "One day goes by without a call, that's okay, but this is the third day and how do I know what's happening there? You could be in traction in a hospital somewhere."

Laura laughed. "You love to worry, Franny. It's your favorite pastime."

"Well," the woman said, "maybe I did overreact a little. I'll feel a lot better when you're home."

Laura chewed on her lower lip and hesitated too long.

"Are you biting your lip?" Franny asked.

Laura released her lip immediately. "How did you know?"

"I can smell bad news. Come on! Let's have it. If you're chewing your lip it's got to be real bad."

Laura took a deep breath. "I've got to stay here for a while, Franny. I can't come back just yet."

"How come?"

"It's a very bad situation. I can't go into it all. I need time to come up with a solution."

"I'm sorry to hear that," Franny said. "I already miss you too much."

"I know," Laura said. "And I miss you, too. But I don't have a big choice here. It's much worse than I thought."

"Okay. You must know what you're doing."

"And I need a favor," Laura murmured.

"What kind of favor?" Franny sounded wary.

Laura plunged ahead. "I need to borrow some money. I want you to know this is real hard for me. I don't like taking advantage of our friendship, but I don't have anyone else to turn to."

Franny was silent for a long moment. "How much do you need?" she finally asked.

"I found a small apartment this afternoon," Laura said. "It's not much, one big room, but it sure is expensive. I had to put most of my money down as a deposit."

"How much, Laura?"

"The lawyer wants five thousand, but I can't ask you for that much."

"Where should I send it?"

"Franny?"

"Don't get mushy, love. Just tell me where to send it, and I'll wire it right away."

Zeke Perez informed his answering service that he would be gone for the day. He locked his office and walked to the far end of the medical building where Paul Murphy had his office. He entered the small waiting room, which was unoccupied, and noted that the red light above the inner door was not lighted, meaning that his colleague was not in session. He tapped lightly on the door and entered when Paul called, "Come in."

Murphy's office was furnished like a living room with a desk. He was slouched in his high-backed leather chair, feet up on the desk, a book propped up against his knees.

"Hi, Paul," Zeke said as he entered and closed the door behind him.

Murphy shut his book, dropped his feet to the floor, and swiveled around to face his friend. "Hiya, Zeke. What's up?"

Zeke moved to the patients' couch and sat down.

"Uh-oh," Murphy said. "If you're on my couch it must be important."

Zeke shook his head. "Sometimes I think you can read my mood while I'm still down the hall."

"I can," Murphy said. "Haven't you heard about my magical powers? Haven't you been talking to any of my patients lately?"

"Only the failures," Zeke said. "And they don't think you're so wonderful."

Murphy groaned and grimaced. "You sure know how to hurt a guy." He slapped his hand over his heart. "Never talk to a shrink about his failures. You know better than that. We save that kind of talk for interns. How else can you make them feel hopelessly inadequate?"

Zeke nodded. "I remember the days when you were supervising me. I wish I could forget."

"I couldn't have been all that bad, Zeke. You're here again, I assume, to consult."

"Yeah," Zeke said, "but not about a patient."

Murphy grew curious. "Oh?"

"I need a lawyer, Paul."

"Uh-oh," Murphy said. "This is serious."

Zeke waved away Murphy's sudden concern. "It's not for me. It's for a friend."

"What kind of lawyer?"

"Criminal."

Murphy leaned back in his chair and scrutinized his friend. "You know as many criminal lawyers as I do, Zeke. It doesn't make sense to ask me for a referral."

"Yes, it does," Zeke said.

"Okay. I'm listening."

"A woman I've just met has asked me to find a lawyer to represent her stepson, who's being held on an attempted murder charge. The stepson is represented by Bob Haines, who brought me in to evaluate the kid." Zeke frowned. "The stepmother doesn't trust Haines, doesn't think he'll fight for the kid. He's trying to get the boy to agree to a plea bargain. He believes the case is hopeless."

"*Is* it hopeless?" Murphy asked.

Zeke paused while he studied his friend's face, then said, "I don't know. There's no possibility of an insanity plea, if that's what you're asking. It's the case of a teenage boy who attacked his father with a knife and damn near killed him. The boy's not psychotic. He is, however, clinically depressed. He must have been really pissed to go after his father with a knife. It's hard to believe that this kid is capable of violence. He's the type who'll drive you crazy by refusing to interact."

"What does the stepmother say?" Murphy asked.

Zeke shook his head. "She hasn't been in the home for a couple of years. She lives in Ohio. I had to bring her out here myself. The kid didn't even want me to know where she was living. They're all terrified of the father. I would guess that he's pretty tyrannical. The kid was probably trying to protect Laura by not revealing her whereabouts."

"I sense that you have some interest in this lady," Murphy said.

"How do you sense that?"

Murphy chuckled. "You call her by her first name. Your voice softens when you talk about her. You're putting yourself out on a limb for her."

"Jesus, Paul. I hate it when you play detective."

"Am I right?"

"Well," Zeke said, "she's awfully pretty."

"I'm right."

Zeke nodded. "You're probably right."

Murphy rose and searched through a Rolodex file. "I'm going to give you the number of the best goddam criminal defense lawyer around. You probably don't know her, but she is the absolute best, especially if you need a gunfighter. But your friend probably won't like her."

"Who is she?"

Murphy spoke as he wrote on a message slip. ''Her name's Harriet Doyle.''

''Why won't Laura like her?''

''Well,'' Murphy shrugged. ''First, she's a woman. Then, she's black. She's as tough as nails. Swears like a streetwise home boy, drinks like a sailor, fights for her clients like a son of a bitch without any regard for who gets hurt. She's a killer, Zeke. And if that isn't enough, she's the sexiest, hottest, most beautiful, longest-legged goddam turn-on I've ever met.''

Zeke grinned like a kid in a locker room and winked at Murphy lasciviously.

''Phyllis won't even let me mention her name at home,'' Murphy said.

TEN

"Two cappuccinos," he told the waiter who hovered over them.

"With liqueur?" the waiter asked.

He turned questioning eyes to her. She shook her head slightly.

"No liqueur," he said. The waiter departed.

He turned toward her in the booth. "No drink before," he said. "No wine with dinner. No after-dinner liqueur with your coffee. Do I surmise correctly that I have a nondrinker seated beside me?"

They had just completed dinner at Carmine's on Santa Monica Boulevard and were seated in the last booth, as far from the piano bar as they could get, so that the music was just barely audible and did not make conversation difficult. The privacy, the romantic atmosphere, and the excellent food were some of the reasons he had chosen Carmine's—that and the fact that the owner never rushed his customers.

The evening had gone extremely well for Zeke Perez, and he was feeling lucky. It was going to turn out to be the best date he had ever had, in spite of his awkwardness around her. Laura thought the object of the evening was to talk about Dimmy, but somehow it had become a date. As if by accident, Zeke had done everything right. At five minutes before seven he had parked at the curb in front of the motel office. He had sat and watched for her through the plate-glass window, disregarding the desk clerk's curiosity.

He had seen the elevator doors slide open and Laura had stepped out, looking beautiful. Her honey-colored hair ringed her delicate face like a frame of soft gold. She wore a simple black off-the-shoulder dress that revealed to maximum advantage every curve, every rise and fall of her splendid body.

He had jumped from his car and rushed to the door just as she saw him and waved and smiled warmly.

"You're right on time," she had said with a touch of playfulness in her voice as he held the door open for her.

"I left earlier," he said grinning. "I wasn't taking any chance of incurring your wrath this time."

She had laughed as he led her to the car, one hand at the small of her back. Just the mere act of touching her excited him. Something about her, something more than her lovely appearance, had fascinated him, had captured his imagination. During the short drive to the restaurant, although he would have preferred to sound sophisticated and adult, he maintained a continuous babble, like an excited teenager. She had reacted quite well to his obvious anxiety, smiling at his jokes and indicating a genuine interest in each topic of which he spoke.

Dinner could not have been better. They had split a Caesar salad and then enjoyed the veal tortellini in clear broth, followed by gently sautéed white veal scallopini with capers in a light cream sauce with angel hair pasta drenched in olive oil, garlic and fresh mushrooms.

They spoke little while they ate, but Zeke relaxed. Laura complimented him on his excellent choice of a restaurant. The more Laura seemed to enjoy herself, the more Zeke was put at ease. And by the time the dishes had been cleared from the table and they had ordered coffee, he felt almost as if they were old friends.

"No," she said in answer to his question about being a nondrinker. "I drink now and then, if there's something to celebrate."

"I thought maybe you had an aversion to alcohol," he said.

She examined his face as if calculating whether or not to trust him. He was a therapist, after all, and she did tend to hold therapists in rather high regard. But Dr. Zeke Perez was not interested in her professionally. Of that she was positive. He had a personal interest in her, she was sure.

"Not an aversion," she finally said. "Just an intense dislike. Most of the really bad memories in my life are connected to alcohol."

He nodded understandingly. "Tough childhood?"

"Yes," she said. "That, too." She paused as the waiter set the two coffees before them, then continued when he had departed. "But mostly from the years I lived with my husband."

"Dimmy's father?"

She bit her lip, and turned the fear in her eyes away from him.

"I'm sorry," Zeke said. "I'm prying. It's the shrink in me. I can't resist finding out about people." He shook his head. "I ask too many questions."

"It's all right," she said, composing herself. "I can't keep avoiding the subject for the rest of my life, especially if I'm going to help Dimmy. I stuck my head in the sand for a long time. And that didn't help anything. Maybe it even made things worse. I guess it's time to get up and smell the coffee, as they say."

She smiled, pressed her lips together, and nodded. "The

answer to your question is yes. That was Dimmy's father—the man the authorities say Dimmy tried to kill.''

''You don't believe he did it?'' Zeke said in surprise. ''But he confessed.''

''I know,'' she said. ''But it really is hard for me to believe.''

Zeke studied her, the soft dark eyes, the delicate, innocent lips. ''Maybe he's not the same boy you remember from back then.''

Laura shrugged. ''I don't want to believe Dimmy is capable of murder, even though I know how easy it is to want to . . . to dream about killing Nikki. It was a fantasy I enjoyed more than once myself.''

''Did he abuse you, too?'' Zeke asked, attempting to control his voice. He did not want her to hear the outrage he was feeling at the thought that this lovely woman could have been abused by her husband. Zeke wanted more than anything in the world to take her in his arms and hold her close to him. He examined her fragility and could not imagine anyone wanting to do physical harm to her.

She laughed bitterly at her own thoughts, at the memories of life with Nikki Pappas. ''Oh, yes,'' she said. ''He was abusive to me, all right. He was so abusive that the foundation of our relationship became my belief that if he didn't beat me it meant he no longer loved me.'' An expression of incredulity crossed her face and she turned pathetic eyes to him. ''I was actually convinced that if he stopped loving me, I couldn't survive.''

''You had all these fears of being alone, of being abandoned by him, and yet you dreamed about killing him.''

''Yes,'' she said softly. ''Crazy, isn't it? I used to picture myself buying a gun and waiting until he was asleep and putting it to his head.'' She shuddered at the memory.

"Sometimes that kind of fantasy is the only thing that lets you go on. Sometimes it's the only way to maintain any self-respect. Especially when you're so far down that you don't think you can get any lower. When you think there's nothing worse that can happen to you, nothing more degrading or more painful than what you've got at that moment."

She fought back the tears. "And you know it will never end. It won't stop, and it won't ever go away."

She stopped and stared off into space. A small tear, unwilling to be contained, appeared in the corner of her eye, and she wiped it away. Her shoulders fell as if in despair. "Of course, you feel terribly guilty after you have those fantasies," she added with another bitter laugh.

"Guilty?"

She nodded. "At the thought of how ungrateful and disloyal you've been by even thinking of revenge. After all, I felt that I was the evil one. Not him. He was just doing what he had to do to keep me in line because I was so . . . bad." She paused and contemplated that for a moment. "Not bad." She shook her head. "I was selfish and greedy and self-centered. And if I wasn't constantly being reminded of the right way to behave, there's no telling what I might have done that would embarrass and humiliate him or inconvenience him. I was sure I made his life miserable with my inadequacies. I knew he couldn't trust me. I was too flighty, too foolish, I was simply incapable of doing anything right." She sighed deeply and bit her lower lip. "I actually believed all that, Zeke. I actually worried about appearing ungrateful."

"That's always a big part of it, isn't it?" he said. "Being constantly told you should appreciate what you have, and if you don't you're automatically an avaricious person."

She nodded. "But it took me a long time to figure that

out. A long time and a lot of therapy." She gazed at him appreciatively. "You've heard all this before, haven't you? God! Millions of times, I bet. You must think I'm so stupid."

"No," he said hurriedly. "Not at all. I think you were a victim. I admire your courage at telling me all this."

"Don't you get tired of hearing people complain all the time?"

He shook his head. "I don't hear you complaining, Laura."

After a long moment she said, "There are women all over just like me, aren't there? Letting things like that happen to them, even contributing to the abuse."

"Yes," he said.

She sighed. "It's easier now, because I know I'm not the only one. I used to think that no one else in the world would let such things happen to her. I thought I was uniquely stupid and weak. But now I know there are people like me all over the world. And people like him, just waiting to accommodate us." She breathed deeply. "I also know that it wasn't my fault, that I was trained to be like that. It's an old pattern, but I can break it."

"That's a big step toward getting rid of the scars," he said.

"What is?"

"Recognizing that such things happen to lots of other people. Sometimes just that knowledge is enough to diminish the self-disgust. And it's the terribly low self-esteem that perpetuates the cycle of offering yourself for punishment and receiving it and then feeling gratified that you got it because, after all, you deserved it, right?"

"Yes," she said. "That's exactly how it works."

"With Dimmy, too?"

She looked at him quizzically, then said, "The same?"

"And with Irene?"

She hesitated. "I never thought it could be the same with the children. I thought it was only me. I thought the children were different."

"Why?"

"I don't know," she said, sounding troubled. "I never thought . . ."

"That Dimmy could be having the same feelings as you? That he could be as disgusted with himself? That he could be dreaming the same dreams? The same fantasies? That an attack on his father could be justified? That he could have been as desperate to escape from his father as you were?"

He had spoken with such intensity that she was shocked for a moment. Hardly aware of what she was doing, she reached out and covered his hand with hers. She sensed that he was moved because he was identifying with her. He cared about her, she felt. And he cared about Dimmy. At that instant she realized how much of a friend Zeke Perez could be.

"No," she said, shaking her head. "I never thought of that because I wasn't desperate to escape from Nikki. It was Dimmy who made me leave." She bowed her head. "If it had been left up to me, I would probably still be there."

Dimmy lay in the darkness pretending to be asleep. He had been fully awake all evening and would continue to be so, he knew, till the early morning. He had no intention of once again risking the terrors of sleep.

He closed his eyes and slowed his breathing at each inspection conducted by one of the orderlies. If they knew he was lying awake all night plotting, they would find a way to put him to sleep. They would force him to swallow one of their pills. Or they would mash a drug into his food or into his milk or Kool-Aid. Or they would poke needles into his ass.

For months, first in the metal cage and now in this white-washed hospital room, he had been avoiding sleep at night, avoiding the dreams that tormented him and invariably shocked him into a startled wakefulness, sweaty and trembling, petrified. He continually reminded himself that his life at home had been horrible enough in reality and that he did not need the bizarre dreams to remind him of what he had to look forward to if he was released. But still, the instant he dropped off into sleep, when he could no longer resist the tug of exhaustion, his dreaming began. It was usually the same dream, and it carried him into a more terrible place than any to which he had ever been in reality.

In the dream, he was transported to the lonely Greek restaurant in New York City, to the deserted dining room, dark, ominous, the chairs overturned on the tables, their legs protruding upward. The absence of sound was ponderous and he felt mournful and afraid as if the place were dead, as if it had been converted into a mausoleum and he had been sealed inside and forgotten.

He suddenly heard the familiar cry from far off in the distance. It was a human cry and he had heard it many times before. It was part of his life, part of him. It saddened him, but it did not surprise him. He had expected it, even looked forward to hearing it, as if its absence would have disturbed him.

Drawn to the wail, he moved forward through the darkened chamber, down the long center aisle between the tables. Like a sleepwalker, he crossed the tiny dance floor, which felt gritty under his feet, and passed the miniature platform on which a guitarist usually strummed out old-country melodies for homesick patrons. He pushed through the swinging doors into the kitchen just beyond the booth from which the owner scrutinized every happening.

The call now clutched at him with desperate fingers. It

wrapped itself around him as if it were immediately beside him. It pulled him to itself and dragged him toward the basement door, the door that led to the private chamber of horrors. The mere threat of being confined there conjured up the most fearsome images of abuse and torture.

After passing through the door, he stepped onto the shadowed landing and gazed down into the damp cavern below. A single lighted bulb, hanging unshaded from a loose overhead wire, cast a yellow glare in a wide circle around it. As the bulb swung slowly, it allowed its yellow light to splash forward and back over the dark figure of a man bent over an old wooden table upon which was tethered a naked woman. He could not see the face of the prisoner, but he sensed her agony. He did not actually see her bonds, but he felt them as if they were around his own wrists and ankles. He felt them burning, cutting into his flesh, rubbing it raw, drawing blood from the lesions they created.

Stumbling, nearly losing his footing, he charged down the wooden stairway. His mouth was twisted into a bitter, silent shriek of rage as he was propelled forward by an unseen force and thrust toward the dark man who, hearing the frantic advance behind him, turned and faced him.

Dimmy stopped as if frozen when the penetrating eyes of his father bored into him, searing his skin and melting his resolve with their authority. The moist lips beneath those eyes grinned at him with sadistic pleasure. A pale, clammy hand rose and beckoned him forward. With a crooked finger, it pulled him forward as if he were no more than a puppet on a string. *Come!* It commands. *Come see!*

Unable to withstand the power of that injunction, he slowly moved around his father's dark form and drew closer to the table on which Laura lay bound and trussed, waiting to be sacrificed. He saw that she was totally naked, her wrists and ankles bound to the corners of the table.

His eyes pleaded with his father to release the wretched woman who had done nothing to deserve this kind of punishment. The dark man, much to Dimmy's surprise, acquiesced. With a flick of his chin, he motioned to Dimmy to release the prisoner.

Overjoyed, he rushed to the table and, fingers flying, grappled with the knotted ropes until a low moan of appreciation rose from the captive's hidden face. He rushed to the head of the table and freed first one wrist and then the other, carefully avoiding the bleeding wounds in the gentle flesh.

Weeping happily, he reached out and took the tear-streaked cheeks into his hands and turned the tortured face to him. Laura! he wanted to cry out. Laura! But he was shocked into silence, deafened by the rush of his own anguish filling his ears. He could hear nothing but the low chuckle emanating from the beast behind him. Dimmy screamed and threw his hands up before his face, trying to blot out the vision. He wanted to erase the terrible tapestry of violation to which he had become witness. He could not live with that vision. It was not Laura on the table before him. It was Irene, his sister.

Dimmy knew he would not sleep again that night, but soon he would discard the fear permanently. He would create another opportunity to end his suffering. He lay wide awake in the darkness. He was in command of his behavior but not of his thoughts, his memories, or his dream. That constantly plaguing dream, he knew, would not leave him in peace until he entered into a permanent sleep.

Laura sat with Zeke in the front seat of his car in front of her motel. His arm was extended along the top of the seat, but he was careful not to touch her for fear of frightening her away by being too familiar too quickly. Leaning back against the passenger door, her head resting against the cool window, she surveyed him, his youthful good looks, the neatly trimmed hair, the carefully knotted tie, the straight, conventional attitude that was so old-fashioned but seemed so natural on him.

"I had a wonderful time tonight," Laura said, "even though the evening didn't turn out to be what I had expected."

He smiled. "Me too. I was pretty sure we'd be talking about Dimmy all evening."

"So was I." She sighed and shook her head. "It was a relief to forget for a few hours." She bit her lip. "As soon as I leave you he'll be on my mind again. I won't be able to get him out of my thoughts."

"If it helps any," he said sympathetically, "I promise I'll stay with him and help him. I won't abandon him."

"That does help," she said. "But it's not his mental state I'm worried about." She looked away, and Zeke saw the tears that suddenly appeared in her eyes. "I don't want him to go to prison." She dropped her eyes. "He doesn't deserve that."

Zeke studied her. He felt her vulnerability pulling at him. It touched a deep tenderness in him. He wanted to draw her to him. He wanted to fold her into his arms, press her face to his chest, feel her hair on his cheeks, put his lips to her skin. He wanted what he was feeling for her to pour out of him and spill onto her. He could not imagine how anyone could want to hurt her. But he knew that someone had used her mercilessly and that she feared a repetition of that experience. The awareness of that deep fear prevented him from fully expressing himself to her.

"I got the name of a lawyer for you," he said, forcing his attention away from his desire for her. He extracted a card from his jacket pocket and passed it to her. "A friend of mine says she's the absolute best."

Laura took the card and read the name and phone number on the back. "Harriet Doyle." She glanced up at Perez. "A woman?"

"Yes."

"Will we be better off with a woman attorney?" she asked.

Zeke hesitated. He knew that her uncertainty reflected her misgivings about the power of women, her own unconscious notion that men were equipped to come to the rescue while women needed to be saved. Viewing herself as relatively powerless, Laura had little faith in the power of other women.

"She's supposed to be a great trial lawyer," he said. "My friend says that if she takes a case, she goes all the way with it, fights like a tiger, as if it's her own life at stake."

"Will she take this case?"

Zeke shrugged. "You'll have to talk to her, Laura. She doesn't care about the money. She doesn't take many cases. You'll have to convince her that there's something more here than some rotten kid having a feud with an abusive parent."

Laura nodded. "You could help with that, couldn't you? You could tell her about Dimmy. About Nikki." She turned her face into the darkness. "About me."

"No," Zeke said softly. "You'll have to tell her, Laura. She'll want to hear it from you. All of it."

"Oh, God!"

Zeke allowed his fingers to touch her hair and was pleased when she did not pull away from him. "It had to happen sometime. You must've been prepared for it when you came out here." He shook his head. "The trial is going to be full of it. You know that. Eventually, you'll have to tell it all to the whole world. For everyone to hear. Eventually."

"Yes. Eventually."

He caressed her hair. "Eventually is now, Laura. It's nitty-gritty time."

"Yes," she said nodding absently. "I guess so."

A few minutes later Zeke dropped Laura at the motel entrance. From inside the glass doors, she watched his car pull away from the curb and disappear down the street. She was pleased that he was not glib and self-assured, that he held her in such regard that his behavior toward her was tentative and cautious. She liked him for that. The whole idea of being courted respectfully was pleasant to her, satisfying. It was certainly different, she suddenly thought with bitterness.

As she was contemplating what it would be like to be with him, she heard the harsh whisper of her name. She turned and faced a slight figure pressed into the shadows in the corner of the lobby.

"Laura?" Irene said as she stepped into the light.

Laura stared at the fully grown woman whom she remembered as a sad, frightened child in pigtails and Mary Janes.

"My God!" Laura said. "I wouldn't know you."

"I've grown up," Irene said. "but I would have known you anywhere."

The girl was taller than Laura remembered and carried herself straighter. She was dressed in tight jeans that accentuated her hips and her small, round behind; a white sweatshirt, sleeves pushed up almost to her elbows; and high-heeled black pumps. Her lustrous hair, once controlled carefully, now cascaded around her face and fell below her shoulders. Beneath the sweatshirt, Laura detected the evidence of a full bosom, evidence of a woman's body.

"How did you find me?" Laura asked.

"I talk to Dimmy every day," the girl said. "I wouldn't run off and leave him."

The bitterness in Irene's voice struck at Laura, offended her. "Is that what you think I did?"

"Isn't it?" the girl demanded. "Didn't you run away and leave us?"

"No," Laura said softly, glancing over at the desk clerk, who seemed interested in their conversation. "Yes."

She reached out, but Irene stepped back out of her reach. "But it had nothing to do with you, Irene." Laura let her arms fall to her sides. "I wasn't thinking of leaving you."

"No," the girl said. "You weren't."

Laura hesitated. "I don't mean it that way." She paused, wet her lips. "I didn't think you'd be so angry with me."

"This is all your fault," Irene said. "Everything that's happened since you left is your fault. Because you really hated us and didn't care. Because it made Dimmy crazy when you went away. You never liked us."

Laura shook her head vehemently. "That's not true, Irene." She lost her enthusiasm under the girl's cold stare. "You know I cared about you," she said softly, quietly.

The desk clerk moved closer to them, scrutinized them more carefully now, more openly. Laura glared at him, and he turned his attention away from them.

"Come to my room," Laura said. "We'll talk."

"I don't want to talk, Laura. I just wanted to see you and find out how you're doing without us."

The girl moved toward the glass doors.

"Irene! Please!" Laura said to the girl's back.

Irene pushed on the glass, opened it slightly, then stopped and turned back to Laura. "I saw you that night, you know. The night you ran away. I watched you leave. I was awake, in my room. I heard everything. I watched you go. You didn't even remember I was alive."

"Irene!"

"You didn't even glance my way."

There were tears on the girl's cheeks now. And her soft, wet face was no longer stiff with anger. She had softened, and her trembling lips revealed pain and despair.

"You didn't even say good-bye to me, Laura." She stepped out of the motel lobby.

He sat on the hood of his car, feet resting on the front bumper, and watched Laura and Irene act out their brief, pained confrontation. He observed silently, impassively, as his daughter bitterly departed from the motel lobby and rushed blindly down the dark street while Laura stared after her helplessly.

Nikki had followed Irene, assuming that she had left the apartment to meet with some boy. He suspected that she had become promiscuous in an attempt to punish him for something, he knew not what. She had grown bitter toward him, had become surly and disrespectful. They had begun to argue frequently—he accusing her of being loose, she denying any wrongdoing, replying that he was a suspicious, paranoid man.

Determined to catch her in the act, he had followed her as she drove to the motel and placed himself in a position to watch what happened.

He had watched Irene enter the motel, speak to the desk clerk, then move to a couch and sit. A rendezvous, he told himself. Meeting her lover. He would beat her back raw, he promised himself. He would drive the badness out of her, no matter how much beating it required.

While he worked himself into a frenzy, an automobile pulled up near the motel entrance. He expected its door to open and a young man to alight and run into the motel straight to Irene. He could imagine them embracing, kissing, his hands traveling along her back, down to her waist, below her waist. He ground his teeth viciously as he saw them, in his mind's eye, naked, writhing in bed together, sweating, grunting, chirping with delight.

What he saw next shocked him out of his heated fantasy.

A woman alighted from the passenger seat, moved to the glass doors, then turned and watched the car pull away. And that woman was his wife, Laura! His lost wife who had been missing for years. The wife who had abandoned him like a thief in the night. The wife who had stolen his money and deserted him without reason, who had betrayed him so shamelessly.

He watched as she and Irene spoke behind the glass as if in a silent movie. Mesmerized, he watched them argue. Laura moved toward the girl, and Irene backed away from her. Good girl! he thought. Don't let the witch touch you. He felt gratified when the girl turned her back on the traitor and left her standing in the lobby.

His eyes blurred. His face felt hot, flushed. He could feel the rush of adrenaline coursing through him. His blood pounded rhythmically like the wheels of a train clacking at every joint in the rails. His fingers played over the ropy scar on his neck, then caressed his upper arm, where the healed stab-wounds rose like welts under his shirt.

Once again, in his imagination, he was ransacking the apartment in New York, tearing the kitchen apart in search of his hidden money. Once again he was roaming the streets all through the night, haunting the places they had frequented together. Once again he burned with the humiliation of having been deserted by a woman. In his world that was unheard of, a totally unacceptable humiliation. In the old country, she would have been whipped and beaten until she realized the folly of such a disrespectful act. How could she do such a thing to him? Where would she ever find another husband as good as Nikki Pappas? There had to be something wrong with the woman's brain for her to have run from her home, her husband, her children. She had to be insane.

He had promised himself that when she returned—and he was convinced back then that she would return on her knees, begging forgiveness, pleading with him to take her back— he would be magnanimous. He would beat her only mildly, so that she would know that he cared. And then he would receive her back into his family, his bed, and his kitchen.

But months had passed without a word from her, and that promise had grown stale and brittle. His friends were laughing at him behind his back, snickering and enjoying his shame. He was diminished in their eyes. What kind of man was he, he imagined them saying, that his wife could desert him and he did not go after her, seek her out, find her, and punish her?

Had his own son not followed her example and rebelled against him? No son would attack his father unless the mother set such an example. He had been wrong to bring Laura into his home in the first place. She had corrupted his son and sullied his daughter, sending her on a path of sin with her own mother as an illustration. She had brought this tragedy down on him by corrupting his children.

The thoughts continued to flood into Nikki's mind, drowning him, choking him, pounding on the inside of his skull. They were old thoughts, gone over and examined many times, picked over until they were clean and bare like the bones of dead animals bleached under a desert sun. They had become unbearably painful as they continued to fester. They would have driven him mad had he not put them away finally, stuffed them deep into his unconscious. He had left New York City, created a new life for himself, reconciled to the belief that he would never taste vengeance. And now here she was before him, merely a street's width out of his grip, an instant away from him. Like a long-forgotten dream come true, she was almost in his grasp again.

Long after Laura's image was gone from behind the glass doors, he continued to stare, to wonder, to plot. He was not sure how, but he knew he would exact revenge. Now that he had found her, he would redeem his honor. His discarded dream of retribution would come true after all.

ELEVEN

At two o'clock the next afternoon Laura stood on a quiet street, much like a country road, in the affluent community of Bel Air, surrounded by expensive homes. She gazed timidly at the entrance to a two-story white Colonial fronted by two huge elm trees that cast deep shadows on the facade of the house. A brick walkway wound its way across a neatly clipped lawn. She hesitated before moving to the front door and was tempted to turn back to her rented car and drive out of that place as quickly as she could. She could have told herself that she was intimidated by the opulence around her, but she had sworn not to lie to herself anymore. No! It was the thought of facing the woman in the Colonial house that frightened her. She desperately needed Harriet Doyle's help, and she was afraid of being turned away.

Earlier that morning she had called the number Zeke had given her, expecting to use Perez's name to get an appointment with a brusque, businesslike lawyer. She had been surprised when Harriet Doyle herself answered the telephone and still further surprised to learn that she had reached the lawyer at her home and not at an office.

"My name is Laura Devon. I'm sorry to bother you at

home," she had apologized. "Would you rather I call later at your office?"

"I don't have an office," Doyle had said in a light, musical voice.

"I got this number from Dr. Zeke Perez," Laura had said.

Doyle had paused, as if trying to remember Zeke. "I don't know a Dr. Perez. Maybe you have the wrong Doyle."

"He got your number from a friend of his. A psychiatrist," Laura had said, cursing herself for not getting that name out of Zeke. "I really need your help."

She had heard Doyle's deep sigh and sensed her resistance. "I don't practice law anymore," she had said. "I've been retired for some time."

"I didn't know that," Laura had said. "I was told you were the best."

"Laura, I can hear that you're troubled, but there are many good lawyers in Los Angeles. I can refer you to several."

"There is already a lawyer on the case," Laura had said. "I'm just not sure he's the right one."

Doyle had sounded cautious. "Who is he?"

"Robert Haines," Laura had said.

"Look," Doyle had said. "You already have a capable attorney. I'm sure that whatever your differences are, you can straighten them out. And if not, you have the right to seek other counsel. But I can't help you."

"How do you know that?" Laura had asked. "You don't even know what the case is about."

"Trust me! I know!"

"My stepson's in jail awaiting trial, and his lawyer is advising him to make a deal and go to prison for four years. This is a boy who wouldn't hurt a fly. His lawyer is on the prosecution's side."

"Well, if he's guilty—"

"He's not guilty until a jury says so. Isn't that how the system works?"

Doyle had softened. "My reluctance to take this case doesn't have anything to do with you, Laura, or with your stepson. It has to do with me. I wouldn't be able to help you. I don't have the stomach for it anymore. I quit a long time ago." She had sighed and let Laura hear her sadness, which seemed to match her own. "I'm burned out, Laura. There isn't an ounce of courtroom energy left in me."

"That's too bad for me, isn't it?"

"I'm afraid so," Doyle had said stiffly.

"What about Dimmy, my stepson?"

"What's the charge?" Doyle had asked.

"Attempted murder."

"What?" Doyle had snapped. "What's Bob Haines doing on an attempted murder case?" When Laura remained silent, Doyle continued. "Never mind. Forget I said that. Look, I can give you the names of a couple of good lawyers. Got a pencil?"

"No!" Laura had said. "You're not being fair. You can't send me to someone else without knowing my story. Maybe that's how Dimmy got Mr. Haines in the first place. Maybe he just inherited him. Like you want to push me off now."

A long silence ensued during which Laura could hear the lawyer's labored breathing. Finally Doyle had spoken. "You know that pencil you don't have?"

"Yes."

"Get it out. I'll give you my address. You come here, and we'll have a drink. We'll talk, and then we'll see. Okay?"

"Okay!"

Now Laura stood before Doyle's door, pressed the bell with a trembling finger, and waited to be received. She hoped the lawyer would look like Franny, with gray hair, warm eyes, and a motherly aspect. She knew that she was wishing for the nearly impossible, but hoped still that there would be an instant rapport between her and Doyle as there had been between her and Franny, an instantaneous sense of sisterhood and love.

But when the door was finally opened and Doyle revealed herself, Laura feared that there would be no instantaneous sense of sisterhood between them. The woman before her—who smiled and said hello, called her Laura, and stepped aside to allow her into the house—was anything but a replica of Franny. She was a tall, slender black woman with a sharpness about her, like the finely honed edge of a bayonet, and a hardness like that of tempered steel. This was no nurturing earth mother. On the contrary, Laura was already intimidated. She'd had little association with black people and did not know what was expected of her.

"Have a seat," the lawyer said when they had entered her living room. "What would you like to drink?"

"Anything," Laura said. "It doesn't matter."

Doyle turned to the small bar in the corner of the large room. She wore tight jeans that clung to her long, shapely legs and black high-heeled pumps that made her close to six feet tall. Her red silk blouse was open at the collar, and her short hair was swept back over her ears. She was an elegant, beautiful woman by anyone's standards and Laura thought that she would have been envious of her, had she been white. But, Laura thought with some horror, the woman was as black as the ace of spades and had been absolutely right when she had said that she could not help Dimmy's cause.

The lawyer returned from the bar and handed her a glass. "Coke," she said. She raised her own glass. "Something a little stronger for me."

Laura was seated on a long, low beige couch that bisected the long room and faced a glass wall that opened onto a patio. Colorful rosebushes surrounded the lush back lawn. At the rear of the garden, Laura could see a kidney-shaped pool with a plastic slide at one end and a diving board at the other.

Doyle sat in a deep chair and studied Laura. Between them was a black lacquered coffee table with a thick, beveled glass inset. Laura placed her glass on a coaster, averting her eyes from the lawyer's sardonic smile, buying time.

Doyle sipped quietly, then sighed. "There's nothing like twelve-year-old scotch to break the ice. Right, Laura?"

"I don't drink," Laura said softly.

Doyle studied her for a moment. "But you used to, I'll bet."

"Yes," Laura said simply.

Doyle nodded. "And you quit? Good girl," she said. "I hope to do the same someday." She swallowed half the contents of her glass. "But not today," she continued. "I need the booze to deal with your reactions."

"I don't know what you mean," Laura said weakly.

Doyle laughed without any sign of hostility. "It's okay, Laura," she said. "I'm used to it. Don't you think it's happened before? Hell, every time I used to meet a potential client for the first time, I got the same kind of self-conscious glances you've been giving me since I opened the door on you."

"I'm sorry," Laura stammered.

"Don't be. It's not your fault."

Laura started to rise. "Maybe I should go."

The smile faded from Doyle's face. "Don't you want the referrals you asked for? Maybe you think I can't write? I assure you I finished both college and law school."

Laura fell back onto the couch. "I'm sorry. I didn't mean . . ."

Doyle leaned forward and set her glass on the coffee table.

"You sounded like a sensitive lady on the phone. Where's that lady? Bring her back. I want to talk to her."

"I'm here," Laura said suddenly growing a little angry.

"Well, then," Doyle said leaning back and lifting her feet onto the edge of the table. "Let's start all over again. I'm Harriet Doyle. You're Laura Devon. I'm a lawyer. You're in trouble. You called me for help. I tried to beg off. You insisted. I finally agreed to meet with you, right?"

"Right!"

Doyle smiled and her eyes softened. "Now! What the hell has any of that got to do with my black skin?"

"Nothing," Laura said. "I was just surprised, that's all. I was caught off guard. On the phone, you sounded . . . white."

Doyle grinned. "Shit, sister! I can be bad. You wanna rap. Jus' aks me." Doyle grew serious. "Is that better? You feel more comfortable if I'm injuring the English language? I like Mozart and Shakespeare, too. Should I trade them in for rhythm and blues and comic books? Will that ease your mind?"

"Look," Laura said, "maybe I deserved some of that, but you're overdoing it. If I hurt your feelings, I'm sorry. I didn't expect you to be black. You surprised me, and I feel stupid. All right! You've punished me enough. I'm ready now to get down to business. Are you?"

"Okay," Doyle said respectfully. "So there is a woman in there."

"Yes, there is. And right now, I'm worried that maybe you aren't the right lawyer for Dimmy. And you're right, of course. It has a lot to do with your color. I'm not sure that having a black lawyer, a black woman lawyer, is going to help Dimmy. I'm not sure he doesn't need a lily-white yuppie type who's part of the system—"

"Whoa!" Doyle interrupted. "I thought you were going to say a lily-white Jewish lawyer."

"I'm not a racist, Ms. Doyle."

"You can call me Harriet."

"Whatever I call you, I'm not a racist. At least, I don't think I am. Yeah! I grew up hearing 'nigger' this and 'nigger' that. That's a word I never use. But my husband would. I know how it feels to be called names, to be ridiculed. I've been there. And I don't care what you are. I care only that you don't hurt Dimmy's case. Because you're right. I know all about our world, and I don't want a jury crucifying my stepson because they hate his lawyer."

Doyle emptied her glass in one long swallow. She stared at Laura for a moment, then rose and moved to the bar. She poured half a tumblerful of Chivas, dropped a sliver of ice into the liquor, and returned her attention to Laura.

"You're tough, aren't you?" she said.

"I am now," Laura replied.

Doyle nodded again. "Okay, let me hear your story. You may just pry me out of retirement."

Dimmy, so exhausted from lack of sleep that he felt numb, struggled out of the bed and slipped his feet into his paper slippers. As he rose, he stumbled slightly and caught himself on the edge of the bed.

"Watch it!" the orderly said, clutching the boy's arm.

"What's your problem?" he said impatiently.

"I got dizzy," Dimmy said.

"Shit. You aren't even medicated."

"What do you mean, medicated?"

The orderly shrugged. "You know. On the yellows. You know. The fuzzy stuff that makes you walk like a zombie and pee down your leg." He laughed suddenly as if he had told a joke. "They ain't got you on that, so what the hell are you falling all over the place for?"

"I don't know."

"You don't know much, do you, kid?" The orderly squeezed Dimmy's arm until it ached. "You're just a dumb shit, ain't you? Don't know nothin'."

"I know I got to go to the bathroom," Dimmy said, pulling his arm out of the man's grasp. "If you don't let me, I'll do it on the floor."

The orderly laughed sadistically. "You do that and I'll make you clean it up with your tongue, motherfucker."

Dimmy examined the man's face. He searched for a glimmer of humor, but found only anger and cruelty. "Okay," he said. "If you put it that way, I guess I'll hold it in."

"You go ahead and do what you want, fuckhead. Don't let me stop you. Jus' remember, your shrink's waitin', and if you get him pissed off, you can end up in a jacket." The orderly chuckled mirthlessly. "I'd like that. I'd like to tie you up."

Dimmy pulled away from the man and shuffled out of his room into the hallway. The wooden benches lining one long wall were unoccupied. Far down at the opposite end, a patient in a blue striped robe and paper slippers shuffled along with the aid of two canes. He reminded Dimmy of a bug in the way the left leg and the right cane moved simultaneously followed by the right leg and the left cane, this process repeated slowly but rhythmically at a snail's pace.

The orderly followed Dimmy, mimicking him as he walked. He whispered to his back, "When I got done wit you, you wouldn't be able to walk nohow. You'd crawl on your belly like a snake."

Dimmy spun around suddenly. "What you want from me?"

The orderly, startled by the boy's sudden confrontation, stopped and stared at Dimmy. His body tensed, and he drew his right fist back slightly as if to throw a punch. Then, as he perceived that the boy presented no real threat to him, he lowered his arm and relaxed.

"Nothing yet," he said.

"So what's this all about?"

"Depends on what you're gonna tell about what happens around here. You know what I mean?"

Dimmy nodded, suddenly understanding. "I won't say anything," he said.

"You're seein' that shrink every fuckin' day."

Dimmy shrugged. "We don't talk about jail."

"What do you talk about in there?" the orderly asked suspiciously.

"You wouldn't believe me if I told you."

"Try me!"

Dimmy shrugged again. "We talk about my mother."

"Last time we talked, you said something I been thinking about," Dimmy said.

"What was that?" Zeke asked.

Dimmy, unchained now, was slouched in his usual chair, his legs extended, his hands locked behind his head. Zeke sat across the interview table from him. He leaned forward, elbows on the table top, and twirled a pencil in his fingers.

"You said that nobody in this room is nuts. Do you remember saying that?"

Zeke nodded. "I remember."

The boy wet his lips and stared off at the blank wall. "Everybody treats me like I'm crazy around here. Why's that?"

Perez nodded. "You're on a psychiatric ward, Dimmy. That's why."

"Well," he said, swinging his eyes back to Zeke's face. "What am I doing here if I'm not crazy?"

Zeke shrugged. "I didn't put you here, Dimmy. You did that all by yourself. You're the one who attempted suicide."

The boy flinched, then nodded. "Yeah. But does that make me a psycho?"

"Well," Zeke said. "It isn't the most rational of acts, is it? I mean normal people don't go around trying to hang themselves, do they?"

The boy hesitated for a long moment while staring at Zeke. Then he dropped his eyes. "I guess not."

"Why'd you bring it up?" Zeke asked.

The boy shrugged. "I don't like the idea of people thinking I'm crazy."

"Does it matter?"

"Sure, it matters."

"In what way?" Zeke insisted.

"It bothers me."

"Does it mean that you're less than perfect?"

The boy glanced up at him and snorted. "Shit! I'm so far from perfect, it isn't even funny. Who the fuck cares about being perfect? It's tough enough just staying alive."

"Maybe it bothers you," Zeke suggested, "because it means you don't have any control over your own behavior."

The boy paused. "Like I do things without really wanting to?"

"Yes."

"Yeah," Dimmy nodded thoughtfully. "That would bother the shit out of me."

"If it was true?" Zeke asked. "Or if people thought it was true?"

Dimmy laughed. "If it was true, nothing would bother me." Then he sobered. "If some people think so, that would bother me."

"Some people?"

"Yeah," he said. "Not everybody. I don't give a shit

about most people. But I wouldn't want some people to think I went nuts."

"Like who?" Zeke asked.

Dimmy dropped his hands into his lap and studied his entwined fingers. "My sister, for one."

"Who else?"

"Some of my friends."

"Anyone else?"

"My father."

Zeke nodded. "Yes."

"I wouldn't want him to think I didn't know what I was doing when I went after him. I wouldn't want him to think I didn't mean it. Because I really meant it. I would do it again tomorrow. Like that." He snapped his fingers.

"Who else?" Zeke asked.

"I don't know."

"Are you sure?"

The boy stared at Zeke; then his face broke into a grin. "You always want to talk about Laura, don't you?"

Zeke quickly rejected the implication of the accusation. "I thought you did."

"Me?" the boy said, pointing at his own chest. "Not me! You always bring her up."

"Do I?"

"Sure, you do." Dimmy nodded vigorously.

"Okay," Zeke said after a moment of silence. "Let's forget about Laura. Would it bother you if anyone else thought you were crazy?"

Dimmy shook his head slowly. "You're right," he said. "It would bother me a lot if Laura thought I was wacko."

Zeke nodded.

"But not because of what you're thinking."

"How do you know what I'm thinking?"

"I've got a magic eye." He closed one eye. "If I close

this one, the other one can see right into your head. I'm a psychic."

"You're a mind reader?"

The boy nodded. "Just like you can read me, I can read you."

"I never said I could read you."

"You didn't have to." Dimmy chuckled. "I know what you're doing. You're always analyzing what I say."

"What else do you know?"

"Are you sure you want to ask me that?"

Zeke hesitated. He had lost control of the session. He sensed that their roles had been reversed, that his patient had become the therapist and was toying with him, leading him to an awareness of some element of himself of which only the boy was conscious.

"I'm sure," he said, not at all convinced that he was.

Dimmy, head cocked slightly, scrutinized Perez carefully. "I know you'd like to fuck her."

Zeke felt his face growing hot. "What are you talking about?"

Dimmy's grin spread from ear to ear. "See?" he said. "I told you I could read your mind." The boy shook his head then. "Don't let it get you," he said leaning forward on his chair. "I'm not really so smart. Everybody wants to fuck her."

As soon as Zeke Perez realized that he could no longer safely deny what he was feeling for Laura Devon, he drove out to St. Andrew's in Pasadena where, many years before, he had been an altar boy. Four years of college, four years of medical school, and two years of a psychiatric internship had almost completely dulled his memories of those times. Then, as a fellow at UCLA's Neuropsychiatric Institute, he had met, worked with, and become good friends with Father

John Manley, a priest who was also a psychologist. Father Manley had briefly reintroduced him to the gentle satisfaction of possessing knowledge through faith, of having assurance devoid of questioning doubt, but Zeke had not returned to relying on prayer and God's will for solutions.

He had suffered some anxiety back then, however. Being torn between two divergent sets of beliefs had wreaked havoc with his ability to sleep, and for a short while he had even lost his voracious appetite over the inconsistencies he confronted daily in his work. If it had not been for the sensitive reassurances of Father John, he might have suffered an even greater decline. But John had sat up with him into the late hours, drinking too much coffee, smoking too many cigarettes, agonizing too much over contradictions that produced feelings of guilt while enraging him at the same time. The calm, levelheaded John had taught him to view himself a little less seriously, to find the humor in the human condition, especially in his own condition. And John had also helped him resolve the differences between what he did as a doctor and what he was as a man.

He found his friend in the rectory office, seated behind a small wooden desk, spectacles pushed down to the near end of his nose, tongue protruding slightly from the corner of his mouth as he wrote frantically with the stub of a pencil. The tall, balding priest looked cramped in the tiny room, two of its walls covered with shelves of dusty books from floor to ceiling, another with photos of many of the previous pastors and various religious ornaments, and the fourth an inappropriate but desperately needed window that faced a lawn and garden. He looked as though he had been folded onto his chair and would unravel if lifted out of it.

Zeke tapped gently on the doorjamb.

"Zeke!" Father John exclaimed when he saw him. The tall priest leapt to his feet, the top of his balding head coming dangerously close to the low ceiling, ran around the desk and swept Zeke into a bear hug. "How are you, my friend?" he said finally.

"I'm fine," Perez said.

"Come on in."

Father John led him into the small office, pulled a straight-backed chair over to the desk, and motioned for him to sit. John sat behind the desk, his back to the window, and faced his friend. "It's been such a long time."

"A couple of years." Zeke shrugged. "When your life gets busy, you drift away from old friends, but you never really forget them, do you? A piece of them stays with you, and then something happens to trigger the memories, and suddenly you feel lonely."

"You sound troubled," Father John said, the smile fading from his face.

Zeke nodded. "I am, John."

"Like the old days?" the priest asked.

Zeke laughed quietly. "I don't drink much coffee. I don't smoke at all anymore. I'm not very ambivalent about my work. So I guess in that sense this is not like old times. But I've got an unresolved problem that's immobilizing me, and in that sense, I haven't changed very much."

Father John smiled. "For such a gentle guy," he said, "you sure have a lot of anxiety. You're always grappling with one thing or another. Some issue always has you up in arms, but at the same time, you're a wonderful therapist. I don't know how you can be so effective when you're churning inside all the time." He paused and gazed warmly at his friend. "I love you, Zeke, but you're what we call an enigma."

Zeke frowned. "I don't find myself very mysterious, John. I usually understand what's going on with me. I just have a hard time resolving dilemmas. Even when I know what to do, it isn't easy for me. It's a lot easier to help other people decide what to do." He grinned at his friend. "I wish I could practice what I preach."

John laughed. "Now you're stepping over into my territory."

"There isn't that much difference between us, is there?"

"I can remember when you thought there was. I can remember long arguments when you would shout that Catholicism was a diagnosis, being Catholic an illness. Times when you blamed the church for all the ills of mankind."

"Yes," Zeke murmured. "I remember those times, too." He gazed out the window at the lawn. "I was always pretty good at blaming the other guy, wasn't I? Denial was my best sport. I could play it all day long and never get tired."

"Yes, you could."

Zeke sobered. "I can't let myself fall into that trap again. I need you to talk some sense into me. I need your simple logic to give me some perspective."

"All right. Tell me about it."

Zeke squirmed. "It has to do with a woman."

"Well, it's about time."

"Yes." Zeke grinned. "But it's a woman I shouldn't be . . . lusting after. Does that make sense in this day and age?"

"The terminology is old-fashioned, but the feelings haven't changed in thousands of years. 'Lusting' is a good word. It tells me exactly what's going on."

"She's the stepmother of a boy I'm evaluating for the court. A boy who tried to murder his father."

"Is this woman married?" John asked cautiously.

Zeke shook his head. "In the process of divorcing. They haven't lived together for a couple of years. But I'm not worried about her marital status. I'm not even worried about my relationship to her—if one exists. I mean, I would like to have a serious relationship with her, and if it happens one day, that'll be great. But I'm not agonizing over it. It's not my immediate problem."

"Okay," John agreed. He leaned back and steepled his fingers before his chest. "Tell me, then, what is your immediate problem?"

"I'm supposed to be impartial. Objective. I'm evaluating this kid, and instead of being focused on whether he's competent or not, what his mental status is, I'm thinking about ways to get him out of the mess he's in."

"Why?"

"Because that would please her, and I'm willing to do anything to please her."

"What about your obligation to the court, to the system?"

Zeke's face grew sad. "That's precisely my problem, John. I know I'm not doing the right thing. I know what I should be doing regarding this case, but I'm not doing it. I'm stalling. I'm not filing my reports. I'm dragging out my interviews. Anything to prevent a trial from taking place. And the worse part is that the kid knows how I feel about his stepmother."

"Excuse yourself," John said sternly. "Withdraw from the case before you do damage to it and to your career."

"I can't." Zeke bit his lip. "The case is my connection to her. If I stop seeing the boy, there'll be no reason for her to be interested in me."

John grunted. "You sound like a high school sophomore. What's the matter with you? Don't you see that you're doing an injustice to everyone concerned? The boy. The mother. And most of all, to yourself."

"I see that." Zeke slumped in his chair. "But it doesn't matter. I'm going to continue trying to get this kid off."

The priest nodded thoughtfully. "You'll make enemies doing that. You'll get some people very angry at you, and eventually you'll get fired."

"I know."

"And that doesn't deter you?"

"John," Zeke sighed dejectedly, "if I were being deterred, I wouldn't be here now seeking help."

The priest nodded thoughtfully. "What would you like me to do?"

"Help me."

"How?"

"I guess I want you to tell me it's all right."

"Why me, Zeke?"

The two men stared at each other for a long moment. "Because you're my friend."

John nodded. "Yes."

"Because you're also a therapist."

John nodded again. "Yes."

Zeke's voice nearly caught in his throat. "Because you're a priest?"

John murmured, "Yes."

TWELVE

By the time Harriet Doyle arrived at the county jail for her first conference with her new client, she had already arranged to be substituted in as attorney of record for Dimmy Pappas, had submitted a formal request for discovery to the prosecutor's office, had arranged to meet informally with Judge Bauer in his chambers at the end of his day, and had engaged in a minor confrontation with Robert Haines, whose feathers had been ruffled by being fired from the case.

"What do you think you're going to do that I couldn't?" Haines had bellowed at her over the phone.

"Let me see what you've accumulated for the defense and I'll let you know," Doyle had replied calmly.

"Accumulated!" he had shouted. "There isn't anything, goddammit! There isn't any defense."

"I'll send someone over to pick up the file," she had insisted. "I'd like to read what you've got anyway."

"Fine." He had paused and breathed heavily. "You know he's a loser, don't you?"

"No. I don't know that."

He sounded bitter. "You won't get a dime out of them. All you'll get is what the court pays you."

"You mean he's a financial loser," she had said.

"What did you think I meant? They're all losers the other way. You know that. They're all guilty as hell. You'll spin your wheels and then watch him go to the joint anyway."

"It's happened before," she had said. "It won't be the first time or the last."

Her attitude had infuriated him. "What the hell do you expect to get out of this case?" he had demanded. "There must be something going on I don't know about. What is it? Did the family suddenly come into a lot of money? You got some hot angle to get some headlines? What?"

"Listen, Haines," she had finally snapped. "Your client's sitting in jail scared to death, isolated from anybody who might care about him. I suspect that his civil rights have been violated a dozen times over, at least as many times as his body has. Meanwhile, he sinks deeper and deeper into the kind of hopelessness that can make a person want to stop living, make him want to tie a sheet around his neck and hang himself. And you haven't done a goddam thing for him except try to persuade him to cop a plea and put himself in prison. He doesn't need a lawyer for that, for chrissake. But then," she had concluded, "he hasn't really had much of a lawyer, has he?"

But Haines had touched on the very question she had posed to herself. What would she gain from trying this case? How could she benefit from taking on still another lost cause? Her career had been dotted with unwinnable cases. What could she achieve by adding one more?

As she had sat and listened to Laura's detailed description of existence in the Pappas home, of the relationship she had built with the boy Doyle was being asked to defend, of how much she owed that boy who had saved her from slipping even deeper into her private abyss, Doyle had felt herself being engulfed by hatred for Nikos Pappas, the real villain of the story. As she listened to Laura tell of being located by Zeke Perez, of setting out for California, leaving behind her job, her friends, the new life she had built for herself, of bravely and selflessly throwing herself into a dangerous situation in order to save the boy, Doyle had developed a deep respect for the woman. Sitting with Laura, hearing her recount her struggles in therapy, the battle to lift herself from the morass of self-debasement, Doyle had begun to feel the appeal of commonality between the two of them. Once, long before, having despised herself as something unworthy, Doyle would forever be sensitive to other women who suffered from that same malady.

It was for Laura that she was embarking on this defense. There would be little gain for herself. Only, perhaps, the satisfaction of winning, if she could, and denying the monster the pleasure of seeing his son sent off to prison. It was Dimmy who would gain the most—his freedom. And Laura would gain the satisfaction of knowing that she had done her best for the boy, that when he needed her, she had been there at his side; she had not abandoned him again.

Doyle sat at the visitors' table in the interview room as Dimmy was led in by an orderly who towered over him. She observed the boy's sweet, cherubic face, the frightened but intelligent eyes, the slight build, the close-cropped black hair, the stooped shoulders, and the submissive air. She watched as the huge orderly enjoyed pushing Dimmy onto a chair and then looked at her.

''You okay, Counselor?'' the orderly asked with mock respect. ''You need anything?'' He grinned at her as though he had some serious offer in mind. His eyes moved from her face down the length of her body and rested finally on her long legs.

''Leave us alone now,'' she said curtly and waved him out with one hand as if to indicate how insignificant she considered him.

He glared at her arrogantly, then turned and left the room, slamming the door behind him.

Doyle snorted. "Have you had trouble with him?" she asked Dimmy.

The boy, head bowed, shrugged silently.

"If you're ever mistreated, you have to tell me, Dimmy. He has no right to mistreat you."

Without raising his eyes, Dimmy nodded his understanding.

"I'm your new lawyer, Harriet Doyle."

"What happened to Mr. Haines?" Dimmy asked without raising his head.

"Lawyers sometimes have to bring in other lawyers to help out," she said. "No one can be in two courtrooms at the same time."

"I understand," Dimmy murmured, unconvinced.

"Mr. Haines wanted to continue with your case, but it was just impossible."

Dimmy raised his head and studied Harriet Doyle for a moment. A wise grin lifted the corners of his mouth, and his eyes crinkled at the corners as he shook his head. "You're full of shit," he said, not unkindly.

Doyle sat upright, flashes of anger glinting in her eyes. Ungrateful little punk, she thought. How dare he talk to me like that? She opened her mouth to devastate him with one of her famous cutting remarks, but then, recognizing the playfulness on his face, she thought better of it.

She relaxed, sat back, and nodded. "Yes! You're right," she said. "We fired the asshole. Laura and I." She paused. "Are you angry?"

"No," Dimmy said. "He would've bailed out anyway. He told me if I didn't plead guilty he'd get himself replaced."

"You don't mind starting over with somebody new?"

Dimmy shrugged. "It don't matter," he said sadly. "I'm burned anyway. I'll never get out of here."

"Why do you say that?"

He shrugged innocently and spoke without emotion. "I did it. I deserve whatever I get."

"If you feel that way, why don't we change your plea to guilty?"

"No."

"Why not?"

The boy pondered for a moment. "I did it," he finally said. "But I'm not guilty. I won't say I'm guilty."

"That doesn't make sense, Dimmy."

He shrugged as if to say, So what? "That's how I feel."

Doyle nodded thoughtfully, then spoke as if to herself. "You did something. You're in jail for it. But you don't feel guilty about it." She shook her head. "Let's start from the beginning. What exactly did you do, Dimmy?"

The boy gaped at her. "I stabbed my father. Don't you know what this is all about?"

"I know that's what you're accused of. I don't know what you really did or didn't do. I know what the police say and what the prosecutor says. But I don't understand what you're saying now. You say you did it but you aren't guilty. Does that mean you did it against your will? That you didn't mean to do it? Does it mean you don't remember doing it? Did you black out? Or are you saying you were justified in some way?"

"I did it," the boy said, nodding. "I didn't forget. I told them everything. All of it."

"I know that you confessed."

He nodded.

"Did Mr. Haines allow you to do that?"

"He wasn't there."

"Where was he?" she asked, surprised.

Dimmy hesitated. "That was before he became my lawyer."

"Wasn't another lawyer there?"

"I didn't have another lawyer."

"No one was there to advise you? Haines said the public defender . . ."

"Bullshit!"

Doyle sat back, a knowing smile of satisfaction on her face.

"No," Dimmy continued. "They asked me if I wanted one, and I told them no. So I signed that waiver—"

"What waiver?"

"The one that says I waived my right to counsel. You know."

"Yeah," Doyle said, suddenly less happy. "I know."

Dimmy looked at her with interest. "How come you don't know any of this?"

"Mr. Haines's file doesn't have very much in it. I've read your confession, but it leaves lots of questions unanswered."

"Like what?"

She paused and studied the boy's guileless face. "It doesn't tell me why you did what you say you did. And it certainly doesn't explain your statement that you did it but aren't guilty." She softened. "Dimmy, explain it to me. Tell me why."

Dimmy turned his eyes away from her and chewed his lower lip gently. "That's my business."

"No," she said. "It's my business, too. If you want me to defend you, you have to help me understand. If I don't understand, how can I make a jury be sympathetic to you?"

"I don't want sympathy."

Doyle shook her head. "And you won't get any unless you help me here."

She watched as Dimmy seemed to shrink in his chair. She

saw the little boy Laura had talked about emerge from inside the hard, unemotional prisoner before her. She saw the child-like eyes open in wonder, the soft lips tremble.

"Everybody wants me to make a deal," he said.

"I don't."

"Everybody else does. They want me to go away. They don't want to hear about it. But I want a trial. I want them to know about him." He shook his head slowly. "I don't want to tell them. I want them to see." He slumped in the chair. "But nobody wants to know anything."

"I do. That's why I'm here—to listen to you, to help you."

"It doesn't matter, anyway," he mumbled.

"Believe me, it matters."

A tear fell onto Dimmy's clasped hands. "Why should I get a break all of a sudden?"

"We don't have the time for this," Doyle snapped in irritation. "You want to be a whiner, you want to feel sorry for yourself, do it on your own time."

Startled, Dimmy sat up straight and lifted his head.

"Listen, kid," Doyle continued. "I can fight the prosecution and you can help me. Or I can fight you and forget the prosecution. But I can't take you both on. So you better make up your mind. Who's it going to be?" Doyle paused and examined the helpless boy. She wondered why she was feeling so frustrated. Surely she could understand his confusion, his distorted logic. After spending so much time in jail, he was entitled to be a little irrational.

"This is not going to be easy, Dimmy. Juries don't like teenagers who try to kill their parents. No one likes to think that a child can get up in the middle of the night and, without provocation, murder his father in his sleep. Do you know what I'm telling you?"

Dimmy nodded silently.

"You're right when you say that people want you out of sight and out of mind, punished and forgotten. They don't care what you might have endured or what circumstances drove you to strike out. Well, I want to make them care. I want to rub their noses in it. I want to make them live it with you, suffer it just like you did. Then I want them to send you home. I don't want you in jail, and I don't want them to want you in jail."

Dimmy stared at her in silence for a long moment. Finally he nodded. "What do you want to know?"

Doyle leaned forward. "What happened that night?"

"You know what happened."

"What happened to precipitate the attack on that particular night?" Doyle responded, irritated.

"I just had enough," Dimmy murmured.

"Enough of what?"

"Him."

"What about him?"

"He's a bastard."

"Every kid in the world says that about his old man at least once in his lifetime," Doyle snapped.

"Mine really is a bastard," Dimmy said almost too softly to be heard.

"Okay. What makes him so bad? Tell me about him. What did he do?"

Dimmy shook his head.

"Come on, Dimmy!"

He continued to shake his head. "I can't," he said.

"Why not?"

"I can't say it."

"Why not?"

"I just can't."

"Bullshit!"

Dimmy shook his head and pressed his lips together tightly.

Doyle, leaning back, sighed deeply. "You're making it really hard for me."

"I can't help it." He swallowed with difficulty. "That's the way it is."

"Okay," she said, rising to her feet. "If you won't give me what I need, I'll get it elsewhere. Don't you doubt that for one minute."

"Where?" he asked meekly.

"Don't you worry about it," she said. "Just sitting with you, talking with you, is enough for me to know that you're not a bad kid. And I know that something happened, something terrible, to make you attack your father. I know it. In here." She placed her hand over her heart. "I'm going to find out what it was. And when I do, I'm going to use it."

She noted the look of terror on the boy's face. What was he hiding? she wondered. Was he protecting someone?

"And then," she continued. "I'm going to get you out of this filthy place once and for all."

Nikki followed the green cab from the Century City mall west toward Santa Monica and parked down the street from the apartment building where it let its passenger out on Bentley just south of Olympic Boulevard. He made a quick U-turn and slipped in under the overhanging branches of a tree between an old brown Buick and a bright yellow fire hydrant, shut down his engine, and sat back to observe. He watched Laura exit the cab, bend over and speak to the driver through his open window, then straighten and hurry up the few steps to the security doors of the apartment building. The cab, its engine idling, did not move off.

He wondered what she was doing in that building. Was

this the home of the man she had been seeing? he wondered. The man who drove her back to her motel at night? The one who sat with her for so long in the darkness of his car? The one who kissed her lightly on the cheek as they parted? Whose hand touched her so possessively as he bade her good night?

Nikki felt the familiar rage begin to flow through his veins. He had not been able to harness his anger. Since the night she had slipped away from him, without her clothing, without her jewelry, without her makeup, so anxious to escape that she was willing to sacrifice anything, he had lived with an all-consuming fury. His face suddenly grew flushed. He could feel its intensifying heat. Beads of sweat accumulated on his brow and on his upper lip. The muscles in his legs grew taut and leapt in tiny spasms. He clutched a jerking knee with one hand while the other unconsciously fondled the knotted scar on his neck, the scar that he wore proudly, like a medal of honor.

From the very first he had been tormented by the thought that Laura had fled from him in order to vault into some other man's bed. He had pretended to be outraged that she had deserted him. But the truth was that he cared much less that she had left him than he cared that she was being used by another man. In fact, not having her around him was not much different from having her around, since she had begun to annoy him with her whining, her irascibility, her constant drinking.

But the knowledge that she was with someone else had festered in him and grown intolerable. The visions he conjured up in his mind struck at him as viciously as had Dimmy's dagger. Images of Laura locked in some young man's passionate embrace flooded through him. Portraits of her face twisted in ecstasy, soft whimpers punctuated by sharp cries of unbearable pleasure emanating from her, filled his mind. He could feel her pleasure, and he grew hard as he imagined it. He longed for her at those times. He wanted to be that young man thrusting into her. He wanted to hurt her.

Nikki continued to watch as she came out of the building and climbed into the back of the cab. Through the cab's rear window he saw her lips move, saw her settle back into the seat and wave to someone he could not see inside the building. As the cab pulled away from the curb, he started his engine and moved forward, intending to follow, but as he passed the building, he saw an elderly woman remove a sign from the front wall. He stopped, jumped from his car, and ran to the woman.

"Am I too late?" he asked breathlessly.

She smiled at him. "Afraid so," she said. "Just rented it this minute."

"Damn!" he said. "Was it by any chance a penthouse?"

"No," she said. "They're easy to rent. This was on the ground floor."

"Damn!" he moaned. "Just what I wanted."

"I rented it to the nicest girl. Gave me three months' payment in advance. Can't beat that, can you? She's moving in tomorrow, taking it as is. I don't have to paint or anything." The woman smiled kindly at him. "Why don't you leave me your name and phone number in case something else comes up?"

"No," he said. "I'll stop by again in a couple of days."

"You could lose out that way," she said.

Nikki smiled. "No," he said. "I have a good feeling about this place. I feel lucky here. I'll be back. I'm sure there'll be something for me."

"Sit down, Ms. Doyle," Judge Bauer said, half rising from the seat behind his desk. "Might as well be comfortable while we clear this up."

"Thank you, Your Honor," she said. She settled into one of the two chairs facing his desk, then looked at him and said innocently, "Clear what up?"

The judge smiled benignly at her. "We're going to get rid of this Pappas matter, aren't we?"

"I certainly hope so," Harriet Doyle said warmly. "I'd like nothing more than to be sent home with my client under my arm."

Judge Bauer's office was little different from the other judges' offices she could recall. Like most, it was sedate, austere, almost frugal in its decoration, and masculine to a fault. Its hue was the inevitable brown—leather paneling, carved desk, stained pine bookshelves. Two standing lamps, one on either side of the room, wore light beige shades like Easter bonnets, and the carpeting was a dull battleship gray. Otherwise, all was brown, including the judge's tanned face, accentuated by a mane of thick white hair.

"Have you had time to familiarize yourself with the evidence?" the judge asked, ignoring her remark.

"Not yet, Your Honor," she replied. "I received a file from the previous attorney, but I'm sorry to say, it's a little flimsy."

"Flimsy?" The judge appeared surprised.

"More like empty," she said. "It contains a police report from the arresting officer, a copy of the boy's alleged confession, a statement from the victim, a description of the weapon, and a report of the treatment the victim received at County General, with an assessment of his injuries."

The judge leaned forward slightly. "What more do you need, Counselor?"

Doyle scrutinized Judge Bauer. She needed to determine how serious he was. She stared into his cold blue eyes and resisted shivering at what she saw there. She knew nothing about Judge Bauer, and yet his attitude was all too familiar to her. Protocol required her to respect him, however, and to assume that he was a man of integrity. But his opening gambit had caused tiny alarm bells to explode into a warning clamor.

"Hold it a second," she said, raising her hands as if in supplication. "Am I missing something here?"

"I sincerely hope not," the judge said. "I want us to be clear as to what our duty is in this matter."

"I want that, too," Doyle said, wary of him now. She could hear the caution which had crept into her voice. "What is our duty as you see it?"

"To see that justice is done," he said.

"I'll buy that."

"To see that the system works smoothly and quickly."

"I'll buy that, too."

He paused, watched her for a moment, then spoke again. "To avoid spending the taxpayers' money needlessly."

"I don't care about the taxpayers' money," she said. "Every accused person is entitled to a day in court."

The judge's jaw grew tight, and his lips, pressed tightly together, nearly disappeared. Finally he sighed deeply. "When I was told that Haines had been replaced, I was very pleased," he admitted. "I thought that at last we'd get rid of this miserable case. Haines couldn't get anything straight. He was totally ineffectual." Bauer brought the force of his unfriendly eyes to bear on Harriet Doyle.

"So I was pleased when I learned that the new replacement was named H. Doyle. Ah, I thought, an Irishman. A good, levelheaded attorney who knows the way the game is played." He smiled almost nostalgically. "You see, I had feared that I would draw a Shapiro or a Ginsberg, and the thought of sitting through hours and hours of asinine lecturing from some half-assed yuppie kike lawyer turned my blood cold. Yes! I was happy when I heard about you." He sighed and shook his head slowly.

"And then you walked in. I will admit I was surprised when I first saw you, but I quickly realized that having you on this case could be an advantage. A woman. Especially a black woman. You must have had lots of experience with intolerable kids, little terrorists. You would understand the need to strike hard, I was sure. You would agree that we cannot allow these bastards to take complete control of our streets. For a moment I thought you would be perfect. Not that I've completely changed my mind. Not yet, anyway." He attempted a smile briefly, then discarded it. "Although you have shaken my faith somewhat with your naïveté."

Doyle grunted. "It's been a long time since I was accused of being naive, judge."

The judge shook his head disapprovingly. "I want you to understand that I will not look kindly upon a long, protracted trial. Do you understand what I'm saying?"

Doyle nodded silently.

"We have an obviously guilty perpetrator in custody. A boy who viciously attacked his own father while the poor man slept and stabbed him numerous times. Barbaric! An unsolicited attack. A premeditated attempt to murder his own flesh and blood. That's the kind of beast this boy is. We have enough testimony to convict him. The boy confessed, and that confession is untainted. There was not a trace of coercion. He needed no inducement other than his own desire to brag about his obscene deed. He enjoyed describing every detail of the dastardly act." His voice had risen as he spoke, and his breath became short.

"There's no need to drag this out any further," he said reducing the volume of his speech. "Is there? Why make the situation more painful than it already is? Why cause more suffering and embarrassment to the father who has already been shamelessly victimized by his ungrateful son?''

The judge stopped and waited. Harriet Doyle saw the expression of satisfaction that had crept over his face. ''You really think you're going to get me to persuade him to plead guilty?'' she asked in amazement.

''Absolutely!''

''That's what you wanted from Haines.''

''Of course. The state made a very generous offer, and I suggested strongly he accept it. It's a good offer, and it won't hang out there forever, you know.''

Doyle shook her head. ''My client won't plead guilty.'' She raised her chin determinedly. ''Because I will advise him not to.''

The judge glared at her incredulously. ''Am I going to have trouble with you?''

She shrugged, wary of him but not willing to let him know it. ''That depends on what you want from me.''

''I want you to be reasonable,'' he snapped.

''In order to be reasonable,'' she said, ''I need to know something about my client before I send him off to serve four miserable years in a maximum-security prison. I need to know more about this alleged crime and the circumstances surrounding it. I need to know more about the victim, his accuser. What was his role in all this? I need to find out how the police managed to get a voluntary confession—if it *was* truly voluntary. I need to know a lot more about what could make a perfectly lovable kid become a potential killer. I need to know so much that it might be months or even years before I could even consider changing our plea.''

''You're making a mistake,'' the judge said ominously.

"I might never get to that point," she continued. "Who knows?"

"Very clever," the judge said angrily. "You think you have the balls to take me on?"

Doyle rose and gazed down at him. "If it gets down to that, I've got more balls than you could ever imagine, judge."

He laughed coldly, mirthlessly. "You know what, little girl?" he said. "Long after that insignificant Greek piece of shit has been salted away behind bars where he belongs and is forgotten, you will be hauling your ass into court day after day. And you're going to appear before me again and again, whether you like it or not. And trust me, it won't take many of those days to make you wish you had a lot less balls and a little more brains."

Her shoulders sagged as she remembered telling Dimmy that she could only fight one enemy at a time, only the prosecution. Little had she known then that she would be fighting the judge as well. She shook her head and smiled tightly. "Your Honor," she said, "when you finally decide to open your eyes and really look at me for the first time you may still tell yourself that you're seeing some feebly ignorant outsider standing in your courtroom. You may actually convince yourself that you're looking at a toady nigger. You may even believe I'm ready to do a version of a down-home shuffle, and pick up the pennies you toss at my feet. But I'm happy to say, you will be dead wrong."

She grinned at him and her mischievous eyes sparkled with the excitement of war. "I'm going to take this case to trial whether you like it or not. Yes, sir. I'm going to shove this case, along with all its dirty linen, right down your throat. I'm even going to win it. What do you think of that?"

She turned and strode to the door, leaving him speechless. With her hand on the knob, she turned and gazed back at him. "You're going to see more balls and brains flung at you than you've ever had flung at you anywhere, anytime, by anyone in your entire judicial career." She grimaced, and her face grew hard and dangerous. "And you can bet on that, Your Honor."

THIRTEEN

Zeke Perez chose a small corner table and ordered a scotch and soda. It was cocktail hour at the Beverly Wilshire Hotel and the room was half filled with young lawyers from the dozens of law firms in the Beverly Hills golden triangle and smartly dressed young women. At the piano, clad in a tuxedo and wearing an abundance of gold jewelry, an aging entertainer played and sang Cole Porter songs. A group of four young women at a table nearby glanced repeatedly at Zeke, then giggled, whispered, and, he supposed, speculated about him. He could not decide if their behavior meant he was a desirable catch or that he was hopelessly out of place in blue jeans, tennis shoes, and a maroon V-neck sweater. He had dashed right over after his last appointment of the day and, fearful of being late, had not bothered to change.

Harriet Doyle had called him between sessions.

"Yes," she had said when he commented on how lucky she was to reach him at five minutes before the hour. "I'm very lucky that way. Besides, Paul Murphy is an old friend, and he's taught me the ins and outs of the shrink business. I understand he's the one who gave you my name and number. And you turned me over to Laura Devon."

"That's right."

She chuckled softly. "I don't know whether to thank you or clobber you."

"I'm sorry." He had detected a note of seriousness under what was meant, he supposed, to be a joke. "She needed someone and Paul said you were the best."

"I'm flattered," she had said flatly. "But my life was relatively simple until I got involved with your friend. I really don't know if I welcome the complications."

"Then you're not going to take her case?" he had asked.

"I'm already on it," she had said. "That's why I'm calling you. We have to meet. Soon."

"How soon?"

"How about this evening?"

"You know," he had said then, "I've been brought in by Bob Haines. How kosher is it for us to meet?"

She paused for a moment. "How religious are you?" she asked.

"Not very," he said in surprise.

"So what do you care if it's kosher or not?"

He laughed.

"If it bothers you, go to confession after we're done."

They had agreed to meet in the bar at the rear of the Beverly Wilshire Hotel.

"How will I know you?" he had asked.

"Oh, you'll know me," she said, and she laughed musically. "What are you wearing?"

He glanced down at himself. "A maroon sweater and jeans."

"No problem," she had said.

He had ushered his last patient out quickly, thrown his notes into a drawer, turned his answering machine down to two rings, and hurried to his car. He fought the rush hour traffic through the canyons of Century City, turned right onto Santa Monica Boulevard, crept along locked into bumper-to-bumper congestion through downtown Beverly Hills until he reached Beverly Drive, where he took another right and jumped over the three blocks to the hotel. His watch had told him he was late, but still he arrived, was seated, and had a drink in his hand before she showed up.

He recognized Harriet Doyle the moment she entered the bar. He would have known her anywhere. She was at least six feet tall and elegantly dressed in a tailored business suit that accentuated her exceptional body and caught the eye of everyone she passed.

He watched her pause at the piano and efficiently inspect the room until she saw his maroon sweater. Her eyes caught his, and she started toward him. Yuppie eyes from around the room followed her progress as she moved lithely among the round tables, and Zeke knew he was about to become the envy of every man in the room.

"Mr. Perez!" she said as she towered over him, smiling whimsically.

"Miss Doyle?" He stood and extended his hand.

She grasped it with her long, red-tipped fingers, then sat across the table from him. She crossed her legs, then she pulled a dark cheroot from her handbag, struck a wooden match on the bottom of the table, and blew a thin stream of blue smoke into the air over his head.

"Do you mind the smoke?" she asked.

"No."

"What are you drinking?"

"Scotch," he said.

"Good!" She grinned at him. "I'll have the same."

He signaled to the waitress.

"What do you think of our client?" she asked.

Before he could respond, the waitress appeared at their side. "One of these for the lady," he said.

Doyle smiled at her. "But put the soda on the side and

give me a double straight up." She returned her attention to Zeke. "Our client?"

"What do I think about him?"

Doyle nodded.

"Well," Zeke said cautiously. "He seems to be a nice boy."

"I'm not looking for gossip, Perez.," Doyle said. "What's your first name?"

"Zeke."

"Okay, Zeke. The question is, is he legally insane? Do I have a shot at a diminished capacity plea? Does he need psychiatric treatment?"

Zeke shook his head. "Am I allowed to go into this with you?"

The waitress set two glasses down in front of Doyle and disappeared.

Doyle lifted the scotch. "Here's to kids who kill their parents and the lawyers who defend them." She raised the glass to her lips and delicately swallowed half its contents.

When she had returned the glass to the table, she lifted her eyes to him again. No laughter remained in them. "You bet your ass you can go into it with me, Zeke. You can go into it right now, or you can go into it later on, or you can go into it a month from now. Of course, if you want to, you can wait and go into it on the witness stand while I'm cross-examining you about your qualifications to go into it at all."

"Don't get angry," he said.

She smiled at him. "I'm not angry, Zeke. I'm impatient. I've got a kid who's been in jail for more than a year, and no one's been given the opportunity to even contemplate whether or not he's guilty of a crime. His constitutional right to a speedy trial has been misplaced somewhere in the broom closet down in the basement. He's being punished as if he's guilty while he's still presumed innocent, and nobody cares. Hell! Who needs to be found guilty by a jury? This is better.

This way we can lock him up and save all the cost and inconvenience of a protracted trial.''

She set her elbows on the table and leaned toward Zeke. ''Even if I get him off scot-free, he's never going to get that year back. It's gone. One of the best years of a kid's life. So when you resist assisting me, I have no alternative but to show you how impatient my client and I really are.'' She grinned. ''Let me put it another way—''

''I got your point,'' Zeke said.

''Good!'' She sat back and relaxed. ''Now we can be friends.''

At eight o'clock that night Zeke was at Laura's motel, his arms filled with Chinese delicacies in little white containers. He knew that the two of them could not possibly eat all that he had bought, but he could not resist splurging. Even if she ate only one bite of each item, he told himself, it would be worthwhile for him, because he had suddenly discovered that he enjoyed pleasing her. He had ordered Chinese chicken salad, egg rolls, moo shu pork, shrimp lo mein, moo goo gai pan, pressed duck, and twice-fried Manchurian beef.

She opened the door at his knock and found him weighted down with his burden.

''What did you buy?'' she asked as he set the heavy carton down on the luggage rack.

''Everything I could think of that you might like.'' He grinned. ''When I came through the lobby, the clerk watched me like I was a thief. I guess they frown on eating in the rooms.''

''This isn't eating!'' Laura exclaimed. ''This is feasting. How are we going to eat all this?''

''We're not,'' Zeke said as he set the food out on a table. ''We're going to taste it all and give the leftovers to the suspicious clerk out front.''

"How do you know he likes Chinese food?"

"Everybody likes Chinese food," Zeke said. "Especially scrawny, hungry-looking guys like him."

And he was true to his word. Using chopsticks expertly, he fed her a mouthful from each of the white containers, except for the crisp duck, which she ate with her fingers.

She pointed to the chopsticks in his hand. "Where did you learn to use them?" she said through a mouthful of moo goo gai pan.

"I'm an old hand," he said, his mouth just as full as hers. "I've had a love affair with the Orient since I was a kid and my dad came back from Korea with a dragon-embroidered satin jacket and a set of ivory chopsticks with my name carved on them in Korean."

He took her hand in both of his and attempted to teach her how to use the sticks, but she could not master it and ended up spilling rice and bean sprouts on the carpet.

"That's probably why they don't want people to eat in the rooms," she said half seriously.

"Probably," he said. "But since you're moving out tomorrow, we won't worry about it, will we?"

"No, we won't," she said touching his hand softly.

When they had eaten more than enough, he carried the remaining food out to the clerk. While he was gone, Laura cleaned up as best she could. On her hands and knees, she picked the rice out of the carpet nap. The towels they had used as napkins she carried back to the bathroom. The empty duck container and one pair of wooden chopsticks she threw into the wastebasket beside the bureau.

Zeke returned with two cans of soda from the machine down the hall, and they sat on the bed, backs propped up against the wooden headboard, and sipped soda.

"I'm stuffed," she said. "But it was good."

He glanced over at her. "You happy?" he asked.

She nodded. "Yes."

"I'm glad," he said.

"For a while I forgot why I was here," she said.

He took her hand, and she did not pull away. He had initially feared sitting on the bed with her lest she think he intended to force himself on her. He did not want to damage the fragile beginnings of their relationship.

"I met with Harriet Doyle today," he said.

"How did it go?"

"I don't know," he said.

She twisted around to face him. "Did you have a problem with her?"

"No, no," he said. "It's just that I want so much to help you. I want to get Dimmy out of jail, but I can't, and I feel helpless."

She leaned over and touched his cheek. She had never been lucky enough to attract a man like him, she realized. He was kind and sensitive and did not use her for his own gratification. All the men in her life had been hard and cruel and manipulative. She and they seemed to sense each other, like missiles seeking each other out blindly, as if she possessed a certain radar that guided her directly into the most painful relationships. And she was not sure she knew how to relate to any other kind of man. She did not know if she could tolerate kindness for any length of time. "It's okay," she murmured, "It's okay."

He kissed her then, suddenly, without thinking first about doing it. Their mouths were cool from the soda and felt pleasant and sweet to each other. He slipped his free arm around her waist and gently pulled her closer to him. She moved up against him willingly and pressed her body against his so that she was half lying on him, one knee between his legs pressed up against his hardness.

His hands, now on her back, holding her on top of him,

fumbled with the zipper on her dress, found it, and pulled it down to her waist, then slipped inside the open dress and caressed her soft skin. She trembled under his touch, and her mouth opened and invited him to kiss her more fervently, more passionately. Soon he felt her losing herself in him. He felt her entire body become liquid, mold itself to him so that they were as one, hungry for each other, willing to surrender to each other.

Zeke pulled away from her embrace when the shrill cry of the telephone invaded the warm silence of their lovemaking. She laid her cheek on his chest and sighed deeply. Zeke, both hands on her shoulders, held her at a slight distance. That instant when they had entered the eye of a wonderful storm of intimacy had been shattered. They had found their magic moment, but the outside world had coldly invaded their privacy, and it was swiftly slipping away.

Laura leaned across him and picked up the phone. "Hello," she said. She adjusted the instrument against her ear. "Hello," she repeated.

"What is it?" Zeke whispered softly.

"Hello!" she said again.

She covered the mouthpiece with her hand. "I can hear someone on the other end, but he won't speak." She lifted her hand. "Hello!" she insisted.

"Hang up!" Zeke said.

She stared at him.

"Don't stay on with an obscene call. That's what they want. Hang up." He sounded angry. He took the phone from her hand and replaced in on its cradle.

He shook his head. "I'm sorry." He slipped out from under her and stood up.

"What are you doing?" she asked.

"I can't do this," he said. "I'm uncomfortable here."

"It's the phone call, isn't it?"

"I don't know," he said.

"You think it was him," she said. "You think it was Nikki."

He shrugged. "I don't know who it was. Most likely a kid's prank. But I don't want you upset. When I leave, I'm going to tell the clerk to hold your calls."

"All right," she said. "Whatever you say."

He frowned at her. "Not whatever I say, Laura. What's best and safest for you."

She nodded. "Then why don't you stay? That would make me feel safest."

He shook his head. "I don't think so."

"Why not?"

"I don't know," he said. "I just feel that I have to go home. I need to think about my feelings. Need to be by myself for a while."

"Okay," she said.

"Are you being compliant?"

"No. Just realistic. I can't make you stay if you don't want to."

He nodded and moved toward the door.

"Did I do or say something wrong?" she asked.

He shook his head. "It's me. It's not you."

"All right," she said. "Good night."

He nodded again. "Good night, Laura." He opened the door but did not step out. Instead, he turned back to her. "I'm sorry," he said. "You may not understand this, but I have very scary feelings about you and I have to sort them out. I have to know if they're real or some power trip I might be on."

"I said it's all right, Zeke."

"I know you did," he said. "I just wish I felt all right about it myself."

When Harriet Doyle got home, she dumped her handbag on the small desk in her bedroom and flung her clothes off as she moved toward the bathroom and a hot shower. She stood for a moment before the full-length mirror and admired herself completely unclad.

"Not bad for an old broad," she said to herself running her hands down the length of her perfectly firm torso. "But you're feeling your age today, aren't you, baby?" She let her shoulders sag somewhat and grimaced at her reflection. "This case is going to be the end of you. You wait and see," she said to herself in the mirror. "It's unwinnable and you won't bend. So you are going to break."

She turned on the shower, stepped under the dense stream of steaming water, and let it cascade over her head and shoulders. Several minutes later she stepped out, wrapped herself in a thick full-length bathrobe, and strode into the bedroom where she poured herself a hefty shot of Cutty Sark.

Drink in hand, she removed a microcassette recorder from her purse, pressed the rewind button, and made herself comfortable on her bed.

"Okay, Dr. Perez. I thought you'd be a maximum turkey, but you turned out to be not half bad," she said when the tape had stopped rewinding and she had pressed the play button. "Let's hear once again what you've got to say for yourself."

The first voice she heard was her own, stridently priming him, setting him up, getting him cooperative with her lecture about injustice. She pushed the fast-forward control and held it for a moment. When she released it, she heard Zeke Perez say, "You want to know about Dimmy's mental status?"

"Yes," she heard herself say.

"Okay," he said stiffly. "There's no evidence of psychosis or physical brain damage. His general mood is calm, although he appears to be slightly depressed. He's relatively cooperative. After some prompting he engages in conversation freely. You might even say he's cooperative. He's articulate and appears to be of average or above average intelligence. He's obviously suffered some suicidal ideation. As you know, he made one attempt at suicide in his cell. But now he denies any suicidal or homicidal thoughts. He is not highly motivated toward treatment but has expressed some willingness to cooperate with a mandated treatment program."

A prolonged silence ensued. Finally she heard herself say, "Go on!"

"That's it," he responded.

"What do you mean, that's it?"

"That's all I intend to say in court."

"Aren't you going to tell me what happened?"

She heard him laugh. "I thought you didn't want to gossip?"

"That's not gossip. That's the stuff I need to know. Why did he attack his father?"

"It's obvious, isn't it?"

"It may seem obvious to you, but I don't trust obvious. I want to know what was in his head at the time."

"I can't help you with that because I don't know. He won't talk about it. He may not know himself."

"How is that possible?"

"He may not remember. He may have blanked it out, forced himself to forget. It isn't uncommon for people to make themselves forget extremely unpleasant, traumatic experiences."

"You don't know anything about his background?"

"Certainly." He sounded exasperated. "I know a lot about him."

"Like what, for instance?"

"I know he's been brutalized for years. Both Dimmy and his sister. The mother, too. And the stepmother. I know the father was both verbally and physically abusive to the boy. Dimmy was beaten regularly, almost ritualistically. He was handcuffed, tied up, and locked in seclusion for hours. I know that his father threatened to kill him on many occasions. At one time he put a gun to the kid's head and pulled the trigger on an empty chamber."

"How do you know all this?" she heard herself ask.

"From bits and pieces in our interviews. From conversations with Laura. But I don't know why he did it."

"*If* he did it!"

"He did it." Zeke's voice contained a special sadness. "We all know what happened that night. I just don't know why."

"You tell me what happened that night."

"It's obvious. Dimmy waited for his father to fall asleep. Then he crept up on him in the dark and stabbed him many, many times."

"Yes," she said. "But why?"

"You want my official opinion?"

"If that's all I can get."

Zeke's voice, which had become somewhat relaxed, now reverted to that monotone of official, objective, sanctimonious professionalism, which Doyle despised. "In my opinion," he said, "the alleged offense was the direct result of the long-standing abuse suffered by the defendant and his sister at the hands of their father. This abuse was psychological, verbal, physical, and perhaps sexual." There was a pause at this point, and the tape ran silently for a long moment. "He had been threatened with death on numerous occasions.

He became increasingly frustrated, desperate, resentful, and angry. At least, in part, he seems to have acted out of a fear that his father would one day kill him. Dimmy had been under severe, unrelenting stress for many years, and he finally reached a breaking point."

Doyle heard herself clear her throat. "Do you believe what you just said? That he reached a breaking point and snapped?"

Another long pause followed when all she could hear was the soft whirring of the recorder's miniature motor.

Finally Zeke said, "No."

"But you intend to say it?"

"Yes."

"Why?"

"Because it's my job."

"But if you don't believe—"

Zeke interrupted. "The court wants a professional judgment. Judge Bauer is not interested in my personal opinions. I can't walk into court and tell him that my gut feeling is that something's wrong here. That it doesn't add up. That my clinical conclusions make sense, but my instinct disagrees."

"Why can't you? Do you have to do everything by the book? Are you afraid to take a little risk?"

"With my career?"

She heard herself laugh. "Career? Your career takes precedence over a kid's life spent in prison?" Another long silence followed. "Okay," she heard herself continue. "If you won't take a risk in court, at least tell me what you really think. Tell me about your instinct, your gut feelings. Tell me what you wouldn't tell the judge."

She heard him clear his throat. She could see him again, in her mind's eye, squirming in his seat, rubbing the palms of his hands together, eyes darting this way and that, wetting his dry lips with the tip of his tongue. "All right," he said finally. "I don't think he reached a breaking point and stabbed his father. It's an obvious explanation and I'll use it in court, but I don't believe it."

"Why not?"

"Because Dimmy presents a classic picture of hostage syndrome, and hostages don't strike out at their captors."

"Explain!"

"Hostages go through different periods of adjustment—rage, denial, obstinacy, compliance, and if they're held long enough, conversion."

"Conversion?"

"Yes. They begin to see the merit in their captor's point of view. They begin to alter their own views. Sometimes they begin to believe they are truly guilty and deserve to be in bondage. And sometimes they join the cause. We call the process 'identification with the aggressor.' If you can't beat 'em, join 'em. That's what hostages do sometimes. They begin to emulate their captors. They identify."

"Is that what you think happened with Dimmy?"

"Yes," she heard him say. "His demeanor, his attitude, his arrogant posture—they appear to be an imitation of his father."

"If that's true and his father is violent, why can't Dimmy be violent?"

"He could be," Zeke said. "But not against his father. If he was part of that cycle—the cycle of deprivation, it's called—he could easily become brutal. But not against anyone stronger than he is. He would act out his rage, like his father, against someone weaker and smaller, someone who presented no threat of retaliation."

"But he didn't do that."

"That's right! He didn't because he isn't violent. But if he were, he would not direct his violence toward the most feared person in his universe. Besides, he's convinced that he deserved the treatment he received at the hands of his father. He perceives himself as being evil and requiring punishment in order to be good.''

"All right," Doyle said then, "what does it all mean? Give me a conclusion."

"I think," Zeke said, "that he would never have reached a breaking point if something, some incident, hadn't occurred. Some incident that was so terrible that he could not tolerate it. I think he totally identified with his father until something happened that was so unacceptable to him, so abhorrent, that killing his father became a necessity."

"You think his father did something terrible?"

"Maybe. Maybe not."

"I don't understand."

"I can't say that the father did something. I can't think of what he could do that would be worse than what he'd already done. But maybe Dimmy did something or failed to do something. Maybe Dimmy, trying to be more like his father, pushed himself beyond what he could tolerate from himself. Maybe he began to drown in self-disgust."

"Self-disgust? Then why go after the father?"

Doyle reached out and punched the stop button on the recorder. She sat still in the sudden silence and pondered what she had heard. She raised her glass, finished the drink, and set the glass on the carpeted floor. Then she brought the recorder closer to her and pressed the play control once again. Zeke's voice leapt out at her.

"I believe that, in Dimmy's mind at that time, killing his father would have been the same as killing himself. One carefully placed stab wound would have been enough to finish the father. But the many wounds, the wildness of the attack, the hysteria, all indicate that he was trying to kill more than a man. He wanted to kill a monster. A demon. And for all we know, that monster might very well have been inside himself.''

Laura rose from the bed and moved silently to the door. The tapping grew louder. She pressed her cheek to the door and felt the vibration of the soft knocking.

''Who's there?'' she asked tremulously.

The tapping ceased. ''Who is it?'' she asked.

''Laura. Let me in,'' a harsh voice demanded.

Her breath caught in her throat. ''Nikki?''

''Let me in, Laura,'' he said.

''Oh, God! Go away!''

''I want to talk to you.''

''Go away!''

''You stopped taking calls. I want to talk.'' He paused and she heard his quick, heavy breathing. She knew he was excited.

''Go away, Nikki. I don't want to talk to you.''

''Are you afraid?''

''No,'' she murmured.

He hesitated. ''Let me in.''

''No.''

He laughed softly. ''Eventually, you will, and the longer you make me wait, the worse it will go for you. You know that, don't you?''

She heard herself sob, too late to stifle the sound.

''You are afraid,'' he said joyfully. ''You should be. You were always afraid of the unknown, and you have no idea of what I'm going to do to you when I get you.''

She felt her legs grow weak. She began slipping to the floor and braced herself against the wall. ''I'll call the police,'' she managed to say.

He laughed under his breath. ''Go ahead. They don't

frighten me." He grunted, and she felt the weight of his body against the door. "I'm coming in," he said.

Frantically she dashed to the bed and grabbed the phone. "Please!" she said into it. "Please!"

A sleepy female voice responded. "Yes?"

"Get me the police," Laura said. "There's a man trying to break into my room."

"One-seventeen?"

"Yes."

"Right away," the voice said and disconnected.

"I called for the police," she said loudly. "They're on the way." She had difficulty breathing.

The tapping had stopped. The breathing was gone. There was no pressure on her door. All was silent as if it had not happened, as if she had, after all, dreamed it. She had expected to be uncomfortable if and when she was finally confronted by Nikki. But she had not believed that she would turn to jelly at the sound of his voice. She had convinced herself that she could handle him, that she could deal with his intimidation because she had developed a new sense of self-worth. But she knew now that it required more than self-delusion to possess real psychological power. She was not yet in command of her own destiny. She remained vulnerable to the conviction that she was too weak to resist and must comply to avoid punishment. Discouraged, she began to despise herself. She was, after all, still a failure.

She had retained enough presence of mind to call for the police, though, she reminded herself. She could be proud of that, couldn't she?

She wept because nothing had really changed for her; she was the same person who had fled from Nikki's house so long ago. What had she been doing all that time in therapy? she asked herself. She had never really gotten to the heart of her problem. She wondered if anyone ever did. Talking was comfortable, but changing was a painful process, and she was a master at avoiding pain.

Yes. She knew what she had been doing. She had been learning, memorizing all the words, all the phases, all the therapist talk, until she had mastered the therapist's jargon and had convinced herself that she'd become a courageous, well-adjusted, self-sufficient human being.

What a terrible lie.

FOURTEEN

"Oh, it's so good to see you," Franny said two days later as she backed out of Laura's desperate embrace. "Let me look at you."

She held Laura at arm's length and studied the younger woman affectionately. Travelers dashed around them, anxious to collect their luggage and get as far from the airport as possible as quickly as possible, but Franny was in no hurry. She feasted on the sight of Laura for a long moment then pulled the girl back into her arms.

Laura had summoned Franny as a last resort. The last thing she wanted to do was cause upheaval in her friend's life. It was bad enough that she had borrowed so much money from her that she had no idea how she would ever be able to pay her back. But when she finally called her it was because she believed that Franny was the only person she could turn to at a time like this.

Reaching out to Dr. Benson had suddenly seemed hypocritical in light of the fact that she had seen, finally, how ineffectual their therapeutic alliance had really been. She feared him as she would a critical parent, and she did not want to hear him say that he had warned her not to travel to California where she would be within Nikki's reach. Nor did she want to revert to the use of the therapeutic clichés that had become handles to cling to when she felt lost and helpless. She wanted help and protection.

Laura had contemplated calling Zeke, but was restrained by the memory of his strange departure from her bed. She was not angry about that incident so much as she was puzzled. The fact that they had not completed their lovemaking did not disturb her. She had been sexually numb for so long that just the rekindling of desire was gratification enough for now. But she was distressed by Zeke's ambivalence. She understood why he might be apprehensive about embarking on a course that could lead toward making a commitment, but she could not get rid of the fear that he had pulled away because of her unworthiness. She could not protect herself from that old, deep psychic wound. There was little doubt in her mind that she was unattractive and undesirable.

Besides, she suspected that she had pushed him away by being too ready to become involved, too easily available to him. If she went to him now seeking protection from her ex-husband, she was positive he would panic and flee from her forever.

For a brief moment she had considered turning to Harriet Doyle. If there had been no Franny in her life, she might have, even though the lawyer intimidated her because of the control she exercised over her own life. What finally stopped her was the realization that whatever energy she took from Doyle for her own needs she would be stealing from Dimmy's cause, and, desperate as she was, she could not bring herself to do that.

In the end, she had called Franny the next morning. She had managed to tell her story quickly and simply.

What she dared not tell Franny, what she wished she could hide from herself as well, was that for more than a fleeting instant, with her face pressed against the door, listening to

his heavy breathing, his thick voice, feeling his energy
through the wood, she had been ready to fling herself at him.
She had almost felt his arms around her, squeezing the breath
out of her, pressing her to him, dragging her down to the
floor, letting his hands roam all over her, and she had become
excited. She had wanted him to do thrilling things to her.
She had wanted him to punish her. The sickness of that
desire had drained the strength from her body. It had notified
her that though she had put hundreds of miles between them,
she had not drawn very far away from him at all.

"Did you tell the police about him?" Franny had asked
after hearing the story of Nikki's midnight visit.

"No," Laura muttered. "He would have denied it," she
said. "And then they'd think I was accusing him falsely just
to help Dimmy's case."

"God, Laura!" Franny had snapped angrily. "Why would
they think that? Why do you always assume that everyone's
going to think the worst of you?"

Laura had remained silent. She wished she could deny
what Franny had pointed out to her, but it was true. She did
welcome guilt.

"Laura," Franny implored. "You have to tell someone.
You need protection."

Laura had sobbed faintly. "I am telling someone,
Franny."

Franny hesitated. "Yes," she finally said. "But I'm not
there. I can't help you."

Laura spoke softly. "I know."

After another lengthy pause, Franny had said, "All right.
I'll come."

"I didn't mean . . ."

"Of course, you did," Franny said. "Don't cop out now.
That's exactly what you meant. I don't mind. I can hear the
wheels in your brain turning, telling you what a bad, selfish

girl you are. Stop it! I don't mind. I want to be there with you. I could use a vacation in sunny California."

"Thanks, Franny," Laura whispered.

"Sure," the older woman said. "I'll see you tomorrow."

Now they retrieved Franny's suitcase and went out to the street, where they found a yellow cab.

"I moved into my new apartment yesterday," Laura told Franny after giving instructions to the driver. "I feel a lot safer than I did in the motel. At least I know it will take him some time to find out where I've moved to."

"Well, that's some consolation."

Laura smiled and squeezed Franny's hand. "And I feel so much better now that you're here."

"I'm glad," Franny said. "But don't get too comfortable and let your guard down. We should take precautions. If the man's half as crazy as you say, you're in danger. We should get you some protection."

"Okay," Laura said. "We will. I promise. But tonight, let's go out for a nice Italian dinner and not think about him. There's so much I want to tell you."

Franny squinted at her. "Am I in for a surprise?"

"I don't know what you mean."

"You know damn well what I mean, Laura Devon," Franny said, sounding parental. "Have you met someone?"

"Well . . ."

"Well, hell! I want to hear all about it."

"I'll tell you about it over dinner."

"You didn't tell him about Nikki, did you?" Franny said wisely.

Laura shook her head. "No."

"Afraid you'd scare him away?"

She nodded.

"You've got a point there," Franny said. "Nikki is a

problem and now you've got even more reason to take care of it."

"I will. In the morning we'll do something. I promise. Okay?"

Franny relented. She smiled warmly. "Okay."

"At least we have some time," Laura said. "I didn't leave a forwarding address, and no one else knows where I moved to."

"Well, in that case," Franny said, "he may never find us."

Notwithstanding the rubber-soled shoes, Dimmy heard the orderly approaching his door. He heard him from down the hall, from outside the unit, from outside the building. He heard those steps night and day, even during those few minutes when he could not keep his eyes open and drifted off into a fitful sleep. Through the walls and the ceiling he heard the soft thud and slurp of their rise and fall on the slick linoleum floor. He heard them as if they were the ticking of a metronome guiding the rhythm of his heartbeat.

He was thinking of the orderly too much; it was not healthy to think about the man all the time, but he could not shake off the fear. If he let down his guard for a moment, he could be lost. And he would rather be dead.

He knew what the orderly wanted from him. For fourteen months he had been dealing with the hunger around him. It was everywhere. In his cell at the County Jail. In the mess hall. In the sick bay. Here in the hospital. The orderly was no different from the others.

He heard the key turn in the steel door, turned his face, and saw the door open slowly.

"Hello," the orderly said. "It's time for your head shrinker."

Then he was beside the bed leering down at him. He was clamping the metal restraints on Dimmy's wrists. He was lifting the boy to a sitting position, swinging his legs over the side, lifting him to his feet.

"Dizzy today?" he asked.

Dimmy shook his head, but did not take his eyes off the orderly. Like a mongoose in the presence of a cobra, he was wary, cautious, alert.

"What's the matter?" the orderly asked.

Dimmy did not respond.

"What are you lookin' at me like that for?"

The orderly tugged on the chains, and Dimmy almost fell forward on his face.

"Don't look at me like that!" the orderly commanded. "Don't look at me at all. You're as nutty as a fruitcake, you know that? You're missing some spark plugs up here." He tapped Dimmy's head with his index finger.

"Don't touch me!" Dimmy said.

"Shit!" the orderly spat. "Who the hell would want to touch you, you greasy little slob?"

"Just don't touch me."

"I ain't gonna touch you, ever. You remember that when you're falling over and you want me to catch you. I'm just gonna let you fall on your face."

The orderly hooked one finger over the chain joining Dimmy's wrists, then pulled the boy out of his room and down the hall to the interview room, where he slammed Dimmy up against the wall beside the door.

"Stand there!" he said. "Don't move a muscle."

He rapped on the door and pushed it open. His head disappeared inside, and Dimmy fantasized about slamming the door shut on his thick neck. He heard the orderly say, "I got him, Doc."

Then he heard Zeke's kind voice respond, "Bring him in, please."

The orderly pushed his face up close to Dimmy's. The boy could smell the lunch on his breath. "You heard? Get your ass in there."

Dimmy stepped around the man and slid into the room. As he passed, he thought he heard the orderly whisper, "I'll get you later."

Quickly he went to his usual chair and sat.

"You want these off him?" the orderly asked the doctor.

"Yes, please," Zeke responded.

The orderly unlocked the bracelets, pulled the chains off, and left the room. Dimmy dared not look at him. He fixed his eyes on the floor between his feet and did not raise them until he heard the door close behind him.

Zeke noted the change in the boy. Yesterday, he had been relaxed, talkative, responsive. Today he appeared distressed, frightened. His eyes darted about the room like a ferret's, and he slouched in his chair as if he feared being struck from behind.

"What's wrong, Dimmy?" Zeke asked.

The boy shook his head. "Nothing." But his eyes avoided contact with Zeke's and his hands twisted the loose front of his robe.

"What are you doing?"

Dimmy tilted his head. "I'm listening."

Zeke leaned forward. "To what? Is someone talking to you?"

"No," he said softly. "I'm listening for the footsteps," Dimmy said. "I don't hear his footsteps."

"The orderly's?"

Dimmy nodded, then frowned. "He's waiting for me just outside the door. I didn't hear him go back to the ward."

"Shall I open the door and see?" Zeke asked.

"No!" Dimmy said, becoming agitated. "Don't let him know that we know."

Zeke rose quietly. He placed a finger over his mouth and ordered Dimmy to be quiet. Swiftly but silently he moved to the door and flung it open.

"Jesus Christ!" the startled orderly said from his low crouch outside the door.

"What are you doing there?" Zeke demanded.

"Nothing," he said turning and striding away.

"Come back here!" Zeke called.

"I'm busy," the orderly shouted. "I got to get back to work."

Back in the room, Zeke noted that Dimmy had not moved from his seat. The boy sat motionless as if dazed.

"What was that all about?" Zeke asked kindly. He feared for the boy, who seemed to be slipping away from him.

Dimmy dropped his eyes and shook his head.

"I can tell that you're frightened. If you tell me why, I can help you."

"He'll kill me," Dimmy muttered.

"No, he won't," Zeke said forcefully. "I won't let him. I swear."

"He thinks I tell you," Dimmy said.

"Tell me what?"

"He'll kill me if I tell you."

"No, he won't!"

Dimmy opened his mouth to speak, then closed it again.

Zeke sat back and folded his arms across his chest. "If you're going to close yourself off from me, I'm going to close myself off from you."

"I don't mean to close myself off."

Zeke opened his arms and made himself receptive. "Then tell me."

Dimmy struggled with the words as if they were stuck in his mouth and he had to spit them out. "He plays with me," he finally said ashamedly. "He plays with my penis."

"Damn him!"

"He's gonna kill me," the boy said.

Zeke stared at him. "Like hell he is. I'm getting you out of here right now."

"What do you mean, you don't know where she is?" Zeke shouted into the phone.

"She didn't leave a forwarding address, sir," the motel clerk said.

"If she calls in, tell her that Dr. Perez called about her stepson. Tell her it's imperative that she call me at my office. She has the number."

As Zeke hung up he heard the door open behind him and turned to see the orderly standing in the doorway.

"You wanted to see me?" the man asked.

Zeke nodded and motioned him to a chair. "I've filed a complaint against you," Zeke said.

The orderly looked at him suspiciously. "If you're pissed about—"

"Yeah," Zeke interrupted. "I'm pissed. I don't like spies."

"I'm sorry about that, Doc."

"Sorry isn't good enough."

The orderly shrugged. "What more do you want?"

"I want you to resign."

"What?" the man shouted. "For listening in at the door? I should lose my job over that?"

"Not only that," Zeke said. "There's more."

"What else?"

"You know, don't you?"

"I think so." The orderly had suddenly grown cautious. "I can guess what he's been tellin' you."

"How can you guess?"

"That's why I listened," he said. "I wanted to know if he was tellin' you lies about me. He's a god-awful liar, that kid."

"How can you guess what he's been telling me?" Zeke insisted.

"Shit! The little fucker."

"Come off it!" Zeke snapped.

The man stared at Zeke angrily. "That's how he gets what he wants," he said. "He's been threatening to tell lies about me since he came on this ward. From the very beginning, after they brought him in with those welts around his neck, he's been making me do things."

"What kind of things?" Zeke demanded.

"You know."

"No. I don't know."

The man squirmed on his chair. "You know. Extra food, things like that. An extra ice cream at night before lights out. He likes his ice cream, all right."

"How does he make you give him extras?"

The man crossed his legs and twisted sideways. "He said he would tell everybody I was suckin' his dick, the fuckin' little liar."

Zeke smiled, and the orderly flushed. "Let me get this straight," Zeke said. "A kid comes on your ward after a suicide attempt, is recognized as dangerous to himself, is restrained most of the time, tries to extort privileges from you, and you don't report it. You go along with it. Have I got that right?"

"Right!" the orderly said, nodding vigorously.

"Did you think going along was therapeutic?"

"No."

"Did you think it was fun?"

"No!" The orderly flashed an angry look at Zeke.

"What did you think?"

"I thought it was wrong. It was against the rules and I shouldn't do it."

"Why did you?"

"Because that's when he started to lie about me."

"When?"

"When I told him I wasn't gonna get him any extras. When I told him it was against the rules."

"So," Zeke said, "at first you refused to cooperate."

"That's right."

"Then what did he do?"

"He said he'd tell everybody that I did things to him."

Zeke watched the man squirm, cross and uncross his legs. His arms had become burdens, and he could find no comfortable position for them.

"Did you molest that patient?" Zeke said wearily.

"Hell, no!"

Zeke shook his head exhaustedly. "Haven't you been molesting him regularly?"

The man raised his right hand. "I swear to God!"

"Put your hand down," Zeke said. "I wouldn't believe you if you were sitting on a stack of Bibles."

"You see?" the man seethed. "That's what the kid said. He said nobody would believe me and everybody would believe him. That's why I did it."

Zeke studied the man for a moment. "You had no relations with the patient?"

He shook his head. "Absolutely not!"

Zeke gazed at the man and pondered what he had heard. His initial reaction to Dimmy's accusation had been outrage. It had not entered his mind that the boy might be lying. And Zeke was concerned about that. He could have asked himself the very same questions he had asked the orderly. Was he accustomed to automatically believing accusations made by patients? How could he discount the fact that the boy was neurotic, at best and clearly self-destructive? Had he thought it was therapeutic to fail to challenge the boy's accusation? When had he ever accepted the word of a patient as gospel? Had he forgotten that patients lied and hallucinated and harbored delusions now and then?

Zeke was troubled that he had jumped to a conclusion without having investigated, that he had joined forces with his patient as a co-conspirator and blindly become an ally in an endeavor that might be wholly vindictive. And more than anything else, he was bothered by the possibility that his immediate acceptance of Dimmy's story had more to do with his confusing relationship with Laura than it did with his clinical relationship with the boy. Did he want to believe Dimmy for Laura's sake?

Finally Zeke nodded to the orderly. "All right," he said. "Let's put this on hold for a while. Give me some time to investigate."

The man rose. "Thanks, Doc."

"It's all right," he said.

"You know it wasn't my idea, don't you?"

"What are you talking about?"

"It was the boy who said I wanted to do him. He said he knew I was thinking about it. I been here eleven years, and I ain't never done anything like that. I'm straight as an arrow. I got a wife and two kids. But he says he can see in my eyes what I want from him. He says that right out to me. The dirty little fucker stabbed me in the back." The man lowered his eyes and stuffed his hands into his pockets. "What the hell did I ever do to him?"

FIFTEEN

Harriet Doyle held the phone away from her ear and glared at it. Her inclination was to fling it against the wall and smash it into a thousand pieces, but that would not have affected Judge Bauer in the least. She could hear his ominous voice, but she could not make out what he was saying. He was completely lost in his discourse on the responsibility of defense counsel and did not care if she was listening or not.

She was seated on her living room couch resenting the conversation. She was angry that she had no office from which to work and so had to operate from her home. She was angry that the fates had placed her and her client in the hands of a judicial moron. She was angry that the system, and in particular Judge Bauer, had no feelings for the humanity of its victims. And she was enraged that in more than a year no one had done any work in preparation for the court battle she would have to wage in order to save Dimmy Pappas.

"All right!" she finally interrupted. "If you won't give me a continuance at least break loose with some funds for an investigator."

"What?" Judge Bauer screamed. "You want more money from the court?"

"Not for me," she said, struggling to restrain herself. "I

need an investigator. If I'm to be ready for trial in a week, I've got to get cracking."

"This trial's been pending for a year already," the judge reminded her. "That's plenty of time to do discovery."

"It certainly is," she responded. "But I haven't been on this case for a year. I've only been involved for a few days."

"That's not the fault of the court," he pointed out.

"I know that, Your Honor. But can't you cut me some slack here?"

He laughed humorlessly. "Cut your own slack, Counselor. You have a good offer pending from the prosecution. I suggest you take it."

"How do I know if it's good or not, if I don't know anything about the case? How about two weeks for a P.I.?"

"Not a day," he snapped.

Her anger rose to a point just below uncontrollable. "I could make a formal motion."

"I would deny it."

"I'd have it on the record. That's appealable."

"I won't allow it on the record. I'd instruct the reporter not to take it down."

"What the hell's the matter with you?"

"This conversation is over," he said.

"Fine!"

"And, Counselor," he said, "please speak to me just like that in court. I'd love to throw you into the slammer for contempt." He hung up.

She had expected as much. This judge was not going to give her an inch, and she could fully expect the same kind of treatment during the trial. His distaste for her would be displayed more subtly, of course. His prejudice toward her client would be hidden from the jury and withheld from the record, but it would be there in the courtroom, in the air, tempering his judgment in a thousand different ways. He would not risk reversal, but he would see to it that the opposition got all the breaks.

Doyle had been in this position before. She had spent most of her legal career playing catch-up—the price one paid for specializing in the defense of unpopular causes. Or maybe it was the price one paid for being outside the mainstream. Well, she had always been an uppity black woman, and she sure as hell was not going to change now.

She poured her first scotch of the day, marched into her bedroom, and commenced pulling outfits from her walk-in closet. Since the rules had been laid down for her and she had no choice but to play by them, she intended to be better at the game than the rest of the players. If the court would not advance funds for an investigator, she would be her own P.I. and do her own dirty work. Now she had to dress the part.

She decided on a wide paisley skirt that fell just above her knees, soft brown leather boots, and a short brown suede jacket over a green silk blouse. She examined herself in the mirror, turning this way and that, and was forced to admit that she looked pretty good. She had kept her figure well, belying the myth that alcohol was fattening. Of course she ate like a bird, she reminded herself, picking at a salad now and then, nibbling at a grilled chicken breast once or twice a week. One had to compromise somewhere, and she was not about to give up her Cutty Sark.

"Not bad," she said out loud, "for an old, worn out, too-tall street chick." She thought that in the dim light of a bar, she could still hold her own against ladies a lot younger. However, outdoing a bunch of ladies of the night might be a much simpler task than taking on the chief witness against her client. If Nikki Pappas was half as dangerous as he was made out to be, she would have her hands full with him. If anything unpleasant happened to her she would have only an unsympathetic judge to blame, and that would get her nowhere.

She parked her car at a meter on Cahuenga Boulevard and walked around the corner to Hollywood Boulevard where each concrete slab on the sidewalk contained a bronze star celebrating a show business personality who had paid a small fee to be immortalized. Though the boulevard harbored many shops, the street was occupied by more loiterers than shoppers. They clung to the corners like balls of dust rubbed off old carpeting. They filled the fast-food hangouts nursing small orders of french fries, dragging out the afternoon in the hope that evening would bring some excitement.

As Doyle walked along the filthy street glancing at the addresses, the loiterers scrutinized her. Some lusted for her; she knew it from their emotionally starved smiles. Others resented her. She was too well dressed. Her boots were too expensive, her jacket too costly. She meant money to them, the desired commodity that was so difficult to come by. There were no fat people on this street. These habitués wore emaciation like merit badges, like the highest reward of their fraternity. What havoc drugs and alcohol had not wreaked on their bodies, hunger and bad nutrition had.

She turned in at a Middle Eastern restaurant with gold letters on the window that read Nick's Falafel. Inside the long slender room, one wall was fronted by a long counter over which the greasy specialties of the house were sold. The other wall was lined with orange plastic tables and chairs at which one or two customers were seated clutching paper cups of coffee. The odor of too frequently used frying grease stifled the air and made breathing difficult. She inquired after Nikki Pappas.

The skinny, unshaved boy behind the counter pointed his thumb over his shoulder. ''Up them stairs outside,'' he said.

She glanced up at the ceiling. "He's got an apartment upstairs?"

"Yeah," the unclean boy said. "He lives up dere."

"Thank you," Doyle said and smiled at the clerk.

"You wanna eat somethin'?" he asked, motioning toward the delicacies lined up behind him.

"No, thanks," Doyle said. The very thought offended her stomach.

She climbed the long flight of stairs to the single wooden door on the landing. The door, which had been painted green many years before, was warped and cracked, and the top layer of plywood skin was peeling back at the corners. She searched for a bell, found none, and rapped hard on the crusty wood.

"Who is it?" a girl's voice inquired after a moment.

"I'm looking for Mr. Pappas," Doyle said pleasantly.

She heard the metallic thud of a dead bolt, and the door opened a crack. A pretty, dark young woman peered out at her.

"What do you want?" the lovely girl asked.

"You must be Irene," Doyle said.

"You know me?"

"Only what your brother told me," Doyle said. "I'm his lawyer."

The girl scowled. "No, you're not," she said. "I know his lawyer. Mr. Haines. I've talked with him."

"If you let me in," Doyle said, "I'll explain."

"Who is it?" a gruff voice shouted from inside the apartment. The girl's eyes reflected her fear.

"Let me in, please," Doyle said.

The girl opened the door wide and motioned her into the kitchen, which was much cleaner than the world outside.

A sullen man sat at a neat table near the window, a folded

newspaper before him. He looked up. "Who the hell are you?" he asked.

Irene answered for her. "She says she's Dimmy's lawyer, Papa."

Nikki spoke to his daughter. "What happened to that Haines guy?"

"I don't know," the girl said.

"I can explain," Doyle interrupted.

"Okay," Nikki said, his eyes roaming up and down the length of Harriet Doyle's body. He suddenly smiled approvingly. "You want something? A cup of coffee? Tea?" She shook her head. "Hey!" he continued. "Sit down." He kicked a chair out from under the table for her.

"I make good coffee," Irene said.

"I'd offer you better stuff," Nikki said. "But I can see that you're a lady."

"What kind of better stuff?" Doyle said.

Nikki shrugged. "A little wine. A liqueur, maybe."

Doyle smiled. "Got any Cutty Sark?"

Nikki stared at her, then nodded. "I think that can be arranged." He rose and moved to a tall cabinet. Inside were a dozen or so bottles of good whiskey. He pulled out an unopened bottle of Cutty. "Twelve years old," he said. "I'll open it for you."

"You don't have to," she said.

"My pleasure," he said. "Irene!" he barked. "Get the lady a glass."

When she had tasted the whiskey, expressed her appreciation, and set the glass down, Nikki laughed. "Okay," he said. "So what's this lawyer stuff?"

Doyle glanced at Irene, who stood with her back against the sink, then turned back to Nikki. "I'm now representing your son, Mr. Pappas."

"How come? What happened to Haines?"

"Mr. Haines had too crowded a calendar, and I was brought in to replace him."

"But I paid him," Irene said.

Nikki shot her a fierce look.

"You paid him?" Doyle asked.

The girl nodded, then lowered her eyes.

"Did you know he was being paid by the court?"

"No," Nikki said. "Smart guy."

"Not very," Doyle said, swinging her attention back to Nikki. "I need to talk to you about this case," she said.

"What for?" Nikki suddenly sounded hostile.

"You're the victim. You're a prosecution witness, and I have the right to talk to you before we go into court. I could have served you with a subpoena and taken your deposition in the office, but I thought it would be better to be informal and not make a big deal out of it."

Nikki stared at her silently.

"There's no reason we have to be enemies, is there?"

Nikki turned to Irene. "Get out!" he said.

The girl started to protest, then changed her mind and left the room without another word.

Nikki returned his attention to Doyle. "How come a great-looking broad like you wants to do this shit?"

"Lots of great-looking people become lawyers," Doyle said.

"Not for that little bastard."

"Are you talking about your son?"

"Yeah."

"Well, if he's your son, he's not a bastard, is he?"

The humor left Nikki's face. "Don't play with me!" he said. "I don't have time for that."

Doyle dropped the pretense as well. "What do you have time for, Pappas? Have you got the time to send your son to prison for life?"

"He tried to kill me!" Nikki snapped.

Doyle softened. "Okay. I understand that. But he's already been in jail for more than a year. Isn't that enough?"

Nikki squinted at her. "What the hell do you want?"

"I want you to go easy on him when you testify."

"No way!"

"I want you to feel sorry for the kid. Give me something to help him with."

"What are you talking about?"

"Did you beat him up a lot, Nikki? Did you punch him out every now and then?"

"Never!"

"You never smacked him around?"

"Never!"

"Did you tie him up and torture him?"

Nikki rose suddenly. "Get the hell outta here!"

She remained seated. "It wouldn't be smart to kick me out, Mr. Pappas."

"No? Why not?"

"Because then you won't know what I'm going to ask you in court. This way you get to see all my cards and I get to see yours, and there won't be any surprises for either of us."

He examined her for a long moment. Finally he smiled and returned to his seat. "You're a smart broad."

"That's what I've been telling you."

"All right," he said. "What you want to know?"

She nodded. "The only thing I want to know is why he stabbed you that night."

"Because he's a mean, ungrateful kid."

"Why that particular night?" Doyle said.

"That night. Some other night. What's the difference?" He unconsciously fingered the ropy scar on his neck. "He did it; that's all that counts."

"Look. There's no doubt that he stabbed you. The trial won't even deal with whether or not that's true. It's going to be stipulated. But attempted murder is a very serious crime in California. He could be sentenced to life in prison. You don't want that, do you? All I want to do for him is try to limit the length of his sentence. To do that, I need your help."

"I can't help you," he said.

"How do you know that? You'd be surprised at how some little, insignificant things can add up to a strong defense."

"Why should I want to help you? The little bastard tried to kill me. Let him rot in prison. It'll make a man out of him."

Doyle sighed and leaned back. She raised the glass of whiskey and sniffed it slowly, then drank it down. "Well," she said, "at least you gave me good whiskey." She shook her head sadly. "You know, I've taken the wrong approach with you. I'm not going to get to you with kindness, am I? I'm not going to get anywhere appealing to some finer sense in you. I wanted to reach the parent in you. Maybe touch the father who might not want to lose his son forever. I thought that might work."

"I already lost him forever," Nikki said. "When that bitch I married seduced him. After that he wasn't my son no more. He was her son. Not mine."

"Are you talking about Laura Devon?"

"Laura Pappas! We ain't divorced."

"What are you saying about Laura?"

"She took him into her bed!" Nikki shouted. His face turned red and the rage blazed in his eyes. "After she fucked him, he wasn't no good to me anymore."

"Papa!" Irene said from the doorway. "Don't say things like that."

"Get out of here!" Nikki shouted.

"I won't let you talk about Dimmy like that."

Nikki continued to shout. "It's true and you know it!"

Doyle stood and turned to the girl. "Is it true?"

Irene shook her head hysterically. "No! No!"

"It's true!" Nikki snapped.

"Did you punish him?"

"Sure, I punished him, but not as bad as God will punish him."

"What did you do to him?"

"I taught him about sex."

"How did you do that?"

He shouted at her. "None of your business!" He seized her empty glass and smashed it on the floor, and Doyle backed away several steps. "Get the hell out of here!"

Doyle moved farther off. "Okay," she said, her hands outstretched to calm the man. "I'm going. Take it easy."

"You better leave," Irene said softly while Nikki glowered at them both.

"Look," Doyle said. "I'm sorry I upset you. That was the last thing I wanted to do."

"What did you expect?" Irene asked bitterly.

"I was hoping I would learn something helpful."

Nikki looked spent, as if his outburst had drained the last of his energy. "You think I don't love my son? You think I'm a monster?" He shook his head. "I'm a good father. Whatever I do is for their own good."

"I can't believe that," Doyle said.

"You think not? You tell her, Irene. Tell her I never hurt my kids."

"That's true," Irene said. "Papa loves his kids."

"Irene," he said, "when you gave that lawyer ten thousand dollars, tell her where you got the money."

"It's true," Irene said to Doyle. "Papa gave me the money for Dimmy's defense."

''And you say I'm not a good father,'' he said proudly to Doyle.

Doyle gazed at Irene's tortured face. She reached out and touched her arm. ''You tell me,'' she said. ''What happened that night to make Dimmy try to kill your father?''

''Irene!'' Nikki cautioned.

Irene gazed directly into Doyle's eyes. ''Nothing happened,'' the girl said. ''I swear to you. Nothing happened. I think maybe Dimmy went a little crazy. He attacked Papa, and Papa's totally innocent. We don't understand it any more than you do.''

Zeke went back to his office that afternoon, after seeing to it that Dimmy had been relocated to the main county jail. He'd been placed in what the deputies and the inmates alike referred to as the pogey bait unit, which was reserved for young white boys who looked like candy to the more hardened guests of the county. To his great relief Zeke found a message from Laura on his answering machine.

When he had learned that she was gone and had left no forwarding address, Zeke had assumed that she no longer wanted to see him. He could not blame her. How could he expect her to understand his behavior when he himself could not? He felt his face grow hot with shame and embarrassment just thinking about their last night together.

He remembered the telephone's shrill ring shocking him out of his moment of passion. It was like being jerked out of a deep sleep, but he realized that he had actually welcomed the interruption. He had leapt at the opportunity to avoid the need to perform. He was afraid of being more to her than a friend.

Still, he could not get Laura out of his mind. When he was with her, he was as happy as he could ever remember being. And when he was away from her, he longed for her.

He would lie awake at night visualizing her naked body beside him. He saw himself lean across her and take her in his arms, touching her, loving her.

And yet, when his fantasy had almost become a reality, he had panicked. He had felt the fear swarm over him like an army of insects. His breathing had become difficult and labored, his palms sweaty, his skin sensitive and painful as though too close to a raging flame. He was compelled to escape from his fear. Though he understood intellectually that he was safe with Laura, he had felt that he was about to be swallowed whole, lost forever. The same irrational fear he had secretly suffered most of his adult life had returned to him that night. He thought the fear had been banished forever, but it was still part of him and would be part of him until he finally confronted it and walked through it in his own personal rite of passage. He would never be free until he overcame his irrational fear of the power of women.

"Ezekiel," he could still hear her whisper to him. "Isn't your father foolish? You'd think after all these years he'd stop sounding like a beaner. He should've learned better English by now, don't you think?"

He would gaze up at her from his seat at the kitchen table where she insisted he do his homework so that she could watch him while she engaged in some cooking. From the living room the voice of his father, the Mexican immigrant laborer who had married the shanty Irish orphan girl after getting her pregnant, floated to them as he conversed with the actors on the television screen. He spoke to them in a mixture of English and Spanish, joked with them, was critical of them, loved and hated their characters as if they were real people who lived down the street. And the English half of his speech was invariably better than the Spanish half. The Spanish he had learned in the streets of Guadalajara; the

English he had learned from watching soap operas during long periods of unemployment.

"He'll never amount to nothin' more'n a hauler an' a lugger," Zeke's mother would say then and shake her head again. "Big back, small mind."

Zeke would wonder why she had married him if she thought so little of him. He was too young then to understand what function marriage played for the poor. It had nothing to do with love, he was soon to learn. It had to do with survival, escape, independence. It had to do with satisfying raging biological urges without incurring the wrath of the demanding, unforgiving, self-righteous God of the Catholic poor.

"Bridget!" his father would shout from the other room. "Come on! See dis. Sit wit me! Come, Bridget, *por favor*!"

Bridget Perez would frown at Zeke, poring over his long division problems. "See?" she would whisper. "That's all he cares about. That dumb old television. Nothin' up here." She would point to her temple. "Not you," she would finish with a firm nod. "I'm gonna make you somebody."

Of course she did just that, but at a high price. While she was driving him upward and onward, she was pressing Jesus Perez downward and backward. By the time Zeke was a teen, she had moved his father out of her bedroom and onto a cot in the laundry room behind the kitchen. The man had lost most of his affable good nature, had grown sullen and bitter, and two beers during a Sunday football game had become a couple of six-packs and a bottle of cheap red wine.

Zeke's father slowly became a lonely, friendless drunk. Denied the company of his wife, denied his only sexual outlet, denied the respect that might have compensated for his own lack of self-love, he eventually drank himself to death.

"See, Ezekiel," Bridget had said to him from the back of his third-hand Chevy as they were leaving the cemetery after having put Jesus Perez to rest. "This is what it comes to." She was indicating that Zeke's father had not, after all, been a man of substance. He had been a failure at the game of life. There were no mourners, other than wife and son, at his funeral, and no one had sent flowers. No one.

Zeke had driven down from Santa Barbara in the old Chevy he had bought for four hundred dollars. He was in his freshman year at the University of California and had left as soon as he got the word that Jesus had passed away.

On the hour-long drive he had tried to weep for his father, but no tears had come, and he felt guilty that he could not express his overpowering sense of loss. He felt alone, frightened, abandoned, unsafe, in danger, unprotected. He remembered the man who had played marbles with him, hugged him, walked him down the hostile street clutching his tiny hand in his huge fist. That part of his life was gone, and in its stead was a sharp pain in the center of his chest. And still he could not cry.

He had no doubt that his mother would demonstrate her feelings without any difficulty whatsoever. She had never missed an opportunity to humiliate Jesus when he was alive. Now that he was dead, she would publicly weep and wail over losing the man who, she would claim, had been a saint. But alone with her son, she could not alter the course she had plotted for herself so long before.

"He's better off," she had said as she clung to Zeke's arm looking down at the freshly dug grave. "He had a miserable life. He was born. He loaded trucks. He died. What a life. He never did a thing to be proud of."

"He had a son," Zeke had said meekly, his eyes turned away from her. Perhaps he felt the need to validate his father's life.

She turned a surprised face to him. "No," she had said impatiently as if speaking to someone who had totally misunderstood what was there plainly for him to see. "*I* had a son, Zeke."

Zeke shuddered as the old memories welled up in him. Sitting at his desk, he tried to pry them loose from the hold they had upon him. He rewound his message tape and played back the part with Laura's voice on it.

"Hi, Zeke," the cheerful voice said. "I've moved out of the motel. I won't have a phone in my new place until tomorrow, so I can't leave you a number. A friend from Dayton is staying with me, and we're going to dinner at Via Fettuccine over on Melrose tonight at seven. I'd love you to join us if you can. If not, I'll call you as soon as I get my phone." There followed a long pause, then, "Love you!" she said before she hung up.

He leaned back in his chair and thought about Laura, for whom he had such mixed feelings. Did he want her to love him? An hour ago he had thought so. But now, after remembering what he knew about love, marriage, and loyalty, he was not very sure at all.

SIXTEEN

Harriet Doyle was pleased that Detective Beck was at his desk at Hollywood Station at four that afternoon. She stood quietly before him until he sensed her presence and raised his eyes.

"Jesus Christ!" he said. "Look at what the cat drug in."

"Hello, Jerry."

Beck stood up and extended his hand. "Hello, Counselor," he said. "Has it ever been a long time."

She nodded. "Yes, it has."

"Sit down."

"Thanks."

"Wisht I could offer you something," he said. "But this is the wrong time and place."

"You owe me one," she said.

"You got it." He grinned fondly at her and then grew serious.

Beck's desk was in a far corner of the detectives' room beside a window that faced the police parking lot. Half a dozen other desks, most of them unoccupied, filled the remainder of the chamber. A single detective spoke softly into a telephone cradled between his chin and his shoulder. The dull green walls were scarred and chipped. The furniture was old and battered. The atmosphere was heavy, depressed. The air, though no one was smoking, was permeated with the scent of stale tobacco.

"You just passing by?" Beck asked.

She shook her head. "I'm on a case."

"Uh-oh," he said. "I hope it's not one of mine."

"As a matter of fact . . ."

"I thought you quit the business," he interrupted. "I heard you were doing real estate or something."

She nodded. "That was yesterday."

He leaned back, and his wooden swivel chair squeaked loudly. "You missed us, right? It got lonely out there in the real world? Boring, right?"

"Right."

He grew thoughtful. "What've you got?"

She shrugged. "Sorry, Jerry," she said. "I've got the Pappas kid."

He smiled weakly. "I should've known. If there ever was a loser, it's that kid. I should've known if you came back it was to take on a no-win like him."

"Just like old times."

"Don't remind me."

Beck recalled the day he had first met Harriet Doyle—his first day in lawyer hell, the day he was cross-examined by defense counsel Harriet Doyle for the first time.

He had testified on direct examination as to having elicited a confession from a Los Angeles gang member who had allegedly driven the automobile involved in a drive-by shooting in which an innocent teenager was killed. The alleged perpetrator had written out his confession in longhand and signed it in the presence of several witnesses. Beck had testified that the confession was made voluntarily, that no coercion was employed, and that the defendant had been anxious to cleanse himself of the burden of his guilt.

Then Doyle, holding a copy of the confession, rose and gazed at the detective. She asked innocently, ''Detective, is it the department's policy to ask for confessions to be written out by the accused?''

''No, ma'am,'' he said.

''What is the policy?''

''To have them typed by a reporter or tape-recorded and then transcribed.''

''In fact, the shooter in this incident also confessed, didn't he?''

''Yes, ma'am.''

''Did he write his confession out?''

''No. He spoke into a tape recorder.''

''I see,'' she said and lowered her eyes for a moment. ''Can you explain why this document was handled this way?''

Beck squirmed slightly. ''We didn't have a recorder handy, I guess.''

''Why didn't you send for one?''

Beck smiled. ''The defendant was so anxious to confess, he didn't give us time.''

She nodded. ''I see.'' She pondered that for a moment. ''Okay,'' she finally said. ''I understand.''

Beck leaned back and relaxed.

''How did you know to arrest the defendant, Detective?''

''I beg your pardon, ma'am?''

She pointed to her client. ''What led you to arrest this man in the first place?''

''Oh,'' he said. ''We had some eyewitnesses. They gave us a description.''

''And what did you do with that description?''

''I don't understand.''

''Did you run it through a computer?''

''No, ma'am.''

"What did you do?"

"Nothing."

"Well, now it's my turn to be confused. You say you found the defendant because of witness descriptions, but you didn't do anything with those descriptions. How did you connect the defendant with the description?"

"Well," Beck said, sitting upright now, tensed. "We confirmed we had the right man *after* we arrested him."

"Oh, I'm sorry," Doyle had said. "I guess I misunderstood." She dropped the confession onto the table as if it had lost its significance. "You didn't arrest the defendant because he matched any descriptions?"

"No, ma'am."

Doyle lifted another sheet of paper and approached the witness. "Do you recognize this document, Detective?"

"Yes."

"Would you tell the court what it is?"

"It's a police report."

"What kind of police report?"

"It documents the verbal descriptions of a perpetrator taken from eyewitnesses."

"Does it contain the description of the man accused of driving the car in this case?"

"Yes, ma'am."

"Would you read that document, please?"

"All of it?"

Doyle shook her head. "Just the description of the driver."

Beck, uncomfortable, lifted the document and read aloud in an angry monotone. "A tall black man wearing a large Afro." He stopped and stared expectantly at her.

"Is that all? How many witnesses were there?"

"Six. But all of their descriptions are pretty much the same."

Doyle paused, lifted her eyes, pressed a fingertip to her

lips, and seemed to ponder. "And those descriptions, all pretty much the same, were enough to justify arresting the defendant?"

"We also had his name," Beck said.

"Oh?" Doyle pretended surprise. "How did that come about?"

"We got his name from his partner, the shooter."

"Ah," she said. "I see. You got his name from a confessed murderer in your custody, matched him up with the descriptions, which were all pretty much the same, and you had your man."

Beck nodded.

Doyle turned to her client and motioned him to stand. Then she returned her attention to the witness. "Detective Beck," she said, "how long have you been a police officer?"

"Eleven years."

"How long have you been a detective?"

"Four years."

She smiled warmly at him. "Do you consider yourself a trained observer?"

"I do."

"Someone who can remember fairly accurately what he has seen?"

"Yes, ma'am."

"So, if you gave me a description of someone, I could expect it to be fairly accurate?"

"Yes, ma'am."

"Would you describe the defendant for the court?"

"He's right there," Beck said.

"Please, Detective."

Beck sighed and shrugged his shoulders. "He's black. About six feet tall. Maybe two hundred fifty pounds. With a wide Afro."

"Thank you." She turned to her client and indicated that

he should return to his seat. She turned and faced the jury. Then she spoke to Beck, but her eyes were on the jury.

"Do you think, Detective Beck, that your description is consistent with the descriptions from the eyewitnesses?"

"I think so."

"But none of them said anything about two hundred and fifty pounds."

"Well . . ."

"No one described him as fat."

"Well, no . . ."

"But you mentioned his weight."

"Yes, but—"

"Detective Beck, do you know the defendant's gang name?"

"Yes," he said softly, almost inaudibly.

"Please, tell the court."

"Fat Albert."

"What does that name refer to?"

"To a Bill Cosby character."

"Can you describe that character?"

"He's obese."

Doyle approached him slowly. "Did any of the eyewitnesses describe the driver of the vehicle as obese?"

"No."

"Did any of them call him fat?"

"No."

"Did any of them describe him as overweight?"

"No."

"But you confirmed the defendant's participation with the descriptions given by those witnesses?"

"Yes."

"Thank you!" Doyle turned back to the defense table, where she stood silently examining another document.

Beck leaned forward expectantly.

"That's all, Detective."

Beck started to rise.

"Oh, wait! One more thing."

Beck sank back onto the chair.

"I'm curious," she said. "How exactly did you get the defendant to confess?"

"What do you mean?"

"Well, did you say, 'Hey, some people said they saw you there so you better confess'?"

"No."

"What did you say?"

"I don't remember exactly."

"Well, not exactly, then. Roughly?"

"We told him his partner had confessed and named him and there was no point in holding out."

"And he believed you?"

"Why not?"

"That's the oldest trick in the book, isn't it? Separate two people and tell each one the other named him?"

"We didn't do that!" Beck said.

"You just said you did exactly that."

"No," Beck said. "You described a technique where we imply that the suspect has been named when he really hasn't. In this case he was really named."

"You knew that?"

"Yes."

"But the defendant didn't know that."

"Yes, he did."

"How could he have known it?"

"We told him."

"And he believed you?"

"Yes."

"Just because you said it?"

"Yes."

"He trusts cops?" Doyle spat. "Cops don't lie? They only speak the truth? Cops are trustworthy?"

"No."

"But he believed you?"

"Yes."

"Come on, Detective. Do you want this court to believe that simply on your say-so, the defendant sat down and wrote out his confession because he believed he had been named by someone?"

"Yes."

"He didn't question you?"

"No."

"He didn't demand to see his so-called partner?"

"No."

"He didn't demand to read the transcript of the other man's confession?"

"No."

"Why not?"

"Because we played the tape for him."

"On what?"

"On a tape recorder."

Doyle paused. After a dramatic moment she nodded and turned to the jury box. "But the defendant wrote out his so-called confession in longhand because you didn't have a tape recorder available. That was your testimony not ten minutes ago, Detective. How could you have played the tape for him?"

"I . . . forget," Beck stammered.

Doyle dismissed him, and he rushed from the courtroom.

A month later she invited Beck to lunch on his day off. She met him at Musso and Frank on Hollywood Boulevard and bought him the most expensive lunch on the menu.

"What's this all about?" he asked after the waiter had brought their drinks.

"A peace offering," she said.

"Yeah," he said. "I feel like Custer looking into the eyes of Sitting Bull. When can I expect the arrow through my heart?"

"I wanted to let you know that, like you, I was just doing my job. Also, like you, I'm very good at it. On that day you weren't so hot. Someday I won't be so hot, either. It's like the tennis pros say: anybody can beat anybody on any given day."

She smiled at him, and he relaxed.

"You guys messed up," she continued. "I found out about it. What can I say, Detective?"

"Call me Jerry," he said. "If we're going to be friends, you can't go around calling me Detective all the time."

"Okay, Jerry." She reached over, and he took her hand. "And you call me Harriet. Fair?"

"Fair enough."

They touched glasses and drank to their truce. She had known all along that she would like him, actually. When checking him out, she had learned that his favorite drink was Cutty Sark. How bad could a Cutty man be?

"You know," Jerry said when they were digging into their lamb chops. "That asshole will do it again. You got him off, but he'll do it again."

"You think so?"

"Hundred percent," he said.

She stared at him for a moment. "I hope not," she said.

Six months later she received an urgent call from her client. He was in jail again on another murder charge. She did not take his case. On that occasion he had been the shooter and someone else had driven the vehicle.

Now, Jerry Beck said, "So you've got the Pappas kid and you want me to roll over."

"No," she said. "Not yet, anyway."

"So?"

"You were there when they took his confession, weren't you?"

"Don't start with me and confessions," he said. "Talk to the D.A."

"I'm not trying to trash the confession," she said. "I'm going to stipulate."

His eyes opened in surprise. "That doesn't sound like you. You don't give an inch."

"This is a different kind of case."

"I interviewed the victim," Beck said. "The guy had fifteen, sixteen wounds in him. Not superficial wounds. I mean real cuts. Deep. Serious. The kid wasn't fooling around. He wanted to put a real hurt on his old man. He didn't just want to kill him. He wanted to kill him dead, if you know what I mean."

Doyle nodded. "I figured that from the wounds described in the coroner's report, but I can't figure out why."

"Did you look at that kid's history?" Jerry Beck asked. "He's an abused kid."

"Abused?" the detective said. "That kid's been beat up and tortured so much it's a wonder he isn't on the funny farm."

She smiled. "Are you telling me to go for insanity?"

"I sure as hell would."

She shook her head. "The shrink says it won't stick."

"Who's the shrink?" Beck asked.

"Zeke Perez. You know him?"

Beck frowned. "Yeah. I know him."

"You don't like him?"

"He's okay. But he isn't the best. You get Paul Murphy on the case and you've got a good shot at temporary."

She shook her head. "It's not just the shrink," she said. "There's something else here. I have the beginnings of an idea. But there are pieces missing. One piece in particular."

"What's that?"

"That's what I need you for, Jerry," she said. "It's worth a case of Cutty to me if you come through."

He eyed her suspiciously. "I'm almost afraid to ask," he said.

"I want to know what pushed him over the edge," she said. "What made him finally do it?"

"It didn't happen overnight, Harriet," Beck said.

"I know it built up over time. That's part of my point. Let's say he thought about it for a long time, maybe a couple of years. Thought about it and brooded about it, but didn't do anything about it. Then, all of a sudden, bang! You see what I mean? Why, all of a sudden?"

"He just had too much," Jerry said. "You know how that is. It builds up in you. A guy takes shit from his wife for years, day in and day out, night in and night out. Then one night he walks in and she starts dumping on him again like she always does, and all of a sudden he takes a Saturday night special and blows a bunch of holes into her, which he can't even remember doing."

Doyle frowned. "You would give me that example, you male chauvinist pig."

Beck laughed. "Okay. I take it back. How about this one. A woman takes crap from her husband for years, day in and day out, et cetera, et cetera. Finally, one night, he's beating the shit out of her and she runs into the kitchen, grabs a big knife, and plunges it into his gut."

"Those killings are not calculated. They happen in the heat of the moment. This kid waited for his father to fall asleep. Then he went into the bedroom, looked down at the sleeping man, and started to carve him up with a frenzy like a hungry shark."

"Right!" he agreed.

"It's not the same, Jerry. He stabbed his father again and again, coldly, unemotionally, as if he had carefully planned the crime."

"I don't see the difference."

"Okay," she said, nodding. "Let's go with the woman who stabs her husband because he's beating her physically at the time or the guy who shoots his wife because she's beating him psychologically at the time."

"Okay."

"But what was happening to the kid when he went after his father? You see? I could buy the connection if something was going on, or had just gone on, that could have provoked him finally to do what he had probably dreamed about doing for years."

"You want the immediate motivator," Jerry said.

"Exactly!"

"Okay, but you don't need one."

"Yes, I do," she said. "If I want to win a jury over, I need that kicker."

Jerry shrugged. "You know better about that than I do, Counselor."

"I had a case once," she said thoughtfully, "a long time ago, early in my career. A young couple who lived in one of the little frame houses over on Fountain where the tennis courts are now."

"I remember those houses," Jerry said.

"Two o'clock in the morning the guy goes into the kitchen, just like you said, and shoots his wife six times. Then he goes and calls me and says he just killed his wife. God! I remember like it was yesterday. I kept asking him why, and always he gave me the same answer. He said she tortured him; he couldn't trust her; she was cheating on him. Over and over again. But what happened that night? I asked him. Nothing, he says. Nothing." She stopped suddenly and grew even more thoughtful.

"Go on," he said.

"Damn!" she said. "You were right, Jerry. About Paul Murphy."

"What about him?"

"I brought him in on that case. I remember his report." She pointed to her forehead. "He recommended sodium pentothal and got the court's permission to use it. That was old Judge Barrett. Man, could I use him on this case."

"Go on," Jerry Beck said impatiently.

"It took seventeen hours, seventeen sessions with Paul Murphy, before my client remembered. For sixteen hours, he kept saying he was asleep. He got up in the middle of the night, walked into the kitchen, and shot his wife. He didn't know why she was in the kitchen in the middle of the night, why he got the gun from the closet, or what had happened to make him do such a thing. Then, during the seventeenth hour, Paul walked him through it all over again. My client said he was sleeping and he got up. Paul asked him why he got up. And the guy said, without batting an eye, that the phone woke him. Only he'd never mentioned a phone before, not in sixteen sessions.

"So Paul jumped on that and kept pushing it until the guy remembered lifting the extension in the bedroom and listening to his wife, in the kitchen, whispering with her lover about how he was going to come over the next afternoon while the husband was at work and fuck her brains out. Then the guy remembered going to the closet, getting his gun, walking to the kitchen, and shooting her. He had blocked it out completely, but Paul got at it with the drug."

"What happened to the guy?" Jerry asked.

"It doesn't matter," she said. "What matters is that he had an immediate motivator."

"What do you mean, it doesn't matter? I want to know if you got him off."

"No." She shook her head. "I wasn't that good back then. He got life. But who knows? Today anything could happen."

Jerry smiled. "You're the only lawyer I know who talks about the cases she lost."

Doyle leaned forward in anticipation. "When the Pappas kid was questioned, the night he confessed, did he say anything that might lead us to the immediate motivator?"

Jerry leaned far back in his chair and reflected. "Not that I can remember," he finally said. "I remember that the D.A. kept asking questions that would get to that, but I don't remember him getting any answers. All I remember is the kid saying his father deserved it."

"How about during the subsequent investigation? Anything come up?"

He shook his head. "Not a thing. The old man claims that the kid is rotten. Led the life of Riley and then went bananas for no reason."

"How about the sister? What did she tell you?"

"Not a thing. She wouldn't talk to us at all. Always had some excuse. She was sick. She was in school. She had to work. The most we ever got out of her was ten minutes of I-don't-know-anything."

"Did you look hard?" she asked. "Or did you just go through the motions?"

"You sure know how to hurt a guy, Counselor."

"Come on, Jerry."

"We had a case," he protested. "We got a confession. And it's a good confession. There's nothing can taint this one. The D.A. is so sure of this case, he didn't see any need to waste time and money—"

"Good!" Doyle said. "That's what I like to hear."

Beck eyed her cautiously. "You've got something up your sleeve."

"No magic," she said, grinning at him contentedly. "Just good old police work."

"Ha!"

She rose. "I'm going to find that immediate motivator, and when I do, I'm going to break this case wide open. You watch me, pal."

"Good luck," Jerry said, rising with her.

"You better call the D.A. and wish him luck," she said. "He's going to need it because Harriet Doyle is back in the saddle again, and she's itching to ride."

SEVENTEEN

Zeke battled the Melrose Avenue traffic, which was thick and slow all the way from Fairfax to La Brea, and although he had left home with plenty of time to spare, he arrived at the restaurant twenty minutes late. When the headwaiter led him to Laura's table, she and Franny had already finished their salads and were just starting on heaping platters of pasta smothered in marinara sauce.

He was a little uncomfortable and not sure how to greet her, but Laura jumped to her feet, took his arm and pushed her lips out for a greeting kiss. Then she said, "This is my friend, Franny Gouch, from Dayton." Zeke shook hands with the older woman, whose grasp was solid, confident.

"Pleased to meet you," he said.

"Me too," she said and smiled warmly at him.

Zeke sat down and ordered a glass of wine and a Caesar salad.

"No, thanks!" he said when Laura offered him a forkful of spaghetti.

"You'll ruin my appetite."

"That's what you're here for," Laura said. "To have your appetite ruined. Among other things." She squeezed his knee under the table and whispered, "I'm so glad you came."

Throughout dinner they joked, and he and Laura teased each other. Franny seemed very relaxed, and commented about how cute they looked together. Zeke sensed that Laura was trying to impress Franny with the nature of their relationship. He felt as though he were being sold like some new and improved product.

When they had finished their meal and had all agreed that the meal had been perfect, they lingered over coffee, feeling too contented to rush away. They felt protected in the restaurant, warm and comfortable surrounded by the rich garlic aroma, the tranquil lighting, the effects of the house Chianti.

"What brings you to California?" Zeke asked Franny.

The woman glanced at Laura before responding. "A well-deserved vacation," she said. "I'm lucky that I have such a good friend to stay with."

"You're staying with Laura?"

Franny nodded. "In her new apartment."

"That reminds me," Zeke said, turning to Laura. "You moved and didn't give me your new address."

"I know," she said.

"Maybe that's my fault," Franny hastened to add. "I've been keeping her so busy she hasn't had time to do any of her chores."

"No," Laura said, growing serious. "That's not why."

Zeke noted the change in her demeanor. "What's the matter?" he said, a note of concern entering his voice.

"I'm trying to keep my address a secret, Zeke."

"From me?" he said in surprise.

"She has a good reason," Franny interjected.

"Oh, yeah? What could that be?"

"Please, Zeke," Laura said. "Don't get angry. Let me explain."

He nodded. "Okay."

"The other night," she said, "after you left . . ."

He felt his face flush.

". . . I fell asleep," she continued. "And something woke me up. Some sound. When I looked around, I heard someone outside my door, trying to break in."

"Oh, God!" he said.

"It was Nikki, Zeke," she said hurriedly. "He sounded crazy. He told me he was going to get me, do terrible things to me. He scared the hell out of me."

"Why didn't you call me?" he said. "I would have come over."

She shook her head. "I called the police and he ran away."

"Goddammit!" Zeke said. "I knew it! What's he think he's doing?"

"I called Franny the next morning and asked her to come and stay with me."

"Why didn't you let me know?" he insisted, sounding hurt.

"I didn't want to . . . you know . . . bother you," she said.

He saw Franny studying him and knew she was wondering how he was going to handle himself in this situation. She wondered, as he did, how serious he was about Laura, for that would determine the extent of his commitment. Was he prepared to admit that he was in love with her, even to himself?

"Bother me?" he asked. "You think doing things for you, making you happy, is a bother? You think protecting you from harm is a trouble for me?"

"I didn't know," she said.

He took her hand. "Well," he said, "now you know. You're not a bother. Whatever you need, whenever you need it, I expect you to call me. I want you to. Do you understand?"

She nodded and squeezed his hand.

"Listen, you two," Franny said, leaning forward and

breaking into their self-absorption. "It's clear to me that you care about each other, and if you want my advice, you'll stop testing each other."

Laura started to protest, but Franny stopped her.

"I'm older than you, Laura, and more experienced. Take a well-intended word of advice. If you two give each other a chance, you may discover that your relationship is something worthwhile. But that means you have to start trusting each other. You can't run and hide from each other every time you feel insecure. Those are the times when it's hardest, but most helpful, to stick it out and share. Believe me, I know. I've made the mistake I'm talking about too many times in my own life."

Laura turned to gaze at Zeke. He nodded thoughtfully, then spoke to Franny.

"Is it that obvious?"

"You mean that you're in love?" Franny asked. "Or that you're insecure and not trusting of each other?"

"Both," he said.

"It is to me," she said.

"Are you?" Laura asked him.

"What?"

"In love?"

He pondered her question for a moment, glanced at Franny, and was grateful for her friendly smile. Then he leaned closer to Laura.

"Yeah," he said. "I think so. What about you?"

She shook her head. "You don't even have to ask."

"Well," Franny said, "now that that's taken care of, let's go home. I was up all night and I'm dead tired."

Seated in his car, parked on the street in front of Laura's new building, watching Franny enter with her key, Zeke slipped his arm around Laura's shoulders. She wrapped her arms around his neck.

"She's a good friend," Laura said, her lips almost touching his.

"Yes," he said. "I can tell."

"So are you," she said.

"You better believe it."

She slid down and pressed her face to his chest. "I feel so lucky," she said.

"Me too."

"And so guilty at the same time."

"Why guilty?" he said to the top of her head.

"Because of Dimmy. I came here to be with Dimmy, to give him support, and instead I'm all involved in my own life."

"There's just so much you can do for him, Laura. I know I can't help him anymore."

"You can't?"

"No," he said softly. "I had to move him out of the hospital. I put him in County Jail."

She sat up. "Why?"

"I didn't think he was safe in the hospital."

"Why not?"

"There was something going on with one of the orderlies. I think the man was torturing him. I need time to investigate, and I couldn't leave Dimmy at the mercy of a hostile staff."

"What was going on with the orderly?" Laura asked suspiciously.

"I'd rather not say."

"I thought we just agreed not to hide things from each other, Zeke."

"This isn't me hiding. I'm protecting Dimmy."

"From me? He doesn't need protection from me."

Zeke nodded. "You're probably right. It's just hard to tell you. I know it'll hurt you." He sighed deeply. "It's a sexual matter."

"Oh, no," she moaned. "That bastard!"

"I'm not so sure the orderly is at fault."

"I don't mean the orderly," she said. "I mean that bastard Nikki. Look what he's done. He's a curse on everyone who comes near him. Look what he did to me, and to his first wife and his children, and now this . . . with Dimmy." She suddenly began to weep.

"Laura, I'm sorry. I didn't want to tell you. I knew it would hurt you."

"Oh, Zeke," she cried. "Hold me! Please! Oh, God!"

He wrapped her in his arms and pressed her firmly to him, then stroked her hair and pressed his lips to her forehead.

They sat that way for a long time while, down the street also seated in the front seat of a parked car, Nikki watched from the shadows. He saw the two dark figures move together, saw them kiss, and his mind created lustful visions as he burned with rage and envy. He felt a madness sweep up and over him. He wanted to bite her flesh, to taste her blood.

When she left Jerry Beck at about five-thirty, Harriet Doyle stopped at a convenience store and bought a package of melba toast and a large cup of black coffee. She drove back to Nikki's and parked on Cahuenga just south of Hollywood Boulevard, facing north, from where she was able to watch both the entrance to Nick's Falafel Restaurant and the stairway to the upstairs apartment.

When she had eaten several pieces of the toast and sipped half her coffee, she lit up her third cigarillo of the day. She wished she were not addicted to the long, dark imported cigarettes and was proud that she had been able to limit herself to so few. That was an extraordinary achievement for an anxiety smoker who had been known to chain-smoke two or three packs a day during a difficult trial.

The boulevard was busy, but the players had not changed from the afternoon; they were simply more mobile at night. They marched up and down the boulevard, greeting friends, trying to score, stopping to chat, begging for change, spitting on the street. Nothing had really changed from the afternoon. The street was merely darker, perhaps more ominous, even more dangerous.

Irene emerged from the stairwell at about eight o'clock. As she started down the boulevard on foot, Doyle swung out into the street, tires squealing, made a wide left turn through the traffic, and pulled up at the curb beside the girl. She rolled the window down and leaned across the passenger seat to call her name.

The girl stopped and stared at her.

"It's me," Doyle said. "Harriet Doyle."

The girl moved closer to the car. "What do you want?"

"You want a lift?"

"No," the girl said. "I'll get the bus on the corner."

"Where you going?"

The girl shrugged. "The Strip."

"Hop in. I'll drive you."

The girl considered the offer for a moment. She glanced down the street in both directions, cast a glance back at the stairwell, then climbed into the car. "Okay," she said. "Let's go."

Doyle pulled out into the flow of traffic and drove west toward the Sunset Strip.

"Okay, what do you want?" Irene said. "You weren't just passing by. You were waiting for me." The girl stared out the window as she spoke.

"You're right," Doyle said. "I wanted to talk to you alone, without your father."

The girl nodded. "So, talk."

They were forced to stop just before Highland Avenue

where the traffic was gridlocked. Doyle could see that the signal light on the corner had become superfluous; it changed from red to green and back again while nothing moved. The river of cars moving north to the Hollywood Bowl had clogged the streets.

"You love your brother?" Doyle asked.

"Of course," Irene answered without hesitation.

Doyle nodded. "You want to help him?"

"What do you want?" Irene snapped impatiently.

"I want you to help me so that I can help your brother."

The girl turned to face Doyle. "You think for one minute that if I could help Dimmy I wouldn't? What kind of person do you think I am?"

"I don't know. I just know that I need help and you're not even trying."

"That's not true."

"Isn't it?"

Irene hesitated, bit her lip. "There's nothing I can do."

"Of course there is," Doyle said. "You can certainly supply me with information."

"You want me to tell you stories about my father? You want me to tell you what a terrible man he is? Is that what you mean by information?"

Doyle nodded. "That's part of it. Yes. But I need to know more about Dimmy, too. I need to know how they were together, what caused this thing to happen."

Irene laughed ironically. "You know enough about them already." She glared at Doyle. "You've talked to Laura, Mr. Haines, Dimmy, and the shrink. You've read all the reports. What more do you want?"

They passed through the bottleneck and sped on toward La Brea. Around them cars filled with teenagers, hooting and hollering, cruised the boulevard.

Doyle turned left onto La Brea, sped down the one long street to Sunset, and made a right turn onto the wide thoroughfare. "All that information doesn't mean a thing. It doesn't help me, and it doesn't help Dimmy, either. What I really need to know, I don't."

"What's that?"

"I need to know what happened that night before the actual incident. Earlier too. Even earlier that day and the day before."

"What for?"

"I need to know what made him finally do it."

"What for?" the girl persisted, her voice rising almost hysterically.

"Because, legally, the fact that he was abused doesn't mean shit!" Doyle said angrily. "It doesn't mean a damned thing. He didn't have the right to try to take his father's life. Unless . . ." She stopped and breathed deeply as much to control herself as to catch her breath.

"What do you want from me?" Irene said. Silent tears were streaming down her cheeks.

Doyle pulled over and parked. She turned off the ignition and twisted in her seat to face Irene. "Look," she said as kindly as she was able. "Your brother's going to go to prison for a very long time unless somebody helps me. I'm counting on you. You're all I've got. Try to understand that I can't save him if I simply tell the jury that after years of abuse he got up one night, stole into his father's bedroom, and stabbed him seventeen times. Because even if the jurors know that Dimmy was abused all his life, they still won't condone his taking the law into his own hands. They won't reward him for attacking his father. The jurors will wonder why he didn't try something else first, why he didn't take more acceptable measures."

"Like what?" Irene snapped.

"Like why didn't he run away?" Doyle said. "Why didn't he tell someone? Why didn't he go to the police?"

"Stupid!" Irene spat.

"What?"

"All of you. You're all stupid."

"Why?"

"Because," she said, "you say stupid things. You talk like you and me are not in the same world. Where the hell do you come from, anyway?"

"I come from a pretty tough place," Doyle said.

"Then you forgot what it was like. You got fancy clothes now. You drive a Mercedes. You got all kinds of money. You must've forgot what it's like."

"Being poor?"

"No!" Irene shouted. "Being helpless!" The girl reached for the door handle. "Let me out of here!"

"Wait!" Doyle pleaded. "Don't go!"

"This is useless. You don't understand me and I don't understand you."

"Try me," Doyle begged. "I want to know. I'll listen to you."

"All right! I'll give you one chance." Doyle could hear the rage in the girl's voice. "Can you peel off your skin and put on mine or Dimmy's? No! You can't do that, can you? You've got to stay who you are, right? Just like me. Just like Dimmy. You've got no choice. Just like me. Just like Dimmy. Your jury wants to know why he didn't run away or go to the counselor at school, go to the police?

"Tell them there is no place to run. Tell them there is no counselor because Dimmy didn't go to school. Tell them he worked in the kitchen like a slave since he was twelve. Tell them the police don't help. They can't be bothered." She paused and breathed deeply. "You can't help, either. Nobody can help. Nobody wants to."

"Did you ever go to the police?" Doyle asked.

The girl threw her head back and laughed again. "You want to hear about the social workers who came, talked to Papa, told him how they understood it was tough being a single parent? Not one of them ever talked to me. We were eating. We had a roof over our heads. The house was clean. What more is there?"

"What about the police?" Doyle asked again.

"Oh, sure. There's always the police. I remember the cop who told Dimmy to shape up and quit giving his father a hard time. In New York a lady downstairs complained that Papa was beating us, and this cop came to see for himself. He and Papa became good friends. They used to go out drinking together. Papa got him tickets to all the fights and to football games. Good tickets. One time Papa punched a Housing Authority cop, but his friend Officer Dillon fixed it up."

"Your father punched a cop?"

The girl nodded sadly. "Papa beat him up, kicked him, and threw him out of his restaurant. Dillon fixed it for him at first. Later, though, they wanted to put Papa on trial. That's when we moved out here to California."

Doyle made a mental note to inquire about Nikki Pappas with the New York Police Department. "Go on!" she said.

"That's all," Irene said and seemed suddenly exhausted. "You just tell the jury that."

"I want you to tell it," Doyle said. "I want you to testify for your brother. You get up there and tell the court the same things you've just told me."

The girl stared at her. "You must be nuts," she said. "You want me to tell stories about my father in public?"

"Yes."

"Didn't you listen to me?"

"I listened."

"But you didn't hear. You were too busy thinking about how you were going to use me." She pushed the door open.

"Don't go!" Doyle said.

"It's hopeless," Irene said. "You can't beat my father by getting me to talk about him. Not a chance. I will never testify against my father."

"I could subpoena you," Doyle said.

"Go ahead!" she said. "It won't help you. If you ever repeat anything I told you tonight, I'll deny that I said it. If you make me testify, I'll say 'I don't know' to everything you ask me. 'Sorry. I don't remember a thing.'"

"I understand that you're afraid, Irene. I won't put you in danger by asking you to testify. But at least tell me what happened that day."

"Nothing happened," she said. "Not a damned thing." The girl stepped out of the car, slammed the door shut, and leaned in the open window. "Nothing happened. Got it? *Nada!*"

"Think about this, Irene!" Doyle snapped. "Do you want your brother to go to prison?"

"I got news for you, lady. My brother's been in prison all his life."

She turned and strode away down Sunset Boulevard. Harriet Doyle watched the girl disappear into the crowd, taking with her most of Doyle's confidence and hope.

The phone was ringing when Zeke got home. He ran to answer it and caught Doyle just as she was about to hang up.

"Hello!" he said breathlessly.

"What the fuck have you done with my client?" Doyle shouted. "Where'd you put him?"

"Hold on, Harriet. Take it easy," he said calmly.

"To hell with that," she shouted. "I went over to the hospital to see him just now. They refused me entry, informed me that my client was no longer a patient there, and could not tell me to what facility he had been transferred. They also told me he was moved on your order, and that really pisses me off." He could hear her rapid, heavy breathing as she fumed at him. "Let's get something straight, Doctor. I'm responsible for that boy's defense. I don't want you making decisions about him without conferring with me."

"I'm sorry," Zeke said. "I didn't think it was necessary."

"You didn't think it was necessary?" she screamed.

"When Haines was his lawyer, he didn't care."

"My point exactly," Doyle snapped. "That's enough to let you know how important it is. Listen, Doc, I'm less than a week away from trial, and I don't want anything to happen that could take this case out of my control. It's a war now and I'm the commander in chief. Got it?"

"Yes, ma'am," Zeke responded somewhat sarcastically.

"If I sound pompous, I apologize. I'm going to sound pushy and pompous a lot in the next few weeks, so consider this apology valid for all of those offenses. Okay? That way I don't have to keep saying I'm sorry, and we can continue to be friends."

"Okay," Zeke said. "But I want it on the record that you intimidate the hell out of me."

"That's my stock in trade," she said.

"Okay," he said. "I'll remember that."

"I'm done beating you up if you're done being ornery," Doyle said.

"I'm done," he said.

"I need a favor," she said, sounding much more conciliatory.

"Shoot!"

"First of all, tell me where you put our client."

"In the County Jail, for his own protection."

"What does that mean?"

"Trust me on this," Zeke said. "It was a medical decision. He's better off where he is."

"You got him with the pogey bait?" she asked.

"Exactly."

"Okay, I'll trust you."

"Thanks."

"I need to see him in the morning."

"You won't have any problem. You don't need me for that."

"Oh, yes I do," she said. "I need you very much."

"What for?" he asked.

"I'll tell you on two conditions."

"What's that?"

"That you don't interrupt and you don't disagree."

"I can't agree to that."

"What's the matter, Doc, don't you trust me?" she asked.

He thought for a moment. It seemed to him that he had heard the word "trust" used more this night than in any group therapy session. "How about a hint?" he asked, finally.

"All right," she said. "You deserve that much. We're going to play investigator, Doc. You and me. We're going to probe our client's mind. Hidden in there somewhere is the memory of the incident that caused him to grab a knife and slice his papa to shreds. We need to know what that was. And we are not going to give up until we get it. That means, if necessary, you're going to pump him full of sodium pentothal and suck the truth out of him."

"Whoa!" Zeke said. "Who said I'm going to do that?"

"I said."

"You don't have that kind of power, Counselor."

"No, but you do."

"Yes," he said. "But I wouldn't dare use it without the court's permission. You get that and then we'll talk."

"I'll never get permission from Judge Bauer."

"Then, that's it," he said. "Without a court order, you can't make Dimmy submit."

"Could you talk him into it?" she asked.

"I doubt it."

"Would you be willing to try?"

"I don't think so."

"Even if I told you it could save him?"

He thought for a moment. "Maybe."

"I'll meet you at the jail at seven tomorrow morning."

"What?" he shrieked.

"And, Doc," she continued, "would you tell his stepmother that we need to have a meeting tomorrow? How about two o'clock? At my house?"

"Hey, Doyle," he said. "I'm not your secretary."

"I want you there, too, Doc. We're going to devise a strategy. No good general goes into battle without a plan."

"All right," he said, surrendering. "We'll be there."

"Oh, Doc," she said before hanging up, "about that secretary crack. If you ever get backed up and need some help, call on me. I owe you one, and I'm one hell of a typist."

EIGHTEEN

Doyle was shocked at how much Dimmy had changed in the few days since she had last seen him. He had lost some weight, and the skin on his face hung loose from his cheeks, like a dog's jowls, emphasizing the dark circles under his eyes. His hair, unruly and uncombed, had grown longer and hung shaggily over his ears. His jail clothes were too large for him. The seams of his shirtsleeves hung over his shoulders, and the cuffs nearly covered his hands. The trousers, baggy in the rear, were artificially pleated in the front and belted with tape.

But it was his eyes that disturbed her most. Their vacant stare passed over her almost as if he had never seen her before. They shone like the eyes of a child with a high fever. And they looked wet, as though he was crying.

They had waited for him, she and Zeke, in a private visiting room. They had been talking about which approach would be most effective in getting from him the information that Doyle wanted. They anticipated some difficulty, expected him to balk. If he was not willing to discuss the circumstances surrounding the attack while he was conscious, it was a safe bet they would have a difficult time convincing him to allow them to question him while he was unconscious. They had therefore prepared themselves for an argument.

However, neither of them was prepared for the boy who shuffled into the room, trailed by a burly guard, and fell onto a chair before them, weak and compliant, as though he were already hypnotized.

Zeke rose and moved to him. "Dimmy? What's the matter with you?"

The boy smiled weakly.

"What happened to him?" Zeke demanded of the guard.

"Nothing," the deputy said, shrugging. "That's the way he's been since I been on. I've never seen him look no different. I know he doesn't sleep, and I guess he must've stopped eating, too."

"I saw him only two days ago," Doyle said to Zeke. "He was okay then. Maybe you shouldn't have moved him."

"Dimmy," Zeke said, "do you know who I am?"

The boy nodded. "Dr. Perez."

"Yes," Zeke said. "And who is this?" He pointed at Doyle.

"That's my lawyer," Dimmy said.

Zeke visibly relaxed. "You scared me, Dimmy. The way you came in here, I thought you were really sick."

Dimmy shook his head. "Tired," he said.

"Aren't you sleeping?"

Dimmy grinned at him. "You don't sleep in here," he said. "It ain't safe."

The guard stood by the door, his arms crossed over his chest. "Can I go now?" he asked.

"Yes, of course," Zeke said.

The guard slipped out and closed the door behind him. The room they were in was bare but for a wooden table and four wooden chairs. A thin plastic ashtray stood in the center of the table surrounded by burn wounds in the wood. The single window faced east, and the bright morning sunlight filled the room.

"Are you being mistreated here, too?" Zeke asked.

Doyle interrupted. "What do you mean, mistreated? Is somebody giving him a hard time?"

Zeke glanced at her and shook his head, then spoke to Dimmy. "The same way as in the hospital?"

"Yes."

"What's he talking about?" Doyle demanded.

Dimmy looked at her, and his expression seemed to melt into one of sadness. "Everybody wants to fuck you. That's the way it is."

"Jesus Christ!" Doyle exclaimed.

Zeke led her off to one side. "Don't get so excited," he whispered to her. "He's been incarcerated for a long time. A little paranoia is acceptable."

"You mean he's imagining things?"

Zeke shook his head. "There's some truth in most paranoid delusions. He's always been a little sexually phobic, at least since I started seeing him, but it's become much worse in the last couple of weeks, since Laura came out."

"Look," Doyle said harshly. "If he's being sexually abused, I want him out of here. I want him someplace safe. I'm not going to conduct his defense while he's being raped nightly in the County Jail."

"What do you want me to do?" Zeke asked defensively. "I can't put him back on the ward. It isn't safe there, either. You know what these jails are like, Doyle."

Doyle glanced over her shoulder and noted that Dimmy was watching them eagerly. She knew that Zeke Perez was no more responsible for Dimmy's devastation than she was, or any of them for that matter. She and Perez had not put him in jail. She and Perez had not made the system what it was. Perhaps no one had made it so. Dimmy had described his situation most accurately when he had said, ''That's the way it is.''

Whatever the outcome of his trial, whether he was found guilty or innocent, she thought, he did not deserve to be degraded like this. He did not deserve to be pulled out of one brutal situation just to be deposited in another. She resolved that she would not allow it to continue. She would put an end to it, no matter what it took.

''I'll get him moved to a holding cell during the trial. I don't want him housed with other inmates. He doesn't need this kind of pressure,'' she said.

She turned and walked away from Zeke. ''I'm going to get you moved again,'' she said to Dimmy. ''I'll do it today. Is that okay with you?''

He gazed up at her and nodded gratefully.

''Paranoia, shit!'' she snapped at Zeke. ''Listen, Dimmy. I promised to do something for you, right?''

The boy nodded again.

''I want you to do something for me.''

''All right,'' he said.

Zeke moved to the table and stood beside Doyle.

''I'll get you moved, but first you have to help me. You have to try to remember what happened the day you stabbed your father. Can you do that for me, Dimmy? Please!''

The boy gazed at Doyle sadly. ''I remember,'' he said.

''Tell me.''

''All day?'' he said.

''No,'' she said. ''Just what happened that made you angry.''

He looked puzzled. ''I wasn't angry that day.''

''How about that night? Did something happen that night?''

He grew thoughtful. ''No,'' he finally said. ''Nothing special.''

Doyle slumped back in her chair. "You don't remember," she said.

"I remember everything," he protested.

She turned to Zeke. "You want to try?"

"I don't see what else I can do. You asked him and he answered you."

Doyle spun around to Dimmy. "Listen," she said angrily. "I need to know what your father did that day or that night that pissed you off bad enough to make you go after him with a knife."

"You're angry at me." Dimmy seemed to shrink even further into himself, becoming smaller and even less significant.

Doyle relented. "I'm sorry," she said. "Now *I'm* beating up on him." She shook her head and frowned.

"Look," she said. "Suppose a guy is minding his own business and another guy breaks into his house and starts to trash it, rob it, maybe even hurt his family. The first guy gets a gun and shoots him. That's called justifiable homicide, Dimmy. But if that first guy gets his gun and goes looking for someone and finds the second guy not doing anything and shoots him, that's called murder." She paused. "Do you see the difference?"

"Yes," Dimmy said.

"Tell me the difference, in your own words."

"Well," he said, "in the first story, that was self-defense. In the second story, the guy had no reason."

"Okay," Doyle said eagerly. "If I asked you which of the two stories is most like yours, what would you say?"

Dimmy thought about the question for a long moment. "Neither one," he finally said.

"Why not?"

"Because."

"No, Dimmy. You can't say 'because.' You have to tell me why. If it wasn't self-defense and it wasn't murder, then what was it?"

The boy shrugged and pressed his lips together.

Desperate, Doyle leaned across the table and spoke directly into Dimmy's face. "Isn't it true that your father hurt you all your life?"

The boy nodded.

"Isn't it true that he hurt your mother?"

The boy nodded again.

"And your sister?"

"Yes," he whispered.

"That he was always hurting you?"

Dimmy nodded again.

"On that day, isn't it true that he beat you? Didn't he tie you up? Didn't he chain you in the basement? Hang you from the ceiling? Push your head into the oven? Didn't he put his gun to your head and threaten to kill you?"

"Hold it!" Zeke said. "What are you doing?"

"That's what went on in that home!" she shouted. She wheeled back to Dimmy. "Did he, Dimmy?"

"No," the boy said calmly. "He didn't do any of those things on that day. If he had, I would remember."

"I know you've got a great memory, Dimmy," Doyle said, "but what if, just this once, you really didn't remember? Think about that! It was self-defense all the time, but we didn't know that because just this one time you didn't remember. Wouldn't that be awful?"

"What are you trying to get me to say?" the boy asked. "I'm not going to lie. That would make things even worse."

"I don't want you to lie. I want you to admit that maybe, just maybe, there is one chance in a thousand that something happened to set you off that day, something so bad that you don't remember it. Sometimes things are so bad that people with perfectly good memories forget them. Isn't that right, Doc?''

''Absolutely!'' Perez said. ''It happens frequently.''

''Maybe that's what happened to you, Dimmy.''

''No,'' he said, shaking his head slowly. ''I don't think so.''

''But you can't be sure,'' she said. ''There's always that one chance, isn't there? There's always that long-shot possibility. Think about it, Dimmy! If that was the one thing that could keep you out of jail and we were negligent enough not to find it, not even to look for it, wouldn't that be a terrible injustice?''

''Nothing happened.''

''But what if it did?'' she insisted. ''Let's say we know that nothing happened. Let's say we're ninety-nine percent sure of that.'' She paused and studied Dimmy. He watched her as well. After a moment a look of amusement crossed his face. She smiled. ''What about the other one percent, Dimmy?''

''What about it?''

''Isn't it logical that if we're all ninety-nine percent sure, we would want to eliminate that one percent so we could be one hundred percent sure?''

''Okay,'' he said.

''Good!'' She smiled with satisfaction. ''Here's what I want you to do. Dr. Perez is going to give you some sleep medicine, and while you're asleep he's going to ask you to remember that day. Now, we all know that nothing happened on that day, so it stands to reason that you won't remember a thing. But afterward we'll be one hundred percent sure and we won't have to bother with it anymore.''

Dimmy laughed.

''What?'' Doyle asked.

He laughed louder.

"What, Dimmy?"

He sobered suddenly. "Fuck off, lady! You know what your job is. I want you to do it. I don't need you sticking needles into my arm. I don't need any truth serum, because I always tell the truth. And besides, what do I need some dumb fucking lawyer poking around in my head for?"

Prosecutor Marvin Jehnke, tall, slender, and impeccably dressed, as if it were early in the morning instead of the end of the day, arrived at the City Café early, seized his favorite table in the rear corner beside the window, and ordered a coffee and a blueberry tart without waiting for his guest to arrive. He settled down to read his notes, perhaps for the fifth time, but did not concentrate upon them. Instead, his mind was focused on priming the witness for whom he was waiting.

Though this was not his first big case, it was without question his most important. It had already garnered serious media interest—this kind of case always did—and that would mean interviews on television, quotations in the press, perhaps even his picture in the *Los Angeles Times*. That his opinions and interpretations would be recorded on the eleven o'clock news was as good as a given.

Success had been a long time coming, and Jehnke was ready for it. He despised every day he spent in the prosecutor's office. His evenings and nights were filled with thoughts of manipulations that would catapult him into the public eye and eventually into a partnership in a private practice. That was where he belonged. He had been convinced of that fact since the day he graduated from law school.

The first time he appeared in court, as a new addition to the district attorney's office, and saw the private lawyers in Armani suits, Bally shoes, silk ties, and embroidered silk shirts, he had known exactly where he belonged. But graduating sixteenth in his class from Loyola Law School was a far cry from the top ten at Stanford, Harvard, Yale, or even UCLA.

Since that first day, he had become even more committed to effecting an escape from public service. He had not only come to despise the D.A.'s office, he had learned that he despised the practice of law in general. He did enjoy the dramas on television that glorified the profession through tense and exciting stories while ignoring the boredom, the routine drudgery, the hours of research and homework, the overload, the pressure, and of course the total lack of anything even faintly resembling justice.

Well, fuck it, he thought. Since it was all a pretense anyway and since nobody really cared, why not make the most of it? He had already decided to go for the jugular on this one and win it in a big way. No attempted murder trial in the state in recent times had attracted so much attention. He could push for life in prison if he wanted to. If he won it, an outcome of which he was fully convinced, there might even be a book deal in it for him. Nothing added to the prestige of a big firm lawyer more than the publication of a best-seller.

At times, when thoughts like these flashed through his mind, he would caution himself that he was extending the bounds of grandiosity, that he should beware of falling victim to an overactive imagination. But at other times, when he thought of the many successful lawyers who had started as prosecutors and carved major careers for themselves by putting poor souls on death row, he knew that his ambition was not so farfetched. The Pappas boy could be his ticket to a penthouse office in Beverly Hills.

He saw Jerry Beck enter the restaurant and waved him toward the back.

"Hello, Marvin," Beck said as they shook hands. He sat across from Jehnke and glanced at the partially eaten tart.

"A sugar fix," Jehnke explained. "It's five o'clock. Some people unwisely imbibe in martinis or whiskey sours. I limit myself to a cup of coffee with three sugars and the richest piece of pastry on the menu."

Jerry Beck surveyed Jehnke's lean frame and shook his head in wonder. "How the hell do you stay so thin? You must run six miles a day. I'm gonna gain weight just watching you eat that shit."

"Nervous energy, my friend," Jehnke replied in all seriousness. "I burn calories while I'm thinking. My most strenuous exercise is studying the cases my colleagues have fucked up over the years."

"You've got plenty of those, haven't you?" Beck said, grinning broadly.

"A pretty good number. Equaled only by the number of assholes who have walked because of police stupidity. Never let it be said that I'm an unfair guy."

"Hey!" Beck said. "I also give credit where credit is due. We both fuck up and why not? We're only human, aren't we?"

They both laughed. They had never liked each other, but each could say that the other was a straight guy. In police jargon that meant a good guy as opposed to a civilian, who could not be good even if he tried.

"We're not going to fuck up on this one, are we, Jerry?" Beck shook his head. "Piece of cake."

Jehnke cringed. "Why do I shudder when I hear that expression?"

"Because you're the nervous type, Marvin. Nothing makes you happy."

"A conviction in the Pappas case would. I want the little

bastard to get the max. Then, as the kids say, I'll be one happy dude."

Beck nodded. "Okay. Go get him."

"I intend to. Come Monday, I'm going into court loaded for bear. Big guns, Jerry. All I want from you is some very precise testimony."

Jerry squinted at him. "Should I be insulted by that, Marvin?"

Jehnke waved the remark away. "Of course not. I merely want you to be very careful, Jerry."

"What's to be careful about? I was a witness to the confession. I didn't interrogate the boy, and I didn't arrest him. I was a witness. I never saw him again after that."

"But you will be asked about his mood, Jerry. About his general demeanor. About his physical appearance."

"Okay. So what? He was scared. Isn't every perp when he's surrounded by cops? He was nervous, agitated. He sweated a lot."

Jehnke leaned forward and spoke softly as if he were proposing a conspiracy. "Here's what I'm concerned about, Jerry," he said. "I don't want to leave any suspicion in the minds of the jurors that he was abused just prior to his confession."

"Nobody touched him!" Jerry exclaimed.

"I'm not talking about you guys. I'm trying to tell you that my guess is they're going after a self-defense plea. If that's the case, I don't want anyone on the jury believing the kid was abused just before the attack. I don't want them thinking that he might have been provoked."

"He wasn't, was he?"

"No, Jerry, he wasn't. But if a juror thinks so . . ."

"Okay," Beck said. "I understand."

"It's very important, Jerry. It doesn't matter if he got beat up the day before, as long as it wasn't on the same day. As long as he had some time to think between his last beating and the attack on his father, I'll shoot the defense full of holes. As long as you don't give some bleeding heart a chance to feel sorry for him."

"But you know," Jerry Beck said, "I remember that he had some fresh bruises on his face, high on his forehead right by the hairline."

"Shit, Jerry," Jehnke said. "Those are the marks that you guys did."

Beck was startled. "When did we do that? We never touched him."

"Sure, you did," Jehnke said, smiling warmly. "The doctor at County General remembers the bruises, too. After the confession, when the kid was being transported into custody, he tripped and fell getting into the bus. Don't you remember?"

"After the confession?"

"Yes," Jehnke said with confidence.

"Is that straight, Marvin?"

Jehnke grew serious again. "I'm going to win this one, Jerry. That murdering bastard is not going to walk. I'm sending him to prison where he belongs if it's the last thing I do."

"Okay."

Jehnke spoke slowly, emphatically. "You remember when he fell? You remember seeing him hurt himself?"

"I guess so," Beck said. "I guess that was what I saw."

Jehnke nodded. "Of course it was. How could it have been anything else? No one, I mean no one, touched that kid for weeks before he made that totally premeditated, unprovoked attack on his own father. If there was ever an act that cried out for punishment, it's this one. If there was ever a time for society to protect itself from its deviants, it's now. And that, Detective Beck, is exactly what I intend to do.''

''What are we going to do?'' Laura asked. ''It sounds so hopeless.''

She was sitting on Doyle's couch with Zeke beside her. Franny was seated in a soft lounge chair across from them, and Doyle stood at the bar, a glass of Cutty in her hand. There had been tears in Laura's eyes almost from the beginning of Doyle's briefing, and Zeke looked helpless sitting next to her.

Doyle had just completed putting them into the picture, as she called it. She had enumerated the various obstacles she faced in the presentation of an effective defense. She was faced with a prejudicial judge who could influence the jury, if not in terms of what they heard certainly in terms of how they interpreted what they were hearing, and her client did not appear anxious to help his own cause. On top of that, the evidence accumulated by the prosecution seemed insurmountable: Dimmy's voluntary confession, his knowledge of the whereabouts of the weapon, the testimony of the victim who unequivocally identified Dimmy as his attacker, and the sister's statement that she had seen Dimmy leaving the father's room, bloody knife in hand, just after she heard the man cry out in pain.

''In addition to all of that,'' Doyle said, ''the courts have a tradition of dealing harshly with children who attack their parents. Parricide is not tolerated in the United States. Even when juries have shown sympathy for the child, they have traditionally punished him or her severely—and that from a society which refuses to stop child abuse. The courts have always held the view that domestic violence is a personal problem and should be solved in the home. That's how kids like Dimmy get to live a whole lifetime being beaten and put into jeopardy."

Under any other circumstances, Doyle would have agreed that the best course of action would have been to accept the plea bargain, serve the time, and get the incident behind him. But, as she told the three guests in her living room, the fact that Dimmy had been so badly and so consistently abused nagged at her. It seemed to her to be incredibly unjust to deliver onto the boy the very punishment which, in Doyle's estimation, caused him to strike out in the first place.

"What are you going to do?" Franny said.

"We don't have lots of choices. There aren't half a dozen alternatives to choose from. There aren't even two that we can compare and examine.

"Here is a kid who went after his brutal father with a knife. There's no getting away from that. And that's a bad act. Keep in mind that the law intends to punish people who are blameworthy. On the face of it, that description fits Dimmy Pappas. In Dimmy's case there are no mitigating circumstances in the eyes of the law. The only meaningful defense would be a plea of self-defense, but that is almost hopeless. The time that elapsed between the last brutal act perpetrated upon him by his father and the moment he attacked the man is just too great. That indicates premeditation. If he had time to think, he had time to make a more appropriate choice.

"In order to prove self-defense I would have to show that Dimmy had reason to believe he was in imminent danger of death or serious bodily harm and that he could save himself only by using force. As you know, I've been unable to find any evidence of that.

"What's more, even if I could show that, I'd have to also show that Dimmy availed himself of every means possible to avoid physical combat before resorting to it. And if I could do that, which I can't, I'd have to show that Dimmy didn't use any more force than he absolutely needed to protect himself.

"I can't do any of that. One, he waited and planned the attack. Two, he made no effort to wake his father and negotiate with him. And three, he stabbed the man seventeen times, and many of those blows fell after the victim was already incapacitated."

Zeke stared at Doyle helplessly and seemed to be waiting for some word of salvation. "Is it hopeless?"

Doyle nodded. "It seems that way."

"So," Franny said, "I'll ask again. What are you going to do? It's obvious that self-defense is out, and you can't agree to make a deal, so what's left?"

Doyle, making the most of the dramatic moment, paused to drop an ice cube into her glass and refill it from the green Cutty bottle. She sipped, thought a while, then returned her attention to them.

"Why, I'm going to plead self-defense, of course."

"But you said—" Zeke began.

"And if necessary," she said, ignoring Zeke's interruption, "by God, we'll make new law."

PART
FOUR

NINETEEN

Dimmy sat alone at the defense table after his lawyer and the prosecutor were summoned to the judge's chambers. He kept his hands clasped on top of the table in full sight, just as he had been instructed, and held his head high. He was dressed in a dark suit that Laura had bought for him, a white shirt, and a maroon tie. His hair had been trimmed and his nails cleaned and clipped.

Just a moment before, he had glanced back and seen Irene sitting at the end of the last pew in the courtroom. She had smiled and waved at him, then thrown him a kiss. He quickly looked away before any of the spectators could catch his eye. They were always trying to get his attention, trying to lock his eyes into a stare with theirs. They really wanted to touch him, he thought. They wanted to tell their friends that they had been right up close to the monster, had looked into his eyes, had touched him.

He turned his gaze to the jury box and examined each of the jurors again, as he had been doing every day since the trial began. The motherly black woman, third from the end in the front row, smiled faintly and nodded shortly at him almost as if she were asking him to take heart. But the silver-haired old gentleman next to her stared at him blankly, coldly, as if he were some mutant who had intruded upon his peaceful world.

The foreman, a heavyset truck driver, would not look at him at all. No matter how hard Dimmy tried to gain his attention, the man always managed to slip his eyes away just in time. Dimmy wondered if that meant the man was trying to remain objective. Perhaps it was easier to send an unknown quantity to San Quentin than to sentence someone at whom you've stared for a month, Dimmy thought. If that was true, the judge should have locked the jury in a sealed room and made them listen to the proceedings over a loudspeaker. That would have really made him seem unreal.

He rubbed his eyes with two fingers. He was not tired, but he was weary of court procedure. He had actually been sleeping quite well in the private holding cell Doyle had arranged for him, and the nightmare that had plagued him for so long had finally vanished. Was that due to being in a safe cell? he wondered. No! He knew better than that. The dream had departed because he had told Zeke about it.

"What does it mean?" he had asked Zeke after describing the dream.

"What do you think it means?" Zeke had replied.

"I should've known you'd say that," Dimmy said.

Zeke smiled. "You know how this works by now."

The boy nodded. "Yeah. I'm an old hand." He looked up at the ceiling. He knew the process. He knew that he was avoiding the truth with small talk. "Okay," he said. "The obvious is that I'm scared that my father is going to do those terrible things to Irene." He sighed. "But that's too obvious, isn't it?"

"I don't know," Zeke said. "Does it feel right to you?"

Dimmy thought about that for a moment. "No," he finally said. "It doesn't feel right."

"Okay." Zeke nodded.

"No," Dimmy said. "It's a dream, not a movie. Dreams don't tell a story straight up. They do it in sneaky ways." He stared at Zeke. "Tell me what it's saying to me."

"It's your dream," Zeke said. "You wrote it. You tell me."

Dimmy grimaced and squirmed on his chair. "They're all me, aren't they?" He slapped the wooden arm of the chair. "They're all me. My father is me. My sister is me. And I'm me. All of us are me in the dream."

"Okay."

"So what am I afraid of? What am I doing?" He questioned himself as if one part of him was interrogating another. "When I'm my sister, I'm being raped. I'm being killed. When I'm my father, I'm doing the raping and the killing. And when I'm me, I'm trying to stop it."

"What does that tell you?" Zeke asked.

"What do you mean?"

"If in your dream you are the victim and the perpetrator and the rescuer all at one time, what are you telling yourself about yourself?"

Dimmy grew agitated. He could not sit still. He twisted and turned in his chair. His face curled into a grimace of pain.

"What is it?" Zeke asked.

"I hate this," the boy breathed. "I hate doing this."

"Of course."

"It hurts."

"Yes." Zeke nodded. "It does."

"Do I have to?"

"No."

"But I want to."

"So?"

Dimmy ground his teeth. "Okay," he said. "All those things are in me. There's part of my father in me and part of

Irene, too. And that's why I didn't do anything, maybe. Because the part of me that's like my old man wouldn't let me, and the part of me that's like Irene knew it was supposed to be that way, and that stopped me, too."

"Stopped you from what?" Zeke asked.

Dimmy shook his head. "I don't know."

"What could you have done?"

"I don't know."

"You were powerless, weren't you?"

"Yes. I thought so."

"Well?"

He gazed at Zeke. "I know you're trying to help me, but this isn't helping."

"Isn't it?"

"No."

"How do you know?"

The boy sighed deeply. "Because I suddenly feel so guilty I want to die again."

"We're really going ahead with it, aren't we?" Judge Bauer said, glaring at Doyle who stood before him.

"I guess so, Your Honor," she said.

"You're some piece of work," he said angrily.

They were in his chambers, she and Marvin Jehnke and the judge, where they had been summoned. Judge Bauer was not in his robes. He sat behind his desk leaning back in his chair in his shirtsleeves and suspenders, glaring up at her with an arrogant smirk on his face. Jehnke stood beside her, dressed at the top of fashion, and remained silent. It was clear to him that he was not in the hot seat and he had no intention of taking any of the pressure off Doyle.

"I'm giving you your last chance," Bauer said. "Before you two go out there to make your opening remarks, I'd really like to see one more serious attempt at a compromise.

What do you say, Marvin? If you waive time served? Recommend leniency? Look for an early parole?"

"I'd rather not, Your Honor," Jehnke said respectfully.

The judge frowned at him.

"Of course," he hurriedly said. "If you feel strongly about it—"

"What about you?" the judge said to Doyle, cutting Jehnke off in the middle of his remark. "What's it going to take for you to bend a little?"

"No jail time," she said.

"That's ridiculous," Jehnke interjected.

"How about a minimum?" the judge suggested. "Some token time?"

"No way," Doyle said. "No time in prison."

"You," Bauer said to Jehnke, "offer her two years, one already served. And you," he said, turning to Doyle. "Don't just brush it aside out of hand. Take it to your client. It's his decision."

Doyle shrugged. "All right, Your Honor. But I can tell you now, he's adamant."

"What the hell's the matter with you people?" the judge exclaimed. "That little fucker is guilty as hell. What does he want for nearly killing his father, a medal?"

"No, Your Honor," Doyle said softly. "Just a fair trial and a little justice."

In the wide hallway outside the courtroom, Zeke, who had canceled all his appointments for the next two weeks in order to be with Laura during the trial, attempted to comfort her. For the past several days she had been chastising herself for having caused the entire affair by abandoning the children in the first place. No matter how often they went over it, no matter how often she finally agreed that she had the right to protect herself, that it was her duty to herself to save her own life, she arrived ultimately at the same conclusion: she had failed the children and caused the calamity.

He held her arm tightly as they paced slowly up and back. The dreaded moment was drawing near, and he could feel the tension in her.

"None of this had to happen," she whispered. "If I had stayed . . ."

"You couldn't stay," he said. "You did the right thing."

"I know," she said. "But I should've stayed anyway."

"You couldn't have prevented it. It had to happen eventually."

"I know that, but—"

"We've been through this so many times, Laura," Zeke said wearily. "Still, you insist on punishing yourself."

She squeezed his hand. "Old habits die hard."

"This one is really destructive," he said. "Instead of seeing only the dark side, I want you to look at all the good that's happened to you. Look at how much better your life is today than it was two years ago."

"Yes," she smiled at him. "You're referring to us."

"Partly, yes. But what about Franny? You wouldn't even know her if you hadn't hidden out in Dayton."

She laughed softly. "You're funny," she said. She kissed his cheek softly. "I like that. 'Hidden out.'"

"Well, it's true. Of course, that's over. From now on, you won't have to hide. You'll stay here with me and live a normal life."

"I can't even think about that yet, Zeke. Not until I know what's going to happen to Dimmy."

"Whatever happens to Dimmy, your life has to go on. And instead of fearing the worst for him, think in terms of the best happening to him. He's got a good lawyer who's going to fight like hell for him. He has just as good a chance of getting off as he does of being convicted."

"You believe that?"

"Absolutely!"

"It must be wonderful to be optimistic," she said. "I wish I could think like you."

"There's nothing preventing you. All you have to do is decide. Then do it."

"That's easier said than done," she said sadly.

He shook his head. "You see why you have to stay with me?" he said. "If I'm not around you'll slip into those ugly frumps of yours. You need me around to keep your spirits up."

She stopped pacing and looked up into his face. "I need you for a lot more than that," she murmured.

Marvin Jehnke unbuttoned his suit jacket and allowed his tailored vest to show as he rose and approached the jury. He relied on his clean-cut good looks to win sympathy from the twelve people in front of him. In his mind, he was not a yuppie lawyer, an object of derision; he was a knight on the field of battle, his cause one of justice and right, his maiden fair the twelve members of the jury. Marvin's attitude was one of courageous sacrifice. He would do what had to be done. He would fight the forces of evil in the name of these twelve people who were not equipped to fight for themselves. He would protect them. He would suffer for them. He would win for them.

He stood before them and smiled warmly, confidently, as if he were their leader about to prepare them for a long and arduous mission.

"Ladies and gentlemen," he began, "the matter before us is not a pleasant one. I might say, of all the kinds of cases that could have been placed before you, this one might be considered the most unpleasant. Since the beginning of recorded time, throughout Greek and Roman mythology, the most terrible tales were those about the ungrateful, jealous son who plotted against and finally took the life of his father. We could read those stories and cringe because they were so distasteful to us. We could wonder how such a thing could happen and never really understand it. It is a crime beyond our comprehension. For most of us, it is an unforgivable sin against God's law.''

Like a professor lecturing an adoring class, he rose up on his toes and then settled back on his heels. ''Such is this case. It is as much about terrible sin as it is about the crime of attempted murder. On the face of the issue are the facts of the crime.'' He held up one hand and counted off by folding his fingers down one by one.

''Fact!'' he said, and a finger disappeared. ''Demetrios Pappas, without provocation, stole into his father's bedroom during the night, while the man slept, and stabbed him with fatal intentions. He stabbed him once, twice, thrice, then stabbed him fourteen more times in the head and body and arms.'' He paused for effect.

Another finger went down.

''Fact! In his possession was the kitchen knife he had used in the attempt to murder his father. He washed it clean, replaced it in the drawer from which it had come, and later led the investigating officer to it.''

Still another finger.

''Fact! Demetrios Pappas, after attacking his father, went to the Hollywood Division of the Los Angeles Police Department and surrendered himself. He gave the police an oral account of his act and signed a typed transcript of that account.''

His hand became a fist.

''Fact! To this very day, Demetrios Pappas has never once denied the accusation that he attempted to murder his father. To this day he has never denied any of the above stated facts.

''Those are the facts. But they do not constitute the entire story. The state intends to show you not only how Demetrios Pappas committed this reprehensible crime but why he did it. The state will allow you to see into the hidden motives of jealousy and envy that corrupted this boy. You will see his ambition. You will see his hunger for possessions, for ownership of his father's business, his father's money, his father's lifestyle. You will learn that he repaid parental dedication with deviousness and deceit.

''The defense will appeal to you on the grounds that the boy was abused. What teenage boy in America doesn't at one time or another feel abused? They will attempt to convince you that he was driven to act violently, that his behavior was that of any reasonable man. And the state will produce a psychiatric report which will prove that the defendant is and was of sound mind and was able to choose his mode of behavior.

''Finally, the defense will attempt to discredit the victim in this case. They will deluge you with stories of parental abuse until you are bored to tears with them. They will defame the victim shamefully. They will accuse him of every foul deed imaginable, every foul deed ever conceived by man since the beginning of recorded time. They will attempt to put the victim on trial in this courtroom.''

Marvin paused and slowly, silently walked the length of the jury box, fixing his gaze on each face as he passed.

''Don't let them!'' he finally said. ''Don't let them convince you that it was the victim who precipitated the attack on his own life. Don't let them do it! Ladies and gentlemen, this case is about a young man who, out of greed and malice, decided to murder his father in order to benefit himself. Only through the grace of God has his victim survived. Had it not been for the Lord's intervention, this might be a murder trial. Don't let the defense mislead you. Nothing about Nikos

Pappas is relevant here except the fact that he was attacked with a deadly weapon. Nothing about his past is relevant. Nothing about his personality is relevant. Nothing about his disposition is relevant.

"There is nothing more to consider here than the simple, calculated, despicable act of attempted murder committed upon Nikos Pappas by his son on a dark, moonless night while the unsuspecting victim lay asleep in his own bed." He stopped and, taking his time, examined the faces of all the jurors once again, then nodded. "Thank you."

He moved back to the prosecution table, turned, and, out of sight of the jury, winked at Doyle, then sat down.

Doyle stood and nodded respectfully at Marvin Jehnke. As she moved to the jury box, she threw him an admiring smile, conscious that the jurors were all watching her. She was not going to fall into the trap of appearing to be the enemy of society. In front of a jury she was keenly conscious of what the jurors saw when they looked at her. Her success had been as much a result of her realistic attitude as of her skill as a litigator.

She knew, for example, that to the foreman, the truck driver, she was "that nigger." To the matronly black woman, she was "a sister." To the silver-haired man beside her, she was "one of the good ones." She knew exactly who she was to each and every one of the jurors in that box, and she would play to them exactly as was needed in order for them to be sympathetic to her. Doyle knew, based on years of trial experience, that if the jury liked her, if they trusted her, they would set her client free. Good trials had very little to do with truth and justice.

"Ladies and gentlemen," she began softly with as much humility as she could generate in her voice, "everything you've just heard from Mr. Jehnke is absolutely true." She stopped, walked a few steps, and allowed the drama of that remark to take effect. Then she continued. "On May 15, 1992, Dimmy Pappas"—she turned and looked back at Dimmy—"seated at the defense table"—she brought her eyes back to the jury—"did enter the bedroom of his father, Nikos Pappas, and did, in the darkness of the night, stab his father seventeen times." She sighed deeply. "That's the truth. We will not insult your intelligence by trying to deny it."

She paced for a moment as if collecting her thoughts, started to speak, thought better of it, stopped, paused again, then spoke. "But it's not the whole truth." As if groping for words, as if unfamiliar with her surroundings, as if new at the game, Doyle seemed to grapple with the difficulty of articulating her message.

"You see, it's the defendant's claim that he's not guilty of the charges against him because he was acting in self-defense. Whoa! you're thinking. In the night? While the victim was sleeping? You've got to be kidding! But it doesn't really matter what the victim was doing if the defendant believed that he was in imminent danger of death or great bodily injury."

She leaned forward intimately. "You see, because of a lifetime of physical and mental abuse, and because of the numerous threats on his life made by the victim, that boy"—she pointed toward Dimmy again—"believed that killing his father was necessary in order to save his own life."

She straightened up. "I don't want you to think that I'm trying to get you off the track. I'm not very good at being clever. I'm much better at straight talk."

The black matron in the front row smiled warmly and nodded at her. Encouraging but not meaningful, she thought, as the woman had already been counted in Doyle's camp. It was the silver-haired man next to her whose sympathy Doyle wanted.

"The law says that killing in self-defense is justifiable and not unlawful when, one, the person who does the killing has reason to believe that the other person will kill him or cause him great bodily harm and, two, when any other reasonable person in the same circumstance would believe that it was necessary to kill to save his life.

"Actual danger is not necessary to justify killing another person. What's needed is that the circumstance is sufficient to create the fear in any reasonable person that there was danger of death or great bodily harm. And if the person doing the killing acted only because of that fear and the belief that such killing was necessary to save himself, the killing is deemed to be justified."

Doyle smiled at the jurors, then shrugged embarrassedly. "The law, in its attempt to be precise, gets a little nit-picky now and then," she said. "But what it really means to say is that actual danger is not necessary to justify self-defense. It's enough that you believe that the only way you're going to survive is to kill that other guy. If you honestly believe that you are in danger, you have the right to defend yourself. And that right of self-defense is the same whether the danger facing you is real or merely apparent."

She stopped to study the jury for a moment, allowing her eyes to move from face to face and pause at each one. To some she offered a slight nod. To others a pleading stare. To a couple of others she rendered a warm smile. Finally she pursed her lips, nodded, and commenced moving again.

"Now," she continued, "when someone receives threats against his life or person, that one is justified in acting more quickly and taking harsher measures for his own protection in the event of an assault, whether it's actual or threatened, than someone who has not received threats.

"This means that if Nikos Pappas had never threatened his son, but on a given day decided to attack him, we would have to examine if stabbing him seventeen times was justified. After all, how would the defendant know, since there were no threats, that his life was in danger?

"But after you've heard all the evidence, if you believe that Nikos Pappas did make threats against the defendant and that the defendant, because of such threats, had reasonable cause to fear greater peril in the event of an attack from his father, you have to take that into consideration. You have to calculate if the defendant has acted as any reasonable person would act after receiving numerous threats upon his life and after having been beaten and abused for years."

She nodded emphatically. "And that brings me to the matter of incomplete truth. The defense will not try to put the victim on trial here in this courtroom. But the defense has an obligation to challenge the credibility of the victim when he testifies as a witness. That's the law, ladies and gentlemen. There is no restriction prohibiting the admission of evidence that a person has committed a crime, a civil wrong, or other dastardly acts when that evidence is offered to support or attack the credibility of a witness.

"All right! What, then, is the whole truth?" She shrugged and turned around. She gazed out at the spectators in the courtroom. She turned and looked up at the judge. She turned and stared at the jury.

"That's what we all want to know, isn't it?" She took a deep breath. "The defense is going to prove to you that Nikos Pappas indulged in a fifteen-year course of systematic assaults and threats against the defendant, that he systematically tortured the defendant, that he routinely abused him both mentally and physically over most of the defendant's life, and that he did so with impunity, with the tacit approval of the authorities, the schools, the social agencies, and society in general. We're going to prove to you that the defendant is a young man of incredible restraint, a young man invested with a true belief in God and profound moral judgment. We're going to prove that any other reasonable person might have acted as the defendant did long before the defendant did. That no man could be asked to exercise the degree of restraint that the defendant exercised.''

Her nostrils flared. She stood before them defiantly, legs apart, head cocked slightly. On her face was an expression of total confidence. She nodded once.

''That, ladies and gentlemen, is the whole truth!''

When court adjourned for the day, Doyle requested a witness room in which to confer with her client privately. She stood by the window smoking a long black cigarette, blowing the smoke toward the air conditioner.

Dimmy sat at the small table staring at her admiringly. ''You were pretty good,'' he said. ''I forgot you were talking about me.''

Doyle nodded a thank-you. ''Don't get too excited. It's only just the beginning.''

''I know,'' he said.

She closed her eyes and concentrated for a moment. ''Dimmy,'' she said softly, ''I want you to tell me about your dream.''

''What?'' he said warily.

''The dream that you talked to Zeke about.''

''That bastard,'' Dimmy said angrily. ''He's not allowed to tell anyone what I tell him. You're a lawyer. You know that.''

Doyle nodded. ''He didn't tell me what was in the dream.

He only told me you were having one and he thought it might be significant in terms of your defense."

"My dream doesn't have anything to do with this."

"How do you know?"

"I know!"

Doyle sighed. "Don't you think I'm a better judge of that?"

"No!" he shouted.

"You can tell me to fuck off again," she said. "But I think, just from your reaction, that you know it's important. You don't want to talk about it because you think it'll give me a clue to what I've been after from the beginning."

"Dammit!" he said under his breath. "He had no right! I can't trust anybody."

"Sure," Doyle said ironically. "He's an asshole. He doesn't give a shit about you, right? He only thinks of himself. We know that, don't we? What did he ever do for you? Dr. Perez found your stepmother. Big deal. Anybody could've done that. He brought me in to defend you. Well, that's no big deal. He puts his neck on the line to get you moved out of a bad situation. Hell! He was probably just covering his own ass, right?"

Dimmy stared at her, and his mouth fell open.

"Shut your mouth," Doyle said. "You look stupid.

"I'm sorry," Dimmy said. "I got angry. I didn't think."

"Yeah, I know. That's one of the reasons you're on trial, because you didn't think. Well, how about doing some thinking now? You really want to go to San Quentin? You think you'll like it up there, huh, kid? You want to get an advanced degree in laundry or in license plates?"

"Stop it," he said quietly.

"No, Dimmy," she said. "You stop it. Stop fucking around with me. Okay?"

"Okay."

"Zeke says you should tell me your dream. He thinks it's important. I'm fighting this battle for you with one hand tied behind my back. I've got a good left jab, but I could get my clock cleaned by a real sharp hook. You know what I mean? Cut me loose, kid. Let me have both hands."

Dimmy bowed his head and spoke to the floor. "Okay," he said. "Okay."

He began to sob, and Doyle suddenly knew that she had found what she had been searching for all this time. She suddenly knew that the next day in court she would have both hands free, and she planned to come out swinging.

TWENTY

The next morning Marvin Jehnke started building his case against Dimmy Pappas carefully and methodically. He called upon an array of witnesses to establish the chain of events on that fateful night of near death, commencing with Detectives Peter Hogaboom and Antonio Sanchez, the arresting officers who had conducted the interrogation that resulted in Dimmy's confession. He followed that with Malcolm Phillipot, the paramedic who was first on the scene and who, along with his partner, Sidney Whitman, had transported the victim to Hollywood Presbyterian Hospital. Nikos Pappas was treated in that establishment's trauma center by Dr. Raymond Statler, who testified that it took more than seven hours of surgery to repair the damage that had been wrought upon the victim.

Phillipot testified that the sight of the room in which he found the victim stunned him. He stated that the wall near the bed was bloodstained to such an extent that it appeared to have been painted red. The victim, he also stated, had crawled from the bed, leaving a wide trail of blood, and was found unconscious on the floor in another huge pool of blood. Phillipot and Whitman administered oxygen while rushing the victim to the trauma center. They attempted to stanch the flow of blood by applying a tourniquet to the victim's left arm.

Doyle remained impassive during most of this testimony, coming to life somewhat only when Detective Jerry Beck took the stand to testify that he was a witness to the defendant's confession and could attest to the fact that it was made voluntarily and was not solicited with coercion or force of any kind. Jehnke questioned Beck about the presence of a bruise on the boy's forehead. Beck replied that to the best of his knowledge the defendant had acquired that bruise following the dictation of the confession and not prior to it. During his testimony, Doyle watched him closely, at one point nodding her approval of his demeanor, and smiled at him as he left the stand.

The surgeon, Dr. Statler, testified as to the extent of the injuries sustained by the victim. He enumerated the various wounds, described exactly where they were, their depth, the damage they had caused internally and what efforts were required to repair that damage. In addition, he testified to the amount of blood administered to the victim while on the operating table and painted a portrait of terrifying brutality causing irreparable damage and almost death. He likened the victim's condition to that of some of the wounded he had treated in Vietnam. At one point he said that his operating room looked as if it belonged in a war zone. He was, of course, referring to the amount of blood that continued to seep from the victim's copious wounds.

A forensics expert, Jonathan Laxineta, testified that the victim's bedclothes had been sliced and rent as if by a ferocious beast. He described the twelve punctures and rips in the sheet under which the victim had been sleeping, gave their measurements, their locations, and concluded by stating that, judging from the nature of the tears, which corresponded with some of the wounds on the body, some of the perforations were straight and deep while others were more superficial but much longer, as if the instrument had been driven into the flesh and then pulled downward, like the slicing of beef.

Doyle remained silent through most of the morning's testimony, objecting now and then, more to build a record for appeal than to strike any of the testimony. She managed to accrue a series of overrules from Judge Bauer that had spectators sympathetic to Dimmy grinding their teeth. However, Doyle appeared to be unperturbed. When court recessed for lunch, she rose easily and offered Dimmy a word of encouragement as he was led out. Then she left the courtroom walking jauntily, head held high, the picture of confidence.

"There's no point in objecting too much," Doyle said over lunch. "We're not going to make any points fighting the technical stuff. We're better off just letting it go. We don't intend to deny any of it, so why risk alienating the jury?"

She was responding to Laura's inquiry about why she had allowed so much damaging testimony to go unchallenged. They were lunching in the Music Center Restaurant, where lunch was more elegantly served than most dinners in most restaurants in Los Angeles. Doyle sat facing the room with Franny and Laura on either side of her and Zeke across from her. The room was crowded with lawyers and their clients from the many courtrooms across the street. They sat at a table in the rear, in a well-lighted area, as far from the noisy bar as they could get.

"The good part is coming up," she continued, after eating a shrimp. "I think we're going to see Mr. Nikos Pappas this afternoon."

Laura gasped at the mention of his name.

"Would you rather stay away?" Zeke asked her with concern.

She shook her head. "No. I want to hear what the lying bastard has to say."

"He may not lie," Doyle said calmly.

"He always lies," Laura countered.

"That would be a big mistake on his part," Doyle continued. "All he has to do is tell the truth and get off the stand. Any straying he does from the facts of the attack will open doors for me on cross that he'll wish he had never opened. I don't think Jehnke will let him do that."

"What kind of doors?" Zeke asked.

Doyle hesitated. She toyed with the remaining two shrimp on her plate, pushed them here and there with her thin silver fork. Finally she looked up at them. "I have a theory," she said. "I've been thinking about it most of the night. I hesitated discussing it with you because, frankly, it's not the most pleasant idea I could come up with, but it seems to be the one that fits best."

"A theory about what?" Laura asked.

Doyle nodded thoughtfully. "About what finally drove Dimmy to go after his father."

They were silent for a moment, fidgeting anxiously as if no one wanted to hear what was about to be said, while at the same time they longed to know.

"You see," Doyle continued, looking directly at Zeke, "it all comes from that dream of his."

"He spoke to you about it?" Zeke queried.

"Yes."

"Was he angry that I told you?"

"At first, yes."

Zeke lowered his eyes. "I really shouldn't have told you."

"I'm glad you did, and so is Dimmy now."

Laura seemed confused. "What dream are you talking about?"

"Zeke told me that Dimmy had been having a recurring nightmare," Doyle said. "It was so scary that the kid was afraid to go to sleep. We had already speculated that whatever had motivated Dimmy to try to kill his father was so terrible that he blocked it out of his memory and was not divulging it because he simply didn't remember it. When I heard about the nightmare, a bulb lit up in my head. I thought, maybe what he had blocked was what he was dreaming. Maybe his unconscious mind didn't want to let him forget totally."

"Is that possible?" Franny asked Zeke.

Zeke shrugged. "Anything's possible with the human mind."

"Anyway," Doyle continued. "Yesterday I asked Dimmy about the dream. He was reluctant to discuss it, but I finally convinced him that I needed that information. At first he broke down."

"What do you mean?" Laura said.

"He cried like a baby," Doyle said. "Later he got a hold on himself and told me the whole thing."

She turned to Zeke and said, "You want to explain the dream?"

"All right." He turned to Laura. "In the dream Dimmy walks down a long flight of stairs into a cold basement. His father is down there, and when he hears Dimmy's footsteps, he turns and blocks something that he has been working over. Dimmy wants to see what it is, but his father is in the way. They have a confrontation. Then Nikki backs off and lets Dimmy see what he has been hiding. Stretched out on a work table is a naked woman who is suffering great pain and who is bleeding from her vagina. Dimmy rushes to her, afraid that it is Laura, only to discover that it is his sister, Irene, who has been brutalized and ravaged."

"That's some nightmare," Franny said, grimacing at the horror of it.

"That poor kid," Laura said sympathetically.

"He's been having that dream on and off for the whole time he's been in custody," Zeke continued. "I suspect it was one of the reasons he tried to take his own life. His reactions to the dream are very strong. I am happy to say, though, that since we worked on it, he has been free of it. Maybe by interpreting it, he killed it off."

"How did you interpret it?" Laura asked.

"I didn't," Zeke said. "He did."

"Yes," Doyle said. "He told me that. And he's convinced that he understands the dream. I'm less convinced, however." She turned to Zeke. "What do you think of Dimmy's interpretation?"

Zeke shrugged. "It's impossible to know. Dreams can never be explained accurately. Who's to know for sure? But if the dreamer gets comfort from his own interpretation, that's sufficient because it reduces the anxiety the dream has produced, and that's what therapy is really all about—the reduction of anxiety."

"So," Doyle said, "if his interpretation makes him feel better, you don't push any further."

"That's right."

"Even if it's wrong?"

"Correct."

Doyle grew thoughtful, then said, "And if some other interpretation, which might be closer to the truth, would increase his anxiety level, you might willingly step around it?"

Zeke grinned uncomfortably. "Truth isn't one of my top priorities," he said. "You lawyers talk about truth all the time, although many of you lie like champions. For us, for me, 'the truth' is much less important than the ability to cope, and coping often requires maintaining an illusion. It's not the job of the therapist to sacrifice a coping technique by destroying an illusion for the sake of truth. On the contrary, reality is relative to an individual's subjective perception. Most of what we think about things we see is really untrue, but it can be comforting because it is illusory." He shook his head. "I hope that made sense to you."

"I don't understand how any of this ties in with the trial," Franny said.

Doyle smiled. "We did digress slightly, but it's important to understand that what Dimmy gets from his dream may not be what the dream is actually saying. If we forget what Dimmy thinks the dream means, we can get closer to a meaning that is more significant but which Dimmy may not want to bring back into his conscious memory."

"Well said," Zeke injected. "That's exactly what I thought when he and I discussed the dream."

"But you didn't push him toward another interpretation."

"That's right. I didn't."

"Because in your work, you don't need him to know the truth."

"That's correct. Not right away, at any rate."

"But in my work," Doyle said, "it's crucial to get at the truth, and that's why I didn't let it go. That's why I took the problem home with me and lay awake most of the night thinking about it, debating with myself about using what I believe to be the truth."

"What *is* the truth?" Laura demanded, finally showing her frustration.

Doyle stared at Laura. "You're not going to like it."

"That won't be anything new. I haven't liked any of this."

"Okay, then," Doyle said. "I think the incident that pushed Dimmy over the edge—the immediate motivator, if you will—had to do with his sister." She paused and breathed deeply. "I don't think Dimmy would have tried to kill his father because of anything that Nikki did to him. I think he is too completely reconciled to his fate to try to change it now. But what I do think, and what Dimmy's nightmare seems to signify, is that Nikki Pappas raped his daughter in the presence of his son and thereby set this whole disaster into motion."

As Nikos Pappas took the stand, every pair of eyes in the courtroom followed his progress down the center aisle, through the gate, past the defense and prosecution tables, and up to the witness box. He was dressed in a double-breasted gray pin-striped suit over a black shirt and a white silk tie. He looked like an old-time movie gangster and seemed to be proud of his appearance. He stood in the box and allowed his eyes to rove around the room. He smiled briefly at Irene, seated in the back, anguish displayed on her face. He ignored Dimmy at the defense table, but when he spotted Laura sitting in the first row of spectators, his eyes rested on her and his face hardened into a mask of hatred.

Judge Bauer studied him with curiosity, a smirk on his usually impassive face.

The clerk said, "Please raise your hand."

Nikki did so and was sworn in.

"Please be seated," the clerk said.

Nikki sat carefully, his back straight, leaning slightly forward, the crease in his trousers protected.

The clerk then said, "Please state and spell your full name for the record."

"Nikos Pappas," Nikki said. "N-i-k-o-s P-a-p-p-a-s."

The judge nodded to Jehnke. "All right, Mr. Jehnke."

"Thank you, Your Honor." Jehnke rose and moved toward his witness.

"On May 15, 1990, were you the operator of a restaurant—"

Doyle jumped to her feet. "Objection! Counsel is leading the witness, Your Honor."

Judge Bauer gazed down at her as if from a great height. "Ms. Doyle," he said. "This is just preliminary. Are you going to interrupt every time the mood seizes you?"

"I know it's preliminary, but—"

"Overruled!" the judge snapped. "Go ahead, Mr. Jehnke."

Marvin continued. "Were you the operator of Nick's Falafel Restaurant, located at 5722½ Hollywood Boulevard in the city and county of Los Angeles?"

"No," Nikki said. "My children were the operators."

"Were you the owner of the restaurant or were they the owners of the restaurant?"

"I opened it in their names," he said proudly. "I oversaw it."

"Do you mean you managed it?" the prosecutor asked.

"We did the whole thing together."

"I see. On that date what were your children's names?"

"One was Demetrios. The other was Irene."

"Is your son Demetrios present in this courtroom?"

"Yes."

"Would you point to him and tell us what he is wearing?"

Nikki pointed to Dimmy. "He is dressed in a dark suit with a white shirt and a tie."

Jehnke turned and stared for a moment at Dimmy, seated beside Doyle. After that prolonged moment, he turned back to Nikki.

"Where are you from originally, sir?"

"Salonika. Greece."

"How long have you been in this country?"

"Since 1972."

"Have you always been in the restaurant business?"

"Yes. From almost the first day I came here I'm in the business."

Marvin moved away from the witness and turned to the jury box. He questioned the witness then more or less over his shoulder while his eyes remained focused on various members of the jury. "On May 15, 1992, were you living and working at Nick's Falafel Restaurant in Hollywood?"

"Yes."

"Were your children living and working at that restaurant with you at that time?"

"Yes."

"Where in the restaurant did you all live?"

"Upstairs. We had the store downstairs and the apartment upstairs."

He turned to Nikki. "Sir," he said, "behind you there is a chalkboard. Do you see it?"

"Yes."

"Would you please step down from the witness box, draw a floor plan of your apartment on the chalkboard, and put your initials, N.P., in the bedroom where you stayed."

Nikki stepped over to the chalkboard and drew a rough outline of the apartment. Then he put his initials inside the largest of the five boxes in his plan.

"All right," Jehnke said. "Now, where did your son sleep?"

Nikki pointed to a box on the far side of the floor plan. "They lived in this room."

"Your son and his sister shared a room?"

"Yes."

"Is that room closer to the front entrance than yours?"

"Yes," Nikki responded. "It's right next to the front door. My room is in the back. To get to my room, you got to go down a long hallway, here. You got to go by the kids' room."

"On May 15, 1992, were you actually living in the apartment above the restaurant?"

"Yes." Nikki nodded.

"During that night did something happen to you?"

Nikki nodded vigorously. "Yes."

"What happened to you?"

"I got stabbed. I was in bed, sleeping, and I got stabbed."

"About what time was that?"

Nikki paused. "In the night, late," he said. "After we closed the restaurant."

"What time do you close?"

"On most days we close at ten o'clock. On Friday and Saturday we close at twelve o'clock."

Jehnke seemed to calculate for a moment. "So, on Tuesday, May 15, 1992, you closed at ten o'clock?"

"Yes."

"Then what happened?" he asked.

"I read the paper. I drank a little ouzo, and I went to bed."

"At what time was that?"

Nikki shrugged. "Maybe eleven."

"Then what happened?"

"I was asleep and I woke up all of a sudden with a pain in my neck like someone was chopping my head off."

"What was causing this pain?"

"I was cut with a knife."

"Did you see a knife?"

"Yes," Nikki said. "I saw a big knife over my head, with blood dripping."

"What part of your body was stabbed with that first blow?"

"Here!" Nikki twisted his head and revealed the thick scar on his neck. "In my neck."

"Then what happened?"

"He stabbed me many times. Seventeen in all."

"What part of your body was stabbed subsequently?"

"All over my top," Nikki said, running his hands down the length of his torso.

Marvin moved halfway to the witness stand. "Please stand and face the jury."

Nikki looked at the judge questioningly. Judge Bauer nodded to him and he stood.

"Please open your shirt and indicate the areas on your body which were stabbed."

Doyle felt Dimmy stiffen suddenly. She placed her hand on his arm and whispered, "Easy, Dimmy."

Then she was on her feet. "Your Honor, I object."

"Why?" Judge Bauer, asked.

"May we approach the bench?" Doyle asked.

Judge Bauer waved her forward. "Come ahead."

Doyle moved swiftly to the bench with Jehnke right beside her.

"What's all this about?" the judge demanded.

"Your Honor," Doyle said. "Mr. Jehnke is attempting to get the jury to examine Mr. Pappas's scars. I'm going to object to that on the grounds that it's prejudicial."

Judge Bauer snickered. "You want to give me a hint as to what you think the prejudice is?"

"Those scars make the wounds look a lot worse than they were."

"Could they be worse?" the judge asked in astonishment.

"They're going to inflame the jury, Your Honor," she insisted.

"So what?"

Jehnke said, "Your Honor, I would like to say—"

"Not necessary," Judge Bauer interrupted. "The objection is overruled."

"Your Honor—" Doyle began to protest.

"Get back there," the judge snapped.

Doyle and Jehnke returned to their tables. Doyle looked sullen.

Jehnke, careful not to smile at his victory, continued as if there had been no interruption.

Nikki removed his jacket and opened his shirt. Thick scars, some as long as four inches, crisscrossed his body. Perhaps a dozen were visible.

Beside her, Dimmy gasped, turned his eyes away and stared at the wall.

"If you want the witness to walk slowly past the jury," the judge said to Jehnke, "that would be all right. I don't know if all of the jurors can see."

"Thank you, Your Honor," Jehnke said. "Mr. Pappas, please walk past the jury."

Nikki, holding his shirt wide open, paraded slowly past the jurors, flaunting his gruesome scars, then returned to the witness stand.

"During the repeated stabbings," Jehnke continued when Nikki had dressed and was seated, "what did you do?"

"I screamed at him," Nikki said. "I tried to push him away. I tried to protect my face. That's how he stabbed my arms."

"Were you able to see your attacker?"

"Of course."

"Is he in this courtroom?" Jehnke asked.

"He's right there." Nikki pointed at Dimmy.

Dimmy raised his chin at the accusation and stared stoically at his father.

"You're indicating your son?" Jehnke asked.

"He used to be my son. He's not my son anymore."

"Mr. Pappas," Jehnke said, turning and walking toward the prosecution table, "during the attack did you say anything to your son?"

Nikki nodded. "First I called him a bad name. Then, when

he didn't stop stabbing, I begged him. 'Don't do it. Don't kill me,' I said. 'Dimmy! I love you! Why do you do this to me? I never hurt you.'" Nikki's face grew hard. "But he didn't stop, and I passed out. I didn't speak to him again."

"You mean that night?"

Nikki nodded. "That night. The day after. A long time after that."

"You have not spoken to your son at all since that night?"

"One time," Nikki said. "In the jail."

"What happened at that time?"

"I said, 'How could you do this to me?' He said, 'Papa, forgive me that this happened and try to get me out of here.' And I said, 'Why should I do anything for you? I don't understand why you tried to kill me.' He said, 'It was the restaurant, Papa. I wanted the restaurant and all the money for myself.'"

Dimmy leaned close to Doyle. "That's a lie," he whispered. "I never said that."

"Our turn will come," Doyle reassured the boy.

Nikki paused to wipe a tear from his eye, then continued. "He said to me, 'I couldn't wait, Papa. I wanted to be the boss of the family.'"

"At that time, did you offer to help your son?"

"Yes."

"Did he accept your offer?"

"No." Nikki shook his head sadly. "He got angry and he said, 'I will get out of here myself, and when I do, I will come after you again and finish you off.'"

"Another lie!" Dimmy whispered to Doyle. "I never said that."

Jehnke gazed at Nikki and nodded his head while he seemed to contemplate that last bit of testimony, thereby implying that it was weighty. Then he turned away from the witness and moved toward his seat. "I have nothing further at this time."

Judge Bauer looked up questioningly at Doyle. "Ms. Doyle," he barked.

Doyle rose. She glanced at her watch. "Your Honor, I expect to question this witness for several hours. It's now almost four o'clock. I respectfully—"

"All right!" Judge Bauer said. "We'll adjourn till tomorrow at nine."

He banged his gavel authoritatively, rose, and disappeared into his chambers, leaving Doyle with the remainder of her statement still in her mouth.

By the time Irene arrived at the Hamburger Hamlet at the west end of the Sunset Strip, Doyle had already put away two double scotches and a tall beer chaser, consumed half an order of fried zucchini, and was on her fourth cigarette of the evening. She was unwinding slowly, could feel the tension in her shoulder muscles easing. She was no longer grinding her teeth, and the dull ache in her lower jaw had subsided. She saw Irene enter the back room, which was decorated in black and red like a Roaring Twenties speakeasy. Doyle waved to her, and Irene walked toward her.

Doyle had found the girl's message on her answering machine after her final conference with Dimmy following the close of court. Nikki's lies had infuriated Dimmy, and Doyle had promised to address those lies on cross examination.

Weary after the grueling day, she had arrived at home wishing only to take a hot shower, down a tall Cutty, and fall into bed. She did not even want to think about the trial. She wanted to be at the top of her form when she returned to the battlefront, but she did not want to overtrain. She needed to get away from it all for a few hours, to clean out her mind so that she could engage Nikki Pappas the next day fresh and exhilarated.

Irene's message waited for her: "This is Irene Pappas. I was in court today when my father testified. I must speak with you. Please meet me at the Hamburger Hamlet on Sunset at eight. Please! It's really important."

Doyle had played the recording again and heard the anxiety, the sense of urgency, and the despair in the girl's voice. She had pampered herself with a shower, but she'd passed on the Cutty, glanced longingly at her bed, and headed back to Hollywood.

Irene approached the booth and slipped into the seat opposite Doyle. She was clutching a shoe box, which she set down beside her. "I'm very worried about my brother," the girl admitted.

"You should be," Doyle said. "I didn't understand why you weren't more worried last time we met."

Irene shook her head slowly. "I didn't know what my father was going to say. About the business, I mean. About Dimmy wanting the money, to be head of the family."

"You're telling me that isn't true?"

"Of course it's not!" She smiled ironically. "The head of the family? What family? There is no family. My mother is dead. My stepmother deserted us. And my father never really cared about us. There's only the two of us, and Dimmy's always been the head of the two of us." She gazed down and shook her head despondently. "As for the restaurant," she said, "I can't think of a single thing that Dimmy and I hate more than that filthy place. It's not a real restaurant. It's a toy for my father. It's his hangout. It's where the young dopers hang out, where he gets runaway girls for his fun. And all the losers on the boulevard sit around and worship him, like he's a big man or something."

"Is he in the drug trade?" Doyle asked.

"I don't know," Irene said, shrugging. "I stay away as much as I can. I don't want to know. I never go in there except when he makes me work in the kitchen. He does a lot of bad things, my father. He drinks too much. He bets on horses. Fools around with a lot of girls. Dirty girls." She shuddered. "But dope? I don't know."

Doyle studied the girl as she spoke. Finally she asked, "Why are you telling me all this?"

The girl bit her lip nervously. "I don't want Dimmy to go to prison. I don't want his whole life to be ruined."

"We may not have a choice," Doyle said.

"There must be something you can do," she pleaded. "If you show the jury how my father lied . . ."

Doyle shook her head. "The lies are not important."

"How can you say that?"

"Because they have nothing to do with the real issue here," Doyle said, not unkindly. "In a trial people tend to get excited about a lot of insignificant things. Tiny points get argued about. That's a lie! No! That's the truth! Tempers flare, and self-righteous pronouncements are made." She paused and smiled at the girl. "Like you're upset now because your father told a lie."

"He told many lies," she said.

"But none that will really affect the outcome of the trial. The truths he told were much more damaging than any of his lies."

"I don't understand," she said.

"Those scars," Doyle said. "They're worse than any lie he could tell about Dimmy because they show the jury what Dimmy is capable of doing. They had impact! For a boy to do that to his father with no motive—"

"No motive!" Irene interrupted. "What do you mean, no motive? Do you know what it's like living with my father?"

The girl's face grew flushed. "Do you know how many times he beat Dimmy? How I used to beg him to stop and he wouldn't? Do you know any of that?"

"What about you?" Doyle asked quietly. "Did he beat you?"

The girl looked away. She seemed to withdraw into herself. "Yes, but not like he beat Dimmy. When we were real little it wasn't so bad. But after Laura left, it was terrible."

"Because . . . ?"

"Because Papa blamed Dimmy for Laura's leaving. Every time he remembered that she had run away from him, he took it out on Dimmy." Her eyes pleaded with Doyle for understanding. "He did terrible things to my brother."

"Didn't he do terrible things to you, too?"

She shook her head. "Not like Dimmy."

"Let me tell you something, Irene." Doyle leaned forward and spoke softly as if she were about to share a secret with the girl. "There is no way I can convince a jury that Dimmy was justified in stabbing your father based on beatings and cruelty that he suffered in the past. The prosecution will counter with too many questions about alternatives to murder. Why didn't he seek help? Why didn't he go to the police? Why didn't he run away? Then, when those aren't answered satisfactorily, they'll ask why Dimmy attacked at that moment. They'll tell the jury that if Dimmy had time to think about doing it, then he also had time to realize that it was wrong. And if he realized it was wrong, but did it anyway, that's premeditated attempted murder. The jury may feel sorry for Dimmy. They may even want to set him free. But they won't. Not under those circumstances."

"You're telling me it's hopeless?"

"No," Doyle said. "There's always the possibility that the jury will ignore the law. They may even ignore the judge's instructions. And this judge is going to sock it to us.

He's going to do his damnedest to get your brother convicted. Still, there's always a chance. True, it's a slim one."

"Oh, God!" the girl moaned. "Is it that bad?"

"It is," Doyle continued, "unless I can give them something so evil that it will make the jury forget about Nikki's scars."

Doyle watched Irene closely. "If I knew what drove Dimmy that night. If I could attach his violent outburst to something other than the beatings . . . something that would seem even worse to the jury. Something that might have sent him off the deep end." She continued to watch the girl hopefully, urgently. "Do you know of anything like that?"

"You asked me that already," the girl said impatiently.

Doyle nodded. "Yes. But you didn't answer."

"I did," she said. "I told you there was nothing."

"I didn't believe you then, and I don't believe you now."

"You think I'm lying?" she asked incredulously.

"I know you're lying!"

"How can you say that?"

"Because I know what happened that day!" Doyle snapped.

The girl gasped. Her face lost color, and her lips commenced to tremble. "What do you know?"

Doyle's words struck the girl like hammer blows. "I know that your father raped you."

Irene turned ashen.

"I know that he forced Dimmy to watch, and I know that's why Dimmy tried to kill him."

"My God," the girl muttered, "are you crazy?"

"You can deny it, Irene, but I know it's true."

The girl rose from her seat. "You better not say that to anyone. If my father thinks I told you that, he'll kill me. Don't say it!"

Doyle looked up at her. "It's the truth, isn't it?"

"No!" she shouted. "And if you say anything like that, I'll sue you!" She turned and stormed off.

"Wait!" Doyle shouted.

"Go to hell!" the girl spat back over her shoulder.

Doyle, watching her leave, shook her head despairingly. She had taken the wrong approach, she told herself. She had misjudged the degree to which the girl would continue to defend her father. She should have been more careful.

As she started to slide out of the booth, she caught sight of the shoe box the girl had left behind. She lifted the box and examined it for a moment, then removed the lid and looked inside.

The moment she saw what the box contained, she understood that the purpose of the meeting was to allow the girl inadvertently to leave it there for her. Doyle smiled to herself. She had underestimated Irene's commitment to her brother.

"Well, you got what you wanted," she said to herself. "But you sure don't deserve any credit for it."

Laura looked in on Franny, found her fast asleep, pulled the covers up to her chin, and slipped quietly out of the bedroom. She went into the kitchen and poured herself a glass of milk, popped a chocolate chip cookie into her mouth, and returned to the unlighted living room.

Resigned to the hopelessness of Dimmy's situation, she had resolved to give up crying. Dimmy would need her to be strong. She had to be there for him during his incarceration and later, when he was released. No matter how long she had to wait for him, she would one day make a home for him.

She stood at the living room window and stared out at the moonlit patio in front of her apartment, a common area shared by all the ground-floor tenants. It had a fire pit, a couple of barbecue ovens, several small palm trees, and a wooden picnic table.

She had failed Dimmy when he needed her. She shuddered at the thought that she was a jinx. A curse. In his most difficult time, when he needed her most, she had decided to fall in love and concentrate on her own well-being instead of throwing herself into his cause. She sipped at the cold milk and despised herself. Staring out into the darkness, she reprised thoughts of self-punishment, which she had not suffered since her time with Dr. Benson. She felt rotten, worthless. She felt that she deserved a whipping.

And Nikki sensed that in her as he watched her through the glass. He saw her with her milk, dressed in pajamas, looking depressed, and knew that she was ready for him. He almost stepped out from behind the palm tree and presented himself to her. He wanted to crash through the window and take her by surprise. He felt himself getting aroused just thinking about it. But he would wait. He would have her, when the time was right. Nothing and no one could prevent that from happening.

He leaned against the tree trunk and let his memory roam over her body. Yes! He would take her. And after that no one else would ever want her again.

TWENTY-ONE

"This better be important," Judge Bauer announced, slamming himself down into the chair behind his desk and glaring at Doyle. "If you're wasting the court's time, you'll regret it."

Jehnke sat off to one side, letting his opponent and the judge fight it out alone.

Doyle placed a shoe box on the judge's desk as she began to speak. "If I had brought this into court without disclosing it to you first, you would've screamed foul."

"What is that?" the judge asked.

"It's evidence," Doyle said. "I acquired it last night."

Jehnke decided this was too important to ignore. He rose and moved over beside her.

Doyle lifted the lid off the box and revealed a collection of photographs separated into groups, each bound with a colored rubber band. "When I got the box, these pictures were just shoved in here any old way. I wanted them to tell a coherent story, so I put them in order."

When she had returned home with the box she was too troubled by what she had seen to sit down and objectively organize them. She had called Zeke and asked him to stop by, alone. She did not tell him what she wanted, but she hinted that it had to do with Dimmy and his case.

While she waited, she poured herself a tall Cutty, kicked her shoes off, fell onto the couch, and stared at the small box while her mind raced with the possibilities it presented. She had seen just enough to be disturbed by the photographs. She found them to be so upsetting that she wanted someone with her when she went through them carefully.

When Zeke arrived, she led him into the living room and poured him a drink. "You're going to need it," she said when he protested. "What I'm going to show you will be hard to take, even for a shrink."

They had spread the Polaroid photographs out on the coffee table. Some depicted Dimmy and Irene as small children, some as teens, others as young adults.

Initially, Doyle attempted to organize the photos chronologically, but Zeke, outraged at the tale they told, insisted that they be separated according to the activity depicted. He wanted the more unspeakable separated from the mildly revolting. They soon discovered that the degree of of baseness correlated with the time period. The older the children appeared to be, the more horrific the contents of the photo.

Both Doyle and Zeke stared at the pictures in horror. Neither one could speak. Doyle did not know what Zeke was experiencing, but she knew that the sight of the savagery dredged up memories of her own terrifying childhood in a ghetto where girls needed protection at all times, but were never protected well enough. It tugged her back to her own earliest experience with sexual violence. Back to a darkened hallway where she was forced to endure groping hands over her body. She felt again the humiliation, the belief that everyone who looked at her could tell that she had been violated. For an instant, as she stared at the photos, she relived the agony of a nine-year-old girl who was suddenly no longer the same as she had been.

"What do you think?" Doyle asked in a constricted voice

after their final pass through the photos. She shivered and raised her glass of Cutty to eliminate the chill.

"I always suspected violence," Zeke said, shaking his head in disbelief. "But never dreamed it could be like this. The father is a sadist."

"I'd like to put him in a cage and throw the key away." Zeke's voice sounded husky, as if he was fighting tears. "That might be too good for him," he croaked.

"Some of the early ones must have been taken while Laura was with them," Doyle said.

"She's not in any of them," Zeke observed.

"True," Doyle agreed. "But does that mean she wasn't a participant? Or she could have been the one behind the camera."

Zeke stared at her in shock, then shook his head wearily. "God!" he said finally. "I hope you're wrong."

"So do I."

Zeke stared at the wall in front of him, but Doyle was sure that he was seeing Laura.

"What are you going to do with these?" he asked finally.

"I'm going to take them to Judge Bauer," she said, "and shove them under his nose. He thinks Dimmy is a monster? I'll show him how monsters are manufactured."

Now Judge Bauer rifled through the photos, passing them on to Jehnke after viewing each one. The judge remained impassive, but as he progressed, his face darkened and he could not hide the fact that he was disturbed by what he was seeing.

"What do you want to do with these?" he asked Doyle after he had passed the last of them to Jehnke, who was groaning.

Jehnke interrupted. A light film of sweat covered his upper lip. "I'd like to object at this time to any reference to these photographs with respect to whatever relevance they show on the issue of self-defense and so-called terror that this man has put into the hearts of his children. I don't think these photos should be presented to the witness on the stand so that the jury has an opportunity to see them before—"

"I won't show them to the jury," Doyle interrupted.

"You bet you won't!" the judge snapped.

Doyle snapped back. "I had planned to show them to Nikos Pappas and ask him if he recognizes any of the people in them."

The judge stared at her and pondered her words. After a moment he nodded shortly and turned to Jehnke. "Since the defense wants to show that the defendant was intimidated by his father by such conduct as is demonstrated in these photographs, I think they are admissible."

Doyle smiled at him. She actually felt kindly toward him at that instant.

He frowned at her. "What are you smiling about?"

"Sorry, Your Honor."

"Your Honor," Jehnke said. "My objection has to do with the highly prejudicial nature of these photos—"

"You can't have it both ways, Marvin," Bauer said. "Her photos are equivalent to your scars. If she lays a foundation, they're admissible." He returned to Doyle. "I'm going to hold you to your promise. You can question the witness about them, but don't you dare show them to the jury."

"I won't, Your Honor," Doyle said quietly.

Judge Bauer continued to stare at her, and she thought she detected a glint of new respect in his eyes. "All right," he said. "Let's go to work."

During the morning session Doyle took Nikki through much of his testimony on direct. She focused primarily on Nikki's claim that Dimmy wanted the restaurant and the wealth and position of the father. She emphasized as often as she could that the victim had offered no motive other than greed for his son's attempt to kill him. She led him skillfully through a series of questions that allowed him to contend that he was a good and loving father.

She questioned him about punishing his children and allowed him to speak at length about a father's duty to discipline his children in order to prepare them to succeed in the world when they grew up. He explained to the court that he never used physical punishment but was more inclined to withhold dinner or some fun activity.

"Are you saying," she asked, "that you have never beaten your son?"

"I only beat him one time," Nikki said.

"When was that?"

"In 1982, maybe."

"All right," she said. "What does 'beating' mean to you?"

Nikki grew impatient. "It's a way to discipline the child."

"When you disciplined your son in 1982, did you punch him with your fist?"

"No."

"Did you beat him with a belt?"

"No."

"Did you use a bat of some sort?"

Nikki glared at Doyle suspiciously. "No."

"Did you ever punch him with your fists?"

"I never hit him in the face," Nikki protested.

"But you hit him somewhere else. Where did you hit him?"

"In the rear."

"What did you hit him with?"

"My hand."

"How many times did you hit him on that one occasion in 1982?"

"I hit him once on the behind and put him in the corner. That's all."

"I'm sure that was all," Doyle said sarcastically, then turned away before Jehnke could jump up and scream his objection.

She took Nikki through his relationship with his second wife. She questioned him about her leaving. Although Jehnke objected frequently, she managed to get on the record that Laura had left during the night and had stolen all his money.

She then went through his departure from New York City, his relocation in Los Angeles, the opening of his restaurant in Hollywood, and the life he had led up until the fateful attack on May 15. By that time the morning was gone, and court recessed for lunch.

"Let's go across the street," Zeke said to Doyle as she folded her notes away in her leather case.

She shook her head. "No," she said. "I need some time alone to do some thinking. I'll see you here at two."

"You know everything he said up there was a lie?" Laura said.

"I know."

"How can he get away with that?"

Doyle smiled thinly. "If it's the last damned thing I ever do, I'm going to see that he doesn't get away with it."

Over lunch, Zeke told Laura and Franny about the photos. He spoke slowly and watched Laura's face carefully. He did not want to shock her, but he wanted to know if she was aware of the existence of the pictures. When she reacted with horror and disbelief, he finally asked her straightforwardly.

"Did you know about the photographs, Laura?" he asked.

"My God, no!" she replied. "Do you think I could have kept silent about that?"

"I didn't know," he said.

"I would've known," Franny said. "If you had asked me, I could've told you she would never be involved in anything like that."

"I didn't think she participated voluntarily," Zeke said, suddenly feeling defensive. He understood what Franny was telling him and wondered once again if he truly loved Laura. If he did, he asked himself, wouldn't he also have known that she could not have been involved in such depravity?

"What did you think?" Franny asked coldly.

"Laura was a victim, too," he said. "They were all held hostage. They were all in bondage."

Franny nodded. "If you can't beat 'em, join 'em. Is that it?"

Zeke frowned. "Sort of."

Franny nodded. "Up until this very minute I thought I liked you, Zeke. Right now I'm not liking you very much at all."

"Franny!" Laura exclaimed.

"Do you want me to lie, Laura?" the woman asked. "If a man loves a woman, he believes in her. He trusts her. How can you love someone and suspect her of being a monster? Who could love a monster who would do those things?"

Laura looked sadly at her friend. "I did," she said softly, tears in her eyes. "I loved the monster who did those things, Franny. That's why I understand Zeke's doubts much better than you think."

Doyle sat near the fountain at the Music Center. Some distance from her a young black man, his violin case opened on the ground before him, played Mozart on his violin. A small group of children gathered around him to watch and listen as if mesmerized by the sounds he drew from the instrument. Passersby, on their lunch break, dropped coins into the open case and hurried away.

The young man appeared to her to be lonely out there, playing for his supper, relying on the approval of others for his sustenance. Or was she simply projecting onto him her own secret feelings?

It was she who was lonely. The young man had his music. She had nothing like it. She had a financially comfortable life, but one that was devoid of love. She shook her head sadly. She had avoided love like the plague. Love meant pain, sorrow, and deceit. She had always believed that. And now, looking at the Pappas family, she was even more convinced that relationships did not work. Human beings were a brutal, selfish species.

She remembered reading that a famous New York psychiatrist had once said, "Show me the kinds of murder you have, and I'll tell you what kind of society you live in." She could say something similar now, she thought. She could say, "Show me how you treat your children, and I'll tell you how fucked up your society is."

Tough as she was, or pretended to be, she was pained deeply by the situation in which Dimmy found himself. More than pained, she was embittered. With cruelty all around her, she had opted to remain alone, safe, uncommitted. And now, for perhaps the first time in her life, she was annoyed by thoughts that she could have been a good parent to that boy and his sister, that she would not have run off and left them, that she would have fought for them to her dying breath, that she would have won out eventually, would have taken them with her, as far as Mexico, if necessary.

She despised Nikos Pappas and what he stood for, but she recognized illness when she saw it. Laura was another matter. Harriet Doyle was contemptuous of Laura, who told

herself that she had flown to California in order to help her
stepson, but who had come to his aid not for him but for
herself. Her act of generosity was suspect. To Doyle it appeared to be an act of contrition. Was it Laura's feelings of
guilt that brought her here, rather than her love for the boy?

What a pity, she thought. If she lost this trial, Dimmy
would go to prison. But if she won, what then? Where would
Dimmy go? To whom? What was waiting for him? What
did the boy know other than the lifestyle that had formed
him? Doyle grew despondent as she realized that when this
was all over, if the boy was set free, he would go back
to his father. He would return to that filthy restaurant on
Hollywood Boulevard and continue cooking and washing
dishes and absorbing abuse. What a waste, she thought.

She glanced at her watch, noted that the time was near,
rose, and strolled over to the violinist who was now into
Sarasate's "Carmen Fantasy." She dug into her purse, found
a ten dollar bill, and dropped it into the open case. The young
man, chin pressed tightly over his instrument, nodded briefly
and thanked her with his eyes.

She smiled and nodded to him then turned and walked
back toward the courthouse.

"Okay," Doyle said after Nikki had been reinstated on
the witness stand and reminded that he was still under oath.
"Let's go back to something we talked about earlier." She
lifted her yellow notepad from the table.

"This restaurant in Hollywood, is it yours?"

Nikki nodded. "I opened it for my children."

"But who is the actual owner?"

Nikki twisted in his seat. "I gave it to Dimmy because
he's a smart boy."

Doyle smiled. "So your son Dimmy is the owner of the
restaurant?"

"In a way, yes."

Doyle nodded thoughtfully. "Can you tell us why, then, this morning when you testified, you kept saying 'my restaurant'?"

"Well, my things went into it. I brought tons of things here when I came from New York. I put everything I had into that restaurant."

"But it is actually your son's restaurant?"

"Yes. But I'm the father."

"Are you saying that whatever is his is yours?"

"There's no mine and his. We're family."

"But it's Dimmy's restaurant?"

Nikki hesitated. He wet his lips nervously, shrugged, and seemed to surrender. "Yes."

"Don't you think it's strange to try to kill somebody to get something you already own?"

"Objection!" Jehnke shouted, leaping to his feet.

Doyle looked at Judge Bauer, who was scowling at her. "I withdraw the question."

She returned to the defense table, laid her notes down, and, leaning forward as if studying them, spoke softly. "Did you ever tell the child welfare people, 'This is my child. I made him, and I can destroy him'?"

Jehnke shouted, "Calls for hearsay, Your Honor."

Doyle was prepared to abandon the question when she heard, much to her surprise, the judge say, "Overruled!" She glanced up at him and noted that his expression had softened somewhat. "The witness will answer the question."

Nikki said, "Never!"

Doyle smiled. "We talked about discipline earlier. Did you also discipline your daughter?"

Nikki stared at Doyle as if he had failed to understand the question and did not reply.

"The same way you disciplined your son?"

''No,'' he finally said.

Doyle hesitated. She turned her eyes to the jury and saw that all the jurors were watching Nikki closely. Their expressions were not pleasant. The silver-haired man scowled as he watched Nikki squirm.

She asked, ''Didn't you frequently tell your son, 'If you're bad I'll kill you'?''

Nikki shook his head. ''I never said the word 'kill.' ''

''Did you ever threaten to cut out his heart and drink his blood?'' Doyle asked. She heard a gasp from the jury box.

''I never did that,'' Nikki insisted.

''And didn't you tell him, 'You can't run away from me. I'll find you where ever you go'?''

''Never!''

''Did you ever threaten your children with a gun?''

''Never!''

''Okay,'' Doyle said. ''By the way, did you know that it's against the law to make a child stop going to school before age sixteen?''

''Sure. I know that.''

''Didn't you take Dimmy out of school to work full-time in the restaurant?'' she asked.

''No!''

''Didn't you shave his head and prevent him from going back to school?''

''No!''

Doyle stood straight and locked her gaze onto his. ''Is it your testimony that you are a good father and a hardworking man who always made a living for his family and never brutalized his children?''

''That's right!'' Nikki exclaimed. ''That's absolutely right!''

''Do you remember going to a hardware store and buying ten yards of link chain?''

''That never happened,'' he said.

"Do you remember chaining your son in your apartment?"

"That's not true," he said in self-righteous anger.

"Did you ever put chains on him anywhere?"

"I never did anything like that."

"Did you ever hang him from the basement ceiling?"

"Never!"

"Did you ever force him to eat from a dog's dish?"

"No!"

"Did you ever stuff his head into the oven?"

"No!"

Doyle sighed and dropped her shoulders as if she felt weary. She glanced up at Judge Bauer again. "If the court please," she said, "I would like the record to reflect that I have marked these photographs as defendant's A through double R, and may I approach the witness, Your Honor?"

Judge Bauer nodded. "Yes."

Doyle walked slowly to the witness stand. In her hand she carried a stack of Polaroid photographs from the shoe box. "Would you look at these photographs, sir? And please keep them to yourself."

Nikki accepted the stack of photos and rifled through them quickly. His hands trembled slightly, and he turned pale.

"Do you recognize any of those people?" Doyle asked.

"Yes," he whispered.

"I beg your pardon?"

"Yes, I said."

"Who are those people?"

Nikki placed the photos down before him. He lowered his head and spoke very softly. "How did you get these?" he asked.

"Who are the people?" Doyle insisted.

Nikki raised his face. There were tears on his cheeks now. "How did you get them?" he asked again.

"I ask the questions here," Doyle said. "You give the answers." Doyle turned to gaze at the jury. "Who are the people in those pictures?" she said, looking directly at the jurors.

Nikki wet his lips with the tip of his tongue. "Me," he said. "My son and my daughter."

"Do you still say that you are a good father?" she demanded.

Nikki did not answer. He turned to the judge, who stared at him unsympathetically.

Doyle continued. "Isn't it true that those pictures show a boy in chains, connected to plumbing under a sink. They also show a boy eating from a dog's dish and a boy with his head shaved. They show you holding a gun to your son's head. They show your children in various positions of bondage. And they show your son with bruises and contusions on his face and over most of his body. Isn't all that true?"

Nikki, eyes downcast, nodded slowly.

"Isn't that true?" Doyle charged.

"Yes," Nikki mumbled.

"I have one more picture, sir." She strode to Nikki and handed him the last picture in her possession. "Sir, do you recognize the people in that photograph?"

"No!" Nikki said. "I don't know them." He put the picture facedown on the bar before him.

"Isn't it true," Doyle said, "that the picture shows a naked young woman in bed and a naked man lying behind her?"

"I didn't see anything like that," Nikki said.

"Did you look at it?"

"I don't want to look at it."

Judge Bauer interrupted. "Mr. Pappas, I'm telling you to look at that photograph. Pick it up and look at it."

Doyle was surprised but pleased.

Nikki lifted the picture and stared at it.

"Mr. Pappas," Doyle said, "that is a picture of your daughter, Irene, is it not?"

"Yes," he said, his twisted face displaying great pain.

"Do you recognize the man in the picture?"

"I can't see."

"But they are in bed together, isn't that true?"

Softly. "Yes."

"And your daughter is tied up?"

"Yes."

"And the man is in the act of—"

"Yes."

"Raping her?"

"Oh, sweet Jesus," Nikki whispered.

"Isn't it true that the man in that picture is you?"

"No," he moaned.

"Isn't that you in the process of raping your own daughter?"

"No! I swear to God!"

Doyle confronted him, a mask of disgust on her face. "Who would you like us to believe it is in that picture, Mr. Pappas?"

Nikki looked up at her. The torment on his face was very real. He lifted his hand and pointed beyond Doyle. "It's him," he said. "It's Dimmy, my son!"

The courtroom burst into raucous sound. There was pandemonium all around her. She heard the judge pounding futilely for order. She heard Laura's sharp scream and Irene's profound weeping. She turned and studied the stunned jurors as they gazed at one another in confusion.

"That's outrageous!" Doyle shouted, wheeling back to face Nikki. "How dare you accuse—"

"I know it's him," Nikki insisted.

"How do you know that?"

Nikki sobbed. "I took the picture."

TWENTY-TWO

Doyle lowered herself into a steaming bubble bath. A half-filled tumbler of neat Cutty Sark rested on the ledge beside the tub next to an ashtray with two dark cigarettes, one lighted and burning and one for later. An immense pink bath towel, folded like a blanket, waited for her to emerge.

Soaking gratefully, she recounted the day's events. Eyes closed, facial muscles relaxed, she smiled softly as she reflected to herself once again how unpredictable life truly was. "Expect only the unexpected," her ex–law partner, a marvelous litigator, used to say frequently. No matter how well prepared a trial lawyer might be, someone on that witness stand would, without doubt, utter something so off the wall that it would shatter even the best laid plans. This day had certainly validated that advice. And it had been days like these that had persuaded her to retire in the first place.

She had quit the practice of law convinced that she was a burnout. She had resented being dragged back into it by Laura's pathetic appeal. But here she was lying in a hot bathtub reflecting upon how much she had missed her work without being aware of it. She reflected upon how good she was at it. She lay in the foamy water wondering how in the world she could get back into it full-time.

She loved the almost sensuous sensation of victory, which she had enjoyed this day. And she most certainly had been victorious today. As far as she was concerned, although one could never predict a jury's decision, this case had been overwhelmingly won on this day. By the time she finished with Nikos Pappas the next day, no jury in the world would convict her client. My God! she thought. They ought to give that kid a survival medal.

She recalled that one bad moment when Nikki had accused his son of ravaging his sister, and she shuddered. Fortunately, she thanked heaven, the judge had adjourned at that very moment, probably because he recognized that everyone concerned would need time to digest the new and confusing development.

She had rushed her client into a private chamber and confronted him.

"What the hell was that all about?" she had demanded. "Where does he get off saying that about you?"

Dimmy, sullen, had moved away from her. He stood by the barred window chewing his lip and staring down into the street. "It's the truth," he said quietly.

"Jesus Christ!" she exclaimed. "Why didn't you tell me? When did this happen?"

He drew a series of lines in the dust that covered the window. "The day I stabbed him," he said. "That afternoon."

She was angry. She felt betrayed, even though she knew that all clients lied, cheated, and deceived their attorneys. She had no right to feel outraged, she told herself. After all, it was his life he had chosen to throw away. Still, she felt abused, as if he had hurt and embarrassed her on purpose.

"Why didn't you tell me?" she demanded. "How am I supposed to protect you if you hide things from me?"

"You're joking," the boy said. "You're angry because I

didn't tell you something that's none of your goddam business? Who the hell do you think you are?"

"I'm not joking," she spat. "You little bastard."

"Then you're stupid," he said.

At that instant she felt the urge to kill him herself. She wanted to place her hands on his throat and squeeze.

He shook his head as if in amazement. "You expect me to announce to you that I violated my own sister? Are you crazy? How could I do that?"

"I don't care how you could do that. I have a bigger question," Doyle said. "*Why* did you do that? Between that and the stabbing of your father, the jury is going to see you as a local Jack the Ripper."

The boy shrugged. "He had a choice," he said. "I wasn't given any choice, I can tell you."

Doyle moved toward him, placed a hand on his arm. "What does that mean?"

"It means what it means," he said, annoyed.

"Okay, smartass," Doyle said, equally annoyed. "You wanna play? I'll play with you. What's the fucking riddle?"

"No riddle." The boy turned away from her and faced the window again. "How did you get your hands on those pictures?" he asked sadly.

"Your sister."

"She gave them to you?" He sounded truly surprised.

"No," Doyle said. "She pretended to leave them near me by mistake."

"Yeah," Dimmy laughed mirthlessly. "That sounds like her. She likes that secret agent stuff." He chuckled to himself for a while.

"You going to tell me what really happened?" Doyle finally asked.

He turned away from the window, brushed past her, and

sat at the small table. "I already told you," he said. "I didn't have any choice."

"Explain that to me!"

"You want me to draw you a picture?"

"If that's what it takes," she shouted. "Yes."

He leapt up from the chair, knocking it over behind him, his eyes blazing with uncontrolled anger. "Papa tied her up like that and told me someone was going to fuck her, either him or me, and I better hurry up and choose."

"Oh, shit!"

"That's right!" he screamed. "Only with Papa, you can't say, 'Oh, shit,' because Papa means everything he says. He was gonna get her raped that day one way or the other." Suddenly the anger left him and he seemed deflated. He grew sad. "It was either him or me or a Coke bottle." He looked down at the floor. "She begged me not to let him do it to her. She begged me." He began to weep, softly at first, then harder. "She was afraid of the bottle." He sobbed deeply now. "She asked me to do it because she knew I wouldn't hurt her."

"Damn!" Doyle sank onto a chair. Her legs felt weak, and she was ashamed of her anger. "That's what you blocked out, isn't it?"

"No," the boy said, shaking his head, drying his tears with the back of his hand. "I didn't forget. I just didn't think . . . You know . . . It's a bad way to get out of trouble, to tell on her like that."

"But it's happened anyway," Doyle said. "Everyone knows now."

"That was her doing, wasn't it?" He shrugged and sat down. "It's what she wanted to do, I guess."

"Why did he do it?" Doyle asked. "Tell me. I want to understand."

The boy shrugged again. "Who knows?" he said. "He was always saying she was getting to be like Laura. He really hated Laura, especially after she escaped. He was always saying to Irene that before she became a whore like Laura, he would do it to her first himself." He sighed deeply like a sad old man. "With my father you don't take those threats lightly. He enjoys doing things like that. You saw the pictures. He took an awful lot of them, didn't he?"

"What do those pictures mean?" Doyle asked. "Why did he take them?"

"That's his hobby." Dimmy smiled sorrowfully. "He's a fucking collector."

Doyle reached over and covered the boy's hand with her own. "So that's why you went after him," she said. "That's what pushed you over the edge."

He nodded. "I guess so."

"That was your immediate motivator," she said.

He nodded again, then started to cry but struggled to control himself.

"You could have saved us all a lot of aggravation if you'd told me right away," Doyle said.

"That would have been fine for you, maybe, but not for Irene. I kept silent to spare Irene. I don't care about anyone else."

Still hearing Dimmy's words in her memory, Doyle crawled out of the tub and wrapped herself in the pink bath towel. She carried her nearly empty glass into the living room, poured herself another, and dialed Paul Murphy's number. Phyllis answered on the first ring.

"Hi," Doyle said. "Your husband there?"

"Hell, Harriet," Phyllis said. "Say hello, why don't you!"

"Hello, Phyl. And I'm sorry. I'm preoccupied, and that was rude. Didn't mean it and will never do it again."

"Stop apologizing," Phyllis said. "I don't like you so humble. I'll get Paul."

Doyle heard Phyllis call out that she was on the phone for him.

"Hello, Harriet," Murphy said, slightly breathless.

"Hi, lover. How you doing?"

"Better than you," he said. "I heard about what happened in court today."

"Don't tear up your ticket just yet," she said. "If you're smart you'll stick around for the next round."

"Uh-oh," he said. "You've got something."

"Something? I'm going to blow the lid off that courtroom tomorrow. When I get done, that jury's going to want to lynch that son of a bitch of a father."

"Want to tell me about it?"

"No," she said. "This call is about something else. I need a favor."

"Anything. You name it."

"Watch out," Doyle said. "Or your wife will come after us both."

"You've got a point there."

Doyle paused for a moment, then said, "I want to go back into practice."

"Wow!" Murphy said. "What brought this on?"

"The taste of it," she said. "I don't want to join a firm. I want to work alone. Maybe with one young associate. But alone. Will you help me?"

"Of course. What do you need?"

"I need an office. Is there any space in your building?"

"There's space. What else?"

"I'm starting fresh," she said. "I need someone to get the word out. I'll have to build a practice all over again."

"Shit, Harriet!" Murphy said. "You'll have clients lined up in the hallway the minute you open your door."

"From your mouth to God's ear," she said.

"I've got a pipeline."

"I'm glad you've got something, because I don't have shit."

"Just a low-down homegirl, huh?"

"Listen," she said. "I'm in a trial with Judge Bauer. He hates women. He hates Negroes. And he hates lawyers who don't kowtow to him. I've got so few points with him, I might as well be Jewish, too."

Zeke held Laura in his arms and allowed her to lean on him. Seated on his couch, she curled up on his lap like a small girl. He stroked her hair, touched her cheek with warm fingers, rubbed her shoulder with a comforting hand. Afterward, he heated up some canned soup and fed it to her, spoonful by spoonful, as if she were an infant. He tried to be nurturing and considerate with her. If he had been stunned by the revelation in court that day, he could imagine the effect the news had on her. These were her own kids—at least, she thought of them that way.

"I thought I hated him before," she said to Zeke. "I didn't know what real hate was like."

"You have to forget him now," Zeke said. "This is the end of it. If I know the D.A.'s office, they'll be filing charges against him in the morning."

"You think so?" she asked anxiously.

"I know so," he said. "Child abuse is a serious crime in this state. And what he did to those kids falls into a category all its own. It isn't child abuse; it's psychosexual sadism. He belongs in jail. If it was up to me, I'd lock him up as a mentally disturbed sex offender and forget about him."

That night when they went to bed, he drew her to him and kissed her gently, convinced that she would not be in the mood to make love. To his surprise, she took charge. She pressed him down onto his back and climbed on top of him. She was careful to lift the phone off the hook first and place the receiver out of sight.

They made love very slowly, very carefully. They were extremely gentle with each other. She whispered her love for him frequently, into his ear, his mouth, his chest. And at one point, he put his lips to her ear and told her he was crazy about her, wanted to marry her, and probably could not live without her, now that she had seduced him. And when she laughed at that, he knew that he had made a good choice.

Zeke was especially pleased to notice that he suffered no more fears about her, that he felt very strong with her. She would not, could not, discount him, he realized, would not reduce him to someone less than who he was. He no longer compared her to his mother.

Having held her and comforted her and realized that her tough exterior had been an act, he felt better about himself. He would have to think about his attitude, he told himself. He worked all day long to raise his patients' self-esteem. He established as a goal for them the achievement of emotional independence. And yet here he was enjoying Laura's weakness. Her apparent strength had frightened him; he felt much safer with her now that she had shown herself to be needy.

He laughed softly as he had these thoughts. He turned his head and watched her as she slept beside him. He was overwhelmed with love.

He raised his eyes to heaven and whispered, ''Physician, heal thyself.''

Franny heard the tinkle of breaking glass, but rolled over and ignored it, unable to rouse herself from the deep sleep in which she dreamed pleasantly of rolling cornfields and sunshine and home. Then she heard a heavy footstep in the next room and remembered that Laura would not be home this night. She opened her eyes and stared into the darkness of her bedroom.

After a moment, when she heard nothing more, she rolled over onto her side and returned to her pleasant sleep. In her dream she was entering her office to begin a new day when the rough hand clamped itself over her mouth and pulled her head back painfully. She grunted, unable to speak while the hand locked her jaws together.

Suddenly, without warning, her attacker flipped her over onto her stomach and pulled up her nightgown, exposing her to the cool night air. He released her mouth, but pressed her face into the pillow. "Please," she begged, "don't hurt me." When she began to push up, she felt a thunderous blow to the small of her back. She fell forward in agony.

She felt him lift his weight off her, and for an instant she thought he had decided to stop. Then the pressure was on her again, worse than before. She wanted desperately to resist, but knew that any such move would probably infuriate him and might result in even more serious physical injury to her.

She made herself relax, half in fear, half in resignation, and let him have his way. She wanted to hate him. She wanted to stay distanced and enraged while he was doing his filthy work. She did not want to become part of his evil deed. If she had to be a victim, she would be a totally divorced one.

She felt his release, heard the breath leave him, as he quickly withdrew and rolled off her. She sensed that he was lying on his back beside her, enjoying the aftermath of the rape. She knew his guard was down. Like a bear after a huge meal, he wanted to rest.

Instantly she was on her feet and out of the bedroom. As she ran toward the kitchen, she heard his heavy footsteps coming toward her. She could not know how close he was, would not take the time to look back and see. But she believed she could feel his hot breath on the back of her neck, and that caused her to run all the faster.

Then she was in the kitchen, at the counter, in the silver drawer. Oh, Franny, she said to herself silently, if you ever had any luck, let it be now. Find something quickly! she screamed inside her head. Her hand curled around the wooden handle of a long, sharp kitchen knife. Her fingers caressed the metal rivets that held the wood in place. Quickly she lifted it out of the drawer and whirled around just as he was upon her. A huge, dark shape reached out for her. She felt both his hands grab her head and sensed that he was going to pull her to him. Instead, she fell into him and thrust the knife into his side as far as she could push it.

She heard him grunt and utter a short cry. She felt his hands fall away from her. He staggered backward a few steps, fell back against the refrigerator door, and doubled over, then rose up again. In the blackness of the night she could see only his dark outline, a figure twisting and turning in great pain.

"Laura!" The voice was filled with agony. "Laura!"

Then, as mysteriously as he had appeared, he was gone. She heard the front door open and close. Her mind raced. What should she do first? She could feel his essence on her skin, and she was revolted. She staggered to the phone and called the police. She told them she had been raped by an intruder, and they promised to send someone over immediately. She hung up, then went into the bathroom, turned on the hot water, and shivered as she cleaned herself in the shower.

Dimmy did not sleep well that night. He could not fall off, but not for the usual reason. He was encouraged by his lawyer's assurances. For the first time since he was arrested, he felt that he might not have to go to prison. For the first time, since being placed in jail, he sensed that he had some future left. He felt very much like a little boy on the night before leaving for summer camp. He was excited with anticipation. He was anxious about court, but excited as well.

He regretted the disclosure that would damage Irene so badly. He knew that the world around them would not judge her. After all, these were modern times. People were more understanding today. But he also knew where he and Irene had come from. He knew to what conditions they had been subjected. Irene would be her own worst critic. She could no longer suffer quietly in the knowledge that she had a secret. She would now suffer knowing the world knew all about her. He wished he could fix that. He wished he could make it all better for her. After all, that was all he had ever wanted, for both of them, Laura and Irene.

He lay awake staring at the metal ceiling of his cell, feeling safer there than he had outside in the clutches of his father. He had prepared himself so well for his fate that he felt more comfortable with the idea of going to prison than with the thought of going home. Who was there waiting for him? Was there still a place for him somewhere?

He knew that he had no home. He had no father and no mother. And now he had no sister, either. He could never go back. He could only go on. But to where? To what? What was he good for? For what was he prepared, trained, educated? He had absolutely nothing to offer to anyone.

Perhaps, he thought, it would have been better not to expose his father. Perhaps it would have been better for everyone if he had made the deal with the prosecutor. Perhaps it would have been best for all of them if he'd been sent away and forgotten, because his presence in anyone's life would serve only as a reminder of evil times. He knew.

He served himself as a reminder. And in that sense, he was a pariah.

Dimmy wept, deeply, sadly, as if his heart would break, because he realized that, even in winning, he was and would always be the loser.

TWENTY-THREE

Laura and Irene had agreed to meet at Figaro's on Melrose near Doheny, where the young set liked to hang out. Laura had received a phone call that morning from Irene, who had moved in with a boyfriend and was attending Santa Monica City College. Although Laura had been pleased to hear from the girl, she remained cautious, recalling Irene's volatility during their last confrontation. But Irene had merely asked her to meet for coffee, and Laura quickly agreed.

Now Laura waited for Irene at an inside table in the corner by the huge plate-glass front window. They had not seen each other since that day in court when Nikki had testified about the photograph.

Nikki had failed to appear the next day, and the proceedings had been held up while everyone waited for him. He never appeared. The prosecutor, in an attempt to locate him, sent Jerry Beck to Nick's Falafel Restaurant. The detective jimmied the door to the upstairs apartment and found it empty.

Remembering the floor plan, Beck made his way to the rear bedroom, where he found several blood-soaked towels on the floor, but nothing else. The closet was empty of clothing, and there were no toilet articles in the bathroom.

He returned empty-handed, except for the towels, and finally Judge Bauer issued a bench warrant for Nikki's arrest.

The judge and the two lawyers then met in chambers to discuss how to proceed with the trial now that the victim and star prosecution witness was no longer available for cross-examination. Judge Bauer was of the opinion that there was not much more Doyle could have pulled out of him anyway, but if she wanted to make a real issue of it, he could declare a mistrial or the prosecutor could dismiss the case.

Doyle had allowed the court to decide what to do, and when the judge announced that the charges had been dismissed, Laura could not contain her joy. Zeke had scooped her up in his arms and laughed and shouted his joy, but all she was capable of doing was weeping exhaustedly through a saddened smile.

The judge thanked the jurors for their efforts and then dismissed them. But the matronly black woman juror approached Dimmy, waited for Laura to release him from the bear hug in which she held him, and hugged him and kissed him herself. "You never would've been convicted," she had told him, "because I intended to see to it that you would be set free." She had backed off then and said, "God bless you, child."

When Irene entered the restaurant, Laura was struck by how lovely she looked, and her first thought was that Irene had recovered well from the shock of her ordeal.

Laura stood when Irene approached and was taken aback when the girl reached out and kissed her. "Hello, Laura," she said.

Laura hugged the girl. "Hello, Irene."

They held each other for a moment, then sat across from each other.

"Have you ordered?" Irene asked.

"No. Not yet."

"What would you like?"

"What's good here? I've never been here before."

"They have great salads," the girl said.

"No. Just something to drink, I think," Laura said.

"The coffee's good."

Laura nodded. "That would be fine."

Irene signaled the waitress, who rushed over. "Two coffees," Irene said, then turned to Laura. "A piece of cake?"

Laura shook her head. "No. Coffee is just fine."

"Just two coffees," Irene told the waitress, who nodded and moved off.

"I'm glad we're here together," Laura said. "Last time we met wasn't a very pleasant experience."

"I'm sorry about that," Irene said sincerely. "I was just so angry. It didn't matter who I hurt so long as I hurt someone. Did you ever feel like that? Just so blindly angry that it didn't matter who you let go at?"

Laura nodded.

"Of course, you have," the girl said. "What am I saying? We come from the same place, don't we?"

"Yes," Laura said. "From the very same place."

"We all have our miserable memories, don't we, Laura?" the girl said. "You and me and Dimmy."

Laura nodded. "Poor Dimmy. What a waste of a life."

A tear appeared in the girl's eye. "I'm going to miss him," Irene said sadly. "He was my best friend."

"Did you see him before he left?" Laura asked.

The girl shook her head. "No." She caught her breath. "I haven't seen him since the trial. Have you?"

Laura nodded. "He stayed with us after he was released."

"Us?"

"Zeke and me," Laura explained. "We're getting married."

"That's nice," Irene said sincerely. "What happened to your friend, that woman who was staying with you?"

"She went home."

Laura's face clouded. She debated quickly whether or not to reveal to Irene what had happened, or what she suspected had happened. Suspected, because no one really knew. But then she decided that the girl had suffered enough at the hands of her father, as they all had. She did not need an additional shock.

Besides, Franny had survived the ordeal. She was a strong woman and had pushed it out of her memory. At least, so she contended. Laura recalled seeing her off at the airport. She remembered the tears they had shed together, the promises to visit each other frequently, to call, to write, to stay in touch.

"I'll come to Dayton once a year," Laura had promised.

"Sure!" Franny had responded. "Why would anyone who doesn't have to come to Dayton, want to?" She grinned at Laura. "Let's play it by ear." They had hugged and kissed and said one more good-bye.

Laura shrugged off the recollection. "We offered to let Dimmy stay with us permanently," she continued. "But he wouldn't hear of it. Zeke really likes him. We told him our place could be his home, but he refused."

"I can understand that," Irene said.

"Can you?"

"Sure!" The girl shrugged. "He couldn't go back to being somebody's kid again. Not after jail and all."

"I bet you're right," Laura said thoughtfully.

Irene nodded. "Trust me! I'm right. That's exactly how I feel, and I didn't go through what he went through." She shook her head. "No. He'll be alone from now on. That's his fate. I'm really going to miss him."

"I understand you have a boyfriend now," Laura said.

"It's not the same thing," she replied. "Nobody will ever replace Dimmy in my life. Papa knew that. That's why he did what he did."

Laura was puzzled. "I don't understand," she said.

The waitress brought their coffee and set the cups down, one in front of each young woman.

"Thank you," Irene said.

"You're welcome," the waitress answered and walked off.

"What is it you don't understand?" Irene asked Laura. "He did the same with you. He interfered when he thought you loved someone."

Laura didn't fully comprehend what the girl was saying.

"Remember Mrs. McNamara?" Irene asked. "Didn't Papa kill that friendship? Didn't he forbid her to see you?"

"But that was because he thought she was interfering in our lives, coming between us."

The girl shook her head. "He wanted to be the only person in your life. You could have friends, but he wanted you to need only him."

"Okay," Laura said. "In what way was that like this?"

The girl stirred her coffee absently and stared out the window. "You know," she said woefully. "He made us do that, me and Dimmy. I don't know what Dimmy told you, but Papa would've killed us if we didn't."

"Don't say that," Laura pleaded. "You don't know how guilty that makes me feel."

Irene gazed at her warmly. "But that's just why I wanted to meet with you, to tell you not to feel guilty. All of this had nothing to do with you. I'm really glad you got away. Dimmy was glad, too. Believe me. We never blamed you for leaving. I wish we could have left with you. But you were smart to go."

"I wish I could believe that," Laura said.

"Believe it! Listen! You didn't do anything to us. It was always Papa. And Papa knew what he was doing. He was bad, but he wasn't stupid. He wanted to finish me with Dimmy. He didn't want us ever to be friends again. That's why he did what he did."

"Explain that to me," Laura said.

Irene looked at her sadly and shook her head. "You know," she finally said. "When Dimmy was doing it to me, and Papa was taking the picture, Dimmy was crying and begging me to forgive him. When that was happening, when the worst part of it was happening, I thought that I liked it. I was humiliated, but I was also glad it was Dimmy doing it to me."

Laura gasped.

"I knew that would shock you," Irene said. "But it's true. I sensed that Dimmy liked it, too. That's why we can't be together anymore. It can't be. You see that, don't you?"

"Yes." Laura nodded.

"That's why Papa did what he did. And that's why I did what I did."

"What did you do?"

Irene stared at Laura. "I had to do it," she said, looking off into space. "I stabbed Papa."

"But Dimmy—"

"Took the blame for me."

"Oh, God!" Laura murmured. "Nobody ever knew."

The girl continued to shake her head. She smiled slyly. "Papa knew. He knew Dimmy was protecting me. That's why he paid for the lawyer. He never spoke about it, but I knew that he knew." She sipped her coffee. "You understand," she continued. "I could be in big trouble."

"Yes, of course."

"So, Laura, you must never say anything about this to anyone."

"Okay."

"Swear!"

"I swear."

"Good."

Laura watched her lift her coffee cup and drink. "You're dealing with it very well, aren't you?"

Irene smiled. "I wish I'd killed him," she said, then shrugged offhandedly. "But that's history."

"Irene," Laura sobbed.

"Don't cry for me, Laura," the girl said. She lifted her hands in the air and displayed her wrists, which were free of watches or bracelets. There were no rings on her fingers, either.

"I'll never be held in bondage again," she said. "Never, ever again."

On the way back to their apartment, Laura stopped at an Italian grocery and bought some exotic items with which to prepare an extra special meal for Zeke as a surprise. She had a desperate urge to show him how much she loved him. She felt lucky that she had found him, that he loved her and wanted to be with her for the rest of his life. She wanted him to know that as long as they had each other—doubts, internal demons, sad memories, and all—they were going to make it together. And somehow, she believed, Dimmy and Irene would make it, too.